PRAISE FOR
THE FIRST CASUALTY

"A lot of fun . . . A refreshing change from the standard good guy / bad guy divisions in military SF."
—Jack McDevitt, Nebula Award–winning author of *Firebird*

"Fast-paced military adventure that presents a grim look at the reality of war and the cost to those who risk their lives for the causes of others. A good choice." —*Library Journal*

PRAISE FOR
THE KRIS LONGKNIFE NOVELS
by Mike Moscoe writing as Mike Shepherd

"A whopping good read . . . Fast-paced, exciting, nicely detailed, with some innovative touches."
—Elizabeth Moon, Nebula Award–winning author of
Echoes of Betrayal

"Shepherd's grasp of timing and intrigue remains solid, and Kris's latest challenge makes for an engaging space opera, seasoned with political machination and the thrills of mysterious ancient technology, that promises to reveal some interesting things about the future Kris inhabits." —*Booklist*

"Enthralling . . . Fast-paced . . . A well-crafted space opera with an engaging hero . . . I'd like to read more." —*SFRevu*

"I'm looking forward to her next adventure."
—*The Weekly Press* (Philadelphia)

"Kris is a strong female character . . . The book focuses on action, with some interesting sci-fi twists thrown in . . . It excels as a page-turner." —*Boomtron*

"Fans of the Honor Harrington escapades will welcome the adventures of another strong female in outer space starring in a thrill-a-page military space opera . . . The audience will root for the determined, courageous, and endearing heroine as she displays intelligence and leadership during lethal confrontations."
—*Alternative Worlds*

THE
PRICE OF PEACE

MIKE MOSCOE

ACE BOOKS, NEW YORK

THE BERKLEY PUBLISHING GROUP
Published by the Penguin Group
Penguin Group (USA) Inc.
375 Hudson Street, New York, New York 10014, USA

USA | Canada | UK | Ireland | Australia | New Zealand | India | South Africa | China

Penguin Books Ltd., Registered Offices: 80 Strand, London WC2R 0RL, England
For more information about the Penguin Group, visit penguin.com.

THE PRICE OF PEACE

An Ace Book / published by arrangement with the author

Ace Books are published by The Berkley Publishing Group.
ACE and the "A" design are trademarks of Penguin Group (USA) Inc.

For information, address: The Berkley Publishing Group,
a division of Penguin Group (USA) Inc.,
375 Hudson Street, New York, New York 10014.

ISBN: 978-0-441-00695-3

PUBLISHING HISTORY
Ace mass-market edition / January 2000

PRINTED IN THE UNITED STATES OF AMERICA

12 11 10 9 8 7 6 5 4

Cover art by Scott Grimando.
Cover design by Diana Kolsky.

To the Men and Women
Who put on the uniform every morning
When the victory parades are over and there's still work to be done
Who pay the Price of Peace with their sweat and pain, loneliness and fear

and to Trudy Moscoe
and all the wives and kids, and now husbands, like her
"They also serve who only stand and wait."

THE
PRICE OF PEACE

ONE

WHITES CRISPLY STARCHED and gig line perfect, Commander Izzy Umboto, captain of the Society of Humanity cruiser *Patton*, started her day as she stepped from her cabin onto the darkened bridge. The stink of tense sweat washed over her, just about wilting her uniform where she stood.

"Captain on the bridge," the Officer of the Deck's voice cracked.

"As you were," she overspoke the lieutenant. "Any change in our unknown?" she asked as she had every hour through the ship's night. Izzy studied the main screen; it answered her before the OOD could.

"No change, ma'am," the OOD shot back. The young man's Adam's apple bobbed nervously. Recently qualified, this was his first time to sweat out a possible hostile approach with the entire ship his responsibility. Izzy had accepted the risk, wanting her best team well rested for today. She gave the young officer an affirming smile as she again measured the distance between the *Patton*, leisurely crossing this system at one gee like any heavily laden freighter, and the unknown galloping down on her at three gees. It was exactly where she expected it to be.

Izzy glanced around at the rest of the bridge crew, tired, worried young faces lit in multi-hued reflections from their stations. "Well done, all of you. Quartermaster of the watch, jack up the blowers." The hum of the air circulation fans went up several notches. For the night, the lights and blowers had been reduced to aid the crew's rest. It was time to get the crew up—and the smell of fear off Izzy's bridge.

"Bos'n, pipe the crew to chow. Announce battle stations in twenty-five minutes." She was cutting it close, but just as Nelson had calculated how fast the wind would drive his liners down upon the French and Spanish fleet, physics decreed how quickly a ship accelerating at three gees could overtake a ship making one gee. *When* would not be the surprise today. Who did what to whom—now, that would get exciting real soon.

"I'll be in the wardroom. Call me if anything changes."

"Yes, ma'am" and "Captain off the bridge" followed her. She'd only had this crew for two months, but they'd shaken down well. *If only the damn boat was as good.* All her career, Izzy had dreamed of commanding a ship in space, lusted for it in the worst way. She doubted it could get worse than the *Patton*. Izzy shrugged, as she had so many times in the war. No use complaining about what you can't fix. The potential pirate bearing down on her—now *that* was something she'd enjoy fixing.

The whiff and clatter of breakfast greeted her well before she entered the wardroom. As she did, a steward's mate started fixing her usual breakfast plate. Izzy noted he went light on the reconstituted scrambled eggs and bacon, and blessed him. This morning, she'd share a hearty meal with her band of officers. Still, she didn't want to lose it as she hurtled the *Patton* through battle maneuvers. And leaving half her breakfast on the plate would not be a good signal to her team.

The exec, Guns, Damage Control, Engineering, Comm, and the leader of her marine detachment had an empty place at their table; she joined them, removing a white linen napkin from the dark blue tablecloth, and settling it in her lap as the steward deposited her plate in front of her. "Thank you," she smiled.

"Think we got ourselves a real pirate?" Guns grinned through a heap of eggs.

"Don't know many merchants that charge around a system at three gees." Izzy smiled in agreement. "Hell on the bottom line. Right, Vu?"

The bald, round chief engineer, last remaining member of the ship's old merchant marine crew, nodded like a silent Buddha, then went back to chasing his curried rice with chopsticks.

Lieutenant Commander Stan Gabon, her exec, wiped his lips with a linen napkin. "Could be hostile. Then again, it could be a courier ship or a fast private yacht."

Izzy nodded, wondering if this guy had been a nervous ninny all his career, or had just adopted the role after reading her career brief. "But three ships have disappeared without a trace, or one squawking life pod. If that ship is a pirate, it's in for a very bad day."

"You got that right," Guns chortled. Surrounding tables joined him. Izzy felt a rush, pure joy at leading these men and women into combat. For twenty-five years she'd dreamed and trained. Today, she'd put it all together.

"If this damn bucket of bolts and chips holds together," Comm muttered as the wardroom quieted. It got real quiet as his words sunk home.

The damage control officer looked grim. "We still haven't figured out why the stern sensor suite keeps dropping off line. The cable routing on this ship would drive a spider mad."

"That's why warships are full of redundancies," Izzy said. Her overworked maintenance chief didn't look very convinced.

The exec's face was also a cool mask, telling her nothing. He was a troubling unknown. His file said he was solid, but something had gone out of him a month ago. His kid brother disappeared just before he was to testify before a senate committee investigating corporate connection to the enemy during the recent war. Tom had been an up-and-coming corporate man. Now he was long gone, or sleeping with the fish or whatever happened to hard-charging company men who knew too much of the wrong things. Stan had gotten quiet and withdrawn.

The leadership books said everyone had a right to grieve. Today, nobody had a right to mess up Izzy's battle plan. She glanced at her wrist unit. "We go to battle stations in three minutes. Let's make it a day to remember."

"Unknown in main battery range," Sensors reported.

"Are they armed?" Izzy snapped, staring hard at the main screen, as if her eyeballs might see something *Patton*'s sensors had missed. The unknown was getting awfully close—and not saying a damn thing.

"Stern sensors are down again, ma'am. I'm doing the best I can with the bow suite." Lieutenant Commander Igor McVinty waved a dark hand at the dozen screens on his board with straight lines across them. And Izzy cursed the spare parts shortage for the forty-eleventh time this cruise. *Damn budget-cutters.*

Suddenly Igor's lines became dancing squiggles. "Skunk powering up main battery. His passive sensors are humming now." He shook his head. "Commander, that skunk is making music like the Mormon Tabernacle Choir. She's a warship."

"Society or Unity?" the XO shot back. Officially, Unity was as dead as Shakespeare, to quote Izzy's old boss. But what they said back on Earth and what a lone cruiser found far out on the rim of human space weren't always the same.

Igor tapped his board. Red lines appeared right on top of the yellow ones that skittered over his screens. "I make it a Daring-class Unity light cruiser."

Izzy eyed Igor's board. *Yep, a damn Daring.*
Every mother's son of which was supposed to be scrap!
So much for the fine points of peace treaties.

"Communications here, Captain. We're being hailed."

"Comm, give me audio. No visual output on these transmissions." Izzy could fake the outside of the *Patton*. There was no way to fake the bridge of a Navy cruiser with its crew at battle stations.

"Yes ma'am," answered communications.

We're ready. It's show time!

"Howdy, stranger," Izzy drawled. "This is Betsy Corbel, skipper of the *Pride of Portland*. What'cha want?" Betsy Corbel *did* captain the *Pride of Portland* . . . on the other side of human space.

A window opened on the main screen; an unshaven face stared out with a smile just one degree shy of a sneer. Then it went to puzzlement. "Your picture ain't coming through."

"Lost our bridge camera a month back," Izzy assured him. "Haven't had the money to replace it."

"Oh." The man on screen looked none too happy about that. But with a shrug, he went on. "There're pirates around here. We'll escort you. Keep you safe. For a slight fee."

Izzy expanded the picture of the man to fill the entire main screen. That gave her a good look at the bridge activity behind him. His crew was a rough lot in rumpled clothing; some of it had started life as uniforms. None of it had been washed lately. In addition to the watch-standers, there was a clump of extra men and women with rifles, knives, and assault weapons lovingly in hand. Izzy glanced at her XO; he returned a grim nod.

Izzy had heard from several merchant captains who'd paid what these guys asked. She had no idea what the three ships that had failed to make their next port of call had said and done. That was why the *Patton* was crossing this system with fake containers squaring off her cruiser lines. On visual, radar, and laser, the *Patton* WAS the *Pride of P.* If the lieutenant in charge of the *Patton*'s electronic countermeasures was half as good as she claimed . . . and her gear was working . . . this skunk was still in the dark about nine six-inch laser cannons charged and ready.

"Sorry, friend," Izzy answered, "but I'm just barely breaking even these trips. I'll have to pass on the escort." Izzy tried to sound grateful for the offer. *Come to Momma.*

There was silent laughter among the armed crew behind

the face on screen as it lost any hint of a smile. Now it was pure cold evil, only slightly softened by greed. "I don't think you understand the situation, sister. You see, it's just you and me, and an awful lot of space. Cough up a charge number and you might live. Keep on the way you're going, and you're gonna end up in deep shit."

"Helm, go to two gees." Izzy let a tremble shake her voice. What she wanted to do was shout for joy.

"Bad choice, girl." The screen went blank.

"Sensors, talk to me," Izzy snapped.

"They just powered up their active range-finding gear. They'll need about half a minute before they can range us."

"Distance to skunk?"

"Coming up on fifteen thousand klicks."

Izzy settled herself back in her chair—and tightened her belt. Around the bridge, the crew did the same. The quartermaster of the watch whispered, "Skipper just tightened her seat belt, folks. I'd do the same." Not a regulation announcement, but Izzy wasn't about to squelch the initiative. She was having too much fun. Twenty-five years she'd waited for this. Finally, she was commanding a ship in space *in combat. If* that ship was a pirate, and *if* it would just take a swipe at her.

She hit her comm button. "Crew, we got a possible pirate off our stern quarter. In a few seconds, they may range us. If they do, I'm gonna start evasive maneuvers real fast. As soon as they miss us, we'll steady down and shoot back. This is what we trained for. We're good. Let's do it." She switched to gunnery circuit. "Guns, hold main battery fire until I give the word."

"Turrets B and X won't take a charge. We're working on them. The rest are ready, skipper."

Damn the budget-cutters to hell and the spare-parts crunch right behind them. There was nothing she could do about that at the moment. The skunk was closing; it looked like she was going to get her fight. "Helm, prepare to flip ship and execute a down zig. Put spin on the ship when I order the down zig."

"Flip ship, standing by. Down zig, standing by. Spin, standing by," was the curt response from the young JG at the helm.

"Guns, as soon as I order the zig, you active-range that bastard with everything we got. I want that target dialed in when I order a shoot."

"Yes ma'am" came back with a grin in it.

"Ping! We've just been pinged, laser and radar!"

"Flip ship!" Umboto snapped. The *Patton* quickly started rotating along its central axis. Now, instead of her vulnerable engines, her ice-armored nose faced hostile fire.

"Zig down," she snapped as soon at that maneuver was done.

In a blink, the *Patton* dropped out from underneath Umboto. As the helmswoman initiated the defensive spin along the ship's long axis, the captain was slammed into her seat. That was planned. Then the stern plunged and the bow shot up. That wasn't. The *Patton* took off on her own, cartwheeling through space. The ragged broadside from the self-proven pirate cut through where the *Patton* had been—almost.

One ray sliced into ice armor. The *Patton* lurched; pumps whined as they redistributed reaction mass to balance the spinning ship. Umboto held her breath. Was the armor thick enough, the spin fast enough to keep the pirate laser from burning through? The pumps cut off as suddenly as they had started. The pirate had done his best. Now it was her turn.

"Hold fire, Guns, hold fire. Helm, steady as she goes."

"Going to manual," the young helmswoman answered. "Damn jets," she muttered as her hands twisted both joysticks at her station. Scores of attitudinal jets, normally balanced by delicate computer modeling, responded to her deft coaxing. After wild seconds, the *Patton* held steady, pitch controlled. "I think I can hold her here for a few seconds, Captain."

"Guns, we got them ranged."

"Did before that last jig, skipper."

"Main battery, fire salvo, pattern C," Umboto ordered. Even with laser and radar range finders, at fifteen thousand kilometers there was plenty of wiggle room for a five-hundred-meter-long ship. Guns and Umboto had worked out an approach to that problem. Each gun aimed for a slightly different section of space, and zigzagged through it for the three seconds of the salvo. With luck, one gun would find the target, and the next salvo would center around that hit. Hopefully, the attitudinal problem hadn't destroyed her carefully laid plans.

The lights dimmed as five 6-inch lasers reached for the threat. In empty space, nothing colored the laser light; it passed invisible to the naked eye. Umboto concentrated on her battle screens. Rays ranged around the target, but there was no sign of a hit. Damn!

The *Patton*'s spin brought two new guns to bear. Using the misses, Guns modified their salvo pattern. Damn, Umboto missed the two broken guns. But wish in one hand and spit in the other . . . see which one you get the most out of.

The target turned red as a single gun nipped it just as the salvo ended.

"Got a piece of 'em," Guns shouted with glee.

The *Patton* lurched. "Sorry, ma'am," the helmswoman answered before her captain said anything.

"Do your best," Umboto said, hoping Gun's fire solution hadn't been hashed again. "XO, tell me something nice."

"Damage control reports they've got attitudinal control back. Helm, go to backup."

"Yes, sir." There was a pause while the *Patton* did nothing . . . exactly the way it was supposed to. The XO and Umboto breathed a sigh of relief at the same moment. And Umboto went back to her main problem. One damaged pirate.

"Sensors, talk to me."

"Target is putting on spin. Only a few RPMs, though. Ranging us constantly." That told Umboto the bastard knew how to fight his ship, but probably didn't trust his crew and equipment to a standard battle stations twenty RPM—and was still very much spoiling for a fight.

"Sensors, time since last enemy salvo?"

"Coming up on ten seconds."

"Helm, zig right."

Patton slewed to the right even as the helmswoman repeated the order. No enemy fire came.

"Batteries are charged," Guns reported.

Sending out the next salvo meant committing the *Patton* to a steady course for five seconds. "Sensors?"

"Bandit is charged, ma'am."

So which one of us fires first? "Hold course steady," Umboto said, while counting in her head one thousand and one, one thousand and two, one thousand and three. "Zig up."

As the *Patton* zoomed up, the hostile lasers cut through the empty space where she'd been. Umboto had outguessed the bandit.

"Guns, pattern B."

"On its way," he said as the lights dimmed.

Five rays stabbed out, reaching for the pirate. One of them connected. The last two guns walked right into the target, slicing it.

"Good hits," Guns growled.

"Well done, Guns. Target their engines next salvo."

"Won't get many prisoners," the XO whispered softly.

"Three ships have disappeared and not a crew member to tell the tale, XO. I don't want prisoners. Let the other pirates sweat what happened to this one. Sooner or later, the marines will dump someone in my brig. I'm in no rush." Lights dimmed again. The five lasers slashed through the pirate for a second, then where a ship had been was only an expanding cloud of glowing gas. In only a moment, that too was gone.

"Yes!" Izzy crowed at her first kill . . . and immediately went back to work. "Comm, any distress signals, pods squawking?"

"Quiet as a tomb, Captain."

Izzy leaned back in her seat. "Helm, belay the spin. Take us back to one gee. Damage Control, report to the XO on anything needs fixing. And do an autopsy on that damn thruster. I want to know who, why, when, where and how it went bad."

"Yes, ma'am" came with a familiar sigh from damage control. Chips had been doing postmortems on too damn much of the *Patton*'s hardware and software. The ship was a jinx. She'd spent the war as a yard queen, tied up waiting for parts. Postwar, the other merchant converts had been refitted back into freighters. Not the *Patton*. Nobody wanted her.

Still, the Society of Humanity's Navy was now responsible for patrolling one hundred and fifty planets, not the forty-eight they'd had before the war. And what with war losses, there were even less ships to do the job. So cruisers like the *Patton*, that nobody wanted, were being given to people like Umboto, whom, if she was honest, nobody wanted. *Girl, you should have asked for the gripe sheet on the* Patton *before you said you'd take her.*

Then she shrugged. The choice was between early retirement and the *Patton*. For Izzy, that was no choice, even if the peace-becalmed Navy Department hadn't included the promotion to captain that the skipper of a cruiser deserved.

So the skipper of the good ship *Patton* . . . whose every officer was drawing pay for one rank less than his or her job deserved . . . stood. "Stan, have division heads report to my day cabin in fifteen minutes. Let's critique this while it's still hot."

She headed for her cabin off the bridge, not turning back to acknowledge Stan's "Yes, ma'am." Only after the hatch closed behind her did she let out a yelp. "Hot damn, that was . . ." What? Scary. Fun. All of the above and a lot more.

She'd outsmarted the bastard! She knew she had to be a better ship-handler than any jerk who didn't bother to shave in the morning.

Her knees began to shake. He could have gotten lucky.

Izzy shook her head. *No way! Lord, that was good!* She'd have to get these feelings out before the others reported. If Stan even half suspected how much she loved hanging it all out and winning, he'd get out and start walking for the nearest navy base—with most of the crew ambling along right behind him.

Tigers get people killed. How often had Captain Andy warned her during the war that she needed adult supervision? Well, now the tiger had the conn. She almost pitied poor Stan; providing the mature judgment for this command was going to be a hell of a job for the guy.

A light blinked on her desk. Mail must have come in during the shoot. Personal mail was rare; her navy career left little room for attachments. Izzy's sister Lora rarely wrote, but her kid Franny was writing regularly, grateful to Izzy for paying her college tuition. There had to be a way out of the slums that didn't mean putting on a uniform. Izzy had begged Lora to emigrate; there were planets begging for women, even a woman with a kid. Lora refused to leave Mom, as if the old drunk noticed her kids. Enough of that. Franny was fun, working hard to get out, getting close to husband-high. Izzy wouldn't mind paying for a wedding, or even the penalty for an unlicensed conception. Kids were cute, so long as they were someone else's to take home.

Izzy tapped the mail button; her screen filled with a weeping Lora. "Franny's dead. I should have called. I should have kept closer tabs on her at school. But she was at *school*!"

Lora's image broke down. Izzy took a step back from the vid as if she'd been slugged in the gut. Navy people died; you knew the job was dangerous when you took it. *But college kids?*

Lora controlled her wailing. "Franny loved gaming. We joked she was addicted, but I never *thought* . . . Izzy, there's this new drug going around. They say it makes VR real, that you forget there's a real world, that it makes every pleasure ten times better. She and her roommates hooked themselves up to a game and plugged themselves into a drug bottle."

Izzy slammed her fist down on her desk. "Not dehydration," the professional in her choked, the anger of foreknowledge almost overriding Lora's final sob.

"They died 'cause they never came out for a drink of

water. Oh, God, if I'd only called. Just dropped by. I'd been meaning to. Honest, Sis, I'd been meaning to."

Izzy hit the close button. The pleading in her sister's eyes faded to blank as Izzy collapsed into her work chair. What was wrong? What was missing? How could Franny have done this? How could Lora have missed the signs? Izzy shivered; the world was crazy. She'd just risked her life to burn a pirate, and Franny had thrown her life away on a thrill.

Izzy sat slumped in her chair until the computer reminded her she had a meeting to run. Lora's message could wait for an answer. With a wrenching sigh that could not fill the void in her heart, Izzy went to do what duty demanded.

Lieutenant Terrence "Trouble" Tordon was troubled. He was not used to that. Trouble to his enemies. Trouble to his friends, even Trouble to himself, and regularly in trouble, he wasn't often troubled. Now, he sat at the captain's conference table a very troubled man. His back was as ramrod-straight as the world expected a marine's to be, his face a study in military blandness, but behind the exterior, his mind was spinning. *What have I gotten myself and the platoon into?*

He'd worked with Izzy before. He knew she was a bit wild, but as a card-carrying member of the "Who Wants to Live Forever Club," Trouble expected no problems. The joke was that after twenty-five years with the defense brigades, Izzy asked for marines for the *Patton* because she didn't want to go anywhere without her security blanket. Since Trouble's choices were between a paltry exit bonus or taking a cut to second lieutenant and a platoon when what he wanted was a promotion to major and his own battalion, he'd jumped at the chance to staff six of the *Patton*'s secondary guns with his marine detachment.

After today's live fire exercise, Trouble wondered if he'd jumped right. The commander had bet her ship and their lives on some pretty crappy equipment, savvy moves, and a lot of luck. She'd won. Had she learned anything? Or would she be chasing the same thrill tomorrow? Trouble eyed her without staring.

She was strangely subdued. Still, her first question was a good one. "Chips, what's wrong with my ship?"

Lieutenant Chippanda Eifervald shook her head. "I told you before, skipper, and I'll tell you again. There ain't nothing wrong with this tub that couldn't be fixed by parking it alongside a pier and combing every square inch of it. I bet we'd find seven or eight good subassemblies to put back in stock to help the spares crunch. The rest, we sell by the pound."

"Yeah, Chips, but if we do that, what'll I command?"

"One hell of a beer bash," the exec offered.

The skipper took a deep breath. The stale, processed air was no different from what she'd breathed on a dozen stations. The gray walls around her could be any of a score of offices she'd worked out of or cubicles she'd lived in. But the proprietary twist to her lips told Trouble all there was to know. *This* air and *that* wall were *her* ship's. The skipper would give them up over her dead body. "Okay, crew, enough jokes. Start with the most important gear in your areas and make sure it'll work next time we need it. Guns, that means those six-inchers. Chips, that means maneuvering. Engineering"—Izzy glanced at Vu Van—"we got any problems?"

"If I had any failures, we would not be here to discuss them." The old Buddhist smiled, confident he could keep the plasma demons from eating his ship.

"Well, then, what did our little live-fire exercise tell us about the opposition?"

The XO shrugged. "There be pirates here, or was. They had a Unity cruiser that was a long way from the scrap heap. They may be bold and brassy against unarmed civilians, but they can't stand up to a fighting ship. That about sum it up, skipper?"

"In a nutshell," the skipper said with a scowl. "Let's go find ourselves another sucker."

The comm link buzzed at her elbow. She tapped it. "Yes?"

"We've got an all-ships message from a businessman on Hurtford Corner. Says he's being threatened by bandits and requests the assistance of any ship in the vicinity."

"Who?"

"A Paul Withwaterson, licensed on Pitt's Hope to sell farming equipment and related gear. Sounds like a legitimate call."

"Yeah," scowled Chips, "but is he really facing bandits, or does he just want us to overawe some rubes that don't want to pay what he wants to charge?" Trouble nodded; businessmen and the Navy rarely saw eye to eye on the proper use of naval presence.

"Has he made a previous request for help?" the captain asked. While Communications checked its database, the exec called up the star map. Hurtford Corner was five jumps away.

"Withwaterson has never made a request for assistance from the Navy. This message is a week old," Comm reported.

The skipper worried her lower lip. "Seven days to cross five jump points. No rush there." Each jump point had a buoy marking its place in space. Message traffic passed from buoy to buoy, but stayed in-system until the buoy jumped through just ahead of a ship, or until its message buffer filled and it dropped through the jump point to pass messages along to the next node. Ships could actually cover the distance between major planets faster than message traffic did between backwater systems.

"Not much of a dispersion," the XO noted. "The Hurtford Corner system is pretty isolated. Doubt if any other ship has gotten this message. It could be a month or more before it gets to District HQ and we get orders."

"Yeah." Now the boss was grinning. "Trouble, could your animals use some dirtside exercise?"

There was only one answer to that. "Marines always love getting their boots muddy, ma'am," he said with innocent relish. The skipper gave him a wink.

"XO, lay in a course for Hurtford Corner. One and a quarter gees, if you will."

Tom Gabon stood before the full-length mirror. He adjusted his tie a smidgen. This might be the frontier, the rim of human space, but a businessman still needed to make a good first impression. This was the big promotion he'd been looking for. As senior vice president for Z&G on Riddle, he would not only manage their planetwide facilities and construction projects, but would also be one of the thirteen who sat on the planet's council. This sure as hell beat testifying at a senate hearing.

Besides, what could he have told them? Sure, corporations kept their lines of communication open across the battle lines of the last war. Information was money. Just because Unity and Earth couldn't talk civil to each other didn't mean business had to stop. And maybe he had heard his board of directors brag that he could turn Unity's President Urm off and on like a light switch, but hey, anyone listening with one ear in the right bars during the war knew that.

All right, maybe I do know more than a lot, but that just means I know when to keep my mouth shut and listen more than a lot of them. Tom grinned; that's how he'd found out about this opportunity. Keeping his mouth shut and listening.

Tom glanced at his wrist unit. The station's elevators had been lifting passengers out of the *Goethe* for a half hour. It was time he made his appearance. As expected, four men were waiting for him as he exited the pier elevator.

"Mr. Gabon," a blue suit said with a smile. "We have a shuttle holding to take you down to Riddle. We can just make the meeting. Everyone wants to meet you." Tom had calculated that just right. He'd even remembered to include where the station was in its orbit around Riddle. Stan, his Navy puke brother, would be proud of him. Just because Tom understood how business worked didn't mean he was illiterate about how the stars and planets turned.

Tom followed his escort down the promenade, heading for more elevators. They chatted lightly about the planet's weather . . . hot and damp, as he'd been warned. The suit aimed Tom toward a small elevator. "I've reserved one for you."

Tom entered it; as he turned to face the door, his eye caught a gleam in the hand of the man behind him. A small cylinder with a needle. Before Tom could react, the needle was jammed in his neck.

"What the hell?" Tom got out even as his knees went weak and his eyes grayed out.

"You didn't think we'd let a snoop like you boss up one of our biggest concerns, did you?" The blue suit snorted as Tom collapsed. "But don't worry. We have work for you. Oh, will you work."

The sun ruled the blue summer sky with authority questioned only by two dust clouds showing where other tractors were at work on the rolling croplands. This was the high summer that Ruth Edris-Morton loved. Long, hot days full of hard work followed by cool summer nights and dreamless sleep.

Ruth reached the end of a row and carefully brought her tractor around, aligning the sprayer for the next pass. Pest control was only a minor part of the mixture this morning . . . and the least expensive. The activators in the mix would turn the modified soybeans into the initial feedstock the biocompanies paid hard money for. Pa would have a good cash crop this year. With luck there'd be enough left over to stake Brother and Miriam to a homestead of their own, and none too soon. Slim looked about ready to bring a wife of his own home. Pa wouldn't be shorthanded, not with Ruth around. She scowled at Pa's blessing.

Ruth settled the tractor in the groove. Just to make sure, she verified it against the Global Position Satellites. Plus or minus .000 meters the GPS told her. Pa proudly said she had a farmer's eye. Yes, she knew the equipment, the crops, and

the fields. Maybe if she'd spent more time with Ma, she'd
have landed a better man than Mordy.

Then the radio squawked.

"Anybody, can you help us?" The voice was young, female, and very scared. It hit Ruth in that place women held
sacred for children. For Ruth, it echoed hollow.

She grabbed for the mike, but Grandma Seddik, who
guarded the emergency channels now that her arthritis was
too bad to let her work the fields, was already talking.
"What's your problem, honey?" she said, soft and warm like
the quilts she made.

"Brother spotted slackers on the ridge. They had rifles.
Dad and Mom are getting the guns out. Dad told me to call
in."

"Good, honey. What's your name?"

"Oh! I'm Lizie. Lizie Abdoes." Embarrassment tinged the
answer to this basic question. The girl was eight, maybe
nine, and knew radio discipline. That she'd forgotten told
Ruth how terrified the little one was.

"Good girl, and what did you get for your birthday this
year?" Grandma Seddik was going straight into the security
check that had become standard while the Unity bullies
were around. No matter how scared a young girl like Lizie
might be, she knew what she got for her birthday—and how
to say it wrong if a gun was already pointed at her head.

"A doll, a rag doll, and shoes. Boots, really."

"This is a legit distress call," Grandma snapped. "Who's
in position to help?"

Ruth had been listening, even as she kept the tractor on
course, spray darkening the beans, no overlap, no misses.
Now she zoomed her guidance map out, and frowned. The
Abdoes place was thirty miles away. Dots lit up as people
reported their location and availability. Grandma would be
getting a full readout on armament as well. Ruth was about
to report her presence when someone at the house beat her
to it.

"Sis, Pa wants you in fast," came on the family channel.
"Slim's already in. Mom, Miriam, and the youngsters will

hold the station." Brother, Slim, and Pa were the usual contribution from the family to the community's Quick Response Team. While she and Mordy had been working for the Seddiks, QRTs were the only times she'd seen family. Now, she was back on Pa's team.

"On my way," Ruth answered. She detached the sprayer; in a moment she was gunning down the row, careful of the bean plants on either side of the tractor's big balloon tires. Once into a fallow field, she angled straight for home. Surrounded by barn and outbuildings, the white-painted two-story house with a new wing for Brother, Miriam, and their twins gleamed in the sun under a mat black roof of solar collectors. Pa, Brother, and Slim were waiting in the dusty yard between the house and the barn, ready to screw metal plates to the cab and vitals of the tractor. Miriam handed up Ruth's rifle, extra ammo boxes, and a basket of food. Mom held the twins, one to each hip; Tina held all three of the women's rifles. Ruth's youngest brother and sister, ten and twelve, already peered from the sandbagged lookout post atop the barn, the family's practice rifles pointed out. The kids looked scared and trying to hide it.

"Take care," Ma said, blowing Pa a quick good-bye kiss. Miriam climbed up the tractor to give Brother the same. Ruth looked away, missing someone to say good-bye to.

"We always do," Pa answered Mom, then turned. "Ruth, you drive. Boys . . ." His nod sent each of the men to a side view slot in the tractor's makeshift armor. He settled into the seat next to Ruth as she put the rig in gear. "Head for the Krogers' place," Pa told her; Ruth gunned the tractor. The armor about balanced out the lack of something dragging behind, though it made for a top-heavy drive. When they were kids, Pa listened to the net on earphones. Today, he listened through the speaker. Reports of availability rolled over Ruth. She ignored them, concentrating on getting where she was going fast . . . and safe.

Still, Ruth couldn't ignore the change. *Slackers weren't supposed to be problems.* They were just people who didn't want or couldn't find work. Before the war, they'd begged and sometimes stolen a few things. During the war, they'd been rounded up and put in the army—the army Mordy was drafted into. Now Mordy was still gone, and the slackers were back with guns. She'd gone home . . . and Pa sandbagged the lookout post above the barn.

Ruth made it to the Krogers' in twenty minutes.

Close to a dozen rigs were parked haphazardly between the Krogers' house and outbuildings. Ruth hadn't even brought the tractor to a halt before Pa swung out the door and trotted for a clump of elders. "Stay with the rig, crew," he said without looking back. Slim was already getting out, his eyes on the Zabossa rig with Becky. With a sigh, Slim dropped back into his seat. Becky waved to him; Slim waved back.

Most of the crews left behind were alertly eyeing the open fields and rolling woodlands around the farm. A light smudge marred the horizon where the Abdoes' place was. Ruth checked her motor readouts; storage was at eighty percent. She spread the solar wings to catch some rays, then called up the latest photo of the Abdoes' station and the land between it and her tractor. Balancing distance against cover, she plotted the best course.

She'd just finished when Pa came back. "More are coming, but we got to get somebody there pronto. Those here are going now." He glanced at the display. "You got a route planned?"

She quickly sketched her path. He nodded. "We're lead tractor. Do it, Ruth. Boys, look sharp, lock and load."

With a hard swallow, Slim pulled back the arming bolt on his rifle, then safetied it. Brother did the same. Ruth folded the solar wings as she gunned the rig. As usual, Pa was leading the first reaction team. Before he emigrated, Pa had put in his time with the army on LornaDo. Pa usually ended up with the lead on days like this, and Ruth had been studying how he went about it since she turned sixteen. Now Pa rarely modified her approach drives for fires, floods, and slacker problems.

Ruth covered the first half of the ten-mile drive at a good

clip, keeping both eyes on the road and letting Pa and the boys worry about surprises. The other tractors and trucks followed in single file behind her, allowing plenty of room for her to spring any trap they were heading into. Ruth glanced at Pa; did he want her to slow down? His eyes were straight ahead. Swallowing her growing fear, Ruth kept the throttle forward as the smoke plume grew in the sky.

At the woods this side of the Abdoes place, Pa called a halt. He signaled for the rifle teams to dismount and hoof it through the trees, then went forward at the head of the men and women. Ruth edged the tractor off the dirt road, hunting for a path through the trees. She didn't have to be told the road was no place for her today. She was almost through the woods when the net came alive.

"Don't look like there's nobody here. Let's close in."

Since that wasn't Pa talking, Ruth continued her cautious advance. When she finally did come up on the plowed fields, several trucks were already parked in front of the blackened house. The homestead had been built with tough local wood; it smoldered more than burned. Ruth's eyes were drawn to the front door. It had been blown in . . . explosives, or some sort of rocket. Pa would know. Carefully, she drove across the field and looped around back. Damage there was limited to windows and doors blown out. No bodies, just a few dead chickens. She spotted Brother and Slim kneeling beside tracks where the cows and horses had been herded off. Around the pig and goat pen were decapitated heads, guts, and blood.

"Looks like a quick butcher job," Brother surmised.

Around front, the human casualties were already under blankets. "Who'd they kill?" Slim asked.

Becky was leaning over, her last meal splattered on the dirt. She wiped her mouth and looked up. "The kids. The little kids," she whimpered. "Why kill kids not big enough for schooling? And their pa," she added.

Slim knelt beside her, an arm around his future wife. Brother's eyes had turned toward home, and his wife and twins. Ruth knew the answer. Kids slowed you down. These slackers must be planning on moving very fast. They'd better; if this posse caught them, they were dead. Ruth called up her map again. If she was running, where would she head?

North, east, south was open farmland—no place to hide there. To the west were mountains, with heavy forest and brush for cover. Lots of places to hide, no roads, no place to take tractors. But hills had rivers and lakes. She searched. Yep, there was the General Store. Old man Sanchez traded for pelts and herbs. His place was on Lake Guadalupe, easy to reach by boat. And he had boats that could reach back into the mountains faster than people could ride. "Brother."

Both siblings looked over her shoulder as she outlined a pursuit. Brother nodded when she was done. "Let's tell Pa."

Pa was in the middle of the elders, and the elders were in the middle of an argument. Old man Seddik was all for going home. "We can't catch 'em. Better we get ready for next time. Let's talk next Thursday at the dance. We got to plan."

The younger men, many friends of the dead Abdoes, wanted to hit the trail right now. "We got to stop these bastards. They're loaded down with the stuff they stole. We can catch them. I say chase 'em 'til hell freezes."

"And what's to keep them from bushwhacking you?" Ms. Zabossa cut in. That brought quiet for a moment.

Pa rubbed his chin. "You watch your step chasing them, and they get away. You chase them fast and reckless, and they set up an ambush. The damn army may not have taught them much, but it would have taught them that."

"So what do we do?" came an anguished cry from the back. "Just sit on our thumbs while they kill our kids and steal our wives?" Ruth saw her chance in the silence and took it.

"Pa, we don't have to chase right behind them. We could get ahead of them if we used the boats from Trader Sanchez to get up valley before they can."

There was a long silence as people called up maps in their heads and roughed out what Ruth had done. "Yeah" came from several. Pa gave her a tight smile. Old man Seddik settled it with a nod. "Okay. You folks chase them, but not too close. Joe Edris takes half and heads for the trading post."

"I'll get horses."

"I'll start the chase on foot. You give me a call when you got the horses."

Quickly, the teams organized themselves. In five minutes Pa was seated beside Ruth as she led five rigs for the trading post.

Ruth gunned the tractor, going for every bit of speed she could. Each curve was a challenge, each straight section a race. Pa said nothing. In the silence she felt his pride in her. That was something she hadn't felt about herself in a long time.

Caution was what she felt as the Sanchez place came in view as they crested a hill above the lake. One glance showed none of the usual activity around the post. Even the dog was just lying there. Five minutes later, Pa ordered a halt. Through the trees and across a bay, Ruth had a better view. "The boats are gone," Brother reported. The door to the store was hanging open. The dog was lying in its own blood.

Pa waited for the other rigs to catch up. Then he ordered the rifle teams to slip through the woods and surrounded the place. Pa kept his eye on the store for a good fifteen minutes before he had Ruth slowly edge the tractor forward. He and Brother entered the store while Slim checked out the dock.

"Boats have been stove in," he quickly shouted.

Pa was slower in reporting. When he came out of the store, he whistled in the folks from the woods. Brother sat heavily on the steps. "Poor Paco didn't even know it was coming. He's there behind his counter, a shot between his eyes. Place has been ransacked." Brother choked on his words.

"Where're Agnatha and the kids?" Ruth asked, scared of the answer.

"Don't know." Pa sighed through a scowl. He reached through the tractor door for the phone. "Edris here. Stop the pursuit, Jeb. Sanchez's place has been sacked. Old man's dead. The rest are gone. Boats are sunk. Edris to everybody, we are gonna have to rethink ourselves."

The acknowledgments were slow and bitter. Pa's face was the deepest scowl Ruth had ever seen . . . and something else, hard and cold . . . as he handed back the phone. "Looks like I got to go to Hurtford City."

"I'm going too," Ruth added.

Zylon Plovdic didn't bother getting out of her truck. She went down the form, quickly checking off one box after another. Yes, the survey team had sufficient supples for ninety days, their safety equipment was in order, and they had an emergency locator signal. True to the founders of Hurtford Corner, she verified only that they had what they needed for their own safety. She had no duty to check for hidden weapons, explosives, or other potential dangers to the community. She grinned; the rifles, ammunition boxes, and rockets were in clear view.

The leader of the "survey party" stood beside her truck. He accepted his official permit with a silent nod. He, along with five others, actually would be surveying for the mineral wealth identified in the permit.

The other dozen or so riders collecting behind the pack mules were another matter. Zylon knew every one of them. Over the last several years, she'd tossed most of them in jail for several kinds of unacceptable behavior. She'd been happy to pass them over to the first Unity Planet Leader when he arrived. Now she was just as glad to turn them loose in the mountains west of town. There, they wouldn't cause her any trouble. Though, unlike the survey team, they would not long be riding west.

Soon enough, they'd be ranging with the other three batches of raiders among the farm stations to the north. But that was none of Zylon's concern.

The survey team leader accepted his authorization from Zylon and passed her the check in the agreed-upon sum on an off-world bank. With mutual smiles, they went their own ways. He to the western hills, she back to her office at the Center for Public Safety. Yes, she had the most volunteer hours of anyone in the city, all of them officially to secure the public safety. What they were securing for her was another matter entirely.

TWO

"THAT'S HARDLY A town," Izzy said, shaking her head at Hurtford City's pretensions. It was the planet's one claim to urban living. She doubted more than thirty thousand people occupied the shallow valley where two rivers merged. The ridge to its east did have a five-kilometer-long landing strip; a dammed river to its west offered a wide reservoir for shuttles who preferred a water landing. "Comm, have we been hailed by the port captain?"

"No, ma'am. I gave up waiting and called the number in the book. Got a recorded message. There're out to lunch. Supposed to be back by one."

The XO frowned at the screen. "Looks to me like nine, maybe ten o'clock local down there," he said dubiously.

"Me too," Izzy snorted. "Comm, did they say what day they'd be back from lunch?"

"Didn't even say what month, ma'am," Comm answered, getting into the humor.

Izzy had enough of the joke. "XO, break out the gig. Make sure any maintenance deficiencies on it have been corrected." She tapped her comm link. "Lieutenant, I'd like a marine honor guard to accompany me dirtside. The emphasis should be more on the guard than the honor."

"No trouble, ma'am."

"On the contrary, I want you with me, Trouble."

"Damn, that's gonna interfere with my afternoon nap."

"See you at the gig in half an hour, Lieutenant. Out."

The XO was rubbing his chin and giving her one of his motherly looks. Izzy set a prim, innocent smile on her face and asked, "You got a problem, Stan?"

He leaned close and kept his voice down. "Ma'am, if there is a problem down there, a captain's place is not in the middle of it. If you want, I can lead the marines."

"Stan, we don't have a problem. This is a formal call by the skipper of a visiting warship on the governor or whatever they're calling their boss man this week. I'll arrange for some liberty, see if they've got a rural hospital that needs painting. You know, do the nice stuff. And if Mr. Withwaterson wants to be at my elbow, making friendly sounds, he just may see some movement by the locals. I'm not going in there shooting, Stan, despite the stories you may have heard about me."

The XO chuckled and shook his head. "And since you've made up your mind, butt out, boy."

"I didn't say that." Izzy tried to look hurt. With her lack of practice, she doubted she succeeded.

"Then quit thinking it so loud."

"Go check on the gig, Stan."

"On my way," he said, launching himself for the bridge hatch. With no station to swing around, the *Patton* was in for some serious zero-gee time; the crew would need liberty. They'd get it, as soon as Izzy verified the "bandits" were just a businessman's hyperbole.

Two hours later, as they finished their landing roll, they still hadn't heard from any portmaster. Izzy let the marines exit first. At the foot of the gig's stairs, she took her first look at Hurtford Corner. Wheat or some sort of grain crop, spring-fresh and green, covered most of the shallow depression between her and the city to the west. More green stretched away to where rolling hills started the climb toward the mountains they'd overflown on approach. A deep breath took in smells of cooling gig, morning rain, and sun-warmed earth. Several trucks and two cars raised dust on the single-lane road to town.

"Nothing like a sonic boom to let folks know they got company," Trouble observed dryly. The marine lieutenant, in dress whites, sword, and pistol, shook his head at their immediate surroundings. "No hangar, no control tower. Must not expect much business." Izzy nodded. The latest report on Hurtford Corner dated back to the war. Did they still have a governor, or, now that the Unity overlords were gone, had they returned to a group of elders with a city manager hired for the town? Intelligence was mildly curious; Izzy would inform them of what she found.

The first truck disgorged a chubby, balding young man with a broad smile and a hand out. "I'm Paul Withwaterson. I am so glad to see you."

I bet you are. Izzy shook the offered hand. "We are here. You seem to be safe. Where're the port authorities? Their voice mail said they were out to lunch."

"Oh, that. They've been out to lunch since they lost the war. My ship got the same message. It hasn't been changed?"

"No. Who's the rest of the welcoming committee?"

Mr. Withwaterson turned. "The other trucks are from my competitors. That black car is the city manager. He's the closest you'll get to a formal welcome. He's the one you have to talk to about the lack of police services. My warehouse has been broken into five times since I landed."

"You got any cargo in that dinky thing?" came a shout from the next arriving truck. A big man with a mammoth red nose took in the gig and crew with a jaundiced eye.

"Commander Inez Umboto, captain of the Humanity ship *Patton*, at your service," she answered.

"No shit. Well, no trade goods, no interest from me." The man growled and did a U-turn. As he passed the next arriving truck, he shouted, "They got nothing, Dean. We wasted our time."

Not the trusting type, the driver still drove over to them.

A thin, white-haired man studied them through thick glasses. "Navy types, huh?"

"At your service," Izzy smiled, and got a gunned motor for her trouble. The truck narrowly missed the arriving car.

A young man, short and thin, greeted Izzy with a wide smile and a handshake. "Mikhail Shezgo, city manager. We've never had a Navy ship drop by, but what can I do for you?"

Izzy gave the official line by heart. "We're here on a routine visit. To show Hurtford Corner it's a part of a bigger universe. Maybe recruit a few new hands, buy fresh fruits and vegetables, paint a hospital or community center. Think of us as ambassadors from the Society of Humanity." Done with the basics, she went on. "With no station to give us gravity, I'll want to give my people liberty for a good part of each day."

"That may be a problem." Mr. Shezgo answered quickly. Izzy had been expecting a brush-off, but not this soon. She raised a questioning eyebrow. "I suspect," he went on, "your young folks want what any youngsters want at the end of a long day. A couple of cool ones. Well, our local brewmasters make just enough for one day, two at the most. You drop three, four hundred thirsty sailors on us and some folks, yours or mine, are gonna go wanting tonight. Think you could hold your folks aboard for a day? Tomorrow, I can promise you a real cotillion."

Which had to be about the nicest way Izzy had ever been told to bugger off and let us have some time to get ready for you. Before she could answer, a siren went off in town, drawing her eyes to a rising cloud of gray smoke.

"Looks like a building's afire." Trouble broke the quiet as they all turned to watch. A moment later, another siren joined the first, though from the sound of it, this one was moving.

"That was a fast response." Mr. Shezgo grinned. "Volunteer fire department is right on this one. Probably just a kitchen fire," he concluded.

"Or someone who didn't pay up," Mr. Withwaterson shot

back. "You don't pay bribes and strange things start happening."

Mr. Shezgo turned on him. "Trader, you are not a part of our community. You haven't volunteered to spend any time with the local patrol, the fire department, or any of the other community service sections. If you're not going to work with us, you really ought to pay something back to the community."

The businessman's ears showed red. "So a 'gratuity' here, a 'donation' there, a warehouse broken into yesterday, a fire tomorrow and a 'tip' to the boys who turn out so quickly to put it out. This is no way to do business," he roared.

"The founders of Hurtford Corner never intended business to be done your way. And no, our people don't do business that way either. We're different."

"Different! You're not different. You're downright daft. Captain, there is no global network. No stock exchange. Nothing needed to do business."

Mr. Shezgo laughed. "You bet. We don't need them. We don't want them. We get along fine without them."

Izzy suspected she was walking into the middle of a long-running argument, and the source of the call for help she'd intercepted. This planet wasn't doing business the Harvard Business School way, and Mr. Withwaterson had problems adjusting. Well, it wasn't the Navy's job to educate him. "Ah, gentlemen, if you don't mind, I'll leave you to your discussions. Mr. Shezgo, I'll bring down the first liberty party tomorrow, about noon. If you could let my ship know what time you are keeping, the portmaster's message says he's out to lunch until one."

The city manager snorted. "We don't have a portmaster. That's a leftover from the Unity thing."

"Yeah. They went out to lunch about the time they lost the war and haven't come back," Mr. Withwaterson added. "Personally, I think this whole planet is out to lunch."

Shezgo shook his head. "You just bring your crew down tomorrow. Captain, we'll show your people a good time."

Izzy boarded her gig, while the other two returned to their previously scheduled argument.

"How'd it go dirtside?" was the XO's first question when Izzy and Trouble sailed onto the bridge.

"About like I expected," Izzy said as she bounced off the ceiling and dove for her station chair. "The locals and visitors speak the same standard English and can't understand a word. Trouble, turn out your marines in dress red-and-blues to impress tomorrow. I'll also want extra shore patrol detachments. I still don't know what's down there. Probably nothing. But until I'm sure, let's be careful while we have fun."

"Yes, ma'am"s answered her from around the bridge.

"I do not like problems," Big Al growled.

"Well, if you'd just used some of that pull you're all the time bragging about to handle Withwaterson, we wouldn't have a problem," Zef Davis shot back.

Zylon Plovdic kept her mouth shut. Big Al's problems, whether people, places, or things, tended to disappear. The more Zef talked, the more Big Al growled about problems. Pretty soon, Zef was going to disappear. Which was no skin off Zylon's nose. She, like Zef, had been born on Hurtford Corner. She also, like Zef, wanted out of the sameness Hurtford Corner prided itself on. When Zef disappeared, Zylon would be another step closer to where she wanted to be.

Conversation paused as the Hurtford standard fare of stew, bread, and beer arrived. The three sat in the back room of a restaurant whose management understood their need for quiet and privacy.

As the waiter retired, Zef continued. "Now, we have two problems. Two guys from the farm stations have rolled into town. I expect they want to talk to the town elders. It would be a disaster if they chanced upon *your* problem."

"Then you will have to get them out of town before they can." Big Al smiled. Zylon would not want to be on the receiving end of that smile.

"How are you going to handle the navy?" Zef harped on Big Al's part of the problem, ignoring his own.

Big Al pushed himself away from the dining table and the boring food that covered it. He glanced at Zylon. "I understand the Navy is looking for recruits. I believe that gives us an interesting avenue to rush them on their way. Ms. Plovdic, can you help me arrange an appropriate greeting for the crew?"

"I would be glad to." Zylon raised her mug of beer.

Alexander Popov raised his in salute, and drained it. "A quaint local brew. Not unlike a minor one I tasted on Vega. Have you ever been to Vega?"

"Not yet." They exchanged a smile, full of confidence she would see Vega soon.

Ruth hadn't seen Hurtford City for four or five years. Then, like every farm girl who came to town, she'd been husband hunting . . . and she'd found herself one. Mordy, just off a shuttle, had looked at her like no boy ever had. She'd taken him home, just like her Ma had taken Pa home. So what went wrong? Pa said Mordy was nothing like him, but Ruth couldn't help wondering what Ma had that she didn't.

While her life had gone in circles, Hurtford City had grown out. The reprocessing plant for the pharmacologicals had been out in the country then. Now it was surrounded by shops, homes, and a solar power plant with its own collection of small factories. As they came down into the valley, Ruth saw buildings stretching almost as far as she could see.

The hotel they stayed at was the same one, now looking a lot smaller and older than Ruth remembered. As they off-loaded fresh fruit and vegetables, bags of grain and potatoes to pay their lodging, people passed them—lots of people. Folks didn't wave or shout hello. It was as if, surrounded by so many, they didn't see anyone at all.

Not everyone was busy. Slackers, in parts of Unity uniforms, lounged against the building across from the hotel. None showed guns, but Ruth wondered how many would be willing to kill people like the Abdoes or the trader.

After checking into the hotel, the three gathered at a table. Mr. Seddik and Pa represented the stations. Ruth was there because she'd gotten in the truck. Nobody but her husband could tell a married woman what to do. This was the first time Ruth had tested the freedom that Mordy had left to her. She was none too sure how she felt about it.

While they'd been unloading, Mr. Seddik had heard a rumor that a Navy ship was in orbit. "I think that was their shuttle we saw landing as we came in. That might give us a bit more leverage. City elders won't want us raising a stink while the Navy's around. They'll listen to us real well and real fast."

Pa wasn't so sure. "If these folks were going to help us, they would have. I don't think they will, or can."

"Then we go to the Navy," Seddik countered. "It's their job to knock heads, isn't it?"

Pa shrugged; everyone assumed his time with the LornaDo army made him an expert on such things. He might be all the local expertise they had on military affairs, but he was the first to point out that wasn't much. "To make a rabbit stew, first you got to catch a rabbit. Five hundred Navy types, two hundred miles up, with laser cannons aren't exactly what you need to hunt a rabbit."

"So what do we do?" Ruth asked. She might not have a vote, but the least she could do was ask dumb questions to keep Pa and old man Seddik from talking around and around the obvious.

The old man sighed. "I'll see about the next meeting of the city elders. Why don't you try to find out something about the Navy? When you got two bunches that might lend you a hand, it's best to know as much as you can about both."

Ruth would rather have gone with Mr. Seddik. She'd seen all the spacers she needed to see for the rest of her life. But Pa took her elbow, so she went looking for spacers.

Izzy spent the afternoon entangled in details. It seemed a shame to visit a planet whose main product was fresh fruit

and vegetables and not take on a full larder. The price for in-
spected and bug-free veggies would just have to be haggled,
not something her supply officer was comfortable doing.
Izzy's bigger problem was raised by the city manager.

"Uh, Captain, I don't know how long your folks have
been in space, or what their idea of a good time is, but, while
we got plenty of beer for the taking, our young women are
not."

"And your young men?" Izzy couldn't pass up the jab
at old-fashioned attitudes.

The city manager had the good humor to laugh. "What
I'm trying to get at is that our women are free to do what
they want. Dance with anyone. Go for a walk with anyone.
But when they say no, they mean it. Most of 'em will say no
twice if they think someone is hard of hearing, but if a girl
screams for help, you better believe a dozen good folks will
be right there in a second. And they'll make sure the guy
who didn't understand 'no' gets to understanding its meaning."

Izzy wasn't so sure the Navy hadn't applied the same
education to some of its own. Still, this was no topic to be
confused on. "I will get my dumb spacer back in one piece?"

"Oh, yes. Just a bit the worse for wear—the first time."

"Mr. Shezgo, if you will make sure my 'worse for wear'
crew member gets turned over to the shore patrol, I will
make sure he, or she, spends the rest of our stay aboard ship.
Dented heads I can handle. Dead ones will be another
matter."

"Then I think we have an understanding. On Hurtford
Corner, we teach people the right way the first time. We got
too much open space to waste folks."

Izzy had the word passed to her division heads and on to
the chiefs. "Anybody comes back from liberty with a black
eye better not plan on going down again."

Trouble paused while a private from the trailing truck double-
timed up to open the car door for him and the skipper. He,
like the young marine, was in full dress red-and-blues, com-

plete with choke collar, sword, and pistol. Izzy had made it
clear that Trouble and his marines were responsible for the
perimeter security at whatever gala the locals laid on. He'd
gotten the word out to his troops that as soon as the dumb
swabbies proved there were no land mines out there, he'd
turn them loose for some fun. His marines provided smart-
looking door guards, hall guards, and a couple of them were
serving as waiters, making sure the officers' glasses were
kept filled . . . with water and soft drinks brought down from
the ship.

The skipper was one paranoid woman. Trouble liked that.

The party was quite a spectacle. The local women were
turned out in everything from miniskirts with frilly undies
that often flashed into view to floor-length dresses that could
be tight sheaths or swirling skirts. Tight and loose, glitter
and bows swirled next to each other on the dance floor. The
men were somewhat more subdued in slacks and shirts with
colorful needlework, although the city manager and several
others wore something like tuxedos. Each different, the people had come for fun, and, to the tunes of several alternating
bands, they had it.

Regularly, Trouble made the rounds of his own men.
Even though their red-and-blues clashed with the soft pas-
tels the community center was hung in, Trouble assured
them he appreciated their decorative contribution to the gala
night—and that they stood ready to switch from toy soldiers
to real ones. The night stayed hot, so he switched the guard
detail from an hour on and an hour off to one on, two off so
he wouldn't lose any to heat prostration. That meant pulling
the guards off the rear side of the center and covering that
quarter of the perimeter with the roaming NCO, but it
seemed a minor call. He did a quick touch-base with a tall
blond from the local Office of Public Safety and made regular radio checks with the chief heading up the Shore Patrol.
His teams were circulating, but had nothing to report but
sailors and civilians having fun.

After two hours of this, Trouble was starting to relax as he
rejoined the skipper. She was diplomatically declining a

dance. The song being played could be quite sedate, or otherwise, depending on who was leading. To her raised eyebrow, he answered with a thumbs-up. She turned back to a small circle of people and their discussion as he moved up to cover her back. Mr. Withwaterson was in full sail.

"Your communications are narrow-band. I can give you ten times the bandwidth. Your solar power cells are twenty years behind, your storage cells at least fifty. I can update every part of your economy."

"Why?" asked an elderly man in a tux.

"Why!" the businessman echoed in wonder.

"Yes, why?" A younger man in a nearly transparent lace shirt cut in. "They work fine. They get the job done. Why change what is doing the job for us?"

"But you can do it so much better, faster, cheaper with my equipment," Withwaterson sputtered.

The young man shook his head. "But what we have is paid for. It's doing what we want. What off-planet exchange we've got needs to go for expansion where we see a need. We don't need a central fusion plant, or fancy doodads. The mines we've opened meet our needs. What you've got costs too much."

"If you'd quit stonewalling me and let my products onto the market, you'd find them indispensable. Whoever has been ripping them off from my warehouse already knows that." The glances exchanged around the circle didn't seem to agree, as to whether that related to the "indispensable" claim or the part about stolen goods, Trouble couldn't decide.

"Lieutenant"—the city manager broke the silence before it ripped—"let me introduce some of the city elders to you." Mr. Donovan was the older man. Mr. Poniatow had to be in his twenties. Trouble tried to suppress any surprise, but it must have showed.

"I speak for the younger and less experienced," the young man said as he eyed the older. "Maybe less hidebound." The two locals shared a knowing smile. "Still, innovation for its own sake is not why my great-grandfather came to Hurtford

Corner. We are quite content to be a bit slower than the rest of humanity so long as we are comfortable and enjoying ourselves." He turned to the band.

Four women had just finished backing up two others, one on sax, one singing a slow torch song. The couples on the dance floor had enjoyed the slow dance even if the sax had missed a few notes, and the singer's voice broke on the final high one.

"We see nothing wrong with the real and natural. Why give up so much to chase the perfect, the flawless, the plastic? Next time you come, Mr. Withwaterson, bring a catalogue of what you can deliver. Most of what's in your warehouse is just taking up space. I believe both your rent and restaurant tab are overdue. You should pay them."

"I can't pay until I sell something."

"Then sell it. We are not stopping you," said Mr. Donovan.

"For a tenth or a hundredth of what it's worth." The color was again rising up Mr. Withwaterson's neck.

"Which is what it is worth to us. Now, if you'll excuse me, I've been promised several dances by a certain someone." With that, Mr. Poniatow bowed slightly and joined another man. They disappeared onto the swirling dance floor.

"You know, Mr. Withwaterson," Captain Umboto raised her glass in a mock salute, "that is just about what Earth said to the frontier worlds when they set the price for resources and finished goods before the war."

"I had expected more support from the Navy."

"I'll have supply go over what you have and see if we need any of it. That might at least allow you to pay your bills."

From the glare the businessman gave his skipper, Trouble seriously doubted the man appreciated the navy's help. Captain Umboto just shook her head as Mr. Withwaterson stomped away. "Someday, Trouble, when I'm old and got nothing better to do, I'm going to get myself a professorship at some big university and teach MBAs a course on the proper application of military intimidation to the negotiating process."

"The way you applied six inches of laser to that pirate's butt," he grinned.

"No, Trouble. As my old boss used to say, killing them is the easy part. Persuading someone you're not allowed to kill—now, that's what separates the men from the boys."

"Boys?" Trouble tried to raise his eyebrow a tad higher. It was about as high as he could get it and still keep it on his forehead. The skipper was not known for accepting put-downs, sexist or otherwise, placidly.

"Andy had given up on me ever growing into a mature female officer. Said I'd just have to make do with my girlish innocence."

They both laughed. "Well, skipper, with all this water you've been forcing on us, and despite this monkey suit's wool content, I must go where even you can't follow."

"Think you can handle it?"

"About the only thing I'm sure I can." He turned, still chuckling. The skipper was one tough broad. He pitied the poor SOB that got on her wrong side. The head was near the back of the building. He got in just ahead of someone with a cart that looked like he wanted to do maintenance. Trouble wondered how someone got stuck with the janitorial duties on a party night like this, but decided not to ask the dour-faced guy. He quickly did his duty and was washing his hands when the man next to him reached across him for the paper towels.

"Pardon me," the guy in shirt and slacks said.

"No trouble." Trouble smiled, stepping out of the way. The man's hands followed him. For a brief second, the marine got a glance at a small cylinder, tiny needle sticking out. Then it was in his neck. "What the hell" and a weak swing was all he got out before his knees caved in. Stretched out on the floor, he got a view of the maintenance wagon rolling in, the door to a side compartment opening like the third pit of hell. Trouble figured he'd just about fit in there. Then his vision blacked out and he quit trying to figure out anything for a while.

Ruth didn't expect to have a problem finding spacers; she had found Mordy and his friends easily enough five years ago. They'd been decked out in outfits you could spot a mile away and acting as if they owned the planet. Pa ignored the first collection of spacers they stumbled upon that evening. They looked young and pretty forlorn in their pasty white uniforms. "Let's find someone with a bit of authority," he said.

"How will you tell?"

"Trust me, Ruthie, you'll have no doubt when you see one."

Ruth didn't have any doubt when they spotted two spacers. One wasn't all that different from the others, except for a hard hat and a black armband. The other looked like he owned all space, and had covered most of it. Pa sidled up to that one. "How's it going, Chief?"

"Nice night." The older spacer wore a cloth hat, different from the helmet of the youngster beside him and the others walking away. Ruth had seen anchors like the one that decorated his hat on boats on the lake. What was a spacer doing wearing it? The chief's eyes roved over the night sky, taking in the stars. "A nice night to get some fresh air." Ruth wondered how long they could talk about the weather, but then, if this fellow was a kind of chaperone, he wouldn't be interested in telling some stranger if he was having problems.

Pa took another tack. "How would you like some fresh food, apples, pears, lettuce?"

"Now that would make you a man after my own heart. Mess could sure use some chow that hasn't been frozen for a year or nine. Understand the supply officer has set up shop somewhere around Twenty-third and Main, if you know where that is."

"Imagine I could find it. Where are all the officers? They having their own fun?"

"The locals put on a party for them at a community center. Several other community centers got shindigs going for the kids, too. Look for the one with the fancy red-and-blue doormen. It's somewhere over there." He shook his hand in a general southeasterly direction. Pa led Ruth off that way. They passed shops, restaurants, hotels, and homes. They located two large centers sporting dances. One had something to do with a religious group, the other was for some kind of Earth animal with four legs and horns bigger than any cow Ruth had ever seen, but all she actually saw were people having a good time. They were doubling back when they spotted the place with the fancy doormen. They'd missed it the first time when they walked past the back of it.

Pa headed for the front door, Ruth right behind him, but, unlike the other places that were wide open, here the doormen were keeping people out. "Just a second," Pa bristled. "I may be a mud farmer, but I got just as much right to party in there as any city boy."

"I don't care if you're God himself," growled an older marine, gold chevrons covering most of his sleeves. "Nobody's coming in or out of this building until we find our lieutenant."

Pa, who'd looked like he was about to shove past two guys twice his size, even if they did have guns with long knives jutting from their barrels, backed up fast. "Daughter, never mess with armed men when they think somebody's done wrong to one of their own. Especially when a sergeant is pissed about what might have been done to his officer."

They slipped back a ways. Not so far they couldn't see and hear what was going on, but far enough that no one would mistake them for trying to cross the line. Several minutes later a diminutive woman in a long skirt and uniform coat, three gold stripes prominently displayed on each shoulder, came to a scowling halt at the front door. Several city men, full of self-importance, followed on her footsteps, arguing that they and their people had every right to leave. She ignored them the way Ruth did flies around the pigpen. "Sergeant," she said in a voice hardly louder than a whisper.

Immediately, the tall marine with all the gold on his

sleeves was in front of her. "Yes ma'am," he said, standing as tall and straight as a barn door. The chatter died.

"Do you have anything to report on the lieutenant?"

"No ma'am. We've gone through this building from top to bottom, stem to stern. No sign of him. Short of taking it apart brick by brick, I don't think we will." The sergeant sounded quite ready to do the demolition job—with his bare hands.

The woman stared out into the street, right through Ruth. Her face was calm, a jarring difference from the excited men around her. Only the tightness around her eyes told Ruth that something was going on behind the face. Something that made Ruth shiver.

"Captain Umboto," one of the city fellows interrupted the quiet. "Crew are all the time jumping ship out here. They see a nice leg, a well-filled sweater, and suddenly their starship doesn't look so appealing. Ask Mr. Withwaterson. One of the crewmen on the ship that brought him missed the last crew call. He's somewhere out on the farm stations, raising corn and kids. There's nothing criminal behind your man disappearing. I saw a number of our young girls measuring him for husband size. And he wasn't ignoring the looks his fancy suit got."

The Navy woman's eyes narrowed. She whirled on the speaker. "Lieutenant Tordon *is* a *marine*. Always was. Always will be. His kind do not jump ship. They do not leave their shipmates in the lurch."

A short, balding young man raised an eyebrow. "Navy's been pushing early outs. Sure you won't get back to base to find he's already turned in his bonus application and been processed out?"

The woman slowly turned on the speaker. "Mr. Withwaterson, I don't expect your kind to understand duty, honor, service. Don't talk about what you don't know. Sergeant."

"Yes ma'am."

"Recall all liberty parties. Mr. Shezgo." She turned back to the one who thought the lieutenant had taken off with some girl. The fellow stepped back from the heat in the look she gave him. "My officer was drinking water, so there is no reason to believe he is drunk. He told me he would be right back, so the fact that he isn't means to me that he is not free to do so. I want him found. You say your folks are nice and informal. Fine. You've got until ten o'clock your time to have Lieutenant Tordon call me and explain his absence. If I do not hear from him by ten hundred hours tomorrow, I will be in your office and we will begin doing it the Navy way." She turned away. "Sergeant."

"Recall is being sounded." From the landing field outside town, a klaxon went off. "Shore Patrol is deputizing all petty officers to enforce the recall. It will take two hours for the launches to shuttle all liberty parties back to the ship."

"Do it. Gentlemen, good night. Officers, follow me."

Several other uniformed men and women had been waiting in the background. They filtered through the city folks like they were not there and quickly joined their captain. In a moment, they formed a solid block behind her, all in step. Just looking at them, Ruth felt . . . intimidated.

Before Ruth could even touch the feelings storming around her head, her stomach, marines filed out of the building. They didn't pass through the city people; the city folks kind of levitated out of the marines' path. The sergeant divided them into teams of five or six and sent them trotting in different directions. Pa watched them go with a tight smile on his face. "You can bitch all you want about the mickey mouse in the military, but when the boss man, er, woman, gives the word, things do happen fast and efficient."

"Pa, did you like your time in the army?" Mordy had gone to the army, and not come back. Was that life better than what she had offered him?

"No way. Been there, done that, dodged the Unity goons when they were hanging guys for not putting on their uniform. Not interested. That doesn't mean I don't respect those who really know how to do it. Let's head out toward the spaceport. I wonder if all their kids'll make muster."

Ruth followed. The spacers gathered at Twenty-third and Main. Ruth watched groups arrive and others form up to be carried out to the landing field on flatbed trucks. After an hour, Pa edged toward the chief they'd talked to earlier. "You missing any of your kids?"

"Too early to tell," the chief answered, but the worry lines were deep around his eyes. "Why you asking?"

"We're from the farm stations up north. Some of our people have gone missing lately. In some cases, stations have been burned and dead bodies left behind. Wondered if you might be having problems like that."

"We better not be taking any of my kids off this planet in body bags," he growled. "Listen, maybe we got the same problem. Some of us may be back tomorrow. I'll tell the first lieutenant what you told me. Our captain may want to talk to you."

"I think I'd like to talk with her, too," Pa answered, touching his right hand to his forehead in a loose imitation of what the sergeant had done.

"Nice to see an old hand," the chief answered, and gave the same loose wave back.

"Okay, Ruth, let's get bedded down for the night." Pa turned and started a fast walk back toward their inn, his arms swinging at his sides. He moved just like the marines and navy people did when they had something to do. Ruth remembered Pa moving that way when she was a kid. Now his hands were usually in his pockets and he moved a lot slower.

"Pa, uniform or no, you look like you're in the army again."

Pa laughed, but he didn't slow down.

Ruth was physically exhausted and mentally wrung out by the time they got back to the hotel. She headed for her room and the light was out in minutes. Still, sleep eluded her. What had she done with her life? Brother was two years younger. Yet he had a wife and two darling kids and was ready to start his own station. She'd married an off-worlder like her Ma and had nothing. How many times had Pa softly whispered that all off-worlders are not the same? The ones she'd seen tonight were nothing like Mordy. The young spacers were lame and the marines hard, not at all like the laughing young man she'd fallen in love with. But would the marines be looking for a new job every six months, the spacers rushing off to join the Unity Army at the first word of a draft? Mordy was . . . the man she'd followed from station to station, always ready with a joke, always fast with his fists, and needing a new job all too soon. And there were the dark demands from him, the ones that started with "A real woman would . . ." He'd taken her nos with a laugh or a sneer . . . and walked out of her life without her ever really knowing who he was. Or who she'd become around him. Ruth hugged the pillow, but the pain was too old for tears to help. She drifted off.

A hissing brought her awake when it was still dark. Groggy, she lifted her head. A man was holding an aerosol bottle to her face. She tried to cry out, but couldn't breathe. Dropping into blackness, she heard the man snarl, "This ought to keep her menfolk out of our hair."

THREE

THE AGONY OF waking the next morning reminded Trouble there was someone he wanted to hurt—badly. Keeping his eyes closed, he did a quick inventory. Everything was there, but his arms were tied and he couldn't feel his hands. His nose was on line; someone had lost their lunch. That stink was mixed with the scent of earth and growing things. He inched his eyes open.

He lay on bare ground beneath trees of some sort along with several dozen other people. Four wore whites; the rest looked civilian. As he struggled to sit up in the predawn light, his company looked pretty helpless.

"Thought you might be first up, soldier boy," came from behind him. A burly man in dirty jeans and a Unity shirt rolled Trouble over. The marine tried to kick him, and got a kick in his kidneys for the effort. "You just lie there, or the next kick will knock your head off." Trouble struggled to work his hands loose while the other man reached under the marine's dress blouse and cinched something around his waist. The guy's fingernails needed trimming; Trouble's stomach and back got raked liberally as a narrow plastic cord was pulled tight around him. "There," the ex-Unity thug grinned. "You cause me any more trouble, you'll wish you hadn't."

"When's chow?" Trouble muttered.

"Soon enough." The fellow kicked Trouble again, pulled another belt from the sack at his waist, and started fumbling with the sleeping woman next to the lieutenant. She was the one who'd emptied her stomach. A local, her clothes were workmanlike slacks and a plaid flannel shirt. The thug yanked the shirttails out, liberally copping feels, and attached a belt. The thin plastic strand cut into her belly, but it was the four cylinders equally spaced around the band that made a tough marine like Trouble swallow hard. *Animal control pods.* One was enough to tame a bull. Four could kill a man. Trouble's belt had six.

The thug worked his way around the supine bodies on the forest floor. The men he kicked; the women he felt up. Most were too drugged to notice. One of the spacers, a third-class petty officer, looked awake enough to object, but too groggy to know where he was. Trouble coughed, caught his eye, and gave him a quick shake of the head. The man submitted sullenly. The thug must have noticed; he gave the spacer a solid kick as he left him. The petty officer saw it coming and rolled away.

By the time the tough had worked his way around to the young woman on Trouble's right, she was fully awake. As he pawed her clothes, she pitched away from his touch. "Well, maybe I'll just have to strip you, girlie." The scumbag grinned and reached for the fly on her pants. The woman, curled up in a fetal ball, shot her legs out, catching the thug full in the front. He managed to keep the family jewels safe as he pitched over backward.

As the thug sprawled out beside Trouble, the marine gritted his teeth. He didn't want to do this; knights in shining armor trying to save damsels in distress were way dated. Now was the time to wait for these idiots to make a mistake. But the woman's scream of rage, the man's yowl—Trouble could not lie there and watch what came next. Pushing off, he rolled toward the tough, scissoring his legs around the guy's neck. "You aren't doing anything the young woman doesn't want."

"Lemme go," the thug pawed at Trouble's legs. The lieutenant locked his ankles together and got ready to ride this fellow out.

Sudden pain laced Trouble's belly; his breath fled as he fought to keep from blacking out. If this scumbag had the regulator for the control pods, even a marine was dead.

"Let him go, soldier boy." A new voice came from behind Trouble. "Let him go or I'll up the pain."

"Will you keep him off the girl?" Trouble was damned if he wouldn't negotiate something out of his situation.

"Girl, you seen the belts Clem's been putting on everyone. Pull one out of his bag and put it on." The girl approached them gingerly. Despite her tied hands, she got a belt out of Clem's sack. Putting it on was another thing.

"Let me help." The petty officer was on his feet. Between the two of them, they managed the belt.

"Come here."

The girl went to the voice. The marine ignored her; Clem was getting boisterous.

"Lets make that a tad tighter" came from behind him. Then, "Okay, soldier boy, turn Clem loose." Trouble took a deep breath, then started rolling. As expected, Clem fumbled his way to his feet and started trying to kick the marine.

"Clem, get out of here."

"But, boss . . ." The man hardly slowed in his one-legged chase of Trouble.

"Clem. Go get some grub. Now. Or you'll be wearing one of those belts."

Clem made one more kick, missed, and stomped away. Trouble found his back to a tree, so he struggled into a sitting position facing the voice. The man was slim, medium height, and held himself tight as a whip. "Much obliged," Trouble nodded.

The man called boss eyed the marine for a second more, then roved the entire group, his hand coming up to display a small red box. "Listen up, folks. It's time we got the new employee orientation over. Welcome to 'Day's Work, Inc.' As our newest hires, we want you to understand just where you fit in the organization chart." He pressed the black button on the box. Pain shot through Trouble's gut. Not as bad as the last time, but plenty bad. A woman screamed; other folks whimpered.

"The good news is I'll be carrying this little motivational tool for the rest of this trip. The bad news is you get too close to me or wander too far off and it don't like it. It quits sending the 'Good Employee Reward signal.' If your belts ain't getting that message, they're gonna start giving you a motivational session. Soldier boy, you want to come here?"

"Not really," Trouble said as he got to his feet and slowly approached the boss. At ten feet his pods sent pain through him. He inched forward. The agony grew.

"Like that?"

"No, sir."

"Think you could get any closer?"

"No, sir."

"Now start backing up. Get a move on."

Trouble moved. At fifty feet the tingling sensation was back; he halted.

"Boy, I took you for tougher than that." The empty smile vanished from the man's face. "Keep going," he growled.

"Just thought you'd made your point, sir." Trouble used his best boyish grin, but started backing again.

"One of the lessons I strongly encourage new employees to learn," the boss went on matter-of-factly as Trouble backed up and the pain grew, "is you don't want to come to management's attention. Not all bosses will be as kind-hearted as I am. Why, I've known some labor consultants who'd make a new employee who'd cause trouble like that there soldier boy keep right on walking until he keeled over from the pain. It bad, boy?"

Trouble had no intention of trying to out-macho this guy. The pain in his abdomen was past bad to agony. But, hunched over, he still was backing up. "It's got my attention, sir. Real good."

"Nice boy. Now, I could start walking away." And the

THE PRICE OF PEACE • 49

boss took a step back. "In a few seconds you all would see
just how fast a man can die from a bellyache."

The pain level shot up. Trouble risked a step forward.

"See. The man is educatable. He don't want to leave my
company. And I don't want to miss delivering a full levy of
new workers. So, come on back, soldier boy, and the rest of
you get on your feet. We got to get moving."

The petty officer and a woman spacer headed for Trouble.
He stumbled toward them as fast as he could to save them
the pain he knew was growing in their guts. "You okay, sir?"
the man asked, taking Trouble's arm and putting it around
his shoulder. The woman took the other. They half carried
Trouble as they rejoined the milling group.

"Take my word for it. You want to stay where he wants
you."

"We putting up with this shit?" the petty officer growled.

"Folks with shit for brains make mistakes. Let's see
where they goof off, spacer. Don't blow our chances before
then. I'm Lieutenant Tordon, but I go by Trouble."

"Third Class Petty Officer Jagowski, sir, Spacer First Yu."
The woman on the other side of Trouble ducked her head.
"Romez," was a red-haired and freckled fellow. "And
Makingana, but we call her Mac." The last was a tall, rail-
thin woman whose dark skin shone where the sunlight
caught it, but who could have disappeared into the shadows
without a trace.

"What *do* we do, sir?" Romez asked.

"Any of you got a laser cannon in your boot?" The four
spacers glanced at their shoes. "If not, we do exactly what
the man says. Let them relax, go easy. They'll make their
mistake and we'll be ready for it." The marine stepped away
from his two supporters . . . and his knees almost caved in.
"And get me a stick or something to lean on."

It was the woman Trouble had helped who tossed him a
sturdy walking stick. Raven-haired and olive complexioned
as seemed to be the local norm, she stepped around rocks
and roots with the confidence of someone used to taking
care of herself. Still, her left hand had a nervous way of

flicking to the pods hidden under her shirt. "I can take care of myself," she threw at him along with the stick.

"Yeah. I could see you were about to take that slob apart."

"Maybe I would have."

"They would have killed you before you could."

"Funny talk coming from someone in a fancy uniform."

Trouble stepped closer to the woman, lowering his voice. "They would have killed you, and none of us would have been any closer to freedom. Probably farther. If we're going to get out of this mess, we'll do it by a plan, and we'll do it together."

Their eyes locked, Trouble stared into obsidian black orbs seething with a rage he could not account for. The woman whirled and stomped away. "Off-world bossy," she tossed in her wake.

"Civilians," the petty officer breathed in answer.

"What's got into her?" Yu asked.

"I have no idea," Trouble said, not for the first time where a woman was concerned. "Bossy" rolled around in his skull for a moment, mixed with the background material he'd picked up and the experience he'd had with the locals at Izzy's elbow.

"Crew, I don't think these folks take well to being told what to do." He glanced around at a bedraggled bunch clumped together in various groups, and edging toward the boss with the dumb look of cows in a zoo. "Let's see what we can do about helping these folks without pissing off any more of them."

The spacers broke up, hunting up more walking sticks for those in most need. It turned out that the young woman was doing the same. Between shouts from the boss and three other toughs like Clem, folks got moving. The buzzing in their bellies made sure of that as the boss mounted a mule and headed out. A couple of people had bad reactions to the drugs that had been used to capture them. Spacers stepped in to help. Trouble found himself on one side of an older woman who seemed to be the worst case just as his female nemesis took her other arm. "They call me Trouble," he said.

"I can see why," the young woman said across the older one. "I'm Ruth, from the farm stations." She glanced around. "Only farmer here."

"Not too many spacers either. I like the way you're helping. Maybe if we work together, we can get through this."

"Yeah," Ruth sighed. "Think there is any help for us?"

Trouble glanced around; he saw bedraggled people, thugs, and trees. Nothing too hopeful. "Somebody's gonna come looking for us. The Navy looks after its own."

"The Navy looks after its own, Mr. Shezgo." Izzy rested both hands firmly on the city manager's desk and locked eyes with him. "I'm missing a marine officer and four spacers. I want them back. Now."

The young city manager sat forward in his chair, eyes solid on Izzy . . . and gave not an inch. "As I told you, lots of off-worlders take a liking to our planet and its gentler, friendlier pace. I came here for a vacation after college and never left. Same thing probably happened to your folks. Adults make their own decisions. Sometimes, they suddenly swap one decision for another."

This conversation could go on for hours; Izzy cut it off. "Has anyone seen my lieutenant? That uniform does catch the eye." She glanced at the marine sergeant at her side. By means and methods known only to noncoms, the man was once again in immaculate dress blues. Izzy had asked for this uniform. If necessary, she'd put him on vid or whatever passed for mass communications around here.

"I agree, ma'am" were the first words from the city manager that Izzy liked this morning. "I've had my Public Safety people working on it. Risa Powers is the safety lead this year, Zylon Plovdic is her assistant. They've been up most of the night looking for your missing people. I don't think your folks want to be found."

Zylon was a tall blonde that Izzy gladly would have taken on for a security guard. Risa was even smaller than Izzy;

how she'd make out in a barroom brawl was very open to question. But the question wasn't a fight this morning. It was finding her people. Izzy turned her attention full on Risa. "What have you tried?"

Without missing a beat, Risa launched into her report. Izzy liked subordinates who did that. "I've had their pictures on all the video feeds and sent personal mailings to the city's business community. I've got one hundred percent acknowledgments . . . and one hundred percent negatives. Lots of people saw your marine patrols. Nobody saw a lone marine."

The city manager tapped his computer and messages began to flash on its ancient flat screen. "They're all here, if you want to review them."

"Ship them up to the *Patton*. I'll have my people check 'em. What else?"

"I've messaged every trucking firm," Risa continued. "Asked each one to make sure no driver had picked up someone in a gaudy red-and-blue outfit. Nothing."

"And I've been catching grief all morning for that violation of privacy, not to mention that of your wayward officer." The city manager cut in. "Around here, we let people do what they want. Best way to get a bloody nose is to interfere in someone else's business."

Izzy rubbed her eyes, going slowly over the torrent of words the people had dumped on her. Maybe if she took them one at a time, they'd mean something. "Nobody has reported seeing someone in a marine dress uniform leaving town."

"No one in my area of responsibility," Shezgo corrected.

"Farmers come in from the stations all the time," Zylon pointed out. "Most likely, some farmer's daughter drove the rig your man left town in."

"That would be none of our concern." The city manager clearly was happy at the thought.

Izzy wasn't. "Mr. Shezgo, that was a pretty fancy party you threw for me and my officers. How many were farmer's daughters out on the dance floor last night?"

The city manager leaned back in his chair, a frown slowly replacing the invincible confidence he'd worn since Izzy marched into his office at ten hundred hours sharp. "None," he muttered after a long minute.

"Did any of your city's citizens see a very gaudily dressed marine officer leave by himself, or with one of their best friends on his elbow?"

"None that any of my people have talked to. And I've mailed everyone who was at that party a query."

"Anyone find a pair of blue pants or fancy red shirt?"

Risa handled that question. "I warned the trash collection crews to be on the lookout for them when they started this morning. And no, I've heard nothing about the clothes either."

"Then for now, I'm going to assume that my officer is still wearing them, and he should be as out of place here as a drunk at a Baptist church picnic. You keep hunting for him. And I'll start. How do I get in touch with the farm stations?"

Shezgo shrugged. "They guard some emergency channels, and I wouldn't recommend tying them up. Those folks can get very testy where safety is concerned. They have their own nets for business. They do what they want, and as long as they don't create interference on our city nets, I don't bother them."

Izzy had a hard time swallowing that line. "You mean the two of you don't even talk?"

Shezgo's shrug got deeper. "When Unity was causing trouble, the farms didn't want to hear what was going on around here, and didn't want them listening in on what they were saying."

Izzy could see she had her work cut out for her, and nothing more would come from this meeting. With an about-face, she headed for the door. Impatient, she had her XO on the comm unit as her car pulled away from city hall. Stan cut her off. "Skipper, the chief in charge of the Shore Patrol last night had a few words with some civilians. Farm types. They've had people disappear, too. Said they'd like to talk to us. Probably at last night's collection point. Supply wants to know if he's supposed to set up a purchasing station there this afternoon."

"Yes, send Supply down with a large team and an armed escort," she answered. "Driver, head for Twenty-third and Main. Somebody may be waiting to meet us. Sergeant, load your weapon and get a pistol for me." Then she returned to the XO. "Stan, have Comm do a full scan of all communication nets in use. Townies claim they don't talk to the farmers and vice versa. I somehow doubt that. Don't send any messages out before I get back. I want to make this a personal call. Can't believe how allergic these folks are to anything smelling of central organization. For now, let's do it their way. I want this place mapped, scanned, and analyzed to the thirteenth decimal place. We got people down here in this haystack. Find them."

"Will do. When should I expect you?"

"Not for a while. I'll stake out the collection point, see if anyone wants to talk to me. You get Supply moving. As soon as he's here, I'll go back topside."

"Yes, ma'am."

Izzy spent a long two hours waiting for Supply to show up. She hadn't been parked five minutes when a grandmother type stopped to tell her how much she'd enjoyed the dance last night, how nice it was to see someone from Earth, and how a ship's captain shouldn't mind if a few of her people decided to stay on Hurtford Corner. "We like to share with visitors who stay." That was just how it was.

Soon an old man joined the woman, giving Izzy a replay of the same views. Two teenagers showed up, a girl looking enough like Franny to cause Izzy to swallow a lump of grief, and a boy hanging on her, both wondering what Earth was like and wanting to talk about maybe joining up. "Anything has to be easier than working for her old man."

It went downhill from there. If Izzy hadn't feared missing whoever it was that was losing people, she would have had the driver gun his way out of the growing crowd. Instead, she stayed to learn how much people loved their planet, hated Unity, and really wondered what Earth was like. When

Lieutenant Pollux arrived with a dozen storekeepers and as many guards, he'd already been briefed to keep an eye out for a contact. Without a backward glance, she had the driver head for the gig. Somewhere on this planet were five of her people. She wanted them back.

Joe Edris drove the truck, Seth Seddik hunched silently beside him. In Joe's pocket, the note burned.

> If you want to see your woman alive, go back where you belong. Get mixed up in what you don't know, and you'll get her back in pieces. Then we'll come looking for the rest of your family.

Joe had been ready to go straight to the Navy. They were missing people, and whoever had their people had Ruth. Seth had backed away from Joe's anger, shaking his head. "You have no right to make the decision for all of us. Not for my family, not even for Ruth. She's a married woman. We must lay this before the elders. Whatever we do will affect everyone. Everyone has to have a say."

"And while we're talking, what's happening to Ruth? Damn it, Seth, we got to do something now. Not next Thursday."

"Joe, you were not raised on Hurtford, so I know it's hard on you. But you saw how we handled the Unity problem. We'll handle this one our way, too." Seth paused, studying Joe out of the corner of his eye. "Unless you and your family are ready to leave the stations. Go out on your own."

Joe knew how long he'd last without the community when he and his needed more than the hands they had. He had no answer for that. Seth and he did not exchange another word. It was a long, silent drive back to the stations.

As a kid, Ruth loved trips to the forest to gather fungus. The family was smaller then, and Ma and Pa had time for her. The drug company money from fungus helped make the payments on the station in those early years. Today was horribly different.

The boss set a fast pace. Comfortably mounted on a sure-

footed mule, he paid no price for hills and gullies, brambles
and jutting roots that dragged, tore, and ripped at the walkers. Ruth was a big sister again, helping those who couldn't
keep up. Lots of folks had worn dancing shoes last night . . .
wrong gear for today. Others just were not up to the effort.
Ruth did what she could, giving one an arm to lean on, finding a stick for someone else, carrying coats and sweaters a
few people were ready to toss away in the heat of the day;
they would want them tonight. Helping made her rub elbows
with the spacers. The lieutenant, Trouble, told them to help,
and they did what he said without question. Of course, he
was helping, too. He spent as much time at the tail end of the
column as Ruth did. Clem and three uglies like him rode
mules back there, laughing at the half-crippled stragglers,
offering to shoot them if they fell farther behind.

Trouble saw to it that his spacers took breaks, balancing
caring for others with caring for themselves. His break time
usually was spent near the head of the column, eyeing the
boss when the boss wasn't looking. He'd said the Navy
looked after its own. Did he really think help was coming?
After the fiasco at the Abdoes place, Ruth didn't expect anything from her own people. The slim chance that the marine
knew what he was talking about kept hopelessness from eating her alive.

At the crest of a hill, the boss rested his mule. Turning in
the saddle, he smiled at the four big fellows who had kept up
with him, then shook his head dolefully at the rest trailing
far behind. He pulled the red box from his belt, raised it into
view, and pushed the button. Ruth's belt went from generat-
ing gnawing discomfort to shooting pains. Around her,
women and men screamed. Even the marine doubled over.
Up ahead, the same reaction came from those who had kept
up.

"Boss's leadership style needs improvement," the lieutenant observed dryly through gritted teeth. "Stinging those
doing what he wants along with the rest of us is no way to
get promoted in my Navy." Two of the spacers laughed; a

grin escaped even Ruth. What kind of people laughed at times like this?

That didn't keep Ruth's anger from surfacing. "You have four legs moving you along," she called. "We have just two. And some of these folks ain't used to using either one of them. You have to slow down."

"I got a schedule to keep. You just got to keep up. If that means walking all day and all night, I guess you'll just do it. Me, I'd like to get some sleep tonight."

"Some of us could use some chow," Jagowski pointed out.

"You'll eat when you reach tonight's camp, and not before. So, folks, you've had your rest. Let's get a move on." He kicked his mule into movement. As he dropped over the ridge, the pain in Ruth's gut grew. They plodded on.

But now Ruth and the spacers weren't the only ones helping. The better off pitched in to help the worse. But that did little to ease the misery as the day grew hot and humid. Now parched lips gnawed more than empty bellies. She followed Trouble's lead as he edged his spacers upstream at water crossings. That way, she drank less mud. Balancing the need to move with growing exhaustion and the inevitable pain in the gut from being behind left the buzzing insects unnoticed . . . until angry welts splotched exposed faces, arms, and legs.

"Damn death march," Jagowski muttered.

Ruth eyed the sun, which was finally dropping low in the sky. "Night's gonna be as cold as the day was hot. Better collect some dry wood for fires." People who could hardly hobble were soon clutching two or three sticks.

The boss called a halt as they entered a small clearing under a stand of tall, spreading oaks. "Take the rest of the night off," he announced. "You stay to that half of the clearing. I get this half." His half was marked by the remains of a fire; their half wasn't. Scattered over the clearing were trash, buzzing insects, and proof that no care had been taken about sanitation. Pa would never leave a camp like this.

"What do we do?" Ruth asked in the same breath

Jagowski did. The marine officer rubbed the bridge of his nose. As he opened his mouth, Clem interrupted.

"I bet you're hungry," got everyone's attention. Clem's mouth moved as he counted the hungry faces gathering around him. Then he pawed in the pack of the mule he'd been leading and came up with, by Ruth's quick count, exactly half the ration boxes they needed. Clem pitched them out like one might toss dry bones to hungry dogs. Then the thug produced an extra ration. "Any of you girlies want to make friendly with me tonight, I got some extra grub for you." His gap-toothed grin made Ruth want to knock a few more teeth out. She turned to the marine.

He was eyeing the four burly types who had kept up with the boss; toughs who probably wanted Clem's job. That thug had made sure a good chunk of the rations landed near them. The biggest had grabbed three boxes, smirked, and turned away. The marine shook his head, his lips getting thin. "Hate to get the boss's attention again today," he muttered, then stepped forward.

"We got to share our food rations." The lieutenant's voice came out low, but rock-hard in command. Several folks around Ruth started pairing up, though none in actual possession of food boxes seemed overly committed at the moment. The four kept walking away.

"Excuse me, gents, but I need those rations you're carrying," the marine repeated.

The one with three turned, a vicious grin on his face. "I'm hungry. When I'm hungry, I eat."

"Lots of folks are hungry."

"Tin soldier, you seem to have mistaken me for someone who gives a shit." The tough enjoyed the laugh that remark brought from his associates. Behind Ruth, Clem bayed like a donkey. The marine eyed the boss. He'd spread his bedroll; his interest centered on the mattress as it filled with air. The goings-on around him apparently were no concern of his.

Trouble stepped toward the tough. "I want those rations."

"Come and get 'em." The twisted smile was evil, delighted.

The marine took another step forward, but didn't go into a fighting stance. The thug couldn't pass that up. Dropping his ration boxes, he charged Trouble, arms flailing.

The officer ducked, sidestepped, and sent the big guy on his way with a push. The thug went down, sliding to a halt, his nose buried in some particularly messy residue from previous campers. He came up bellowing, blood bubbling from his nose. "You shouldn't have done that, pretty boy. I'm gonna sleep real warm tonight in your red coat. You're gonna be cold and dead."

"Come get it." Again, the marine just stood there.

This time the tough was slower in his approach. Lumbering up to the marine, he kept his arms wide, a big, nasty bear, ready to hug his prey to death.

Trouble waited, then went in with two fast punches. The big fellow stumbled back, shook his body to rid himself of the shock. Then, roaring in outrage, he charged again.

Trouble faked right, then evaded wide to the left, side-kicking the fellow's knee as he went by. The man screamed, "My leg, my leg," as he went down. But not for long, as his skull came up hard against a tree.

"That's gonna cost you extra." The boss was relaxing on his bed, a warm meal in his lap. "You damage my merchandise, you got to make it up to me."

"I guess I'll have to run a tab," Trouble said, collecting the dropped rations and ones offered him by the other toughs.

"Smokey'll share with me. Won't you?"

Sharing had suddenly become popular. Clem and one of his sidekicks attempted first aid on the slow learner. Ruth could probably have done a better job, but at the moment, she had a meal to prepare.

A little shyly, she offered Trouble half of her only slightly warmed meal. "Heater didn't work too well," she apologized. As they split the beans and something, with ancient crackers and gummy fruit bits, Trouble outlined what he wanted.

"Place needs a little work to make it decent. Jagowski, you see about digging latrines. I'll take care of the fires. Ruth, could you get people to gather ferns, leaves, things to put between us and the ground?"

"Right," Ruth agreed, "the ground's gonna get awfully cold before morning. Without blankets, we'll be in trouble."

The meal done, people went about their jobs in the rapidly fading daylight. Two of the spacers got promoted to doctors and assigned to examine the worst blisters. Ruth eyed the rocks around the boss's fire pit. "I could collect some more along the stream," Ruth said innocently as she headed out.

Trouble came close to her. "They'll have water in them. Might explode." Ruth grinned; for a spacer, the guy knew something about dirt. She nodded.

The marine shook his head. "Unlike plastic, rocks got no fuse. They go off when they want to, not when we want. Your heart's in the right place, woman, but let's pass on this one." The marine gave her a thin smile, nothing like the smirks Mordy tossed out at her ideas. "Dry rocks," he whispered.

"Okay." She headed into the gloom. When she got back, three fire pits were being dug, Trouble and two others working on one as near the boss as the pain pods allowed.

"I love watching other people work," Clem giggled, tossing a handful of dirt that had fallen near him back into the pit.

"So do I," drawled the boss. "Clem, get a shovel and help these people. Soldier boy, a word with you."

They walked off a ways. The boss held the red box tightly in his hand; the marine kept a respectful distance. They exchanged words for a few minutes; Ruth understood none of it.

When they were done, Trouble backed away slowly, then paused. "You got a med kit? We got folks who could use a hand with blisters. Maybe do something for that guy's busted leg."

The boss chewed on that for a long moment. "Clem, that hole's big enough to bury someone. Go get a first aid kit." As Clem shambled off, a shovel slung over his shoulder, the boss followed him, his words now singsong as if he were talking to a three-year-old. "Take out the needles and the scissors. Mother can't let them hurt themselves on pointy things."

"Yeah, boss," Clem snarled. But he emptied part of one med kit into another, then tossed the first one none too gently to Trouble. Bandages and antiseptic sprays flew in general formation with the kit. Trouble caught the box, gathered up the scattered contents, and turned it over to the two spacers who were caring for feet. Ruth borrowed part of the first aid kit and took a look at the tough's knee. The kneecap was out of place; she snapped it back in. The leg wasn't broken, but the ligaments were a knot.

"Somebody's gonna have to carry him tomorrow," she told his buddies. They showed no enthusiasm for the chore. With the knee wrapped, she returned to the fire pit nearest the boss, just as the marine was finishing.

"Spare us a match?" Trouble asked.

"Here's the deal," the boss said, tossing Trouble a single match. "You start it with that, and I'll let you take fire from it to start your own. You ask me for a second match, and all my fire stays put."

No one risked a protest.

"Anybody here started a fire recently?" Trouble asked.

"Don't you marines do this all the time?" Ruth snapped. "My Pa did."

"Dirt time on an oxygen planet has been kind of scarce lately. Okay, stand back and let me have some air." For the next minute, as twilight waned, the marine arranged tinder, twigs, and small chunks of wood. He was almost out of daylight when he risked his match. He struck it along the sole of his boot. Got a spark . . . and nothing else.

"That's dumb," Ruth growled, and reached for a grainy rock like Pa used. She handed it to the marine. Trouble drew the match slowly along its flat, rough face, gradually increasing the pressure. The stick smoldered, then caught. After a brief flare, it died away almost to nothing. Holding his breath, the marine moved it the few inches to his tinder. The pile smoldered, caught, crackled, then began to die.

Carefully, Trouble fed the tiny flame, building it, letting it reach out to the larger sticks. *Grow, damn you.* Expectant eyes glittered in its growing light.

Once it was well caught, Ruth wrapped some dry moss around a stick, let it catch, then took it to the next fire pit. Jagowski had a pile of tinder and sticks like Trouble had made.

The third was almost routine.

Then the marine did surprise Ruth. He captured the ends of a couple of saplings, collected their ends together with his web belt and then tied that to a downed log. In one swoop he had a lean-to. While one of the other spacers used her belt to do the same for a second lean-to, people scattered armfuls of leaves and sheaves of moss. "You got two choices tonight, folks," the marine said. "Stay close and warm, or keep your distance and be cold. I never thought I'd say something nice about this old-fashion uniform, but it's got a lot of old-fashion wool in it. I'll take one of the outside edges."

Plopping down with his back to the outside, Trouble eyed the rest. Well, he hadn't been bossy, exactly. Besides, Ruth was exhausted. She lay out beside him, guiding a sick woman down beside her. The spacers settled in next like a pile of spoons. The city folks, depending on who they knew and how well, slowly found their places under the bowing saplings.

"Hope you don't mind if I snore," Trouble said.

"Snoring's better than being pawed," Ruth answered. "Thanks for all you've done today." She wiggled closer to him, the closest she'd been to a man since her own walked out. Strange how this was working. She didn't expect to sleep, but in the warmth of Trouble behind her, she must have.

• • •

Joe didn't know what to say to his wife. Bibi had raced from the house, the kids like a swarm of bees around her. The sight of the empty seat beside her husband had brought her up short. "Where's Ruth?"

"Somebody's grabbed her," he snarled, getting out. "Seth says we got to talk before we can decide what to do."

"This can't wait 'til next Thursday's dance." Bibi dried her hands on the towel she wore wrapped to her waist.

"It's not gonna," Joe snapped. "Son, get the crew saddled up, armed, supplied, and ready. I'm not sure we'll be coming home after tonight's meeting."

"Right." The young man moved off, Slim at his elbow. Bibi gathered the younger kids around her. "I'll get the rest packed. Where will we sleep tonight?"

"Love, I don't know. Maybe we'll have company. Maybe you'll go home to another station. I just don't know." He glanced at the dark western sky. "But this is going to stop."

Zylon Plovdic worked late that night. Nothing about the missing navy personnel surfaced. No surprise for her. It was dark before Risa dismissed her office staff. "You've worked more than your fair share today. Get a good supper. I'll tell Mikhail the Navy's nowhere to be seen."

Zylon came late to supper, but she knew she would not be eating alone. The waiter brought her meal and left the table quickly. As Zylon expected, two men were already eating.

"Any surprises?" Big Al asked. The bland glance he threw her told that none were expected—and none would be accepted.

"No surprises. Everything's under control," Zylon answered the off-world boss. Alexander Popov had arrived with Unity—and survived its demise. His connections went far beyond the rim, Zylon suspected to old Earth itself. It was he who'd talked the elders into signing mineral contracts just before the war with some of the biggest names in space.

"We've got the farmers running back to their stations, tails between their legs," added Zef Davis, the local boss,

junior scion of a third-generation Hurtford family. What he
didn't know about Hurtford hadn't happened. What he
wanted was for exciting things to happen, and real soon.
"We won't see the hayseeds again until they've had a chance
to talk everything over six different ways, and then they still
won't decide anything. You get that damn cruiser off our
backs, and we'll have a free hand. I still say we should have
cut that Withwaterson fellow in. That would have saved us
all this."

"If we have to cut anyone in, it will not be a minor trader
of his ilk. He's out of his league and will learn soon
enough."

"Well, how come your big league couldn't keep one lousy
cruiser off our backs?"

"I'm looking into that. It will be taken care of. In the
meantime, that pretty little skipper has lost five of her crew.
She will be more careful about spending time down here."
That got a laugh from both of them.

Zylon finished her nondescript stew while the two played
their little power game. Like so much of what passed for
food, goods, and services on Hurtford Corner, the stew
lacked taste, and the wine lacked body. Zylon wanted something rich, full-bodied, overflowing. She nodded to the two,
paid attention to both. Her time would come. When they fell
silent, she summed up her day, and the next week . . . and
life on Hurtford Corner.

"Nothing's happening. Nothing will happen. We've tied
up all the loose ends. I'll keep an eye on them to make sure
they don't unravel."

"Have supper with us tomorrow," Big Al offered.

"Be glad to."

Izzy leaned back in an overstuffed chair in her day cabin,
which was more ship's office than personal space. A conference table for big meetings stretched along the wide outside
end of her pie-shaped cabin. Smaller meetings such as
tonight's used comfortable chairs and a sofa grouped around
a coffee table that looked wooden and hid a fully functional

data display. Behind her, a desk occupied the narrow focus of the office. As usual, a dozen red lights blinked from her in-basket—reports, reviews, and items demanding her signature before they left the ship. They'd wait. She had real business to handle. Leaning forward to tap the coffee table, she called up her to-do list. "Found their recall beacons?" she asked Stan.

"All five," her XO answered, no joy in his voice. "They're all together in what looks like the town dump."

"And Shezgo said they'd search the trash cans."

"I think we ought to cut the guy some slack. I read the planet charter. All decisions are made by unanimous vote of the elders. There's a little wiggle room, but these folks are dead set against autocratic rule and unilateral action."

Izzy rubbed her eyes as she mulled over that concept. "Hell of a way to run a warship," she muttered, "or a planet."

"They've been at it for eighty, ninety years and are still here." Stan gave his boss a quirky smile.

Izzy could tell a dead end when it slapped her; it was time to move on. "What have we got on the farm net?"

"That was a bitch. We knew they were there, but couldn't find them. Igor and one of his old chiefs tried a different tack. Everything's digital. You go up the frequencies by point one, point two, but what about what's in between?"

Izzy was physically tired, and her attitude was rapidly going from pissed to downright cranky. "Talk to me, Stan."

A quick nod, and words started falling quickly from the XO's mouth. "Looks like the farmers grow their own radio crystals. None of the frequencies they're using are at the standard digital points on the net. They can jump up the frequency by doubling, tripling, or what have you the base frequency. Igor and his team are working on a transmitter that ought to be able to dial in their net. Be ready by morning."

"Good. I want words with them. Morning ought to be soon enough." Izzy yawned. Her brain was turning to mush, but there was more to do. "What about our survey?"

Stan tapped the table. The screen changed from the to-do

list to a map, centered on Hurtford Corner. "Looks the same as the one we've been staring at for the last week," Izzy muttered.

"Pretty much is. Roads, rivers, and hills don't change much. The farm area's spread out a bit. The town's a little bigger. Nothing significant has changed."

"What have we got real-time?" Quickly the map was overlaid with a picture. Roads became a string of lights. Most buildings disappeared into darkness. The farm stations speckled their part of the map. Izzy zoomed the map onto the hills to the west. Tiny dots blinked. "What's in the back-country?"

"Nothing but a few campfires. Most are herb and plant hunters. Original flora has some interesting hydrocarbon chains. Brings a good price from the pharmaceutical corps. Some are survey teams. Several Earth corporations got contracts to survey for minerals, both here and in the system."

Tired as she was, Izzy had the energy to frown at that. "A bunch of Luddites like these signed on for mining? What are they gonna have, a kinder, gentler strip mine?"

"I don't think the locals much like the contracts. Some Unity types signed them just before the war. But the Earth-side suits are holding the present government to the contracts."

Izzy ordered the screen to zoom to each of the fires. Stan called up a database they'd acquired from the locals. "They keep good tabs on everyone backcountry."

"Isn't that a violation of somebody's privacy?"

"Seems that where search and rescue is concerned, folks are a bit more understanding. People are kind of scarce out this far. They don't want anyone dying if they can help it."

Izzy leaned back, her eyes losing their focus as camp after camp flashed by. What was wrong with this picture? People were few and far between on the rim. Yet, where she came from, folks were crammed into slums by the millions. Governments tried forced immigration, but shipping all those bodies was awfully expensive considering that few survived the first six months pioneering a planet. And folks like her sister Lora couldn't be moved with explosives. In the war, Earth and her seven sisters had built most of the hardware. The other forty developed planets drafted most of the people who did the fighting. Funny how people and things ended up being distributed. *God, I'm tired.*

"Stop the scan. Go back." Izzy sat up, leaning over the replaying scenes. Most camps had one fire. A second fire was usually a ways away from the first, as if somebody wanted her or his or their own part of the night. But . . .

"There, that one. What is it?"

Stan glanced at the camp, three fires forming a triangle, and read the database. "A survey party. Left Hurtford City five days ago."

Izzy eyed it. "Hasn't got very far."

Stan did the measurement. "Not far at all."

Izzy rubbed her eyes, tried to banish the exhaustion that was blocking memories. "Read something about a triangle once. Can't remember now. Stan, tomorrow morning have Trouble's gunny sergeant review these. Also, I want a marine detachment sent down to recover the beacons and anything else they can find in the dump that looks suspicious. Make sure they're heavily armed, and tell them to take no guff from the locals." Stan's eyebrows were up. "But not to start anything. Okay?"

"Yes, ma'am. Now, why don't you get some sleep? Not much either of us can do for a while."

Izzy added two more notations to her to-do list as she glided to her night cabin just off her desk. She closed her door, less for privacy than to shut out the damn blinking lights from her ignored in-basket. A warm shower drained enough of her exhaustion to let her slip quickly to sleep without worrying too much about what kind of night Trouble was having.

Joe Edris fumed, and kept his hand in the air, though the muscles of his arm were knotted painfully and it would do him no good. Seddik had been good to his word. Joe had gotten the first words that night. But the moderator had dutifully followed tradition. Any newly raised hand got recognized before someone who'd already spoken. Old Seddik must have used a database to track who talked and how long. If Joe heard once more about the failed drainage project, he'd explode. The rains had been heavy last year; no amount of project planning could have prevented that. And it had nothing to do with someone kidnapping Ruth. As more and more people yammered on, Joe waved his hand and sat on his thumbs.

His opening statement had gotten through to a few of the younger people. Still, the older folks couldn't seem to get it through their heads that the last month had changed everything. They may have outsat the Unity yahoos, but now somebody was coming after them where they lived.

Two hours into the talkathon, Joe gave up on being recognized a third time. As he stomped for the back of the hall and a glass of punch, others joined him. They took over a corner to talk among themselves.

"We got to protect the stations, or we're gonna be burned out one by one" was the concern first and foremost in their minds.

"What about Ruth?" Joe's question drew blank stares. These people had some ideas how they might protect their loved ones and life's works. They had no idea how to find one woman somewhere on this vast planet. Joe had seen it before; people concentrating on what they could do something about and turning their backs on what only overwhelmed them. He'd done it himself. Now, it was *his* daughter no one could help.

About the sixth time his "But what about Ruth?" was ignored, Bibi locked onto his elbow and hauled him out of the circle.

"You read the letter. You and Seth left town like they told you. We are doing what we can for Ruth. If we do nothing with the navy people, she will be returned."

"You can't believe that." Joe shook his head, incredulous.

"Why not? They gain nothing by breaking their word."

And it hit Joseph Edris just how strange these people

were he'd chosen to live among. No, not strange, just wonderfully rational. It was stupid to harm a woman if the farm stations did what they were told. Therefore, the kidnappers would not. Joe had been one of the few who'd expected the local Unity bunch to be worse than they had been. He'd seen, growing up, what passed for rationality on other planets. That was why he'd chosen Hurtford Corner. Now, Bibi and Seth were putting their faith that people were rational on the line for Ruth.

For a moment, Joe wanted to believe too. Slowly, he shook his head. "The raiders at the Abdoes place didn't act rational." He watched the color drain from her face, as if he'd hit her. "Bibi, something crazy and mindless and evil is out there stalking us. We've got to fight it every way we can."

"Even after twenty-five years with me, you still say that first, with so little to go on. You say I don't understand what's happening. I say when we do, we'll know better what to do. What fills you with anger and hatred and makes you ready to jump off into something you have no idea about? Joseph, you can't risk our daughter's life on just . . . just guesses."

If he could not even convince his wife, how could he persuade the whole community? His daughter's life hung in the balance, and his words carried no more weight than a feather.

Bibi returned to the circle of folks planning how they might protect themselves but still work their fields. After a long purgatory of frustration, Joe rejoined them. Here at least was something he could do. An hour later, Jethro Hakiem raised his hand. Jethro, a man whose quiet Joe had come to realize came not for a lack of anything to say, but a need to carefully order the myriad of thoughts in his mind, had said nothing that evening. Seth immediately recognized him. Slowly, methodically, he outlined the plan that had been developed in the corner.

All the stations nearest the hills should be abandoned. The larger stations would provide temporary shelter for the smaller ones. Work would be done in teams, always three or four rigs together, going from one field to the next. Each occupied station would keep a twenty-four-hour watch. Fire support teams would be on quick reaction alert. Dov Dobruja would turn his electronic shop into a sensor factory. He expected to have enough listening posts grown by next month to cover the entire front range. "We do what we've always done. Stick together. We can turn aside this threat to our way of life."

There were nods, even a few quiet cheers. Some of the younger couples were reluctant to abandon their stations, but fathers and married sons, mothers and grown daughters worked out those problems. Bibi had taken in four young couples, one wife heavy with their firstborn. They trailed her truck in the dark as she carefully led them back to the station. On the drive back, Joe sat across the seat from her, his gut ripped in two. He wanted to trust the way he'd lived the last twenty-five years. But he'd grown up on LornaDo. He'd marched in her army. He knew the senseless purposelessness of evil.

He trembled for his daughter.

FOUR

RUTH DIDN'T SO much wake up the next morning as give up hope of any more rest. She must have slept some during the night. She recalled shivering. Next thing she remembered she was huddled close to the woman on her front, and the marine was just as tightly crowded along her back, his arm warm against the length of her side. It felt good. When she came fuzzy awake to a graying sky, every muscle in her body aching and shivering, it seemed time to get up. Still, she didn't want to move.

"You awake?" came a low question from behind her.

"I guess so," she answered.

"I'm gonna try getting the fire going again. You mind me taking away the warmth to your back?"

"I guess I'll get up and help."

Ruth hunted along the edges of the camp for more wood while the marine stirred the embers for some glow of warmth. A few pine cones helped restart it. Trouble also restarted the boss's fire, keeping his distance to avoid a jab of pain in the gut. "No need having them any grumpier than they have to be," he said with a wry smile.

Ruth would just as soon have let them freeze.

As she helped the off-worlder, Ruth studied him. He was a strange man. Very strange. Everyone had done what he told them to do last night; not one of the city folks had thrown the word "Bossy" at him. And city folks were the least likely to let anyone tell them what to do. At least, that was what they said on the stations. The spacers had followed him without question. Maybe that was what started the rest? Ruth doubted it. You only had to look at the man. When he said do it, you wanted to do it.

Of course, it was something you knew needed doing.

So why hadn't he ordered them to grab rocks and smash these guys' brains out? Ruth shivered at the thought. She'd used an ax to kill chickens, knives to slaughter hogs. Killing people was something she'd never thought of until the Ab-does place got burned. *If the marine said bash out someone's brains, could I?*

He hadn't. Maybe he was smarter than she. Did he plan to just take it? Watching him move around the camp, going from one clump of cold, hurting people to another, he didn't look like someone passively waiting for whatever the boss wanted.

"Shall I ask the boss for some food?" she asked the marine.

"I'll do it," Trouble assured her.

"No," Ruth said, "you stuck your neck out yesterday. I'll take the risk this morning." He did not stop her as she strode toward the boss's campfire. About twenty feet from his bedroll, she stopped. "We could use some grub," she said.

The boss rolled over, yawned mightily, stretched slowly, then looked around the camp. "You're up mighty early. In a hurry or something?" That got a laugh from his cronies. "Clem, get them something to eat. This time, one per. Don't want to lug all that food if we don't have to, now do we?"

"Yeah, boss."

Ruth's ration box didn't warm up, even a little bit. Trouble shared his coffee with her. His came out too hot. They mixed theirs together and got two lukewarm cups. "No wonder Unity lost the war, fighting on cold coffee." The marine shook his head.

They had barely finished before the boss was mounting his mule.

Showered and uniformed, Izzy had breakfast served in her cabin with the XO, Chips, and the Gunny. This allowed her to get her key players together early without having to invite the sergeant to breakfast in the wardroom. She doubted her officers would mind, but to a marine gunny, such things were NOT DONE.

Between pancakes, sausage, and hash browns, she covered the high points of her plan for the day. "Chips, how soon can you get me into the farmers' net?"

Dark eyes gleaming, he said, "Oh-nine-hundred soon enough?"

"Perfect. I've got a few words to tell them. Stan, I want to talk to the chief of the Shore Patrol before then. I need his best recollection of that talk he had with the local."

"I'll have him up here by oh-eight-hundred."

"Gunny, you glance at the camps we mapped last night?"

"Yes, ma'am. Interesting. How sure are we of the database?"

"As reliable as any of the stuff from Hurtford Corner."

"That good," he grunted.

"See anything interesting about one of them?" Izzy had spent her entire shower trying to remember what it was about a triangle of fires. It still eluded her.

"You mean the one with three fires in a triangle?" the Gunny asked. She nodded. The old marine shook his close-cropped head. "Don't know, ma'am. Years ago, before we left Earth, when we were just trying to get our wings, three fires in a triangle used to be a distress signal. Don't know how many people remember that. What with recall beacons in your wrist unit and ID card, not many people bother learning the old survival skills."

"Think Trouble did?"

"He's a pretty savvy young officer. But it was twenty years ago that I had time to read old oxygen-based survival

school handbooks. Don't know if he has. Not part of the regular training he'd get. Ancient history."

Izzy chased a last bit of pancake through cooling syrup.
"When somebody takes away all your modern tools, ancient
history may be all you've got to live by. Chips, see if there's
any way to track those ground teams during the day. I want
a thorough scan of campfires tonight, pronto."

"Yes ma'am"s answered her.

"Gunny, I want you to lead a team dirtside this afternoon.
Bring me back the beacons for our missing personnel. Don't
start anything, but I want all hands back at the end of the
day."

"No problem, ma'am."

"Pa, we just got a message you better see," came Slim's nervous voice over the radio in the cabin of the tractor.

"What is it?" Joe asked his younger son.

"Pa, you better just come in." Slim's young voice cracked
under the stress . . . or pain. "Ma don't think you need to see
it. But Pa, it's the Navy woman asking about missing folks."

Joe dropped the harrow and gunned for the station. There
were five tractors in this work party. Four would have to do.
"Slim, I'll be there in ten minutes."

"I'm asking you, the working people of Hurtford Corner, to
help me." The face of the dark-skinned woman filled the
screen, her hair a thin down on her skull. Joe studied her,
tried to measure her through the flat tube. *Can I trust you
with my daughter's life?*

"I'm told that some of you started life in other places and
chose Hurtford Corner. It's a beautiful planet, and you've
made a pleasant way of life here. But I think five of my people are being held here against their will. If I'm wrong, all I
want is a quick call from them, and I'll process their dis-
charge papers. There'll probably be an exit bonus in it for
them. But I haven't gotten any such request. In that silence,
I'm left worried that they are not gone of their own free will.

"One of you talked with my Shore Patrol chief. He said

you had people disappearing too. I think your problem and mine are the same. You like to work together to solve things. That's my way, too. I'm sending a launch down. We've located the IDs of our missing crew members. We're not going to leave their papers lying around any more than we're willing to leave them. If you won't talk to us on the net, come talk to us at the launch."

The woman's words stopped. Hands clasped in front of her, she stared hard into the camera. "Please help me."

The naked need in those words shook Joe. He'd known army officers. "Help me" was not in their vocabulary. For this woman, commanding a fifty-thousand-ton cruiser high above his head, asking for help must have taken a lot. Joe turned, hunting in his pocket for the truck keys.

Bibi stood in the door to the net room, a baby from one of the young couples in her arms. "Please, don't do it, Joseph."

Two women, one a stranger, one his wife, each pleading with him for opposite reasons. Who was right? Ruth's life hung on his choice.

"I don't know when I'll be back," he said as he brushed by.

Gunny Griz exited the launch first, eyes scanning the tarmac and the green, waving crops beyond. His right hand rested on his holstered pistol. The skipper didn't want any trouble, but she didn't want any more missing troopers either. The dress uniforms were gone; green battle dress, body armor, and locked and loaded weapons were the uniform today. Gunny reached the bottom step and turned. Chief Maximilian, Chips' best ground sensor man, was hot on his heels, eyes locked on his board.

Concentrating too much on his board, the chief missed a step. Gunny grabbed him before he landed flat on his face. "Any targets?" Gunny asked as he steadied him.

"Nothing in front. Maybe something on the other side."

Gunny pulled the chief aside as Corporal Hetec led first squad out of the lander at a trot. "No bandits to starboard. May be one to port," he advised the young marine as he went by. The corporal passed the word as he deployed his squad for perimeter defense. Max ducked under the lander's cooling nose to focus his sweep on the far side.

"Yeah. Heartbeat went up when he got a look at the marines. We got a watcher, Gunny."

"Armed?"

"Not picking up anything magnetic or dense. Let me check visuals." The launch had swept the landing area as it came in. The chief replayed the video, now using the human heart located on his electromagnetic monitor to zoom the picture to . . . "Yeah, there's our man. Lying low. No visible weapons." The screen changed again, switching to infrared. "He walked over from that single-lane track. Yep, there's a truck. Tire marks head off to the north, but the sun's warmed the road too much for me to backtrack him too far."

"Shall I collect him?" Corporal Hetec was back at Gunny's elbow.

"Nope, let's let him stew for a while." Second and third squads were rigging the light transports, three of them, though two could carry all twenty men of the two squads. The captain wanted redundancy; Gunny liked that in an officer. He also had two sensor specialists, Chief Max and a second class petty officer. Gunny had planned to take the chief with him to the dump. With a live one here, he changed his mind. "Chief, Corporal, maintain this position. Whoever that is may be someone the skipper wants to talk to. Then again, he could be a sniper." Gunny fixed his gaze on the young noncom. "We are not losing any more people to homesteading. We are not lifting anyone out in a body bag. Chief, you keep an eye on our visitor. First sign of hostility, you call in the marines. Otherwise, Corporal, you let that joker play out any game he wants. Understood?"

"Yes, Gunny."

"Chief?"

"No problem. I got him dialed in. He so much as wants to scratch, I'll know it before his fingers do."

• • •

Ruth stumbled on a tree root. Trouble caught her before she ended up facedown in the moss and leaves. His arms felt good around her, even in the oppressive noon heat. The humidity sapped her strength, and the welts from bug bites were starting to itch like mad. Since she could do nothing about them, she kept silent, keeping her misery to herself.

"Thank you," she smiled at the marine for the catch.

"Glad to. We got to look out for each other. Doesn't look like there'll be a stop for lunch."

Hunger was a close fifth on Ruth's lists of pains, the boss having gotten ahead of them enough that the pain in her gut made it hard to notice she was hungry. Ruth eyed the trail. They were skirting a thicket. Thorns reached out from low shrubs. People had edged away from them. But red berries dangled beside the barbs, and winged things that passed for insects here were nibbling at them. "We can eat those," she pointed.

"You sure?" Trouble wasn't persuaded.

"When I was little, Ma and Pa used to go fungus hunting, to help them put extra payments down on the station. Brother and I went along, but we weren't much help. Ma showed me things to snack on. The red ones are okay. The blue ones aren't ripe yet. They're bitter and give you the runs."

Trouble edged off the trail to pluck a small pod of the red fruit. He tasted one tiny red bulb. "Sweet" was all he said.

"I used to love them," Ruth said, plucking a handful.

Trouble still didn't look happy. "We ought to go easy on these. These might not be the same berries you remembered. How old were you?"

"Five or six. What's the matter, you don't trust me?" Ruth scarfed down the entire handful of berries and collected two more. Others followed her lead, and quickly the thicket was stripped of fruit. Trouble shrugged. The buzzing of their guts demanded they hustle to catch up with the boss.

The next stream crossing offered more food. "Ma called them red potatoes, though they sure aren't from Earth. The fungus grows near them." And sure enough, Ruth spotted the slim white stalks that the fungus shot up. "See? That's worth money."

While she used her walking stick to pry up a potato, Trouble was using his to gingerly probe around the fungus. "How far does that go down?"

"Maybe thirty centimeters."

He bent down, scrambled around in the dirt for a moment, then stood up, an ugly whitish-brown growth the size of a large watermelon in his hands. "Hey, boss," he shouted.

The boss turned his mule in its tracks, matching looks of puzzlement on the faces of man and animal. The marine got about as close as he could, maybe five meters, then stopped. "You say I owe you. Here's something on my account. Worth a bundle. You got people tramping along out here. You ever look at the gold mine you're walking through?"

The boss had the look of an off-worlder who's never quite sure what he's seeing if it's not straight blue and green. Clem was off his mule and running from behind the prisoners. To see the big, clumsy fellow run almost got a laugh out of Ruth. She swallowed it. Maybe she didn't have to. Clem rushed right by her as if she wasn't there. He grabbed the fungus from Trouble.

"This stuff sells at the trading posts for a couple hundred a kilo. This sucker's five, six kilos for sure." He hefted it. "Where'd you get it? Never seen one before it was cleaned up."

Trouble glanced around. "It's all over. Under those white strawlike things." He pulled a smaller one up, handed it to Clem. "See?"

The thug's eyes got real big.

"I hate to disappoint you, marine," the boss cut in, "but you people are worth a lot more than a couple of stale sponge cakes. But, Clem, stow it in your pack. Now get moving."

Ruth had taken the pause to show other people how to dig red potatoes. She grabbed two more and shared them with Trouble. "Thanks for the break." she said. "I don't know what fungus is selling for this year, but it was worth a five-minute break."

The marine glanced back; Ruth's eyes followed him. Clem and his associates were still grubbing in the dirt, yanking up clumps of fungus, laughing among themselves. The boss had ridden around the next twist in the trail, ignoring their delay. The pain in Ruth's belly reminded her she couldn't ignore him. They trudged along, leaving the toughs rejoicing in their newfound wealth.

"It's so much easier working with satisfied employers." Trouble grinned.

Gunny sniffed. Except for the smell, the dump run had been a cakewalk. He'd taken the long way around, driving the roads along the edge of the town, rather than going directly through. The workers at the dump had come to a roaring halt when three rigs carrying twenty armed marines drove into the place. They'd just stood around, hands in plain sight, while one squad covered the other squad and the sensor specialist. They'd driven right to the spot where the beacons were squawking. And stopped.

"Beacons are about a meter down in some pretty ripe crud," the petty officer had reported to Gunny.

While Gunny considered that, someone who might have been a foreman sauntered over to him. "You need some digging done over there? I can lend you a dozer."

"Be obliged for it."

"Az, take your dozer over and give those guys a hand," the local shouted.

"Up yours, Bossy," a driver shouted, but put her rig in gear. Ten minutes later, the squad was back, a brown plastic bag held gingerly in the petty officer's left hand. The five IDs were in it, along with three watches and five wallets. The remnants of a glass bottle had soaked them in whiskey when it had shattered. Gunny scowled.

The bossy one watched. "Guess that got by yesterday's shift. We were told to keep an eye out for anything that looked Navy, but a bottle of whiskey in a plain brown wrapper, can see how they missed it."

"Yeah," Gunny growled. "Saddle up, crew."

"Got to go so soon? You know, word is, some mines are gonna be opening up soon. Hurtford could use people like you guys. Az don't always look like that."

The dozer driver pulled the hat from her head, slowly shaking out long blonde strands, and seductively lowered the zipper on her coveralls. It was all that was covering her. Several marines whistled. "I like big men," she cooed.

"Saddle up, marines. Now!" Gunny growled as he stepped between Az and the staring privates. Boobs like Az's were hard to turn away from, but a mad Gunny was something to avoid. The troops loaded up. Damned if the girl wasn't totally out of the coveralls, standing there in work boots, a smile and nothing else. She got whistles, marriage proposals, and propositions, but Gunny got the trucks moving, his last out.

"Good try," he called to Bossy.

"For today. See you tomorrow."

The drive back to the airstrip was by a different route; Gunny took no chances now that his team's presence was known. Still, they met nothing that could be called opposition. Some kids, playing ball in the street, had been slow to get out of their way, but he saw nothing that looked organized. As they cleared town, he called ahead.

"Chief, anything interesting?"

"I got a good cardiac fingerprint of two rabbits making more rabbits. Other than that, it's been peace and quiet personified. What about you?"

"Your second class almost got some good cardiacs of people making more people, and me having a heart attack, but other than that, no trouble."

"Gunny, boys and girls give you a heart attack. I'm shocked. I never took you for a virgin."

"How is your reluctant virgin?"

"Watcher's still where you left him. Hasn't moved."

"Tell the bos'n to get ready to cast off as soon as we get back. I'm gonna leave the rigs down here."

"Righto."

Dismounting as the truck came to a halt, Gunny was met by Corporal Hetec and Chief Max. "As soon as my troops are back aboard, recover your security detail," he told the corporal, then turned to the chief. "What's happening?"

"Nothing. Our unknown has rolled over twice, but mostly he just stares at us."

"Time to fish or cut bait. Any sign of a weapon?"

"None, but that don't mean there ain't one."

"Tell me about it," Gunny said, ducking under the nose of the launch to get a better look at where their observer lurked. Nothing was visible in the half-meter-high stalks of grain. "Okay, Chief, you go aboard. Corporal, you get ready to come out here real fast if I need you."

"Yes, Gunny," the corporal and the chief answered.

Straightening his back a smidge to return it to the proper ramrod posture of a Marine Gunnery Sergeant, and to toss off the doubts of the unknown, Gunny began a properly cadenced march across the tarmac. Soon his boots crunched dirt and crops. He kept his eyes straight on the place Chief Max said hid their question mark. About halfway there, Gunny halted. "Stranger, we've got what we came for, so we're leaving. You got something you want to say?"

A man in jeans and a plaid shirt stood. Gray showed around his temples. He kept his hands in clear view. "Don't know."

"I left you alone out here as long as I could. You're gonna have to talk, come with us, or wave good-bye. Your call."

The guy glanced off to the north. "Can I trust you?"

"Good question. You can trust me for a beer, if the locals will take my money. Beyond that, it depends."

"Can I trust you with my daughter's life?"

That gave the Gunny pause. He had no kin that he was aware of, no son or daughter depending on him. "If your daughter is with my lieutenant, you can trust me. We will get them back."

The man's deep sigh turned into a shudder that shook his whole body. "That's the problem. I don't know."

"How many sons of bitches you got running around this planet stealing people?"

"A month ago I'd have said none. I hope to God there's only one bunch now."

"Then I think we're after the same bastards." The Gunny paused, trying to understand the agony chasing across the face of the poor man in front of him. "Listen. We got a good skipper. We got good people here. If there's any way we can get your daughter back, we will. We want the bastards that got our people. We want them bad."

"I want the bastards that got my Ruth." The man walked in.

Izzy studied the farmer seated to her left at the conference table. Gunny Griz sat to his left. The XO and Sensors were on her other side. "You know something about my missing personnel?"

"No, ma'am, but I do know my daughter went missing the same night your people did. Who did it left a note in her room telling me to go back where I belonged and not to talk to you."

"You didn't then," Stan said gently. "Why now?"

The man sighed like it might be his last breath. "You got to understand. Folks around here agree on everything. Most of the time, that's no problem. Even with the Unity heavies, we figured out what they wanted. When the men they drafted didn't show up, we got hit with fines. Paid the fines and everybody was happy. They didn't really want people running around in uniforms. Who'd invade Hurtford Corner? They wanted money they could ship off planet. We got them pharmaceuticals and furs. I understand the city folks signed on for some mining."

"So that's why the mining contracts?" Izzy said. Word around the wardrooms was that there might have been more financial interests promoting the war fever than hit the vids. *Am I staring part of it in the face?*

"Folks at the dump today said there'd be a need for plenty of new hands when the mines opened up real soon," Gunny added.

"Did somebody try to recruit your troopers, Gunny?"

"A mite bit, ma'am. Nothing we couldn't turn down."

Izzy wanted to do something to put her people off limits; that would have to wait. "Are we the only ones losing people?"

"I don't think so," Sensors said softly. Igor might as well have shouted it. Four heads swiveled to him like seekers in terminal lock. "The city net is pretty easy to track. Lots of messages. Pretty overwhelming. But we set up a search on 'didn't show up for work today' or 'didn't come home last night.' We got several dozen hits. Skipper, there are a lot of people missing. Why hasn't the city manager mentioned that?"

Izzy leaned back in her chair. "Curiouser and curiouser." She turned to the farmer. "Mr. Edris, have other station people disappeared?"

"That's what brought us to town. One of our stations was burned last week. Those not killed were carried off. A trading post also got ransacked. Its owner was killed and the rest of the people disappeared. For the last two, three months we've had single folks, usually teenagers, go missing. We don't have runaways like we had where I grew up on LornaDo. If a kid can't get along with his folks, there's usually someone willing to take him in, give him a man-size job and see if he's ready to carry it. A boy or girl don't just take off for the hills. Until lately. Caused a lot of wondering. Then the Abdoes place got attacked in broad daylight. There's no question for me. Something new is going on. Why? I don't know. But something's changed."

"Who's doing it?" Stan asked.

"Damned if I know. We've always had slackers, usually kids, some of them old enough to know better, folks who don't fit in, don't want much out of life. They get along doing odd jobs. City collects most. When Unity showed up, nobody minded when they slapped them into uniform. Most of them didn't know what to do with a gun, but they did like to swagger. Now Unity's gone, and so are most of the guns." The farmer's eyes worked their way slowly around the table. "Now some of our people are gone, too. I was a soldier once, on LornaDo. I never expected I'd want to carry a gun again. But sergeant, if you got a spare weapon, I'd be grateful for it."

Izzy leaned back in her chair, stroking her chin, trying to order her thoughts. Problems you could solve with a personal weapon were nice; she doubted this problem was that easy. She wished it was night; would someone arrange three fires in a triangle again? It was still four hours until dark. She had people missing; the farmers had people missing. They were squawking. Town people were missing, and no one said boo.

"Comm, get me the city manager."

"Yes, ma'am," came immediately, followed only a moment later by a "Hello."

"Mr. Shezgo, I understand that my personnel aren't the only ones who went missing after your party. Some of your town folks didn't make it home."

There was a long pause on the city manager's side. "I haven't heard anything about that. How many?"

Igor counted down his list. "Seventeen, to be exact."

"Seventeen! That's impossible. I'd have heard about it." Izzy listened intently. There was shock and denial in his voice. But cover-up? Without body language, it was hard to tell.

"We've monitored phone calls about them." Igor didn't give any ground.

"Mr. Shezgo, would missing people have been reported to you?" Izzy asked.

"One or two, no. Seventeen—yes, I should have been informed."

"By whom?"

He didn't answer that one. "Do you have the list of people you say are missing? Could I have it?"

Izzy glanced at Igor. He shrugged. "Shoot him a copy of the names." The sensors officer tapped his personal board.

"I have it" came from the comm unit. "I'll call you back in a bit. I need to look into this."

Izzy cleared her throat. "Mr. Shezgo, I'm not sure it would be a good idea to talk that list over with whoever should have brought it to your attention. Looks to me like somebody's introduced a new game in town down there."

"You might be right," Shezgo said distractedly. "I'll get back with you real soon."

Izzy sat forward in her seat. "Anybody want to take a bet we never hear from that guy again?"

She got no takers.

Mikhail Shezgo went down the list. *Yep, seventeen.* He printed it, wiped the call, and stuffed the hard copy in his pocket. As he left his office, he nodded to Henry, who covered his office on Thursdays. "I'm going home for a late lunch. Be back in an hour." He was halfway through his four-block walk home when he turned left instead of right. Five minutes later, he ducked into the cool shade of his cobbler's shop. Nicholas, as usual, greeted his customer by glancing at his feet, not his face. "There is nothing wrong with those shoes."

"No, friend. May I use your phone?"

Now Nicholas did look up, squinting. "So the great man cannot get his phone to work. I always said you should get a real job."

"And someday I will. Now, can I use your phone, today?"

"Yes, yes. You know where it is." And the cobbler went back to his last.

Mikhail called the first two numbers, then skipped halfway down the list, then called the last one. Each call was different, but the same. No, he or she wasn't home. No, he or she hadn't been home for two nights. No, he or she hadn't been heard from. Stuffing the list back in his pocket, Mikhail thanked Nicholas and stepped back outside. *Seventeen people in my town are gone and nobody told me!*

Turning back for city hall, Mikhail headed, his temper heating, for the Office of Public Safety. As he turned the corner, he came to a complete stop. Public Safety would have gotten the calls. Indeed, three of the four people he'd talked to had specifically mentioned calling in the missing person. Public Safety *should* have briefed him on the situation. Seventeen people. That's more than a situation. That's a . . .

Someone in Public Safety had kept the information from him. Mikhail drew the list out of his pocket again, went over the names. He'd never met any of these people. Probably nobody he knew had ever met any of them. They were little people who could go missing and never be missed by anyone who'd raise a stink.

The list was well chosen.

Mikhail turned at the next corner. His path was random now. He needed someone he could depend on. He had no idea who.

Izzy was halfway through her in-basket, and beginning to worry her joke about the city manager never getting back to them was too damn close to the mark, when her comm screen lit up.

"Those people are missing, and somebody down here doesn't want me to know about it," Shezgo started without preamble. "I'm not calling from my office, but I can't talk long. I'll be spending the rest of the afternoon trying to collect people I think I can trust, then I'll take on *my* Office of Public Safety."

"Would you like some marines?"

"I'd know I could trust them, but I'm not sure how people would take to 'em. Not long ago we had Unity hoods swaggering around. I'm afraid your marines look a lot like them."

"I'll follow your lead. Be careful." Izzy paused for a moment. She was used to blowing things up; this cloak-and-dagger stuff was new to her. "If somebody's telling you what to say, call me Izzy. That way we'll know you've lost control, and we'll add you to our list of people needing rescuing."

"Izzy," he repeated. "Call me Mikhail, and you don't have to be in trouble to use it."

"Take care," she said.

"You too," he answered and closed out.

"Stan," she shouted, hitting the ship's comm. "We got friends, but we got problems. When is it dark down there?"

The wood was wet, and the wind was blowing, and the damn match sputtered out only seconds after the marine struck it.

"Looks like I'm the only one that gets a fire tonight," the boss drawled as he handed Trouble a second match.

Ruth didn't know where to look. Not the boss. His grin was boiling her blood. All she wanted to do was claw his eyes out—or rip off what Mordy was so careful to protect when he knocked her around. The marine was trying to keep the boss happy. She dared not look at the boss.

She couldn't bear to look at Trouble. His face, his body were frozen. He was hurting inside, but too proud to let the boss see . . . or anyone else. *Was the fire that important?*

"You really wanted us warm, didn't you?" Ruth risked asking him. Trouble broke his stony demeanor just enough to nod, then struck the second match. The flames taunted them as they flicked to easy life. Trouble knelt by the fire, feeding it carefully as it grew. Others gathered, seeking warmth in the cooling night.

Ruth didn't know why, but they needed three fires tonight. Someone had to face the boss, pry a light from him for the other two fires. Who would risk it? Everyone else had kept their heads down. Only she and Trouble had dared cross the boss. How often could they challenge him before he took the pods to the limit?

Ruth stood. "We need fires to keep us warm tonight," she pleaded to the boss's retreating back.

He settled into his bedroll, his back to her, but she had no trouble hearing his answer when it came. "Soldier boy knew the rules. One match, and he could borrow my fire. Two matches, and there's only my fire. You got a beef, take it out of his hide."

The three big city guys who'd been half carrying their "friend" with the bent leg grinned as they collected clubs that wouldn't be used for firewood tonight.

"But that won't keep our teeth from chattering. Help get any sleep," Ruth pointed out.

"Your loss," the boss shrugged inside his sleeping bag.

Ruth's gut twisted into a dozen knots. She was just making things worse like she had most of her life. Nobody stepped in to help. *What could they do? I started it. I have to finish it.*

What handle could she use on these guys? The fungus? Trouble had tried greed to get at the boss. "If we don't get any sleep tonight, we'll hardly be bright-eyed and bushy-tailed tomorrow. We might walk right through a big bunch of fungus and never notice a thing. Too bad."

Boss didn't roll over to face her, but he wasn't fidgeting around in his roll searching for a comfortable place. "Clem and his guys will keep an eye out for fungus."

"Probably will. Wonder how much they chase down will be worth a couple hundred bucks a kilo, and how much will be poison. Think Clem can tell the local stuff from the crap that's come in from off-world? Put some of those poisons in the same bag with the good stuff, and none of it will be worth a damn."

That got the boss to roll over. He eyed her the way she might a new sown field . . . full of weeds. "Let me guess, kid. You're the only one what can tell money from poison?"

Ruth glanced around. None of the city folks could. None of the spacers either. "Looks that way."

The boss glowered at her. "I could turn you over to Clem and his friends. 'Spect that might make you more willing to go along with us."

"But you'd never know if she was pointing you at poison or profits," Trouble put in quietly.

The boss rolled back over, away from them. "Maybe you're all more trouble than you're worth. Maybe I ought to just turn the trainer up full blast and watch you all curl up and die." He seemed to settle into a comfortable place. Ruth hardly breathed.

"Then again, I only get paid for the workers I deliver," the boss muttered. "Light your damn fires."

"Thank you, sir," Ruth answered, because she'd been raised to be polite.

She hardly heard the "Thank you very much" that the marine officer whispered. But she heard it. And the shivers she got at his words left her warm.

The first nighttime pass over the mountains showed Izzy no camp with three fires—in a triangle or otherwise. She went back to her in-basket. At moments like this, routine kept her from chewing her nails . . . or subordinates. The next report didn't help. It listed all the maintenance deficiencies Chips' team had identified and went on for two hundred hard copy pages. Scrolling through it, Izzy's eyes glazed over. "Hard to believe there's that much wrong with this tub and we're still breathing oxygen." She endorsed it with a strong recommendation that the *Patton* get a yard period at the earliest available opportunity.

She was well into the next report when the screen went black. Before she could cuss the equipment, Stan's voice intervened. "Skipper, got a picture for you. Just starting our second night pass. One of those fires has sisters."

Izzy eyed the dark screen. Yes, there were a few sparkles. "Show me the one, Stan." The screen zoomed, although with so much black on black it was hard to tell. There, in the middle of all that black, were three fires forming a rough triangle.

"Stan, roust out Igor, Gunny, and our visitor. We got some planning to do."

FIVE

THE SECOND NIGHT was also cold, but Ruth didn't remember waking at all. Maybe she was just too tired to notice, or maybe it was because Trouble stayed close. Clem's bellowing roused her. "You've had your beauty rest. It's time to move."

They did, with groans and moans. Breakfast was again in a box. Again, the heaters didn't raise most of the food to lukewarm. Ruth had to force it down; she wasn't about to leave any. When the boss announced, "I'm moving out. You'd best follow," she stuffed half her meal in her pocket.

"Keep your eyes peeled for fungus. Remember, you owe me," the boss reminded them.

"I'd rather watch for a rescue party," Ruth muttered.

"We'll see what we see," Trouble whispered, not looking up.

"Let's see what we can see," Izzy said to Igor and Mr. Edris—no, now he was just Joe. Joe had been there when Igor explained the workings of the Condor to Izzy. "Don't often get to do searches in an atmosphere where these work. Tiny thing, not much bigger than two fists, but once the descent stage cuts it loose, it unfolds a one-meter wingspan and a sensor suite you wouldn't believe."

Now, the Condor circled at fifteen thousand meters. Its sensors scoured the ground; its solar panels fed the engine and sensors, and charged the fuel cells that would keep it up tonight. "Dandy little critter," Joe grinned, echoing Igor.

"Not until it shows me something," Izzy growled.

"Okay, infrared first. There's what's left of the three fires. No one around them now. Let's see. Footsteps lead off to the northeast, just like I thought." Last night, Igor had connected the two sets of fires and drawn a line through them in both directions. Back toward town, it intersected a road. When the line was extended to the northeast, things got interesting.

Ghosts appeared on Igor's screen. "I think we got some people here. Kind of large for a survey party. Not many mules carrying their gear, either. In the lead is a single man on a mule. Strung out behind him are about twenty walkers. Well behind them are four men on mules leading two pack mules."

"Are any of them our people?" was Izzy's one question.

"I'll have to drop the Condor down to five thousand meters to get an electromagnetic reading on a heart. I've got signatures for the lieutenant and two of the missing spacers."

Izzy frowned. Heart signatures were supposed to be part of every recruit's induction, along with DNA, fingerprints, and retina scans. But with the budget cuts, recruiting centers were cutting corners. "Do it, Igor."

Igor took fifteen minutes to spiral his Condor down. "There's the lieutenant. He's got a woman walking beside him."

"That's Trouble," Izzy agreed.

"Two of our spacers are right behind him. A man and a woman walking with them. That probably accounts for our four."

Izzy frowned at the screens. "If there are only five people riding, why hasn't Trouble taken them apart?"

"May have the answer here, ma'am. The guy in the lead is radiating signals on two different frequencies. Both are weak, but one's just a bit stronger than the other. That's the type of signal we get from a restraining system." Igor quickly filled his skipper in on the latest in animal control. "You put four or six of those transmitters on a man, and you can incapacitate him in seconds. Kill him in a minute. A very long minute."

"Damn" was all Izzy said. She called up a map she'd put together the night before. "If they stay on the course they've been following, in two days they reach this lake. It looks to me like there are two other survey teams headed for the same lake. Igor, cruise over to them and check them out."

"It will take most of the day."

"Take it. I also want a fine scan of that lake. You can put a shuttle down in a lake that big, if it's deep enough or all the snags have been removed. Next pass, I want to know everything there is to know about that puddle, including any good places to beach a boat, or a lander."

Igor turned to his sensor specialists. "You heard the lady. Let's make the skipper happy."

"What do we do now?" Joe asked Izzy as they left the sensor team to their work.

She grinned. "First we tell it to the marines. Then, I tell it to a very irate XO who won't want me to do what I want to do. Too bad for him. He *ain't* the boss here."

Mikhail walked the streets of Hurtford City until well after dark. Part of him wanted to go home, ignore what he'd found out, and go to work like normal tomorrow. After all, that navy woman was handling this. There was nothing he could do.

Right! And what do I say when they haul me off?

Which left him walking in circles, trying to figure out who he could talk to. When he'd decided to cooperate with Unity, his circle of friends had gotten a bit narrow. They'd supported his practical approach; they were all practical people. And some of them were probably kidnappers. Murderers, too, if you believed the farmer. Going to the wrong person for help would be worse than doing nothing at all. So he went to Cindy, the first girl who had befriended him on Hurtford Corner. That was about the last thing in the world anyone would expect of him.

Unfortunately, that also included Cindy.

"What are you doing here?" was her answer to his knock.

"I think someone may be trying to kill me," he said, thinking he sounded very melodramatic.

"Four years ago, Mike, that was me." She slammed the door.

Mikhail risked a toe to keep the door open. "Cindy, you're the only one I can turn to."

"You're serious." She hung on the door for a second, giving him one of her sidelong looks. He nodded. She shook her head, long brown curls flying. "Hey, this is Hurtford City. We don't kill people. Some gal from your off-world college days finally look you up?"

"It may be somebody from off-world, but it's also somebody from right here. Cindy, something very strange and nasty is going on. Do you want me to explain it here in the hall, or can I come in?" She opened the door wider; he slipped in.

She listened with the intense gaze Mikhail had found so alluring as he told her what he knew. The list of missing people had drawn a slow nod from her. "I know two of them. They aren't the type to just vanish. We wondered."

"Who wondered?"

"A few of us. Listen. The couch is yours for the night. I've got a spare blanket and pillow in the hall closet. I'll be out for a while. You'll probably be asleep when I get back. We can talk more in the morning." And she left. Sleep was a long time coming; he had only dozed off by the time she returned. She said nothing to him, but went straight to her bedroom. Despite the fears chasing around his head, he must have slept. She greeted him in the morning with a smile, a bowl of cereal, and "I've got someone you should meet."

"I was afraid, last night, when you were gone so long, you might be coming back with, you know, someone who'd be after me."

She laughed. "Mike, you don't know a thing about women. Are all off-world guys as stupid as you?"

"Somehow, I doubt it."

"Hurry up and eat. We have a busy day ahead of us."

The busy day started with a long, circuitous walk, ending at an old house in the middle of town. "Mike, I want you to meet my grandmother, and a few of her friends."

The next orbital pass told Izzy everything she needed to know. The lake was shallow, and full of snags . . . except for a six-by-two-kilometer stretch near the eastern shore. Right next to that prepared water landing strip was a very nice, sandy beach showing plenty of footprints.

"I think we've found where your people are disappearing. Now, if those other two parties show animal-control signatures, we know who our targets are."

"We also should expect company soon," Izzy's exec put in.

She nodded. "Somebody's coming to collect them. No one's in-system yet, so we can prepare a surprise for them. Stan, you put the *Patton* in a low orbit around the small moon, make a hole in space, and put the ship in it. You catch whoever comes to collect those folks. I want prisoners this time."

"That ship may well be full of folks they've kidnapped off other planets," Stan pointed out softly.

"All the more reason for you to go easy on it. Capture it, but in a gentlemanly fashion."

"And while I'm doing that?" the XO asked slowly.

"I'll take the marines dirtside and collect the rest."

The XO showed no surprise. "Why don't we just collect them all up here in orbit?"

"Stan, a lot of things can go wrong. I'm not putting all my targets in one basket. There're three on the ground and one in space. I want them all, but I've got to have one of them."

"Can't Gunny lead the marines?"

"They don't have an officer. I've got the only experience

with ground-pounders on this boat. I'm going with them. Enough said. You want one squad of marines for boarding?"

"I suspect you'll need all the marines downside. We can take care of things topside."

"Good, Stan. Now, what's the weather down there? I'd love a good thunderstorm to cover the lander's noise."

Stan just shook his head.

"So you're the young man from off-world who's been trying to run our planet." Green eyes sparkled up at Mikhail. Grandma Uzeg was a tiny woman. She was seated in a rocker and covered by a quilt of intricate patterns—whether of Irish or Arabic tradition, it was probably too late in human history to tell. Her smile was neither approving nor disapproving.

"I haven't done as well as I thought I had." Mikhail took the small stool offered him.

"These have been difficult times. None of the choices were easy. We here approved of all you did." A hand, wrinkled and spotted, swept around the circle of a dozen others, as old as or older than she was. "Like you, we hoped this day would not come. Unlike you, we feared it would. Tell us what you know."

Since that wasn't much, it didn't take Mikhail long.

"So the Navy says calls were made to the Office of Public Safety, reporting the missing, but it was never reported to you and the Elders." Grandmother summed it up. Mikhail just nodded.

"Three mothers came to me about grown children gone missing." The speaker now was an elderly man. "Their friends had done a search. I know they called Public Safety."

"It appears someone in Public Safety is neither public nor safe." Grandmother leaned back thoughtfully. "I have been concerned about Zylon since she was a little girl."

"She spends too many hours volunteering at the same place." The old man shook his head. "That was not what the founders had in mind."

"And how many hours have you, Frederick, spent at the

water works? The founders wanted us free to do as we chose. Now it appears that some are choosing to use that freedom against the common freedom. Mikhail has brought us the fullness of the threat. What we do in the next few days will decide which freedom will prevail. Who, besides Zylon, has chosen unwisely?"

"I do not trust anyone from off-planet," the old man said.

"Yet it is the Navy that tells us the scope of our problem, and may well save many of our children. And Mikhail is not native born. Come now, let us be more selective." Thus the true Elders of Hurtford Corner began to divide up the population. There were those they would trust, those they would not, and those they could not decide upon. Mikhail was surprised at how few fell into that last group—and appalled by how much time he'd spent among people these Elders would not trust.

"Now that we have our chess pieces"—Grandmother's green eyes glistened—"how shall we play out this game? I far prefer a checkmate to a bloodbath."

Izzy floated beside the guide lines leading into the liberty launch. The marines were not dressed to party. *On second thought, they're probably expecting more fun than they got at the last dance.* Stan floated beside her.

"Skipper, one last time. You sure you want to do this?"

"Stan, your whole career's been ship duty. I bet you've got a dozen different ideas on how to take a merchant ship out without harming a hair on anyone's head." Her XO didn't argue.

"Me, all my duty has been using ground-pounders to do unto others fast. I'm going where I can do the most good. You're going where you can. If we weren't so strapped for people, we wouldn't be having to choose, but we are, and that's that. See you when I see you."

"Yes ma'am." He saluted.

"Give 'em hell." She saluted back.

She was moving fast. They had no idea when the shanghai ship would jump in-system; the *Patton* had to be a hole in space when she did. Thunderstorms were moving through the mountains. With luck, they'd cover the launch's approach. It did make for a rough ride down.

Izzy joined most of the marines in sleeping through it.

They had just crossed a babbling brook when the boss decided to make camp. In the half hour it took to eat and set up camp, the stream went from babbling to roaring. The day's rains had been plentiful in the foothills; higher up, they must have been real heavy. Trouble swung his folks around to the high side of the boss's camp. While Ruth led the firewood collection detail, the marine tried to figure out where to put three fires; tonight would be a very rough triangle.

It took him three matches to get the boss's fire going. Damp wood contributed to his failure. The kindling and moss he'd picked up early in the day when the rains started had not helped. After he had sweated and been rained on, the stuff in his pocket was no drier than the punk around camp. Ruth had returned to camp about the time the second match flamed out. She hung around while he worked the third. Before she could open her mouth, the boss cut her off.

"Three matches, girl. Three. And you didn't find all that much fungus today. No fire."

"You kept us on rocky ground. Fungus doesn't grow there."

"Find me fungus tomorrow, and maybe you'll get a fire. Then again, maybe you'll sleep on a nice warm ship. Go away, girl."

Ruth did; her eyes found Trouble. The question was plain. *How important is fire?*

The marine kept his head down too, as submissive as he could force himself to be. *Damned if I know* was hardly something he could get his face around for a silent signal. *Not worth you risking yourself* was also beyond him. So he faced down and gave her no signal. In the failing light, they made lean-tos to keep some of the rain off, found ferns that weren't too damp to give them some protection from the ground, and huddled together to keep warm.

"Have we done enough?" Ruth whispered.

Trouble was a twenty-third-century military officer, used to going into battle with a full suite of sensors and mayhem at his fingertips. The last few days had reduced him to his bare hands and one of man's oldest tools, fire. Had someone up there spotted his fire signal and understood it? Was help on the way? If the boss wasn't just throwing more smoke at them, and they were to be shipped off-planet tomorrow, time was running out. It was time to come up with his own plan.

"These belts don't have to keep us controlled if we don't let them," he started slowly.

"What do you mean, sir?" Jagowski asked.

"It will hurt like hell, but if I get a running start, I can smash into that shithead before I keel over. If I knock the control out of his hands, and if someone else kicks it out of his reach and away from us . . ."

"Kind of like soccer," a spacer put in.

"Only the goal is to kick it just a little ways, not too far," pointed out the petty officer. "Meanwhile, someone else has got to take out Clem and the cruds."

"A bit complicated," Ruth noted dryly, rain dripping on her. "But Clem has a weakness. He wants us girls in the worst way."

"Honey, he is the worst way," a woman spacer noted.

"All we have to do is distract him. Get close to his pistol. Then, we could do . . . something."

"I hate to agree with Ruth," Trouble said against his will, "but it's time to try anything. As long as we're on this planet, there's hope. They ship us off, and it's their ball game. We've got to do anything and everything before then."

The morning was half gone before Zylon Plovdic put her finger on what was bothering her. The outer office was crowded, and getting more crowded. And too quiet.

By the founder's rules, anyone could volunteer to do anything for the common good. Indeed, those who didn't volunteer were frowned upon. Early on she'd discovered how much fun it was to wear the security armband. She could haul people in for a night in the drunk tank. Occasionally, she even got to beat up a problem. Yes, security was the place for her, even before Big Al introduced her to the added perks. Since anyone could volunteer for any job, she just kept on volunteering for this one.

And she knew all the regular volunteers. Several were very good friends. Most of the people working today in the outer office were new to her. Strange. Very strange.

A quick check with Risa added another oddity. She hadn't briefed Mikhail yet. He hadn't come in.

Maybe it was nothing. She checked the volunteer sign-in roster. Three names were familiar. She flipped through a couple more databases before she hit on the right one. *Oh, shit!* Missing people. Most of the unfamiliar sign-ins had relatives on the missing people list.

A glance at the clock told her lunch was an hour away. Still, she grabbed her coat and headed for the door. "Bara, Din, how about an early lunch?" she called to the only two faces she trusted in the bullpen.

"A bit early, but okay," Din agreed, and Bara joined them. Zylon set a quick pace for the exit, turned left, then alternated lefts and rights at each block. By the fourth turn, she knew a couple was following her.

"Team, I think we have a problem. Ever seen so many strange faces in the bullpen?" That got a rise from the two.

"The city manager didn't come in today. I think somebody's trying to pull off something funny. Those two behind us have been following since we left the office. I need to find some Elders. At the next turn, I want you to wait for those two, detain them while I get lost. Can you do that?"

"No problem," Din agreed. Bara seemed a bit less sold, but she was willing to go along with Din. Zylon made the next turn. The two immediately stopped, backed up to the wall, and waited. Zylon took off running. She was to the next street, across it, and heading up it before her tails tripped into Din.

Zylon needed to talk to someone, but it wasn't an Elder. Maybe Big Al would talk to one or two that were in his pocket, but that was his call. Hers was to Big Al. Something was happening, and it wasn't what they'd planned.

Izzy loved it when a plan came together; last night's storm hadn't dampened her spirits. What was a little rain among good people who loved their jobs? The chief from Igor's team had griped a bit; deprive a spacer of a warm bunk and a full galley, and he tended to complain. She factored his noise out with the thunder and rain. *God, it's good to be back with the Joes.*

The Condor was at fifteen thousand meters, circling between three very solid targets. All three were supposed to be survey teams. All three had been cleared by the same official from Public Safety, a certain Zylon Plovdic. Izzy wanted to talk to that woman. First, she needed more evidence—and her people back. She would hit Trouble's team, then backtrack and take out the others one at a time. She suspected Trouble would like it that way. After three days of taking whatever these dudes were dishing out, she wanted to put her officer back in the driver's seat.

Trouble knew they were getting near the end of this hike. The mules' packs were empty. Clem and his crowd were joking more among themselves. Even the boss seemed relaxed.

All morning, the marine, the spacers and Ruth had hurried their pace, kept up with the boss. Close, but not too close. Ruth had identified several large clumps of fungus. The boss was happy; he'd even spotted one. Yes, the hike was about over, and everyone wanted to end on a happy note.

Then the woods got awful quiet.

Every forest has its sounds. The wind in the trees is a constant. There are always insects, or something small that makes its presence known by rubbing, pecking, or squawking. They might quiet down if Clem and company got to laughing it up too much, but they always came back. At the moment, the trees were making the only sound besides Clem's weak effort at a long joke. Next to the marine, Ruth's eyes were tight slits.

She glanced around in swift, jerky movements. "Take it easy, Ruth," Trouble whispered. "Heads up, crew, and eyes open. Something is going down."

Gut tightening, muscles tensing, Trouble walked along, head dutifully down, eyes searching the underbrush beside the trail. Hunting for something he wanted to find. Something that, if he found it, would result in some private getting a royal dressing-down.

If they were out there, the camouflage was perfect.

Maybe he was just fooling himself. Maybe he'd better make his own play next rest stop. He figured to plant himself on top of the boss. If the others didn't manage to kick the control far enough away from him, he'd be very dead in sixty excruciatingly long seconds. Nice thing to think about for the next hour.

"That's far enough," boomed a voice twice the size of any mountain this planet had. "Put your arms in the air, and no one gets hurt."

The shock was enough to knock Clem off his mule; his hands were going up even as he fell. The boss was another matter. He started going through his pockets.

"Look out, everyone, he's got a pain controller," Trouble shouted, even as he realized the boss could have slapped the controller in a second. No, he was after his personal files. They had his contacts, contracts, everything. Trouble did not want those erased.

"Follow me," he shouted—and charged.

Pain shot through him, lanced his consciousness with agony like a white-hot sun. His whole body wanted to ball up around the hell that was his gut—but his feet kept pumping, propelling him forward into flaming pits of yellow and red. The mule saw him coming and, like any smart animal, tried to get out of the way. Four legs went one way, the boss went another. With his last ounce of control, Trouble aimed for the boss's hands and lunged. Black agony and lightning were all he knew as he lost consciousness.

* * *

Trouble was a long time coming back to awareness. From far off he heard a corpsman defend himself. "Captain, I've pumped every kind of pain reliever I've got, both the standard and restricted. He's still shaking, but he's still here."

"Are you sure?" Trouble mumbled. And immediately threw up.

"Yes, I'm sure," the skipper nudged him with her boot. "Want to go hunting for some more of these bastards?"

"There're more?" Trouble wiped vomit from his mouth. Gritting his teeth and squeezing his eyes shut, he managed to will back a wave of pain.

"Damn it, sir. You just tossed half of the meds I gave you. Want another batch?"

Very slightly, Trouble shook his head. "I'd rather go hunting. Where're the bastards that were pulling my chain?"

The skipper just grinned and pointed. Handcuffed together, they hugged two trees. Their shirttails were out; Trouble spotted the control pods. "Who's got the controller?"

"I do." A man raised the console. "I'm Ruth's pa, Joe."

"Where's Ruth?"

"With Gunny. Learning how to use an M-6."

Trouble struggled to his feet. The ground rolled out from underneath him, and pain washed over him like hell's own baptism. One of the civilians handed him her walking stick. "You got any spare armor, skipper?" he asked.

A private handed him his personal body armor and helmet. As Trouble slapped the armor tabs down, he activated his display. The location of his marines and the topography half a kilometer around him tinted his eyeball. Two flashing red triangles indicated targets off the map to the north. He zoomed out. A Condor had them spotted about ten klicks away. "Looks like we got business." He grinned and stepped off to the north. His leg collapsed under him. The skipper caught him.

"Ever heard about Captain Jinks of the horse marines?" she asked. "You're riding, man." Two privates helped him onto the boss's mule. The skipper held the reins, then started walking north, leading his mount. "Don't go telling me this is embarrassing, man. We got to get north, and I want you there. I got a phone call this morning."

"Phone call?" Trouble wasn't sure he'd heard right.

"Yeah, the *Patton*'s on emissions control, so I got myself an unlisted number on the local net. City manager is on our side, and they're trying to sort out the rest of the sheep from the goats. I expect things will get wild sometime later today, and I want to settle up with everyone here in the woods before then."

"Sounds like fun. By the way, thanks for saving my ass."

"Trouble, that was about the most stupid thing I ever saw, you charging the guy with the pain controls, and, much as I'd like to take the credit, I didn't save your hide."

"Who did?"

"Your friend there."

Ruth waved. "Gunny's been showing us how to use your rifles. Good stuff."

"Am I turning into a wimp? She drop-kicked the damn thing, and went on to rifle practice, and I can hardly stand."

"Wimp, maybe?" The captain gave him an imp's grin. "'Course, it helped that two of her controllers were duds. All six of yours were working. Turns out a third of them were duds. Poor quality control."

Trouble glanced over his shoulder. "I hope you didn't put any duds on that bunch."

"Oh, we tested them. Petty Officer Jagowski was quite insistent. Checked each one to see that the skin was reddening around the controller. Turned it on three times to make sure."

"Jagowski's a good man." He turned to Ruth. "Thanks for saving my life."

"None of us would be alive if you hadn't been here. Izzy told me the fires were a signal. Glad I helped get them lit the second night."

Trouble gave Ruth a wink. So the skipper was Izzy to Ruth. She must have impressed the old lady. "Did you get the boss man's data files?"

"We got 'em," the skipper said. "They're locked down. If it takes the ship's team and computers more than a day to unlock 'em, I'll have somebody's hide for a rug. I want these guys. Just a hunch, but I bet our pirates and these slavers are in cahoots. Maybe not, but I'm looking for evidence to prove it. Meanwhile, we got some folks to save. Let's pick up the pace, Gunny."

Gunny repeated the captain's orders. On his heads up, Trouble watched his teams, some spreading out to secure their advance, others coming together to concentrate their fire. They were a good crew. They knew their jobs. He'd trained them well, and they'd saved his bacon. Now, he had a few things he wanted to fry. Trouble kicked his mule for a bit more speed; the damn thing was falling behind the skipper.

It was good to have places to go and things to do.

Zylon needed a phone, a place to hide, and a way off this planet. She'd start with a public phone. As usual, Big Al wasn't answering. Zef swore it was just his way of showing how important he was. A computer asked her to leave a message. "Zylon here. I got lots of unknown volunteers today. Two tailed me when I went to lunch. Maybe nothing, but I ain't betting on that. I'm going to ground. I'll call you again in one hour."

She hung up and started walking. She ought to get off the streets, but she didn't have a lot of choices. One or two places might be safe. She'd try them.

In an hour, the marines and the targets had closed to within two klicks. As the skipper expected, the slavers were headed for the beach. She and Trouble laid on quite a party for them. Then "I got a radio intercept. Passing it through" filled Trouble's headphones, followed by hissing and crackling as the portable cracker decoded the message.

"Bernie, Elm, and Maurice, we may have a problem."

"What d' ya mean?"

"What's happening?"

"Where's Bernie?"

"I don't know" came in two flavors. The boss had never owned up to a name. Trouble suspected Bernie was tied to a tree, savoring a whole new meaning of pain.

"He could be down in a valley. These mountains are hell on reception."

"We'll see. In town, we have a problem. The locals are up in arms. They cannot void the mining contracts. If they look into the labor recruitment efforts, it could get inconvenient. You may have to dump your cargos in a hurry. Understood?"

"Will we get paid?"

"A reduced sum, but yes, you will be paid."

"Whatever you say, sir."

"I will get back to you when I know better what the situation is here. Try to raise Bernie. I must go now."

The skipper had called a halt while they listened. Now she stood facing the sensor chief. "How old's that message?"

"Almost real time, ma'am."

"Forget the planned ambush," she said, turning to Trouble. "We got a meeting engagement ahead of us. I'll take first and second squad. Trouble, you got third, fourth. We'll split the civilians between the fire teams. Any questions?" There were none. "Move out on the double."

"Gunny, go with the skipper."

Gunny's "Yessir" had serious doubts behind it, but when the lieutenant made a curt signal toward the CO, Gunny went.

The scouts in the vanguard split, one group heading left, the other right. The two fire teams trotted past Trouble, one staying on the trail, the other heading off cross country to the right. If he was going to keep up with his team, Trouble needed to hustle; he kicked his mule for more speed.

It stopped dead in its tracks right in the middle of the trail. He kicked it again. It turned to eye him dolefully, any thoughts of obedience far from its large brown eyes. The civilians had been trailing the marines; now they passed Trouble. "Blow in its ear," Ruth suggested as she hurried by.

"Blow in its ear?"

"Yeah. Hard." The woman didn't even slow down.

Trouble gave the recalcitrant animal one more hard kick. It ignored him. It had turned to the side of the trail and was stripping a bush of leaves. Shrugging, Trouble leaned forward and blew in its ear. No effect. He drew in a deep breath and leaned real close.

The mule took off so fast, Trouble almost lost his seat. Working hard to keep on the damn critter and point it in the general direction of the target group, the marine bounced past the fire team and shot through the scouts.

Now brush and low limbs added to his problem. His helmet visor and body armor protected him, but that still left a lot of exposed skin. At least the heads-up said he was headed in the right direction.

In fact, he was almost halfway there.

"Slow down, girl," he shouted. Nothing happened. He pulled in on the reins. The damn thing speeded up. The target was getting real close. Trouble considered falling off the mule, but the ground looked awfully rocky. Shooting the mule was attractive, but his pistol was holstered, and both hands clutched the beast's reins. Not that they controlled it.

The mule galloped into a meadow. On the far side, the leader of the target group was just riding into the clearing. Trouble's four-legged transport headed for him, or the mule he rode in on. The leader waved a halt; his victims were bunched up a ways behind him. Three toughs with rifles joined him. All four eyed Trouble and his galloping friend, more puzzled than alarmed.

Maybe I am a puzzle. Helmet and visor hid his face. Body armor over a bedraggled red-and-blue dress uniform said nothing about who he was. Now the mule slowed. Probably wants to get friendly with the mules up ahead. *Think, Trouble.*

"Bernie's in trouble. He needs help," Trouble shouted in the best imitation of Clem's drawl he could manage between bumps in the mule's slowing gallop.

The leader turned to his toughs, shaking his head. "I told

you Bernie was too smart for his own good. What'd he do this time?"

"Went chasing after a big brown hairy thing. Said the pelt was worth a fortune. Turns out it had a momma and pappa. His leg's broke," Trouble finished as his mule came to a stop, nuzzling the muzzle of the leader's mule. Trouble slid from its back, a hand grasping the saddle to keep him balanced on wobbly legs. The other hand edged toward his pistol. He had it out before the others had quit laughing at Bernie's fictional distress.

The business end of a service automatic ended their guffaws. "I'm Lieutenant Tordon, Humanity Marine Corps, and if you want to keep living, drop your rifles real slow."

For a second, they just stared at him. Then an evil sneer crept across the leader's face. "There's only one of you, and there's four of us."

"The first of you that moves his rifle dies with a bullet in his heart. I can kill two more before any of you can get a shot off. And I'll get the last one while I'm falling. You want to live, drop the guns."

One thug held his rifle out at arm's length. Trouble eyed him as he dropped it. The leader took the opportunity to bring his rifle up. Trouble put a bullet in his chest before his barrel moved a foot. Two more rifles were on the ground before the leader landed.

The riderless mules took off to tour points of interest. The thugs were having trouble controlling their rides with their hands in the air. One man fell off—too damn close to the rifles. "Go for the guns and I'll blow your head off. You guys dismount. All of you, over against that tree."

They moved, slowly, eyes on the blood pumping from their leader's chest. Trouble had aimed for the heart, and hit what he aimed for. Several would-be slaves took the opportunity to get close. "You want to grab a rifle and keep these guys covered?"

"Would love to," a black-haired woman agreed, "but we can't get close enough to him," she inclined her head toward the leader, "without getting shocked."

"Any of your group sucking up to these guys?" Trouble remembered the four city fellows they'd left tied to the tree with Bernie and his crew.

Disgust shaded the woman's face as she glanced at her fellow hikers. "We weren't that desperate. They killed my husband." Growls of agreement accompanied that. Trouble shoved her a rifle. Once she had the junior toughs covered, he handed a second rifle to a kid, maybe fourteen, then collapsed beside the leader's body. He found the controller and switched it off. Two women rushed to get rifles; another gave the leader a kick.

With rifles covering the thugs, others were ransacking their pockets, removing knives, phones, and other potential weapons. The black-haired woman traded her rifle for a Bowie knife. For a moment, Trouble weighed how important prisoners were to the skipper, then decided it wasn't worth the effort and turned his back.

"Trouble to skipper. I've got the situation with my target well in hand. Had to shoot their team leader." There was a scream from behind him. He didn't look back.

"We heard the shot. You take any prisoners?"

The scream from behind him had turned into a trio. "I don't think so."

"Our team has gone to ground. We're closing on them and will dig them out carefully. You've got witnesses?"

"Yeah, I got the widows of some of the men they killed."

"Explains the static on your signal. If you've got witnesses, this group gets no benefit from killing their hostages. May take me a while, but they're mine. Umboto out."

Trouble struggled to his feet. His fire team would be arriving soon. Probably best he kept them to the far side of the clearing until things separated themselves out here. He was waiting in the sun when his scouts glided out of the woods. Ruth and her dad were with them. The corporal leading the scouts eyed the other end of the clearing. Shrieks and screams and laughs were still coming from that direction.

"Widows are talking things over with the guys who murdered their husbands," Trouble said. The corporal shrugged and set about securing this side of the meadow.

Ruth and her dad settled beside him, their backs to the dell. Ruth's olive skin paled as the screams went on, but she said nothing. It was her father who spoke. "Short woman, black hair showing gray?"

Trouble nodded.

"Agnatha, Paco's wife. Probably ought to stop her. This isn't healthy." He didn't move.

"Not good for a combat unit's morale." Trouble kept his voice steady. A shriek went up the scale, then stopped dead. "But I don't see those folks as combat troops."

Ruth coughed, then leaned over and lost what was left of her breakfast. "Sorry, girl" was all her Dad said.

She wiped her mouth; Trouble signaled to a marine for his canteen. The private offered it, along with a candy bar. Ruth took the canteen but ignored the food. "When we got free, I wanted to do something to Clem, the boss, all of them. Hurt them like they hurt us. But with all the marines around and the chance to go after two more gangs, somehow it slipped my mind. I don't think I could live with myself if I'd done this."

"But your captors didn't kill anyone," her father pointed out. "These women have to live with the memory of their husbands and children being murdered. Maybe this won't make it better, but maybe it won't make it worse, either."

Shots came from their distant left; Trouble called up the last target on his heads-up. A large clump of figures was surrounded by many well-deployed marines. The fire didn't sound like M-6s. Probably poor fire discipline by fools who didn't know they were finished. He switched to the skipper's channel.

"You're the last of the three. We've got plenty of witnesses to what you're doing. Harm one of those people, and none of you'll get out of here alive. Put down your guns, and you'll live. This planet doesn't have a death penalty."

Trouble didn't know that. Behind him, the last scream died. Part of him was sorry some people had found the need for capital punishment. But his sorrow was for the nightmares of the freed hostages, not the slavers they'd executed.

There was more fire, none of it marine-issue. Trouble zoomed his heads-up. The Condor was down to one thousand meters and giving a good infrared picture. People were balled up in a circle; someone must have turned off the proximity pain threshold to get them in that close. One image broke from the center of the circle. The shot that brought him down was in his back. That must have given a marine sharpshooter a good sight picture, because his killer quickly went down. For a long second, nothing happened; then guns were tossed away as three men stood, hands up. Two marines broke cover, guns steady.

Trouble chinned his display off. "They got the last bunch. One killed by his own people, one by marines. Three surrendered. Looks like all the hostages are okay." He tried to stand; Ruth helped him up. The rest of the marines doubletimed into the clearing. Trouble pointed them to the left. "Situation is stabilized. All hostages are safe. Let's join the skipper."

"Want me to get your mule?" Ruth offered.

"I think I'd rather walk," he chuckled, and chinned on his mike. "Skipper, what's the rallying point?"

"Beach where the launch is waiting. Corporal will show you. I don't want to turn on a beacon until we got the ship that was planning on picking up these folks."

"I'll follow the corporal," sighed Trouble.

SIX

ZYLON PLOVDIC HEADED for the hills, her pickup loaded with "borrowed" camping supplies and two men Big Al trusted. He rode beside her. She'd kept below the accepted speed in town. Now she pushed the rig for all the speed the dirt track would allow.

"What now?" she asked.

"We lay low. A ship's coming in with more survey supplies and weapons. It will pick up the labor recruits as soon as the Navy leaves orbit."

"Assuming the recruiting teams are still there and the damn Navy ever leaves orbit."

"I have arranged for the Navy to leave orbit soon. I believe it is time to check in on our teams." He pulled a small radio from his pocket. "Bernie, Elm, and Maurice, talk to me." Nothing. "Any of you there?" Nothing again. Slowly, Big Al closed up the radio. "Our problem may be bigger than I thought."

"When's the ship due?"

"Maybe it is best that it not arrive. Are we well supplied?"

"For three months."

"Fee, three months in this wilderness." He opened the radio again, tapped several keys. "Benefit, this is Harmony. Go away. Come back in a month."

"Benefit here. I won't be back for another circuit, say fifty days."

Big Al shook his head. "See you then. Out."

Benefit made no reply.

"XO, I think things just changed. We intercepted a coded message on a merchant channel. Our bogey's two hours from making orbit. It just hit the decelerator. It'll never make orbit on that course. Looks like it's headed back the way it came."

"Not economical use of reaction mass." The XO grinned. "No merchie would do that. Helm, take us to three gees in a smooth but rapid curve." The alerted crew needed only seconds to start the punishing acceleration. They couldn't have been in a better place in their own orbit around Hurtford Corner's moon.

"Sensors, ping that baby. Let her know we're a warship and she's a target. Comm, advise the skipper we are in hot pursuit and emissions control is no longer necessary." Stan leaned back in his seat as the gees built up. "Okay, folks, let's nail this jack rabbit."

The net got very busy all of a sudden. Trouble's nerves were still frayed, and his brain was far from clear. He passed along to Ruth and her dad what was happening, as much to keep them in the loop as to have someone out of uniform to remind him if he started to screw up. "The slave ship that was supposed to pick us up is running for the jump point. The *Patton*'s hot on its tail, and I'm betting on her in this horse race. The skipper is having Jagowski bring our bad guys to the launch. She wants to get firepower into Hurtford Corner as soon as she can, so she'll load the marines and prisoners back on the first lift, civilians on the second."

Joe patted his M-6. "I got plenty of firepower here. Mind if I hitch along on the first ride?"

"Me, too," Ruth jumped in.

"I'll see what can be done."

The skipper pointedly ignored the rush Trouble's ex-hostages made for the water as soon as they came in sight of the beach. She gave those who needed it time to wash blood from their skin and clothes. By that time, Jagowski had arrived with his little detachment. The boss and Clem looked a bit the worse for wear, but nothing that couldn't be accounted for by a fast hike through rough terrain. Captain Umboto kept her prisoners to one side of the beach, the survivors to the other, and the marines in the middle. She made an exception for Ruth, her pa, and a couple others from Trouble's group who had shown they knew how to use an M-6. The skipper explained her plan.

Agnatha stepped forward, a rifle slung casually over her arm. "There's more bastards like those who killed my husband and kids running around these hills. I demand justice."

"You'll get it, but not now," the skipper answered her.

"We have rifles, food, mules." Several of the survivors had collected around the dozen saddles mules. Several of the pack animals had been stripped of their empty loads and were ready if someone wanted to ride them bareback. "You have sensors. Loan us their service, and we'll find our own justice."

The skipper glanced at Trouble. He shrugged; he hadn't been able to control them before. He wouldn't bet she could control them now. "I need to pull all my people back when it's time to go. I can't have them hiking around the backcountry."

"Then lend me a helmet. Up there"—she waved at the clouding sky—"is a Condor. Your man can control it from here. He's here when you need him and can show me what I need."

The skipper took a step back, as if a rabbit had grown fangs before her very eyes. "Suddenly you know a hell of a lot about my weapon systems."

"My husband was a hunter and tracker. We couldn't afford the bells and whistles in the catalogues. That doesn't mean we never heard of them. Loan me your eyes. These bastards are as much a threat to you as they are to us. We'll kill 'em for you."

Trouble doffed his helmet. "They aren't going home, skipper. Don't know what the bad guys have got. Unless we give these folks a hand, they might walk into a trap," he said, offering his helmet to Umboto.

"Bad bunch of choices." The captain sighed as she passed the helmet along to the widow. "We'll want it back."

"I'll return it quickly." She turned. "Who is with me?" Fifteen men and women, several hardly more than kids, headed for their mules. They were ready to ride, but the skipper slowed them down while a corporal showed Agnatha how to operate her heads-up display. Gunny took the others aside and made sure they knew how to use the weapons they had, while a corporal collected all the rations available and passed them to the civilians.

Gunny was shaking his head when he returned. "These folks know weapons. I don't want to be in those kids' sight pictures."

The marines had already set up a base camp on the beach. Jagowski and one of the able spacers asked to stay behind. "Sensor chief's gonna need some support. Nothing's gonna get near here without us seeing 'em." He hefted his M-6. "Be nice to have some legitimate targets."

"You know, Jagowski, you stay gone too long, your leading chief's gonna decide he doesn't need you anymore," the skipper scowled.

"He'll be wrong. Things aren't finished here. Let us cover this side while the rest of you go to town."

Captain Umboto raised the question to Trouble with a single eyebrow. "Why not? We'll have a full load, anyway."

"Lieutenant, move your fire team out." The skipper ended the matter with an order.

"Gunny, mount 'em up. Move 'em out."

"Aye, aye, sir."

Ten minutes later, the launch shoved off. Petty Officer Jagowski waved; Chief Max was still looking around the camp, shaking his head.

● ● ●

"What was that?" Big Al asked, sticking his head out the window and searching the sky.

"Sounded like a shuttle taking off, but it wasn't long enough. See any contrails?"

"One. Started just ahead of us. Ended just behind us. What do you make of that?"

"Where's that lake you've been using to ship in stuff we didn't want to go through customs?"

"Ahead of us."

"And the main landing field is behind us. Al, I have a very strong suspicion that we're being outmaneuvered."

"The three recruiters are off line. I better have the survey teams check in. Tell them to lay low."

"Is it safe to call all of them up on a single channel? Seems to me we're being out-teched by the Navy." Big Al held the radio in his hand, measuring it like he did some of the recruits Zef brought in. "Back a bit there was a turnoff to the left. Let me backtrack to it. You send to the teams, tell them the situation here and have them stay off the air. Then we get back on this road and pick a good turnoff to the right."

"Woman, you are brilliant. I do believe I must keep you around. You have skills I doubted I'd find on such an innocent backwater as this."

Doing a quick J turn, to complaints from the back end, Zylon got her plan for misdirection started. It was good Big Al was listening to her. It might get them off this planet in one piece . . . with him owing her. She had a few more tricks up her sleeves or in her pants. Big Al was sweating; she had his attention. Very good.

While they were stopped, there was a phone call she wanted to make. A few people did owe her. If the recruiting teams had gone quiet, and a Navy shuttle climbed out of where they'd been, maybe she could deliver a very nice present to Big Al.

It was just a short hop to the city landing port, but it took more than the usual gees. Trouble was aching as he dismounted. The three trucks standing by were only enough to take half the troops into town. Trouble stood by with one squad and the prisoners while the skipper galloped for town. Ruth stayed with him when Joe went with the skipper.

"Sure you don't want to go with them?" Trouble asked.

"And leave you all alone? Remember, the last time you were in town, you got shanghaied." Trouble noticed Ruth had a pixie's grin.

"I know a woman who got kidnapped."

"They had to catch me in *bed*. I am *not* bedding down in that town again."

"Well, they got me in the men's room, and you are not following me there."

"Why not? I'm a married woman. You haven't got anything I haven't seen."

Which put Trouble's attitude toward the young woman into an about face so fast it made his head swim. He wasn't actually attracted to her. She was just fun to be around. He heard women on the frontier planets married young; he should have realized a sharp, good-looking woman like Ruth would be spoken for. *So why is her dad here and not a husband?* Trouble swallowed the undigested lump of this revelation and fell back on what he knew; the perimeter needed touring.

The prisoners were secure, but the overall situation left him feeling a tad naked. It had been a long time since he'd had to rely on just the Mark One eyeball. "Keep your heads up, crew. The bad guys are supposed to be running for the hills, but there's always someone who doesn't get the word."

The launch took off to get however many former hostages chose to come. Trouble began to have serious regrets about giving away his helmet. He was used to instant access to a situation board. Now he had to drop by third squad's corporal to get updated. He shook off the idea of stealing the poor woman's helmet; she had a squad to run. So long as she did her job right, he shouldn't have to worry. He borrowed the helmet and signed on. The skipper reported things were real lively in town; fires were springing up all over the place. A glance toward town showed several roiling plumes rising against the blue sky. Even as he watched, a new smoke trail began.

"Think somebody's trying to destroy the evidence?" he asked the skipper.

"Looks like it. I'm matching marines with local safety volunteers and sending them out on patrol. I'll need the trucks for a while. I'll see what I can do about rounding you up some transport, but you're stuck out there for now."

"No problem, skipper. It's nice and quiet here."

He signed off and handed the corporal's helmet back. She'd heard the conversation. "I'll tell the troops to keep alert." She eyed the prisoners. "They're the best evidence we got."

"Yeah." Trouble said. He headed over to where Ruth and three armed civilians kept an eye on eight very subdued prisoners. He took Ruth aside and brought her up to date on the situation, as two more fires made their appearance on the town's low skyline.

"Someone's awful busy in there," Ruth noted.

"Yeah, but are they busy there, or just trying to distract us from what they really want?"

"You sound like my pa, always wondering if what you're looking at is what you're looking at."

"Probably comes from spending time other than here," he answered, wondering for a moment what it would be like to live your life believing in what you saw, not wondering what it hid, or what was waiting, hull down, just over the next rise. He shrugged the thought off. *Maybe next incarnation.*

"Yeah, last couple of days have been . . ." She trailed off, lacking words that could get their arms around the experience.

"Yes" was all Trouble could offer. He didn't like the feeling of inadequacy that left in his gut, so he went on to what he could get a handle on. "I don't know if the local nasties will try to liberate our prisoners, or kill them. Whichever way it is, I don't think we ought to keep the control pods on them."

Ruth had a studied frown on her face as she eyed the prisoners paired and sitting back to back, flipping the controller over and over in her hand. "I'll keep the pods on them, but turn the controller off. That way, who knows?"

"Good idea," Trouble agreed.

Lieutenant Commander Stan Gabon liked the feel of the captain's chair. What officer wouldn't want that chair all to himself, especially with a live shoot coming up? Maybe he hadn't said everything he could have to keep Izzy on board instead of running around dirtside. From the sound of it, she'd gotten her side of the job done. And was having a ball.

Now it was his turn.

"Comm, send to merchie in-system. Cease acceleration and prepare to be boarded."

"Yes, sir." There was a brief pause. "No answer, XO."

"Continue sending. Add 'or we will fire' to it."

"Yes, sir."

"Guns, you got a fire solution on our skunk?"

"She's just coming in range. I wish I had one of those new central fire controls. With the chance of innocent people on board that bogey, I'd like a better solution."

"Could you send a shot across her bow?"

That brought a long pause. "Deflection angle's shallow."

So now I get to learn why it's called the worry seat. "Sensors, what can you tell me about our bogey?"

"Not much, sir. She's pretty quiet. Engine radiation is masking most of what I might be getting. Engine profile matches several classes, both commercial and ex-Unity." Igor turned from his boards. "That includes the Daring class, sir."

"Wonderful." Stan cycled his own station through to helm. The *Patton* was up to 3.5 gees. The bogey was holding at 2.25. At this rate, they'd overhaul it several hours before the jump. *Unless, of course, we take a hit in the engines. Or they do.*

This was not getting any easier.

"Helm, edge us away from the hostile's track by five degrees. Guns, as soon as you feel comfortable with the deflection angle, let our friend know we've got her in range."

"Yes, sir."

Stan ignored the clock as it ticked away the seconds. He concentrated on constructing a decision tree; it didn't have many limbs. If she wouldn't stop, he'd have to try nipping her engines, without blowing her engineering spaces like Izzy had done to the pirate. It was a lot easier to blow up a ship than capture one. At least this one wasn't shooting at him. Yet.

"XO, this is Guns. I'm ready to try a shot across the bow."

"Do it."

The lights didn't dim for this one; the ship's power supply hardly noticed the drain. The main screen showed a single ray reaching out, passing ahead of the target.

It kept on accelerating.

"XO, we've got a live transmission coming in."

"Put it on main screen." Stan hoped he remembered everything he'd read in his correspondence course on hostage negotiations. It had been part of a lieutenant's promotion requirement ten years back. The face filling the screen didn't look frightened. It was also a woman's. *Damn!*

"Listen, I don't know who you are, or what you think you're doing, but I've got passengers on board. You're endangering innocent people."

"We know about your hostages."

"They aren't hostages. They're labor recruits."

"Right. We liberated the 'labor recruits' you were headed to Hurtford Corner to pick up. If anything happens to your hostages, you and your entire crew will he held personally liable for their deaths. Need I remind you that killing a hostage in the commitment of a felony is a capital offense? Cease accelerating and prepare to be boarded."

"Your signal is breaking up. I'll call you back in a minute on another channel." The screen went back to the battle board.

"Sounds like you scared her," Guns chuckled on net.

"I told her we know what she's up to and we have witnesses. Won't do her any good to dump her cargo to space."

"Sensors here. Target just activated targeting sensors. Six-inch guns are powering up. She's a Daring, and she's hot."

"Guns, do you have a solution on her engines?"

"I'll try."

"Do it. Initiate spin. Prepare to jink ship on my command. Guns, I'll keep her steady until you've got the first salvo out."

"This will be a seven-gun salvo. I fixed two problems, and another two broke." Even as Guns complained, lasers reached out for the stern of the enemy ship. Five rounds were clear misses aft. The next two corrected. They missed closer.

"She's charged." Sensors' voice was steady.

"Jink up," Stan ordered.

Two ragged shots weren't even close. "Not much of a fighter, is she?" Stan muttered. This might make things easier.

Then three more laser rays reached out for the *Patton*. One snagged her briefly. Pumps screamed as they fought to balance the ship. Kicking himself, Stan ordered a down jink. The shoddy quality of this hostile was only making his problem tougher, not easier. Ragged salvos meant he'd never know when it was safe to shoot.

Damn, and I got to take this one alive.

"Guns, I've got to keep zigging at all times. Shoot when you can."

"I'm going to single ranging shots until I get a better feel for where she's at. Maybe I can walk into her slowly."

"Do it."

While the *Patton* dodged the random shots from the target, each one of her own shots got closer to the bandit. The slaver held a steady course, Stan guessed because her crew was not stabilized in battle stations like the *Patton*'s crew. He was grateful for any help he got in this live fire exercise.

"Nipped her!" Guns shouted. There were shouts of glee on the gunnery net. The target veered to the right, wiping out the firing solution for the next shot. "Back to work, kids. We found her once. We'll find her again."

The bandit steadied down on course. "Slowed to two gees acceleration," Sensors reported.

Stan finally allowed himself a smile. Damage Control reported the one hostile hit had only vaporized armor; that's what it was there for. He could give the ship back to Izzy without having to explain a major dent. Maybe it was time to end this. "Comm, send to hostile. 'We can keep this up as long as you want, but you are not getting out of this system.'"

"Sent, sir."

Two more lasers missed his ship. So much for talking. Guns continued to answer, one shot at a time, walking his rays up to the rear of the other ship. He slashed a second engine. "Good going, Guns," Stan grinned.

"Hostile down to one point five gees," Sensors reported.

"Message from hostile. 'If we surrender this tub, can we cut a deal?'"

"Damn, I need a lawyer," Stan groaned. "Tell them no one has died yet; there is no capital punishment charge. Yet."

"She wants to talk to you."

"On screen. Guns, check fire. Repeat, check fire."

The woman was back. "Your last shot damn near slagged our reactors. You want to blow us all up. Listen, me and my crew, we just pick up and drop off cargo. I don't know nothing about what's going on. You want us to talk, I'll talk. But I don't want to waste my life doing jail time. Deal?"

Stan really needed a lawyer. What kind of promises could he make? "I'm just Navy, ma'am, not a cop. I'll do what I can, if no hostage is harmed, and if all of your files and databases are turned over. No erasures. All of them, network and personal."

She fidgeted. "Every system has a few erased files on it. You'd run out of storage if you never erased anything."

"This sounds like stalling to me." Stan made his face as hard as he could at 3.5 gees. "Cease acceleration and allow us to board. Close down all offensive systems. Now."

"Tandy, take us to zero gee. R.S., kill the sensors. Tabby, stop shooting. We'll open our main lock. There's room for a shuttle to dock."

"We'll be boarding by several access points. Please collect all your personnel on the bridge or one mess deck. People wandering around the ship just might get shot."

"Yeah. Okay, nobody wants to get anybody hurt on this side. Let's just settle this nice and easy."

Stan liked that attitude. "Sensors?"

"Skunk's going quiet. Guns are bleeding off their charges. Looks like she's doing what she said."

"Helm, take us to one gee smartly." Stan turned to the Chief Master at Arms. "Put together a boarding party. Take anyone you need with small arms experience and time in space."

"Aye, sir." The old chief stood as the ship steadied on one gee and saluted Stan. He returned the honor with a proud grin. *Skipper said bring them back alive. And, damn it, I did. Now, maybe, I'll get a ship of my own. If there're any left.*

"Comm, advise the captain. Hostile vessel is being boarded. Will advise you when we have boarded and searched the vessel. Gabon sends." He stood, then stretched to get the kinks out of a body that had been tortured by three and a half times its normal weight. "Well done, folks. Very well done."

Stan was having a very good day. Unbidden, his brother came to mind. Stan bet no corporate slob like Tom ever had a day this good. *Oh, God, let Tom be okay.*

Tom Gabon was having a very bad day, just like all the rest he'd had lately. It was raining. His bare feet sank into the mud, and if he wasn't careful, hoeing out a weed could knock over a drug plant. The guard must have lost bad in last night's poker game; his whip was taking his losses out of any farmhand who even nudged the cash crop. Tom hunkered down and moved his hoe with slow, methodical regularity like a good slave.

That was what he was. A slave growing drugs in a steaming hell. He wondered what euphemisms were used on the corporate profit sheet to cover up what he saw. If his cracked lips wouldn't have hurt, he'd have smiled. *Guess I didn't ask as many questions as I should have at that job interview.*

The whip snapped again, yanking the man next to him out of his plodding. "Take it easy," Tom whispered.

"Just let me get that bastard out behind a bar some dark night," the spacer beside Tom growled. Ever the good manager, Tom had evaluated his coworkers. The spacers were hard cases, officers and crew of pirated ships. Yet their toughness had a brittle underpinning to it. When it finally got through their hard heads that they weren't going anywhere, their spirits shattered. Tom had watched as several quit eating and just balled up and died.

There were others around Tom. Farmhands yanked off other planets and dropped in the mud beside Tom. Street toughs hauled out of a gutter drunk some night to wake up in a ship's hold with the others. The street kids could shatter like a spacer, or turn out as tough and stoic as the experienced farm workers.

The corporate outcasts, managers who'd gotten on the wrong side of a boss, could be like the spacers or the farmers. Tom took the long view. He'd been looking for a job when he found himself in this one. Everything changes. Sometimes fast, sometimes slow. He could hold on, bide his time.

Someday Tom would laugh about this over a drink at his favorite bar. This couldn't go on forever. That held Tom together. Sooner or later, something would develop. It had to.

Trouble knew something new was developing. He just had no idea what. The town was an enigma, and he was none too sure about his immediate vicinity. He would not bug the poor corporal for reports. Her helmet monitored only one net at a time; that made for easy maintenance and longer time between failure. Right now, it meant she had to drop off her squad net, manually dial her system into any one of a dozen other nets, and hope something interesting was happening when she listened. Trouble kicked himself; he should have had a trooper give up a helmet. The Book said you didn't give any gear to civilians. The Book needed a footnote about what to do when you didn't follow it.

"We got trucks headed our way," shouted the picket facing the road.

Trouble didn't like the looks of the two civilian flatbed trucks with canvas covers. "Corporal, contact the skipper. Ask her if she's arranged any transport for us."

"Yes, sir."

Trouble kept his eyes on the approaching trucks. "All hands," he shouted, "keep your eyes peeled. This would be a great time to sneak up behind us." No pickets had moved off their assigned areas, but a reminder was in order.

"Skipper's not available, sir," the corporal shouted. "She's in a burning building at the moment, trying to find a lost child. Gunny says they've been trying to rustle up transport, but he doesn't know if the civilians have done it. He's checking, but the civvy net is a bit hard to organize."

"Tell me about it," Trouble growled. Then had to suppress a laugh. The damn trader who'd gotten them here in the first place said this planet needed a new net. Hell of a way to prove it.

Time to get busy. "Corporal, we got an unknown situation developing here. Get your personnel to cover." His eyes roved the runway and the grain fields beyond. They might provide enough concealment to save a marine's life for a critical second or two. "Fire plan for the time being is to cover all three hundred and sixty degrees of the perimeter."

"Yessir." The corporal got busy.

Trouble turned to his civilians and prisoners. They huddled in the clear, where the road and runway met. Right where things might get exciting. "Ruth, mind moving these folks off a ways?"

She glanced at the trucks, now less than a kilometer away. "Izzy said she'd send us a ride?"

"That might be it. Then again, somebody's starting a lot

of fires. Seen any lately?" A haze had settled over Hurtford City. It was hard to tell if anything new was adding to it.

"Don't mind a little walk. All right, everybody, on your feet." The prisoners didn't react. Ruth raised the controller, made a big scene of activating it, and grinned wickedly. "I'm walking. I'm walking. You better be, too." They did.

"Take care of yourself," Ruth said, standing on tiptoe and giving him a quick kiss on his bearded cheek as she waltzed by.

Trouble didn't quite know what to make of that. Rubbing the kiss into his beard, he turned to face the trucks. By all that was smart and holy, he ought to be finding a few blades of grass to hide behind. But that would surrender the initiative to whoever these guys were. They could drive onto the field or anyplace else they wanted before showing their hand. No, he would walk right up to them and find out what they had in mind. "Hell of a situation," he said, stopping in the center of the road, not sure whether he meant the trucks . . . or the kiss. And too busy at the moment to figure it out.

The lead truck halted a few feet from him. The driver stuck his head out. "You folks need a lift into town?"

"Yeah," Trouble answered. They looked on the up-and-up. One driver, one passenger. Canvas hung loose. He sauntered toward the rig. "Things look lively in town. What's going on?" he chattered. All the equipment, all the technology, and it still came down to a jarhead hanging it all out on the line. Trouble climbed up on the truck's step and peered into the cabin. Two guys sat there. In the shadows at their feet were propped assault rifles. The passenger went for his.

Trouble backed off the step. As he hit the ground, the canvas came up in the back. More gun barrels stared him in the face. His knees buckled without even a suggestion from his brain. As he went down, he shouted, "Hostiles!" Once on the deck, he rolled himself under the truck.

Right under an old-fashioned hydrogen/oxygen fuel cell. Even as his body screamed at the new torture, his brain was shouting—explosives!

With bullets whizzing above him, both incoming and outgoing, he rolled himself right out the other side of the truck. Pistol out, he sent one round up through the door. That ended the passenger's shooting. He was the only gun pointed out this side. *Damn, they're going for the prisoners—and Ruth.*

His knees water, Trouble used his left hand to pull himself up. The driver was shouting orders even as he leveled his gun in Ruth's direction. The marine yanked the door open. As gun and passenger fell out, he put two rounds into the back of the driver's head. His knees refused to support his weight, so Trouble did a belly flop onto the bloody seat and grabbed the release for the parking brake. As incoming rounds from his "friendly" marines ripped holes through the cab, as well as the gunners on the truck bed, the entire rig gave a lurch. That brought yelps from the gunners standing behind bags of potatoes piled up like sandbags on the truck's flatbed.

While the truck's roll spoiled their shooting, Trouble emptied his pistol through the rear window, taking down gunners who were trying to get back their aim at the prisoners and civilians diving for the scant cover of the wheat field. When the automatic closed open, Trouble grabbed for the driver's assault rifle. Dead fingers didn't want to let go, but Trouble had more persistence. Not much more, but enough.

Snatching a spare magazine, Trouble rolled out of the cab and lurched and flopped his way to the rear, hearing and feeling a lot of rounds coming in above his head. Usually he was tough on marines who shot high. Today, he prayed they would.

The driver and passenger of the next truck were just getting their weapons out. He didn't try for a sight picture, but walked a burst across the hood and through the windshield. Not looking for danger to their front, they died not knowing what hit them.

Adrenaline finally cut in. Leaping onto the front bumper of the second truck, Trouble sent a long blast through the cab's rear window and into the gunners on the flatbed. He was switching magazines when he heard a click behind him.

One gunner had stayed low, been missed, and now had a bead on Trouble's wide-open back as he pulled back the arming handle. "Dumb jarhead," he grinned.

And dropped forward over his gun, dead from a bullet between the eyes.

"Thought you might need some help," Ruth gasped as she bounced off the fender of the rear truck. Her dash in had not spoiled her aim. *Thank God.* Trouble tumbled off the bumper, his knees no longer caring how much adrenaline was pumping through his bloodstream. Ruth caught him as he went down.

From the field, the corporal shouted, "Okay, people, you can keep dying, or you can drop your guns and live. Your call, but until we hear something, we're gonna keep riddling those trucks."

Whatever surprise the trucks might have once had was long gone. The marine fire was growing in intensity, and from the holes appearing in the trucks, Trouble's crew was getting in some seriously aimed rounds. In the rear truck, there was another scream, followed by, "We quit! We quit! Stop shooting!"

"Cease fire," Trouble croaked. The corporal got something more understandable out on the squad net. Fire stopped like a hose had been turned off.

"Come out slow, and with your hands in plain view," the corporal ordered. "One at a time."

The new set of prisoners did. Marines appeared out of the grass. Two kept their rifles on the thugs. Two more frisked them down, made sure a prisoner hadn't forgotten a pistol, knife or grenade, then got them spread-eagled on the ground.

"We lose anyone?" he asked no one in particular.

"A marine's checking the prisoners. One or two are bleeding, but it doesn't look bad from here," Ruth answered.

"No casualties among the marines," the corporal reported. "Not that you didn't do your damnedest, sir, to be one."

"Just part of the job, Corporal." Trouble sighed, rolled onto his back and stared at the sky.

Ruth and the corporal exchanged the kind of glance Trouble has seen young mothers trade over wayward kids that were still in diapers. Well, he'd gotten everyone out alive. That was what mattered, wasn't it?

Ruth settled down beside him. "How you feeling?"

"Fine, fine. Give me a beer, a good meal, about ten years of sleep, and I couldn't be better. You know, I joined the Corps 'cause I wanted to do exciting things. I really enjoyed the adrenaline rush." Ruth's face screwed up into some kind of doubting Thomas's scowl. "No, I really mean it."

"Well, have you had enough for one day?"

"Five or six." Trouble tried to leverage himself up. Ruth stood, offered him a hand, and pulled him up.

"That was a short rest break."

"No rest for the wicked. At least, not until we get these bad guys into whatever kind of lockup this town prides itself on. Corporal?"

"Skipper just came back up on net. No, sir, she hasn't sent us any transport."

"Nice to know we didn't shoot up our boss's personal gift," Trouble laughed. "Check these trucks for weapons, then have the prisoners toss off the potato sacks. Let's get saddled up and moved into town."

"Yes, sir. You heard him, marines, let's get moving."

Zylon Plovdic was not moving; she'd parked the truck under a tree. They were past the first line of foothills, but she could still see the haze that marked the sky above Hurtford City. She'd expected Big Al to urge her to drive faster. Instead, he'd called a halt. She selected a spot, close to a crossroads that would let them go just about anywhere. Now she waited while Big Al stared at the haze. Things had been coming fast and furious all day. She hoped she hadn't tied herself to someone who couldn't handle sudden changes to well-laid plans.

"We have been reacting to them," Big Al muttered, then turned to her. "We must return to their reacting to us."

"Yes," she agreed. That was why she'd suggested the fires and the raid on the airstrip. Her associates had seen the marines drive into town, but they brought no prisoners. That left a good chance that the only people who could incriminate them were still out in the open. It had been worth a try.

Zylon had expected some report from that effort. Said report was overdue. She didn't want her first job for Big Al to be a mess, but it was out of her hands.

Big Al extended the radio's antenna.

"It will give away our position," Zylon said cautiously.

"We will be gone from here in a moment. All of my children," he said into the tiny handset. "Come back home. Come quickly. Do not play with fire. I will speak with you no more until I see you face to face." He snapped the antenna from the radio and tossed both of them out the window.

"Now, they, whoever they are, expect us to flee for our lives. To hide away, and cause them no more trouble. We must disenchant them with such daydreams." Pulling his personal assistant from his pocket, he plugged it into the truck's display. A flashing red dot appeared on the map. "Go to that location. I have left a few things I doubted I would need, but it seems that I do. Then we will see what resources we have who are not just fair-weather friends."

"We're leaving," Zylon shouted to the two who'd stood a few feet away, smoking. They scrambled aboard as she pulled out. She wanted to be as far from this place as possible before anyone came hunting for them. Big Al might be ready for a return to the old days, but until she saw some proof that was possible, Zylon Plovdic would stay very much out of everybody's way.

Once Trouble had his prisoners safely in the local lockup, he relaxed. He added four marines to the local guards, who sported nothing more threatening than nightsticks, then went hunting for the skipper. He found her at City Hall.

"Trouble, you look like shit" were her first words.

"Skipper, you say the nicest things to a guy." But since he felt like he'd been stunned, run over by a truck, and generally knocked around, he couldn't argue with her.

Captain Umboto turned to the city manager. "Can you put him up somewhere?"

"The Hurtford Inn is a block from here. They owe us big time for putting out that fire not two doors down from them."

"Is it secure?" Trouble asked. He'd had his fill of waking up in surprising locations.

"We'll make sure it is," the skipper assured him. "You and your lady get rooms, a shower, some sleep, and I'll see you tomorrow morning."

With the pressure off, Trouble dropped like a leaking balloon. "His lady" led him down the hall in a fog. A nurse snagged them both as they went by her office and shot them full of painkillers and anything else she thought might help. Trouble made it to the hotel. He had dim recollections of checking in. He must have shed his body armor and clothes, but he didn't remember doing it. He was asleep before someone closed the door behind him.

"You awake, Lieutenant?" and a pounding on the door brought him back to consciousness. The clock beside the bed, and the sun streaming in the window, told him it must be morning. He wondered how many days he'd slept. *Not enough.*

There was more pounding, on the door and in his head. "Go away," he mumbled.

"Skipper wants to see you, sir." It was Gunny's voice. Only that old topkick would dare face his officer this morning. Stumbling over strewn clothes, Trouble stubbed a toe on armor. A check through the peephole showed Gunny, shaved and shipshape. Trouble yanked the door open.

"You look like shit, sir," Gunny said.

"You are not very observant, Gunny. I look like shit that's had a night's sleep."

"If you say so, sir. I got a razor, toothbrush, underwear, the essentials, sir." Gunny examined the room in a single glance. "Don't look like that uniform's gonna be good for much."

"Probably not," Trouble agreed. "While I take a shower, you want to get me something?"

"Yes, sir," Gunny said, but he didn't move. Serving as lifeguard while Trouble showered also seemed part of his assignment this morning. Since Trouble almost lost his balance twice, maybe it wasn't such a bad idea. Gunny covered for the lieutenant by taking the time to bring him up to date. "*Patton*'s heading in with a merchie under prize crew and a hell of a lot of happy people as well as a couple dozen unhappy types."

"Did they get that tub's files intact?" Trouble asked, washing his hair for the third time.

"The XO is proud as punch they did. He scared the bad guys real good. They didn't even try a wipe. Still, they're so encrypted that it looks like a long, hard pull to crack them."

Making a second run at scrubbing himself down, Trouble asked about the situation in town.

"Pretty stable. Skipper will tell you more at breakfast, but it looks like we got them in the brig or on the run. Locals got a real interesting way of doing business. I spent yesterday watching folks vouch for each other . . . or not. In a town this small, everyone knows everyone and what they're doing. Mostly, they ignore what ain't broke, but once the smoke went up, they found the fire starters they were after."

Trouble turned off the water; Gunny handed him a towel. "I'll find you something to wear." He was back about the time Trouble finished shaving, a pair of slacks and a open-necked shirt thrown over his arm. "Courtesy of the hotel. They really were spooked by the fire yesterday."

Trouble dressed quickly and followed Gunny downstairs. Captain Umboto, Ruth, her dad, the city manager, and a young woman named Cindy were sitting around a table with an empty chair. He filled it.

"You look a damn sight better," his skipper assured him.

"I feel a damn sight better. Amazing what a night's sleep and a shower will cure." Trouble winced as a dozen body parts disagreed with him.

"Try a couple of these," Mikhail Shezgo said. "Nurse swears these local herbs can cure anything overactive kids can get into."

Trouble took three of the offered green pills, then frowned at them. "I've already had mine," Ruth assured him. He swallowed them with apple juice.

"The hotel will give you anything you ask for," Ruth informed him, "but I recommend the hot oatmeal, unless your stomach is a lot tougher than mine."

He ordered oatmeal. The waitress was back with a steaming bowl, sprinkled with brown sugar and drowning in milk. The first spoonful was heaven.

"Mikhail was just telling us the bad guys really goofed yesterday with the fires. Anybody who had doubts about whether they needed stopping lost them real fast when they thought their home or business might go up in smoke."

"Gunny told me people were vouching for each other," Trouble said around a full mouth. The oatmeal was good, and his stomach had only compliments for the cook.

"In a town this small, everyone knows what everyone else is doing. Founders made a rule. What's your business is nobody's business. Folks learn to look the other way, unless people are hurt." The city manager put down his fork, his pancakes gone except for a puddle of syrup here and there. "Maybe we've been giving too many people the benefit of the doubt. Heaven knows, after the Unity folks took to the hills, we were glad to have our town back. Guess we weren't looking hard enough at how some folks celebrated their freedom. Anyway, no more fires were set after your attack, so I think you got the last of them."

Trouble glanced at his skipper; she seemed a tad less confident. "What do we do now, ma'am?"

"When the *Patton* gets back in orbit, I'll go topside to see what Stan caught. You handle things down here. Provide whatever assistance Mr. Shezgo needs. I noticed several of your street safety patrols carrying hunting rifles." She turned back to the city manager. "Do they know how to use them?"

He laughed. "This town's almost empty come fall. During hunting season, the brewers hardly bother to bottle anything, those still in town, that is."

Trouble and Ruth graduated to flapjacks. The others left them to the newfound hunger; only Cindy stayed behind.

"I'm full," Ruth sighed, as she stuffed another bit of pancake in nevertheless.

Trouble finished his last bite, considered ordering ham and eggs, then shook his head. "I eat another bite, and they'll have to tote me upstairs and put me to bed for the day."

"Don't you deserve a day off?" Ruth asked with a grin. Was she offering to spend it in bed with him? He wasn't sure how that kiss and her husband went together. Rested up and washed, she was beautiful.

"The skipper's shorthanded. You don't get what you deserve. You get what you got." He evaded the question and stood. "I better make a round of the guard posts."

Ruth fiddled with her fork, trying to figure out what she wanted. Truth was, she had no idea. What she wanted didn't seem to mean much. This tall, strange marine had been dragged into her life . . . and now was running, not walking, out of it. Mordy had done the same. And yet, the two were so different. Ruth remembered the feel of Trouble's hands along her side, bringing warmth to a cold night. The way he'd grabbed Clem when she threw him off her. Then chided her for starting a fight. Mordy would have loved a fight. Mordy and Clem would have . . . No, she would not go there. Mordy was out of her life. Trouble . . . she didn't want him gone. Well, she had nothing else to do with her day. *Mr. Trouble, I'm your shadow.*

"It's not fair." She put her fork down. "You come down here for some time off, and all you get is drugged, dragged all over the place, and a fight."

"Who says that's not a marine's idea of a good time?" Oh,

the boyish grin he had. It made him look like a delightful, huggable kid. Except around the eyes. They stayed old.

"Well, if you can't think of anything better"—Ruth stood up to her full height—"maybe I'm gonna have to show you." Which got her one of Trouble's raised eyebrows; then, with a shrug, he turned for the door. *Another great impression I've made.*

Ruth had to jog to keep up with him. "I've got a pretty good idea what farming is like," he said, holding the door open for her. "Now I'll show you how my day goes."

"No way you know farming," she countered. "You show me marines today. Tomorrow, I'll show you a farm."

"Well, today neither of you know your way around my town," Cindy said, joining them at the door. "Your marines are scattered all over. I'm your native guide." Unself-consciously, Cindy had introduced herself over breakfast as the city manager's ex-girlfriend. It quickly became evident, at least to Ruth, that Cindy would be glad to add Trouble to her . . . no doubt . . . long list of exes. The young woman played up to him, *so* excited about *his* rescue of the hostages, *so* wanting to hear *everything*, as she batted her eyes at him. Ruth was disgusted. Trouble lapped it up. Or seemed to.

He told the story, in immense detail, and every time something important happened, Ruth got the credit for it. The first time Trouble did that, Ruth laughed. Second time, she started to detect a pattern; she kept a very straight face as Cindy's fawning smile took a turn for the puzzled.

"Didn't you do anything?"

"I was just along for a walk in the woods. Ruth here's the one who had the guts to let the jerks know the first time that we weren't theirs for the taking. She got us fires, turned their greed loose on the fungus." He turned to her. "Saved my life when she kicked away the controller. What kind of school do they send girls to out on the stations?"

Cindy started to say something, but they had come upon their first set of marines. Ruth and Cindy hung back as Trouble did his officer thing. The marine was two men in one skin. Talking to his marines, he was formal, even curt, speaking quickly, then listening as his troops replied just as tersely. But they all looked like kids as he promised one hell of a beer bust when things calmed down.

Trouble also didn't seem to hear the parting whisper about the lieutenant having a new girl, maybe two. Cindy grinned. Ruth found herself wondering what it would be like to be a marine's wife. Did marines even have wives? Was Trouble already married? That didn't seem to matter to Cindy. To Ruth, raised on the stations where a marriage, a family, and a farm were as close to one institution as was possible, it did very much.

She wasn't paying a lot of attention to what was going on, her mind jumbled with questions, even as she tried to recognize the woman Trouble kept making her out to be to Cindy. She wanted to take a walk by the creek, listen to the wind, figure out who she was and who this stranger walking beside her might be.

She came full attention to the now when Cindy suggested lunch with her grandmother. On the stations, you only took a guy to the grandfolks when you were serious. She'd heard city folks were a lot looser. Could a girl work this fast?

Trouble set a fast pace; they must have covered half of Hurtford City by noon. Cindy never ran out of brew pubs to point out. But after the third detachment, Trouble's attitude toward Cindy changed. Gunny led that team. His report included several recent tries made to recruit . . . more like seduce . . . marines to stay. Trouble listened, his eyes looking straight through Cindy. After that, his answers to her were short and clipped. Still, he didn't change lunch plans.

Grandmother's large house was near the center of town; or rather, the town had grown up around it, then long past it.Today, it was crowded. Ruth quickly concluded Grandmother was one of the Elders that had moved so quickly to tackle the new challenge. It probably took Trouble less time; he acknowledged the city manager and several of the elected Elders. Just leaving. They had the look of boys who'd been taken out behind the barn and talked to real good by their pa and his belt. That the tiny grandmother who presided over the dinner table could get that reaction from grown men told Ruth much.

Cindy served lunch—soup, salad, and sandwiches. But the main course was talk; Grandmother served it with questions.

"What do you think of our world?" she asked the marine.

The marine left his soup untouched to study the woman. "The land is good."

Grandmother smiled at the half answer. "And the people?"

"The mixed bag I've found most places."

The old woman chuckled dryly. "Yes, no matter where people go, there we are with our wants and needs. Some people seem to have more wants than others."

"Yes, ma'am, that's why I'm a marine. A few folks need reminding of what they can reach for. And what they can't."

Grandmother leaned back in her chair, eyes closing. "That was the hope of my father, and his father when they came here. That a new world would have so much to reach for, folks would remember what belonged to others. We wanted people free to reach as far as their grasp could go. On the old worlds, people were always swatting your hand for reaching instead of letting you have what you needed. Here, in our corner of the galaxy, we turn our eyes away from the problems that freedom brought in the past, focus on the reaching, each man and woman for herself. Some activities just don't deserve notice. You know what I mean?"

"A smart officer knows what not to see and hear. But it seems to me, even on the short visit I've had here, that maybe too much was watched with a blind eye."

Grandmother's eyes came open. "Unity was not something we foresaw. We did what we had to do to satisfy folks whose stomachs were far too big. And whose eyes saw further than ours did. These mining contracts—who would have expected that what we signed here could be sold so quickly and so far?" Grandmother sighed. "I thought when we hired Mikhail that we had acquired a snake charmer. We need to open ourselves up. Not just to seekers who come to share our vision, but to those who question it as well. We need more snake charmers, like you."

"I think this is the second job offer I've gotten in the last week," the marine chuckled. "I admit yours is a lot more attractive, and I appreciate the delivery much more. Still, ma'am, I'm a marine. Born one. Raised one. I'll live one and probably die one. There're lots of guys who've been beached in the last few months. I'm sure I can get in touch with some good ones. Send them your way if you want me to."

Grandmother drew in a deep breath and let it out slowly as her head shook. "We know you. We have seen your work. We'd rather trust you to be our eyes. Trust you to know what to see, what not to see. You rather than someone we don't know."

The marine just shrugged.

"Then I guess one trusted by one I trust will have to do. Your soup is getting cold. It is best eaten warm. Cindy, get this young man a fresh bowl." Lunch followed quickly after that.

Fed, they were leaving Grandmother's when Trouble took Cindy's elbow. "I'm *not* available for recruitment."

With a shrug, she produced a map chip, located the marines on it, and took her leave. Ruth expected to be told to get lost too, but the marine never got around to it. Instead, he got her talking about the stations. "Farming can't be that good."

"Oh, but it is," she shot back, and only stopped talking during the next hour when he checked his marines. She wouldn't have kept talking, but he kept listening. Somewhere in all those words, Mordy came up. That did end her cascade of words.

"I thought the farmers figured out how to avoid the draft." Trouble was puzzled.

"We did. But the first orders were pretty threatening, and Mordy said he'd rather show up for induction than be the one they hung to impress the rest. He went with about

twenty others, mostly young boys who really wanted to see
what the rest of the world was like, but there he was too."

"He didn't come back?"

Ruth found herself looking for a crack in the sidewalk to
fall through. It took her a long while to get the single sylla-
ble out. "No."

"No death notice?"

That "No" was easier to get out.

"Did you check on him?"

"How could I?"

The marine came to a dead halt. "The records are here."

Ruth kept quiet; she knew the records had to be somewhere. Just where, she wasn't sure. But considering how
bad things had been before Mordy left, did she really want
to find him? Was she the kind of woman to go hunting for a
husband who didn't want to be found? Trouble headed
straight for City Hall.

Ruth followed, letting the silence stretch. Her throat was
too choked up to let the words out that would have stopped
this quest. She knew she could stop the marine with a simple plea. The marine would listen to her. But she couldn't
say that word.

At City Hall, Trouble slid into an unoccupied workstation
and quickly accessed the military records. Ruth spelled out
Mordy's name and date of birth. In less than a minute,
Mordy's military record on Hurtford Corner covered the
screen. With a "hmm," Trouble summarized it. "Previous
military training, space experienced, they shipped him off-
planet two weeks after he reported in. Nothing after that."

"Nothing," Ruth echoed, tasting the finality in the marine's word. Probably just as well. *But now what?*

"Let me check the *Patton*. Good, it's overhead; this won't
take but a minute." It didn't. "He survived the war and was
discharged." Trouble sounded like he was giving her good
news.

"Where?"

Trouble snorted. "Doesn't say. A lot in Unity records
don't match the peace treaty's requirements. Troops mus-

tered out but no location, ships scrapped, but no record where or by whom."

"Mordy's alive." Ruth let the words roll around her mouth, unsure how they tasted.

"Yes," Trouble agreed, not embarrassing her with the question of why he wasn't home yet.

"I could," the marine went on, "have the *Patton* search the net directories, see if we can locate him."

Ruth let that hang in the air between them, desperately wishing she knew what she wanted. Mordy back? Mordy gone from her life for good? Mordy the husband she'd dreamed of? How do you live your life if you don't know what you want?

Trouble filled her silence with his lopsided grin. "Then again, maybe not. We've got almost two hundred billion people on file, from Earth to Pitt's Hope. But some of the frontier nets don't follow standard protocols. I'm not sure I'd find you on the net. If he's some place like here, or in transit, or . . ."

"Or just doesn't want to be found."

"Yes." They left City Hall with that word echoing in Ruth's head. The marine had a few more teams to visit. Words got kind of few and far between. Ruth was lost in questions. Why hadn't Morty come back? Did she want him back? What was wrong with her? As a wife? As a woman?

"Why'd you become a marine?" tumbled out of Ruth's mouth before she even thought of the words.

"I was born a marine. Raised by the Corps. Never thought of being anything else. Don't know how to be anything else." The words came at Ruth like automatic weapon fire. Trouble didn't even look at her; his eyes stayed locked straight ahead. A moment passed into silence before he posed his own question. Now his voice was little more than a whisper. "Why'd you become a farmer?"

"I was born one. Raised one. You know the rest."

"Yes."

"You married?"

"God, no. No woman deserves a marine for a husband. No kid rates a marine father."

"That's strange, coming from you." He had her attention. She really couldn't understand the puzzle this man had become.

"I grew up waiting for my old man to come home. The five-month cruise that took nine months. Getting to the new post just in time for him to ship out. Always wondering when he'd come home. If he'd come home." The marine's eyes squinted, seeing beyond the street ahead and into some past only he knew. "No, ma'am, the Corps is a great place to live, but you never want to visit. You going to divorce Mordy?"

So quickly, the marine changed the subject. "I don't know. We don't divorce out on the stations."

"No divorce?"

"Out there, we're a farm, a family, and I guess we're a couple last. How do you split up a farm? How do you take care of the kids? Folks don't stay single very long. Take the Henderson place. He came from off-world. He and Maggie couldn't seem to get along. He chased after a gal, brought her home. She got on with the hired man. When they come to the dances, nobody knows who's going to be dancing with whom, but the kids are being raised and the farm is making it. That's what matters."

That brought Trouble to a halt. "Remember what I said this morning, about me understanding farming and you not understanding marines?"

"Yes."

"Forget it. I don't think either one of us will ever understand the other's world."

"So how come my pa came from off-world and he and Ma get along fine?"

"I don't know."

"Me neither."

Trouble's comm link beeped; he lifted his hand to his mouth. "Trouble here."

"Skipper wants you back topside. We need to insert a fire team to help the civilians chasing around the hills."

"When?"

"Captain's gig is on its way down to get you."

"I'll get out to the runway as soon as I can hitch a ride."

"Out."

"Out," Trouble repeated.

"Inn laid on a feast for us tonight," a forlorn Ruth reminded him.

"Guess I'll have to take a rain check. Wonder who's headed out to the port."

"Maybe we can borrow a rig. I could drive it back."

"You don't mind running me around?"

"No."

An hour later, Ruth watched the gig rocket back to orbit. Fate had brought another off-worlder into her life, and was rushing him out of her life much quicker this time. Probably just as well. Still, the marine was a lot more interesting than Mordy had ever been. Much more complex, too. In love with the Corps, and hating it at the same time. She wondered if he knew that. Probably not. The marine seemed to understand her and Mordy better than she did. Why did you need to stand back to understand what you had to live close up? She put the truck in gear; now, how would she put her life in gear?

SEVEN

IT WAS NOT a good picture that greeted Trouble back aboard the *Patton*. "Whoever those bastards are down there, they got more tech support than they deserve," Igor summed up his sensor feed. "We've set the locals up for two ambushes, and the bad guys sidestepped both of them. They've got to have heart monitors, not as good as ours, but they got them."

"So, Lieutenant, take them down," the skipper ordered.

"No trouble, ma'am," Trouble snapped, then studied the board to make sure he was right. "We drop a fire team outfitted with scout suits and spoofers ahead of them, go in fast, and put them down. What do we do with them?"

"I want prisoners to chat with. These folks are way too smart for dumb thugs. Who sent 'em to school? I want answers to my questions. I want to take these guys with us when we leave." The skipper pulled at her ear. "How am I going to do that?"

Stan hardly let her finish the sentence. "Skipper, I had our legal clerk look into what the local folks call their laws. Turns out Hurtford Corner doesn't have much law. Most crime is handled informally, and not the way they did it this morning.

"However, Joe told us our bad guys have been using rockets to break down doors. A few hours ago, one of them tossed a surface-to-air missile at our Condor. Missed, but got me thinking. Maybe HC has no laws restricting access to weapons. Society's Law Code doesn't require a sovereign planet to have any such laws, but it does demand and require that the importation of such weapons be in accordance with *its* code. Whoever imported that SAM did not pay the taxes." There was a general chuckle at this. Stan went on.

"So, what we need is an agent of the Alcohol, Tobacco, and Firearms Administration. It so happens our personnel clerk is authorized to swear in anyone who might volunteer for such an appointment, not to exceed one year. Joe, you interested in being the lieutenant's cop?"

"Would I have to go off-world?"

"Nope," Stan answered. "Just file an affidavit and cover everything else from your farm. As soon as you arrest them, you can turn them over to our custody for transport to a marshal."

Joe Edris scratched the bridge of his nose. "Sounds like something I'd like to do. So, now we catch them."

"Piece of cake," Trouble assured him.

"I had a sergeant tell me that once."

"The parasail almost flies itself," the Jump Master assured the newest ATF agent in human space. "We've picked a five-meter hole in the forest canopy for you, logged its GPS coordinates in your suit and it'll swing you right down into the target hole. If you think you're headed for a tree landing, just control the sail the usual way." The Jump Master was very confident.

"He's never made a jump before," Trouble informed him.

"Oh." The assurance was replaced by a visible gulp. "Well, sir, if it looks like you're headed for a tree, you probably aren't, so you just let the system land you."

"What else do I need to know?" Joe asked Trouble.

"The scout suit is pretty sophisticated. I've reprogrammed it to respond like the body armor you used in the LornaDo army."

"Thanks. Bet I haven't forgotten a thing in the last twenty-five years."

Trouble let the man have the laugh he deserved. "I've set most of it for auto anyway. Cooling will keep the surface of the suit at ambient temperature. To night vision, you'll look just like the next tree. Don't worry when these hoppers drop off." Trouble thumbed the bumps that speckled the armored suit. "They've got the jammers for the heart monitor. They feed off the chemical heat sink." The look in Joe's eyes told Trouble the man hadn't understood a word. "You'll see, once we get down there."

Joe shook his head as the tech settled the helmet on him. "And I thought qualifying on the M-6 was all this job took."

"Your drop is behind the rest of us. You stay low, and all you'll have to do is read 'em their rights."

"Right."

There was something beautiful about a plan clicking into place. In zero gee, Trouble's marines glided rather than marched to their places in the drop shuttle. Still, the scrape of armor, the creak of weapons on harness, the snap as men and women strapped themselves in brought a rush to Trouble. Good troopers, doing what they did best. You had to love it.

Liberty Launch Four was the only one on the *Patton* rigged for a combat drop. As soon as Trouble reported them rigged for drop, the pilot dropped out of orbit, then went to aerospike, cruising well south of the target at thirty thousand meters. The suits would take care of breathing. They went out the drop ports by the numbers, falling in a pattern through the freezing evening air.

Right on time, the parasails streamed and deployed. While Trouble, Joe, and four of the marines glided north as planned, three other troopers spiraled straight down.

So much for GPS guidance.

At least their chutes opened. The miss-drops tried to redirect their sails in flight, but the programming was not something you did while dangling from silk and cord. They reported as soon as they were on the ground. "Hoof it for town," Trouble ordered, reminding himself it wasn't their fault.

"Slight change of plans, Joe. You keep to my right hand."

"Piece of cake, right, marine?"

"Ever had a slice of cake out of field rations?"

The drop zone was awfully small. The tight spiral the parasail flew was almost enough to make a fresh trooper dizzy, and Trouble was only one night away from a lousy night's sleep. Free of his chute, he started closing the target. "Got to make a few changes," he advised his teams as he went. Blue and red teams were where they belonged—to the north and south of the target. Green team had fallen out of the sky early. He and Joe would have to be the cork in the bottle all by themselves. He revised his fire lanes and approach tracks to reflect that, sent it, and got acknowledgments from all hands. Fifty meters to his right, Joe moved parallel to his approach.

"What was that?" came as a half squeak. Trouble checked Joe's area. There were two echoes there. "Your first hopper just launched. They bleed off heat. When I activate them, they'll jam every sensor the bad guys got."

"There went another one. Okay. How close do you want me?"

Trouble would have preferred to have three marines even with him. "Fall back another twenty meters. You've got the right fire lane. I got the left."

"Piece of taffy."

Trouble didn't mind the job getting tougher to chew. He just didn't want his teams breaking their teeth on rocks.

The bad guys were coming up a canyon, moving rapidly on foot. Blue and red teams were covering them along the ridges to both sides. Joe and Trouble would meet them head-on. "We're coming up on a thousand meters. Sensors figures their rigs to be good for that range. Stand by to launch all ready hoppers." Trouble quickly jogged the distance from a tree to a rock. The targets suddenly quit moving. "Launch hoppers. I'm activating."

His armor had been slowly charging hoppers, shedding one at a time as his own body heat overloaded the cooling system struggling to keep his suit indistinguishable from the background. Now it topped off a dozen and sent them bouncing away from him in all directions. A flick of his wrist activated not only his but all those of the five other marines closing on the target. Trouble wondered what it looked like to be on sensory overload, and grinned.

"We got something ahead of us," Polly shouted.

"What?" Havelock demanded.

"Five, six, oh my God! I don't know. A couple ah hundred. You tell me."

Polly shoved the electromagnetic heart searcher at his boss. Havelock glanced at it and scowled. "They got to be spoofing us. They couldn't have gotten an army up ahead of us."

"You can't jam one of these things. Westinghouse guarantees 'em."

"Right, and sleepy bullets never killed anybody. Okay, everybody. There's something ahead of us. We know what's behind us. Head uphill to the right. We'll drop over into the next valley and see how things are. Donny, your team takes the lead."

"Why us? We're due for a rest. Shit, man, we've been moving all day. Can't we take a break?"

"Sure, if you want to wake up facing some old lady whose husband you killed. Me, I'm moving."

Twenty tired guys started moving upslope.

"Where's this instant army?" Donny asked.

"Polly's magic spells ain't working at the moment. Toss a few rocket grenades out there and see what happens."

"Oh, shit" came in a many-part harmony, but there were several pops as grenades arched out before and behind them.

"Head down, Joe. Incoming." Trouble slipped behind the largest tree trunk available. Body armor was nice. Not getting hit was nicer.

"Humph" came from Joe. "Didn't dodge that one very good."

"You hurt?"

"Nope. Good stuff you got here." It was good stuff, but a sensor scan Joe's way showed a hot spot.

"Joe, your armor's not cooling like it should. I got you on infrared."

"Bad?"

"Not too. You come in about squirrel size."

"Thanks."

While they'd talked, the intentions of the target had become clear. "Okay, crew, they're moving uphill toward red team. Blue, you follow. Red, you hold in place. I'll close on their flank. Select nonlethal. Open fire when you got a good shot."

Trouble switched his M-6A3 to its backup magazine. The needle tips of those rounds were pumped full of sleepy drugs. Phyzer-Colt guaranteed each bullet. If it killed its target, they would write a very apologetic letter to his next of kin. A target was swinging uphill, getting closer to Joe than Trouble wanted. Going to ground, he laser-pinged him for range, set up a solid sight picture, and squeezed the trigger. The target dropped as the firing computer assessed three hits.

Trouble rolled to the left as return fire laced his position. "They got backtrack radar," he shouted, to warn his own crew, and to get Igor busy jamming it.

Coming up behind a rock, Trouble scanned the firefight. While the bad guy's heart scanner was definitely out of business, Trouble's system interrogated the scene every ten or eleven milliseconds, while the hoppers were pausing. Eight of the targets were officially down. Trouble did a scan for electronic activity. Three were hot. He picked one, put him to sleep, and rolled again.

Next check of the fight showed no fight. The last three went down before he could get one of them in his sights. "Red one, blue two, hold your lines. Rest, close with and disarm the targets. Switch to live ammunition." At that range, he would not risk one of his marines.

"When do I get to read them their rights?" Joe asked.

"Got me, but don't they have to be awake?"

"Your guess is as good as mine. They just swore me in. I didn't even get a new employee handbook." The shared laugh didn't take any of the edge off Trouble's caution as he worked his way toward the sleeping beauties.

Somebody scrounged up a helicopter that had been brought on-world by the mining exploration concern. Six hauls brought twenty sleeping toughs, five marines, one ATF agent, and a dozen witnesses out of the hills. Trouble was careful to assign the witnesses and the accused to separate lifts. By midnight, he had all twenty in the lockup and was ready to call it a night. *Liberty Launch Four* had recovered to orbit, so it looked like he could spend another wonderful night on Hurtford Corner. The inn even had his room waiting for him. Figuring Ruth had called it a night by now, he grabbed a quick snack and hit the sack. Tomorrow they could celebrate.

Big Al put his feet up on the coffee table and relaxed into the comfort of a massage chair. Zylon prowled the room, glanced out windows, checked for watchers, and gauged her best escape route. "Relax," Big Al assured her. "Henri is well paid. We are well provided for. We can gather our wits and our strength."

Zylon settled on the edge of the couch across from her superior-for-the-moment. "Can we really go off-planet with our tail between our legs?"

"I said gather our strength and wits, not sulk away."

"We can't let these people think they've beat us."

"And we won't." Big Al closed his eyes and seemed to relax into the gently flexing chair. "When the time is right, we will reeducate these fools to the facts of life. For the moment, the time is wrong. Let them have their day. It won't last long."

"Just so long as we have something to show when we go off-planet."

"You'll have plenty to take with you when we leave."

That was the first time Big Al had made such a promise to Zylon. For the first time today, she smiled.

Ruth was delighted to come down to the inn's public room and find Trouble eating breakfast with her pa. "Didn't you guys have something to do?"

"Did it," Pa answered around waffles. "We now have twenty more prisoners under lock and key, fully booked on capital charges of committing a felony with explosives illegally transported through interstellar commerce. I even read them their rights last night as they were waking up."

"Pa?"

"Daughter, I am the sole officer of the Alcohol, Tobacco, and Firearms Administration in thirty light-years. At least for the next year, I am. I've arrested them and will shortly officially turn them over to Captain Umboto as the only local representative of the Society of Humanity with access to transportation, to get those bastards off our planet and deposited for trial wherever the nearest Society court is."

"You're going, Pa?"

"Not on your life. I've filed affidavits for both me and several of the survivors. If the court wants more touchie-feelie stuff, they can bring themselves here to talk to us. No, the *Patton* will get these SOBs out of our life, and Hurtford Corner will be saved from letting them go free after what they did or having to come up with some legal excuse for hanging them. I think this is the best way to handle our problem."

"I do too," Mikhail Shezgo said from the door. "Can I join you for breakfast?"

So Ruth listened over pancakes to her pa and Trouble's account of last night. "Lord, when you folks decide to do something, it does happen fast," she sighed when it was over.

"We like it that way," Trouble said. "Now, I think I can take a day off."

His communicator buzzed.

"Trouble here."

"Umboto here. How fast can you get your prisoners up here and collect all those affidavits?"

"Affidavits were done last night. Prisoners are ready to move as soon as the locals provide us with paperwork."

"What kind of paperwork?"

Shezgo leaned over. "A list of their names with my signature on one side of the bottom and one of your people's signature on the other. We try to keep the paperwork light." That got a laugh. "Why?"

"We got orders for a yard overhaul. Looks like somebody hollered uncle even before my last long list of deficiencies hit their in-box."

"Full refit! We may actually spend some time at High Columbia."

"No such luck. Just a two-month reduced availability, and it looks like it went to the lowest bidder. A Wardhaven yard."

"But they were Unity?"

"Yeah, and I understood we shot up their space docks pretty good in the last battle of the war. Maybe we didn't do as good a job as we thought. Hope so. Anyway, orders say to get under way for Wardhaven soonest. The sooner I can get this collection of accidents waiting to happen into a yard, the happier I'm gonna be. If I send all the launches down before noon, think you could have everyone ready to lift before dark?"

"Probably sooner, from our end," Shezgo offered helpfully.

This was all happening too fast. Ruth wanted more time. Time to figure out who this tall collection of "Trouble" was. Time to decide if being a farmer was all she wanted to be, or was just all she thought she knew how to be. Time she didn't have.

Trouble put his fork down. "Damn" came softly, but there

was nothing hesitant when he spoke. "I'll have the prisoners up on the first launch. Gunny should have the troops saddled up and ready for the next one." He turned to the city manager. "I'm gonna need that chopper of yours to collect three of my guys who missed their drop zone last night."

"It's yours."

"Skipper, how much fresh fruits and vegetables has Supply got waiting?"

There was a pause before Izzy answered that one. "Couple thousand pounds. Say, two shuttles worth. Headed for Wardhaven; I'm not so hungry for fresh greens, but they're bought and paid for. Mount 'em up, Lieutenant. Move 'em out."

"Yes, ma'am." Trouble tapped his comm link off, then gave Ruth a shrug. "So much for a day off."

"There are days like this on the farm, too," she sighed.

Two weeks later, Izzy was having one of those days. On her viewer was a long and convoluted report from the network team explaining why they still had not broken the encryption lock on the slavers' files. The lieutenant had taken yet another opportunity to explain to her why the Navy needed to update its own encryption system. Since a ship's captain could hardly replace a Navywide system with an off-the-shelf commercial product, she just scanned that part of the report. The bottom line was that Trouble could have saved himself a lot of agony and let the slaver erase the files. She wasn't about to tell the marine that. She endorsed the report with a terse "Keep working" and went on to the next report. She didn't like that one either.

The initial contact with the yard had not gone well. To her preliminary list of priorities had come back a very delayed report requesting clarifications, delays or flat-out remarks that the requested work was not part of the contract. Izzy was seriously considering having Chips in his next report just list the few major subassemblies on the *Patton* that might be applied toward the spare parts shortage and have

Stan start planning that beer bust he wanted to throw on the *Patton*'s scrapping.

"Naw, not yet."

"Skipper, we've got the dock manager on the comm," the XO reported. There was a certain something missing in his tone. Enthusiasm, surprise. Izzy headed for the bridge.

"What have we got, Stan?"

"Spacedock's not ready to receive us."

"When will it be?" she asked the man on screen.

"The war damage was greater than we expected. Number five dock will need several more weeks before it's ready to take you. Even then, the shops will be under repair." The dock manager didn't seem the slightest bit bothered by handing Izzy this bad news. She wondered how low his Unity party number was. *Hey, guy, we won the war. You lost it. Remember?*

"So, what about docks one through four?"

"They're, er, already under contract."

That was not what Izzy wanted to hear. She took in a deep breath, readying herself for a major blast. Beside her, the XO was making calming signs with his right hand. Izzy let out her breath. Half of it. "You have a contract for us, don't you?"

"Yes, but work isn't supposed to start for another month."

"Month! Our orders were to report here immediately." Now Stan was flipping rapidly through their message traffic. In a moment, their orders appeared on Izzy's own screen. Yep, they were supposed to report immediately. Then again, they didn't say anything about when the work would start. So far, she hadn't gotten a copy of the contract between the Navy and the yard. The man on screen was waving something.

"It says right here. Work will begin no sooner than the fifth of next month. You're early."

"You'll pardon me. Could I have a copy of that?"

"Of course, ma'am." That was the first helpful word she'd heard so far. The contract started appearing on her and Stan's boards simultaneously.

"Date's right," Stan agreed.

"Now that you're here, we might be able to get some work started early," the yard manager offered. Maybe the fellow could be helpful.

"You got a pier we can tie up alongside? Get housekeeping support from?"

The man glanced off screen. "Pier eight is between docks three and four and close to the shops. That would be a good one for you."

"We'll take it. Light off its beacon. I have the conn. Helm, lock on to pier eight's beacon." The docking went smoothly after that. That was about all that did.

Housekeeping support along pierside was supposed to include electricity, water, sewer, and air. Gravity came for free as the station spun around its axis. At least the *Patton* got one gee gravity. The electricity was the wrong voltage, the water was brown, the sewer hookup didn't, and the only air came from the open locks. With all the other mismatches, Izzy wasn't so sure she wanted those locks open.

The rest of the day, and a big part of the next, was taken up correcting those problems. The yard personnel were always so apologetic. "Sorry, we thought that was what you wanted." "Oh, we didn't realize our unit didn't have a universal adapter." "Guess the war damage wasn't as repaired as we thought." "Are you sure you need that? Our specs on your class showed you needing class C support." And, since the *Patton* never had fully conformed to the Navy's standard configuration for its class, not all were the yard's mistakes.

Izzy was starting to feel sorry for the yard folks when the quarterdeck hailed her. "Ma'am, we've got some security folks here from Wardhaven. They say they're here for our prisoners."

"Like hell they get my prisoners. Tell them to get lost."

"I've tried, ma'am, but they won't leave until they talk to you."

"Send them to my day cabin. OOD, you've got the bridge. Stan, you and that legal clerk of yours had better report to my day cabin, too. Since when does Wardhaven have a marshal or anyone else authorized to take my prisoners?"

"I don't know."

"Well, find out."

Izzy still didn't have an answer to her question fifteen minutes later as she sat at the head of her conference table, Stan to her right, a yeoman to her left still frantically going through his law reader. For her own sense of security, Trouble sat next to Stan, and two of his marines stood at parade rest beside the hatch to the bridge. At the foot of the table, Special Agent for the Wardhaven Bureau of Investigations Howdon sat flanked by two more agents and a prosecutor.

"Captain," Howdon had begun, "we are prepared to give you receipts for your prisoners and for copies of all evidentiary data files that you have in your possession."

"Can you give one good reason I should provide them to you?"

"Ma'am, when you came alongside, you asked for housekeeping support. Among the modifications proposed for your ship is doubling its frozen food storage capacity. That will require running more chilling ducts through the spaces next to your brig. The brig's being moved forward two frames and down a deck. So we're here to take care of your prisoners while your brig is out of commission."

"You know a hell of a lot about my overhaul."

"Ma'am, the yard just advised us of the nature of your overhaul and requested that we take custody of your prisoners for the time being." Howdon's smile was pure innocence. Izzy doubted he'd been that innocent on his first day at kindergarten.

"That might account for the prisoners. Not the evidence."

"But, of course, ma'am," the prosecutor cut in. "They go hand in hand."

"Copies," Trouble drawled, "not the originals."

Caught, the special agent and the prosecutor exchanged worried glances. Izzy and Trouble enjoyed a smile. Now that the air was clear, this shouldn't take long.

Howdon studied his watch, seemed to be counting the seconds. Before Izzy could wonder what for, her comm buzzed. "Captain, we got a call for you."

"I'm busy," she snapped. "Take a message and I'll call back." That was standard procedure when she was occupied. Some trainee must be standing watch in the radio shack.

"Skipper"—now she recognized Sparks' voice—"you told us to pass a call from Anderson right through to you."

Now Howdon's and his sidekick's mouths were edging toward a grin. Captain Anderson had been her commanding officer during the recent unpleasantness. He was about the only thing that made the 97th Defense Brigade sufferable. His retirement to Wardhaven and the chance to catch up on old times with him was the only pleasant possibility this yard period offered. She'd called him as soon as phone lines had been brought aboard last night. A secretary assured her he was unavailable and might be for some time. She'd asked for a call back as soon as possible. Now was a hell of a time to get it.

"Put Andy through," she said.

"Hi, Izzy. How's navy life?" The words were pure Andy, but the voice might as well have been chalk scratching down a slate.

"Elie, what the hell are you doing here?" If Andy was the best of the 97th, Elie Miller was the worst. A college professor drafted and put in charge of their sensors, she could not open her mouth without lecturing or talk without a flip chart to draw on. Only Andy's sense of humor, and Izzy's lack of hundred-percent certainty she could dispose of the body, had kept Elie alive for the three-month campaign on Elmo Four.

"Andy's secretary told me you wanted to talk to him. He's off-planet for a while. I don't know when he'll be back. We really need to talk."

"About?" If the list of things she wanted to talk over with Andy was as endless as the beer they'd drink, the list she'd share with Elie was as dry as a freshly washed stein.

There was a long pause; then, with a deep sigh, words

cascaded from the comm link. "Listen, Izzy, I know we didn't get along very well. But you have to know you're not the only one chasing what you're after right now. You've got a lot of allies, if you just know where to look. The uniforms may be the wrong color per recent memory, but yesterday's enemy could be today's friend, and vice versa. Could we meet for supper?"

Izzy glanced at her to-do list for today. She hadn't gotten a damn thing done that was scheduled; wrestling alligators had eaten up every second. She didn't have time for supper, certainly not to drop down to the planet. "Elie, I'd love to, but I'm kind of busy. Don't have time for a dirtside visit today."

"That's fine. I'm on the station. Meet you at the Wharf Rat in half an hour."

Izzy never said the woman wasn't smart. And, if she went out to supper, that just might help her get these gumshoes off her ship. She stood. "Gentlemen, we seem to be at an impasse for the moment. Why don't you take it up with your superiors in the morning? I doubt we'll tear the brig down tonight."

"No problem, ma'am," Howdon agreed, far too quickly. *Elie, who have you sold your soul to this time?*

"Trouble, I want you and a couple of marines with me for dinner. Sidearms but civilian clothes. No use flashing uniforms in recently hostile territory. Stan, you've got the ship. Lock her down tight after I depart. I don't want any more people wandering aboard. Post marines in full combat kits at each of the locks. Issue live ammo. Anything I missed, Trouble?"

"No, ma'am. That ought to start the war up again just fine."

Thirty minutes later, Trouble reported to the quarterdeck in slacks and a sports coat, two similarly clad marines beside him. Between their crewcuts and shoulder holsters, he doubted a casual observer would identify them as marines for at least fifteen seconds. It didn't help when they fol-

lowed the skipper off the ship and immediately fell in step.
Well, all the skipper asked for was clothing, not disguises.

"I see you brought the marines," Elie Miller remarked as
Izzy and three towering males were shown to the table
where the woman sat alone. With his eyes, Trouble directed
his two men to the next table. They went, none too sure what
was expected of them. Bodyguarding had never been a part
of their tactical training. It hadn't been in Trouble's, either,
but the Book said to improvise; he was doing his best.

"I often find them better conversation," Izzy shot back.
Trouble didn't know he'd been invited to a cat fight. Did his
duty extend to protecting the skipper from a clawing she
started? For a moment's diversion, he glanced at the menu.
He spotted one item he could identify and probably afford.

"Anything good on the menu?" he asked.

"Several things," Elie assured him, distracted for the moment as she glanced around the room. Then she put her
hands on the table, leaned forward, and fixed the skipper
with the most sincere eyes Trouble had ever seen on a
woman. "I want to thank you, Izzy, and apologize."

The skipper had been about to say something; instead, she
nearly fell out of her chair. Never had he seen a starship captain with the wind taken out of her sails so thoroughly.
"Thank me?"

"Yes. I'd spent my whole life in school or university, stu-
dent or teacher. I can't think of any time I ever had to deal
with the real world. The world where you can't meditate on
a problem for however long you want, where you need
something now that's good enough, not tomorrow that's perfect. You made me madder than hell." That brought a
chuckle from the skipper.

"Yes, I used to try to get to Andy any time but when you
were around. But, damn it, you were right. I did take too
long to spit it out, and I always hedged anything I said. It
must have been hell on you."

"I didn't leave much doubt about that, did I?"

"No, and it was the honest feedback I needed. I could
never have done the job I'm doing here, worked with the

people I have to work with daily, if you hadn't softened my edges."

"And I'm just the abrasive character to sand down rough spots," Izzy drawled. "Okay, now that we've had our little love fest, what are you after?" Damn, but the skipper was a hard case. Throw her a kiss, she'd toss back a hand grenade.

Elie studied her hands for a moment, then went on as if she hadn't heard the last remark. "Wardhaven hired Andy and me to work in their Ministry of Science and Technology. Andy's heading up the Bureau of Exploration. I'm in charge of Technological Review. I study research proposals and decide which ones deserve some of the money that's being switched from the military budget to the R&D side. Deal with a lot of prima donnas that remind me of myself. How do you decide what to fund? What has a good chance? What is something we really need? Puts me in contact with a lot of people. I've learned a lot more than I ever did in university. World's quite complex, you know."

"Seems I mentioned that a few times," Izzy said dryly. Still, the skipper was paying attention.

"You should meet some of the people I've gotten to know."

"I'm a bit busy. Got a boat that's in desperate need of an overhaul and isn't getting nearly what it deserves."

"I know. Getting it ready for its next fight may be more critical than even you imagine."

"Next fight?" Trouble could be very relaxed gabbing about his last fight, or anything that was of purely historical interest. You start talking about his next one, and he got very, personally, interested. The skipper, too.

"I would very much appreciate it if you could meet some of my new associates."

"When?"

"Right now. They are quite close." Izzy moved forward in her chair. Trouble got ready to stand. "Some of them are rather allergic to weapons they don't personally control. Would you mind leaving your beef trust behind?"

"Trouble goes with me," Izzy voice was deadpan.

"It always has." Elie blinked in puzzlement.

"Lieutenant Tordon, usually known as Trouble." Izzy indicated the marine. He nodded his head.

Elie glanced at him, then studied the comm link at her wrist. "Lieutenant, would you mind leaving behind your weapons?"

Trouble noted the use of the plural. Izzy gave him a short nod. He removed the service automatic from his breast holster. Then he slowly removed the needle gun from his back belt. When Elie kept looking at him, he added the short knife from his shoe and the longer one from beneath his collar.

"Trouble recently spent a few days' involuntary leave with some slavers," Izzy drawled. "You'll excuse his tendency to overcompensate for those days of being disarmed."

"I will, but . . ." Elie's glance went from her comm link to Trouble and back again. With a groan, he unclipped the brass knuckles from the back of his belt buckle.

"You can keep that. It's the darts in your shirt collar they want." With a scowl, Trouble put back the knuckles and carefully removed the four sleepy darts that helped keep his collar in place.

"Damn good system your friends got," he growled.

Now Elie stood up. "If you'll follow me."

A word from the skipper kept the marines in their seats as she and Trouble followed the woman out the back. For the next five minutes they went left or right at corners in no particular pattern. They rode several elevators, at least one of which had no numbers and moved without Elie punching a button.

"You can quit now, Professor. I'm totally lost," Izzy growled.

"This isn't for you. We keep this up until my associate is sure we have lost any tail you or I may have had."

"Paranoid bunch you've traveling with," Izzy answered.

"They lived through Unity, and survived a Society admiral ordering all life on this planet vaporized."

"A mistake," Izzy said, but her voice didn't sound as sure as it usually did.

"I'd value your opinion on that after you're fully briefed." Elie's voice held no sarcasm. The next turn brought them onto a busy concourse; they wound their way down and across it. A woman in a dowdy purple dress bumped into Elie. The professor followed that woman through a small door, down a hall, and into another elevator. The woman motioned them in, but did not follow. There were no controls.

Izzy was getting damn tired of this runaround. She'd had a long, nonproductive day and didn't need to play silly-assed games to work up an appetite. She was about to start chewing on Elie when the elevator opened into a small dining room with a round table set for five. Several dishes rested on a lazy Susan in the center of the table. The smell was powerfully oriental and spicy. A large man in a rumpled suit already sat facing them. A tall, thin man stood to his left.

"Come in, come in, I'm Ernest Nuu," he announced cheerfully, "the owner of the yard that's to repair your ship. Captain, this is my friend." His hand indicated the seated individual, but he did not give a name. "You've already met Elie. No need to introduce yourselves. We have already met." A second wave of the hand indicated a wall of monitors, one of which showed the table at the Wharf Rat where all this had started.

"Quite a collection of toys you had, marine." The large man smiled. "I collect toys like those." The voice, the eyes told Izzy this fellow collected a lot of things: people, weapons, bodies. His basement probably was quite an interesting place come spring cleaning. Did he ever do a garage sale?

Elie served herself from several plates on the lazy Susan. The "toy collector" went next, careful to mix the steamed or wokked vegetables and meats together. Mr. Nuu followed his lead. If any part of the meals were drugged, they'd been thoroughly mixed. Had they taken an antidote? Did he trust his thugs to remove him safely, while tossing Trouble and her down a black hole? Trouble served himself; Izzy followed suit. The food was quite tasty—a bit hot, but that was life.

"You said you wanted to share some things." Izzy got down to business as she took her first mouthful.

"But I don't want to lecture," Elie sighed.

"Do you believe in black and white?" The toy man asked around a huge forkload of chicken and oriental vegetables.

"And three or five shades of gray," Izzy added.

"Very good." The big man beamed. "I bet you even have been known to do things for several competing reasons."

"Occasionally." Izzy hoped this little dance wouldn't take forever.

"Good. Then you'll understand that our recent war was many things to many people. On the surface, it was a raw grab for power by President Urm and his Unity thugs, from rich Earth's view point. Out among the poor rim worlds, it was a struggle against an oppressive Earth that kept us weak and in debt. I'm sure you know of those opinions."

"Was in all the papers," Izzy said dryly.

"Slipping around the fringe of the spotlight were several other motivations for the war, less clear, less worthy of dying for. Efforts by certain financial centers to gain advantages in the new order that peace would bring."

"I've drunk a few beers in bull sessions on that idea. Nobody had proof that would interest a court."

"Precisely. Courts are difficult things to interest, and legions of people make their living assuring that what is done does not rise to their level of interest. Unfortunately, Wardhaven has not been able to stay uninterested. When an admiral orders a billion people vaporized, myself included, I become supremely interested."

"But what's-his-name was a mistake. His orders were canceled, he's . . ." Izzy ground to a halt, suddenly very aware that what she thought was true might not be so.

"Vanished. Yes, we can't seem to find anything out about Mr. Whitebred's whereabouts. And believe me, we have tried."

Izzy was getting tired of all this beating around the bush. "Is there a purpose to this history lesson?"

"I assure you, I have no time to waste on history. You wanted to talk to your friend, Andy. He is not here. Presently, he's providing off-planet oversight to a search for a ship that went missing on a routine six day hop. Mr. Nuu's first grandchild is due in five months. His son-in-law was on that ship. Son-in-law is also Wardhaven's Minister of Science and Technology. We want him back."

"I don't see the connection."

"The ship that disappeared had been Mr. Whitebred's flagship. We suspect he left a little something behind for the crew to remember him by. At least as long as they have oxygen. That is one of many items that piqued our interest. Several ships from Wardhaven have disappeared in what has come to be called pirate-infested space. Now you come to us with word that people are being kidnapped on rim worlds and transported off them to serve some purpose. Captain, I find all of this most puzzling, and I do not like puzzles. Do you?"

Izzy let the list of recent crimes roll around her head for a long moment. Alone, each was a puzzle. Formed up in ranks for inspection, they were still a puzzle, but a big, ugly puzzle. "No. I don't like puzzles either."

"Have you cracked the files you captured on Hurtford Corner?"

"No," Izzy spat.

"Then it seems to me that we both face the same distasteful puzzles. What is going on? What is it that we are not supposed to be concerned about, but are? Can we work together?"

Izzy had been expecting that. She shook her head. "I've got a few questions of my own. Why are you talking to me, a lowly cruiser captain? Why don't I see anyone else from my government at this table? If you are so concerned, why haven't you taken it up with my superiors? I was born with the chain of command wrapped around my neck. I've grown attached to it. This doesn't fit anywhere on that chain."

"Quite correct, Captain, this doesn't fit anywhere in that chain. After studying the chain of events that put Admiral Whitebred speeding toward Wardhaven with a ship full of relativity bombs, I am very careful about the chains I become entangled in. You have demonstrated a personal commitment to destroying pirates and slavers. Even burned one of the bastards. You are here. I would rather deal with you than work through channels with trap doors that go I know not where. You no doubt have felt the full intensity of the concern that your superiors have for the well-being of your command. Do you find it strange that you received orders for an overhaul quite suddenly after you stumbled into the hostage situation on Hurtford Corner?" The acid of his words hung for only a moment, etching itself into Izzy.

"My orders were to report here immediately."

"Yet the overhaul was not to begin for a month. Someone did not want you in orbit above Hurtford Corner."

"Who?"

"I do not know," the spy answered.

Izzy did not like the taste of this new piece of the puzzle. She was also tired of guessing games. "Sir, if I had wanted to be a horse trader, I wouldn't have joined the Navy. Shall we cut through all the crap? What do you want, and why should I care?"

The big man pushed back from the table, folded his napkin, and chuckled. "Captain, I am not a horse trader. You are an honorable officer. You have no personal price. Yet we both have needs. I think they are the same. I have things I can offer that I believe you, as captain of a man-of-war, can accept.

"First, I need to know what the pirates and slavers are doing and where they are doing it from. Ships do not operate without a base. I want to know where that base is. I think you do too. I believe we will find that base when we crack the files you are in possession of. You have not cracked them. I doubt a cruiser's resources can. I place at your disposal an entire planet's resources. In return, I promise full disclosure of what we find, when we find it. As soon as I know anything, you will."

Izzy nodded. As much as she hated to admit it, her team had not cracked the slavers' security lockdown. She could use some help there. But what would that help cost her? "Is that it?"

"No." Mr. Nuu took the lead now. "I own the yard your ship is scheduled into. I can have you in dock two tomorrow morning. I can assign two, three times as many people as I am obliged to under my contract. I can make shops and spare parts available to you without reference to any piece of paper. If you want it and it's on this planet, you can have it. In two months, I can give you the best six-month refit you could ask for."

Izzy sat back in her seat. She knew how much her refit was funded for. Nuu was talking about four or five times more. "That's going to cost."

"Nothing compared to what I'm spending to find my son-in-law. Nothing compared to what it will cost me and mine if what I'm afraid of actually happens. Captain, until we get a full download from your files, all I have to go on is the twisting gut of a scared old man. But I've done business with these fellows. They scare me a lot more than an over-run on your cruiser."

Izzy rubbed thoughtfully at the ridge of her nose. They wanted to help her crack files she wanted to read. They were willing to give her ship the overhaul it desperately needed. They were offering her a lot, all in the line of duty, none of it personal. Ha! Offering a captain to remake her baby into a ship that could really fight. Nothing personal. Right! She leaned forward and stared the toy man in the eyes. "You want my files. What else?"

"Two months from now, your ship will require a shake-down cruise. For that, you will probably be authorized to carry extra yard personnel. We want that shakedown cruise to be to the pirates' planet, and those extra personnel to include the best drop troopers Wardhaven has."

So there it was. "You want to fight a little war of your

own, and you expect me to provide the transport." Part of Izzy was horrified at the idea. But not all of her. It would be quite a fight. A real challenge. Maybe even fun.

"And cover," the big man shot back, "if it comes to a ship action."

Izzy chuckled at that. "God, and to think I dreamed all my life of an independent command." She leaned back in her chair. "I can just see myself explaining this to the admiral."

"I am confident we will not be asking you to do anything your superiors will not support . . . after the fact."

"Always was easier to get forgiveness than permission," Izzy muttered. How often had Andy chided her for doing just that? Still, you don't fight a war if nobody shows up. "What if you can't crack the files? What if you can't locate the bastards' base? What about my overhaul then?"

"Then I've bet you an overhaul for nothing," Mr. Nuu put out his hand. His face was solemn, but his eyes twinkled. "But my gut tells me it's a good bet."

Izzy eyed the hand. The *Patton* would get her overhaul. Maybe she would haul some Wardhaven drop troops off to blow up something she and Trouble would love to see gone. If there was a downside to this, Izzy couldn't spot it. Hell, the worst they could do is retire her, and they damn near did that last year. Why not? Izzy reached out to take the man's hand.

"Sounds like a good bet to me. We'll move *Patton* into dock tomorrow morning." She turned to the toy man. "When do you want the files?"

"Tonight, if possible," he said. "And the prisoners, too. They may give us a unique insight into the workings of the encryption."

Izzy paused; the rim was not known for its compliance with the fine points of Society's human rights legislation. Then again, she wasn't sure slavers were human, and they didn't have a lot of rights in her book. "If your Mr. Howdon is available, I believe he can move them out now."

"He has been waiting."

"Why am I not surprised?" Izzy stood. "Elie, you've got

some really interesting friends. Chow sure beats the old 97th, but I've got some things to do. How about lunch in a few days?"

"I'd love it."

"Anybody know the way back?"

"The elevator outside will take you back to the promenade just outside the Wharf Rat." The toy man broke a smile.

"You're a damn good spy," Izzy told him.

"And you're a damn good ship driver," the spy paid her back.

"We'd all better be damn good at what we do if we're going to pull this off."

Izzy was no fool. The second she stepped aboard, she ordered copies made of the encrypted files. Her prisoners were quickly rousted out, but Special Agent Howdon had to wait until her copies were done before taking prisoners and data files off her hands.

Next morning, Izzy had a few quick words with Stan and her division heads, telling them to keep their eyes open and stay alert for surprises during this overhaul. Still, by 0900, the *Patton* was stripped of her ice armor and docked. By noon Izzy was up to her eyeballs in setting the scope, priorities, order, and timing of more task orders than she had ever hoped for. The yard personnel were not only enthusiastic, but knew what they were doing. They'd just done a refit on a County class cruiser; Izzy heard regular references to the *Sheffield*. They knew almost as much about what she wanted as she did. In a few cases, more.

"We've got a Westinghouse SG-180 central fire control system in the warehouse. Would you like it?"

"I'll take it," Izzy and Guns shouted in the same breath.

"It's yours. Hardly any wear on it. Took it off the *Sheffield* when we put in a SG-195. Now then, the trash compactor and disposer. If we don't rework the latch on that sucker, half your crew are gonna be breathing vacuum."

Stan grinned. "What have you got?"

• • •

A week later, Izzy was just coming up for air after a long and productive meeting with the shipyard supervisor when her comm link buzzed. It was Elie, offering lunch dirtside.

"Sure you can't come up here?"

"I can, but my boss wants to sit in on this one, and she's four months pregnant. Definitely down-checked for space, and a bitch on that point, so don't mention it in her presence, okay?"

"If you say so. What do we need to talk about with her?"

"Our mutual friend has information of mutual interest. More will have to wait."

"Damn, I get you out of lecture mode, and now I can't get a word out of you."

"Yeah. Bring your marine friend."

"Why?"

"I think he's kind of cute. Our mutual friend likes him. I don't know, just bring him. Eleven-thirty, at the ministry."

"Will do. Out." Izzy rubbed her hands together. All this and pay too. Her ship was being taken apart and put together the right way. And now they were shoving a hunting license in her hand she would have killed for. Life doesn't get any better. "Trouble, put on your dancing shoes. We're going dirtside."

EIGHT

ELIE HAD A nice office at the ministry, a tad too neat for Izzy's taste, maybe running a bit too much to old marble and plush carpets, but nice. "How'd you get these digs?"

"Unity tossed the previous owners out. We took over when they vacated the lease. Someday, I'll have to do something about all the cold marble. Put in real workstations, not these old antiques. We get by."

Elie showed them next door to an even bigger office, then through several more doors until they found themselves in a small lunchroom. There were plastic-wrapped sandwiches and bottles of soda on the table. "Nothing fancy today," Elie said, taking a seat. "We have work to do."

A woman came in, just beginning to show her pregnancy. She talked rapidly with the big man whom Izzy identified only as the toy/spy guy. Mr. Nuu and a half dozen others filed in behind them. Nuu, the woman, and the spy took places at the table; others settled into chairs against the wall. The last two in carried armfuls of printed reports. They distributed them, then, lacking seats, just stood.

"This may take a while," the pregnant woman said. "Rustle yourselves up some chairs." In a moment, the two returned with mismatched chairs and settled in. The woman spoke a moment longer with the man Izzy still had no name for; then, scowling, she closed a folder and looked at Izzy.

"Excuse the informality, Captain. I'm Rita Nuu-Longknife. I once was a ship driver too—transports in the recent war. You've met my father, who's footing the bill for updating that wreck you brought in. In my husband's absence, I've been designated minister without portfolio. Which means I get all of the headaches and he'll have the fun of answering to Parliament when he gets back." Izzy caught the slight inflection on the "when." Not if . . . when. As important as the *Patton* and the pirates were to Izzy, she suspected Rita had a higher priority. "My friend here"— apparently even Rita had no name for the spy guy—"has damn near closed the planet's net down to get your files hacked. It appears that he has. Spill it."

The large man nodded to a slim woman, who rose from her chair along the wall, plugged a large comm unit into the lunchroom table, and hit a button. The wall in front of Izzy came to life, and the briefing began. "I am Tru Seyd, chief of information warfare. I won't bore you with the infinite amount of fun this cryptographic problem gave my team. It suffices to say that we started reading these files on Tuesday."

"Tuesday," Izzy interrupted. "Hold it. You promised me as soon as you knew anything, I'd know it. You kept me in the dark for forty-eight hours!" Work on the ship was going fine, but Izzy was still looking for the rub in this setup. She was a long way from trusting these folks enough to break orbit with a ship full of drop troops. As of this moment, her trust was zero.

"My call, Izzy." Elie rested a restraining hand quickly on Izzy's elbow. "The operative word was that she *started* reading the files on Tuesday. I saw the raw feed. They were getting maybe one word in four, and half of them were guesses. They only got a better handle late yesterday as they ran more and more of the files through their algorithm and modified it. Trust me, you had a lot more fun with your overhaul that I had with the first reads."

Izzy pulled her elbow away from Elie's hand. The professor had bought in with these folks. That vote was still out for Izzy. *Damn it, where is Andy?* "So, what did you get?"

"A fairly good handle on an ugly nest of snakes," the briefing officer said slowly. "Some of our assumptions we've verified. The pirates have converted a small settlement on the planet Riddle into a going concern. They've established an orbital station to strip the captured ships and maintain their own. They've expanded the original settlement into the hinterlands with a very profitable cash crop, and are importing prefab the kind of urban infrastructure that will support rapid population growth."

"How are they doing that?" Trouble had taken a large bite out of his sandwich. He chewed it thoughtfully.

"By cheating," the unnamed one said.

Tru took back the story. "Earth, Sirius, the first colonized seven sisters have billions of warm bodies. Few are interested in leaving. Even fewer have any idea how to survive on a frontier planet. I think Alpha Centauri was the last one to try shipping unwanted mouths off-planet. So few survived being dumped in the wilderness that it was cheaper to just space the migrants out the station lock than ship them off to somewhere else to die." Izzy nodded; her sister Lora wouldn't even think of moving off-world.

"At one point," the toy fancier chuckled, "Benjamin Franklin suggested the North Americans show their gratitude to their king for the forced colonists England was shipping them by shipping him rattlesnakes in return. My grandfather was so proud he could date our lineage back to the North America of that time. I never forgot that bit of history. Bottom line is that raw human flesh, even by the ton, does not a colony make. You need committed, dedicated, skilled workers, or you're just building a graveyard."

"It appears," Tru continued, "that someone is robbing Peter to pay Paul. Stealing capable labor from one colony to rapidly grow another."

Izzy felt a headache coming on. "This makes no sense.

Why not just support the colonies that are growing? Why go to all the risk of ripping up one to force-grow another?"

The spy cleared his throat. "Tru may have oversimplified one aspect. Robbing Peter to pay Paul is a zero-sum game. No one benefits. However, if I own Peter and you own Paul, your robbing Peter and shipping it off to Paul means a gain for you. Riddle appears to belong to a certain set of financial interests who overstepped themselves before and during the war, and landed hard after it. Riddle is an effort by them to recoup their fortunes. By the way, did I mention that we in this room helped that group land hard? I doubt they hold any love for us."

Izzy was definitely getting a headache. It lurked behind her eyes, drumming a sharp staccato right into her brain. All this talk of finances and people was the farthest thing from her world of show-me-a-target-and-I'll-shoot-it. "So they're stealing people. But people still need gear to build a planet. Stealing a couple dozen ships and their cargo do not a full-fledged urban infrastructure make. What am I missing?"

"Nothing . . . that we could recover from the cracked files. For that, we had to go looking elsewhere." The man with no name grinned. "When you are trying to solve a large problem, it is well to have a lot of pieces to pull from. How do you take over a relatively worthless agricultural planet and turn it into a booming urban world in just a few months?"

Izzy shook her head. "Farming is no way to get rich." She'd seen that in Joe Edris's callused hands.

"Unless you can find a really good cash crop," Trouble went on slowly. "Big cash crop."

"Drugs," Izzy said, and found it hard to breathe.

"On the money, first guess," Tru snorted and took back over. "Earth and the seven sisters teem with over a hundred billion people. They've recently discovered a new drug. A neat one. It enhances pleasure and pain by several multiples. You get laid, it's like no lay in history. You hurt, it's agony like nothing you've ever felt. You take this drug into a vir-

tual world and you can have everything you've ever wanted.
Even better, you forget there's anywhere else. No reality
niggling you around the edges. You want to be King Arthur,
Adolph Hitler, the great Khan, you are. Smart folks tube
themselves for food, water, whatever. Stupid folks overdose
and die of dehydration before they come up. Shit, this stuff
is it."

Franny wasn't stupid, Izzy thought, cringing inside, *just
dumb.*

"All this in four months?" Elie asked.

"No. It's been a growing problem. Some folks in Unity
felt it was a legitimate tool to balance the trade deficit between the rim and Earth." The toy man showed no distaste
for that policy. "Before the war it was a problem. During the
war it grew, despite the supposed cutoff of trade. Since the
peace, it's skyrocketed. Makes you wonder if it's under new
management."

"Makes you want to change its management," Trouble
snarled.

Izzy nodded, but kept a tight rein on herself. *Don't let 'em
see it's personal.* "We've tried guns and they're still there.
Sounds like we need some kind of very combined arms
campaign." Izzy eyed the spy and Mr. Nuu. "What have you
got in mind?"

"Putting them out of business," Mr. Nuu said firmly, "before their unfair competition puts me out of business. The
problem with bad money is that it forces out good. I can't
pay my people a living wage if I have to compete with a financial empire funded by drug money, piracy, and slave
labor. Given a level playing field, I can take on anyone, but
not this way."

"So we level the field," Izzy agreed. *And I'll level them.*
"What do the nav charts and planetary survey look like for
Riddle? I'm assuming this is my primary port visit during
the *Patton's* shakedown cruise."

"Nav charts are ten years out of date. The planetary survey seems to have vanished in the confusion of the war."

"All copies?" Izzy couldn't believe that; every planet had

a central archive of all data about human space. If they'd all been stripped, there were a lot of fingers in this cookie jar.

"Captain"—the spy's eyes locked on hers—"it was a clerical error that promoted a reserve captain to admiral and damn near killed all life on this planet. There appear to be a lot of clerical errors going on. An underpaid temporary clerk is not a difficult person to bribe." It sounded like he spoke from experience; Izzy didn't push the point. She had other fish to fry.

"You don't plan a strike on ten-year-old data. You mentioned a space station. Where is it? What's its layout? What's the damn planet look like? I don't care how many jump troopers you've got and how tough they are, if we don't drop them in the right place, they're no good at all."

The spy nodded. "Glad you see it my way. I'm sending a tramp freighter off to Riddle. Expect it should update most of the basics. That enough?"

"No!" Trouble snapped. "Not near enough. And I'm not sure what to tell your tramp to look for either, until I see it for myself. I assume we don't have time to run a couple of surveys."

"We cannot assume our cover will hold for more than one run," the spy said.

"Could a Wardhaven military type join that freighter's crew?" Trouble asked.

"Not a smart move," Rita cut in. "Most of the rim's professional soldiers know each other. Too likely a Wardhaven officer would run into someone he knows."

Izzy wanted these bastards, but did she have the right to risk a good man? "Trouble, aren't you about due for some leave?"

The marine let one of his lopsided grins consume his face. "I've never been out on the rim before this cruise. I may have exchanged shots with some of your troopers in the recent unpleasantness, but I've spent no time face to face."

"We get one shot at the right data to put together a full-scale, planetwide assault and take over," Izzy continued. "If my lieutenant here doesn't like the data he gets on the run in to the planet, he can make sure they get it right on the run out. This is no time for an unsupervised survey." *Bless you for volunteering, Trouble.*

The spy's chuckle was ugly. "Drawn-out hostile takeovers are such a bitch. We must be quick, before anybody can file a complaint with the Securities and Exchange Commission."

Rita waved at two of the men who'd been sitting along the wall. "For your one ground-pounder, I'll trade you two. Major Tran of the Second Guard Brigade, and Lieutenant Sweetson, his intelligence officer. They'll show your lieutenant what data we have on Riddle and see what we need and how to get it. When does your freighter leave, sir?"

"Freighter's not coming near here. We'll intercept it with a fast packet that had better be out of here in three days."

"No trouble." The marine stood, edging toward the two officers. "We can plan our recon quickly. What kind of sensors can I use?" Tru handed him a reader, already active.

"I think we're done," Rita concluded. "You'll excuse us. Sir, I've got a few ideas I'd like you to run down." She and the spy headed for the door.

Izzy stood; Franny would get one hell of a tombstone. "Pass your data to the *Patton.* I'll have my officers comb through it. See what we make of it."

Elie stayed seated. "Izzy, can I have a word with you?"

Izzy rubbed her hands together. "Professor, I got a hell of a complex exercise to plan. Why don't you walk me to the car?"

"Here." The ex-professor's word was hard, like a vacuum, and just as empty and cold.

"Is there a problem?" Izzy froze; did Elie know about Franny? Izzy had a fight to plan. Would Elie take it away from her? The woman's eyes were hard, bitter cold.

"The pirates and the slavers share the same base." Elie spoke slowly, measuring each of her words. "That was the first bit of data we cracked."

"So?" Izzy said. Elie was back in lecture mode. Izzy swallowed her impatience and let her ramble.

"They also share the same ships."

"Right," Izzy sighed. "That sounds logical." For a moment longer the captain of the *Patton* stood there, waiting. Then the meaning hit home. Suddenly her knees no longer supported her; she collapsed back into the chair. Air was hard to come by. With a convulsive gulp, she gasped breath back into her lungs. On the third try, words finally slipped from her.

"Pirates also pick up slaves?"

"We have reports of ships making orbit on Riddle with a captured freighter in tow, and both crew and slaves locked in the same hold."

Across the room, Trouble excused himself from the Guard officers and stepped quickly around the table to kneel beside her. "You all right, skipper?"

"So any particular pirate," Izzy whispered, "at any particular time may have aboard not only its own crew but also slaves and captured crew."

"Yes, Izzy."

"They've lost one recently." Izzy tried to keep the words in. They tumbled out by themselves.

"The *Reprisal* failed to make Riddle at its appointed time, five days after you encountered a pirate."

"And destroyed it. No quarters asked, none given." Izzy finished the thought for Elie.

"Yes."

Now even the conversation between Rita and the spy had come to a halt. The spy's eyes locked on Izzy and held her until she looked up. "They play a nasty game," he said. "Sometimes we must make it just as nasty for them."

Izzy swallowed hard again. "Yes," she agreed. With a flick of her hand, or maybe just a tremble, she gave them leave to go. The room emptied quickly. Only Trouble and Elie remained.

"You had no way of knowing, skipper. We didn't run into the kidnapping routine until after we burned the pirate."

"If we'd interrogated prisoners, we might have found out sooner."

"Yes, Izzy," the other woman answered. "I've read your report. It's already been endorsed up the chain of command. No one faults your decision."

"Nobody knows how many innocent passengers were on my burned pirate, do they?"

"No one in the Navy," Elie answered.

"But you do." Izzy got back a slight nod. "How many?"

"Possibly as few as one hundred sixty-seven. Could be over two hundred."

The headache struck with lightning force, shooting through both sides of her brain, threatening to tear her skull from her shoulders. Izzy slowly massaged her burning temples. "Two hundred," she whispered.

"Maybe less," Elie assured her. "They don't keep very good records."

Izzy snorted. No, the pirates wouldn't keep good records. And whatever records the *Reprisal* had on board were gone to hell with it. Gone to hell with two hundred innocent people whose only mistake was to be captured, enslaved, and hauled into space by people too greedy to pass up a slow freighter.

"Skipper, it wasn't your fault," the marine assured her.

"Trouble, I'm the skipper. I called that shot."

"But you didn't know."

"If." Izzy spoke the word, but couldn't sort out, among the jumble in her mind, what she wanted to tag onto the word. There were so many might-have-beens. "I got to get back to the ship. Yard supervisor is due at sixteen hundred."

"I'll go back with you," Trouble offered.

"No, you've got your job cut out here. Work with these folks as long as you need. We've got to take Riddle down, all the way and fast. No need for more collateral damage." The words were so clean.

"Yes, ma'am."

"The ministry has a driver. I'll have her take you back to the port. Did you bring your own gig down?"

Izzy nodded; Elie left. For several long minutes, Izzy sat, Trouble still kneeling beside her. Then a cheerful woman in a brown jumpsuit stuck her head in the door. "Somebody here need a run out to the spaceport?"

"Yes," Izzy said and followed her out. The woman chattered during the drive about traffic congestion and new construction. "Wardhaven's really growing, now that the war's over." Izzy managed grunts in the appropriate places. The woman's words were a fine thread, holding Izzy to this place and time, distracting her as the battle with the pirate replayed over and over in her mind. *What could I have done different?*

Those bastards were blowing up ships, enslaving honest folks, and feeding poison to good kids like Franny. They had to die before they killed again. But in killing them, Izzy had killed kids like Ruth. Franny, Ruth, and the face of the captain she'd vaporized ran together in her mind. *What should I have done different?*

Izzy had no idea . . . and a dozen screaming alternatives.

The gig was waiting for her. It taxied out even as she settled into her seat. The copilot had to remind her twice to put on her seat belt before she heard her. Thank God there were only two shuttles ahead of them; takeoff was hardly delayed. Then Izzy found herself wanting something to slow them down, to keep her away from her ship. Stan and the rest would be reading the report, duties allowing. They had to go over the documents; the next fight might depend on one of them spotting some fact or item that eluded the rest. And none of them would miss what Izzy had managed to overlook through the entire meeting. Elie had spotted the connection right off. For Izzy, it had to be pointed out. Her nose had to be pulled down hard and rubbed in it.

"How could I have missed the implication?"

What else have I missed with my "go for it" attitude? How many times had Andy and other COs warned her? Take a second to look past the surface. Oh, but the surface was so attractive. You could see it; you could shoot it. A pirate is a pirate and deserves no mercy. Life was so easy that way.

The gig docked above the *Patton*; it was an easy drop down to her own quarterdeck. The supervisor was waiting for her, shaking his head. "I've got two or three hulks tied up alongside that are in better shape than this scow. Lady, you sure I couldn't swap you one of them?"

"If you could have one of 'em fully gunned, armored, and rigged in seven weeks, I might take you up on the offer."

He shook his head. "It was the push to convert these tubs in ninety days that got this ship in this mess. But"—his eyes lit up—"if you got five, six months to spare, it's a deal."

"We break orbit in seven weeks."

"Then I guess I better get folks busy ripping out two of your main busses. Connectors are way below specs. Half are fused, the rest trip out if you look at them hard."

"How long?"

"Mr. Nuu said you sail in seven weeks, you sail in seven weeks. Just means I get a few more crews turned loose for you. No problem, ma'am. When Ernie makes a promise, nobody wants to be the one who makes him break it."

"You like your boss."

"One of the best, Captain. Now, I'd best be going."

Izzy spent the rest of the afternoon reviewing the reports on the overhaul, then dove into more reports. She was way behind in her paperwork. What else was new? It kept her mind off something she couldn't do anything about. She ordered up a sandwich rather than face her officers in the wardroom. How many of them had found time to review the report on the pirates?

As the mess tech was leaving, Stan stuck his head in her cabin door. "Skipper, you got a second?"

Izzy glanced up from a report, about to take a bite out of a meat loaf sandwich. "Problem, XO?"

"Not sure."

Izzy swallowed and put the sandwich down untouched. "Come in." Usually, she'd have headed for "her" chair around the coffee table. Usually, she liked to keep things informal. This time she waved him to a chair across the desk from her. Today she wanted to keep the desk between herself and . . .

"I've been reading that report the folks dirtside did up on

the slave files we gave them. I can't make out one thing in it."

"What?" Izzy asked. She'd gotten the briefing; she had yet to read the actual report.

"It seems to me the pirates and the slavers are operating out of the same hole. Maybe I missed something, or haven't come across it yet. Are they one and the same?" Izzy nodded. "So a ship may be a pirate one cruise, a slaver the next."

"No." Izzy took a deep breath. "They can be both in the same cruise."

Stan settled back in his chair and gnawed on that bit of data for a long moment. "That's why the skunk I chased had guns ready to burn me." Again Izzy nodded.

"I did see where they were missing a ship a week after we burned that pirate," the XO said slowly. "I didn't find anywhere in the report where they might have listed an expected cargo."

"It's in there." Izzy wasn't going to beat around the bush with her own exec. "The *Reprisal* had picked up slaves before we ran into her. Maybe two hundred."

"Oh, God," Stan whispered. Izzy said nothing. The XO moved to the edge of his seat. "You've been very quiet since you came back up. You're blaming yourself."

"I made a snap decision to take no prisoners. I killed 'em."

Stan's head nodded slowly. "So how do you feel about me bringing back a ship full of prisoners?"

"You did it right." There, she'd said it. "I screwed up, and you did it the way I should have." Damn, this wasn't the way a captain talked to her exec. But, Christ, she'd blown it. Who could she talk to?

"I disagree with you, Captain," he shot back before she could finish the thought.

"Disagree?"

"We had two different situations. My skunk knew it was in deep shit the second it spotted me. They had plenty of time to sweat. To think about my guns. I had time to peel their hide, and their soul. Yes, I took some risks with your ship, but not a hell of a lot. I didn't have the disadvantages you had."

Izzy blinked several times, trying to keep her face a solid mask, trying to figure out where Stan was going. "And what did you see as the disadvantages of my situation?"

"We had to wait until the bastard made the first move. And he had to make it, not us. By that time, we were up close and personal. There's not a lot of time to think when you're dodging six-inch lasers. Given an hour or four like mine had, yours might have had a change of heart. But we were swapping broadsides as fast as we could charge the guns. When we winged him, all I could think was 'Oh, shit! Oh, shit! Do we go for prisoners and maybe get clobbered while we're offering them a chance, or do we just blow them to hell and worry later?'"

"Guess I'm doing the worry latering." Izzy tried to smile.

"Yeah. It was a hell of a call I was glad someone else had to make." Stan shook his head.

"Yeah, hell of a call. Two hundred people blown to bits before they even had a chance to scream."

Stan let out a noisy sigh. "Yeah, I've been seeing that for the last hour. I just wondered if I was seeing it right. Big report. Hard to string all the important facts together."

"Sorry, Stan, I asked for the raw feed. In another day or so I expect to get a more refined read."

"I need to read the raw. Don't want some chair-bound analyst to simplify some critical item out of the read just so he can shorten a sentence and make it read easier."

Izzy stared at the sandwich. There was nothing in the Book about execs giving captains absolution, but that was what she was feeling. "We did the best we could, didn't we?"

"Yes, skipper, we did the best damn job we could, considering the cards we had to play."

"Thanks, Stan, I appreciate the visit." Izzy reached again for her sandwich. "Let's do a better job next time."

"That's what life's about, ma'am, learning to do a better job next time out. See you at breakfast."

"I'll be there."

Trouble was glad the skipper had her color back next morning at breakfast. The unanimous consensus in the wardroom was that it would have been good to bring the *Reprisal* in, lock, stock, crew and slaves. Still, at the time, dodging lasers, it felt mighty good to see the source of their doom go boom. Next time, they'd work something out to disable the skunk. Still, you didn't save many lives after you were reduced to atoms.

Trouble had a rough outline of his recon; he briefed the division heads on it. They offered changes. Guns had several suggestions, and Igor came up with a few spare sensors to add to the tramp freighter's pod. Trouble ran the suggestions by his Wardhaven counterparts, who had done their own briefing and had a few changes of their own. By the third day, Trouble had a consensus plan, a damn good pod, and a handful of disks from Tru, the spy's info warrior.

"This one ought to get you through their firewall," she assured him. "If it doesn't, pop this into one of the computers dockside. All we want to know is what works. I'll take care of the rest once I'm in-system."

"You're coming with the assault teams?"

"Wouldn't miss it for the world. It'll be my first crack at info war, realtime. And I get to put drug bosses and pirates out of business. What more could a girl ask for?"

"All I'm asking for is a round trip, at the moment."

The recon pod was a round cylinder one meter across and three long that had been rigged to plug right into the tramp's hull. Power in and feedback came out from a central shaft running through the plug. Everything was passive. "We'll have to get our topography from stereo photos. Anybody got a computer system still able to process those?" Tru asked.

That drew shrugs all around. "We always use radar topo," Lieutenant Sweetson answered.

"Well, buddy, we are not doing anything active. Not if

you want your boy wonder back. Start hunting for obsolete tech if you need to know how high a ridge is on Riddle before you fly into it." They had a lot of delightful conversations along that line before Trouble's fast packet shoved off. Leaving the Wardhaven officers behind with a long list of things to find, steal, or otherwise acquire, Trouble wasn't sure who had the toughest assignment. The *Loki* was waiting, tied up to the tiniest station Trouble had ever seen, orbiting a gorgeous planet called Jacob's Folly. While the specialists on the packet installed the plug, Trouble met Captain Hood. Gazing down through the viewport, both of them watched the pod being maneuvered into place, then latched down. Its outer skin meshed perfectly into the rough, worn hide of the tramp starship.

The *Loki*'s skipper was just as rough, a paunchy wreck of a man; his stoop-shouldered and trembling frame left the marine wondering how the fellow managed a ship. "Glad to have you aboard. We've been shorthanded since we left Sirius. Fewer people aboard, the fewer you got to worry about trusting." The body might be a disaster, but the blue eyes were as piercing as any officer Trouble had had the luck to ship with.

"Where's the crew?" Trouble asked.

"Dirtside, enjoying a few hours leave. Didn't want anyone looking over our shoulder." Trouble handed over his papers; Hood glanced at them. "So Jerigelski tossed you off the *Salome's Favors*. Never did like the guy. Welcome aboard, Mr. T. We'll get you bedded down."

The room was larger than Trouble expected, but then marines didn't have a union to set minimum personal space like the civilian spacers demanded. He plugged a battered and obsolete entertainment unit Tru had given him, three times the size of a modern e-unit, into the wall socket. He played with it for a second. The external deceit quickly vanished as the wall display switched from a grainy picture of a waterfall to a full-range sensor readout. The top of the e-unit now had as many reaction buttons as an admiral's battleboard. There was even a keypad for word entry to back up the audio. Trouble had spent the ride out getting familiar with it. He was three jumps away from making it tell him more about a bunch of bastards than they wanted him to know. Fine.

"Captain, there's a civilian on the quarterdeck. Says he has to see you."

Three and a half weeks into this refit, Izzy was beginning to entertain hope. Matters between the *Patton* and the yard were going far better than she had any right to expect. With a sigh, Izzy figured she was about due for something to go wrong.

"This civilian have a name?" she asked. With everybody busy, they must have a raw trainee standing the watch.

"He won't give it to me," came the plaintive response.

"Visual on quarterdeck," Izzy snapped. A picture of the *Patton*'s quarterdeck, an elevator gaping in the background replaced the report she'd been mulling over. "Zoom to upper center," she ordered, not believing her eyes. Hm! If he didn't want his name in the log, she'd go along. "Provide the civilian with an escort to my day cabin," she ordered. She wiped her screen, made sure she had nothing she didn't want visible, then met her guest at the bridge hatch.

"Thank you for seeing me."

"Joe Edris, what the hell are you doing here? You're a long way from Hurtford Corner."

"Yes, and so is my daughter, I fear."

Izzy took the time to get Joe settled in a chair across the coffee table from her, then ordered coffee and sandwiches.

"Thanks, I'm starved. I made this trip on a shoestring."

"How did you make it at all?" Izzy asked incredulously.

"Mr. Withwaterson, you remember him, finally gave up and called in a ship to pick him up. Turns out an ATF agent has a certain call on ships for official transportation. Using nothing more than the ID card you issued, I wrangled myself aboard his ship headed back to Pitt's Hope. From there to here. I imagine when somebody audits their bills I'll be in a hell of a mess, but that can wait. My daughter can't."

"What happened?"

"Damned if I know. For the first ten days after you left, everything was wonderful. My wife even forgave me. Then one morning we woke up to find more than fifty people gone. Some maybe went voluntarily, but Ruth didn't. It was a slap at us. Show us we couldn't protect our own. I heard a sonic boom from a shuttle late that night. Seemed strange. Stranger when it left before dawn. Come morning, Ruth's room was empty. A Miss Uzeg, city manager's new girl friend and granddaughter to one of the new elders, was gone too. They slapped us in the face with a club. I was the only one on Hurtford Corner that had any chance of getting here. They all, city elders, station elders, my wife, want your help."

"You didn't message?"

"Withwaterson's ship was due that day. I figured I could get here as fast as any message. Besides, Izzy, I want to get my hands on the people who did this. Can you help me?"

"As it turns out, yes. I and a lot of other people are already doing all we can. As soon as the *Patton*'s out of the yard, it heads for the planet where your daughter probably is. Lieutenant Tordon is already out there, doing a predrop recon. We're going to take those slavers apart."

"I hope he doesn't run into Ruth. That could be a mess."

"Damn, let me see if I can get a message out to him." Izzy hit her comm link. "Get me Elie Miller."

Quickly Izzy explained the problem to Elie. It took a long five minutes to connect the call with the still unnamed spy. He listened, shaking his head before Izzy was half done. "That is something we cannot do. They should be at Riddle already. Any message will get there too late. Your lieutenant will have to tough this one out on his own. Mr. Edris, I am very sorry about your daughter. My analysts had a strong hunch that several of the hard-hit planets would be in for further attention. Hurtford Corner is rich in mineral resources. They want you, and they've just let you know they will not let a minor setback take you off their hit list."

"That's what I figured, too. Izzy, you got a berth aboard for a ATF agent?"

Izzy always had room for a good man. "I'll see what I can do." *Well, Trouble, you're deep in it again. Take care, boy.*

NINE

THE SECOND THE *Loki* jumped into the Riddle system, Trouble activated the pod. An hour later, Captain Hood dropped by. "What you getting, boy?"

"Not a hell of a lot. No electronic signals at all from the planet?"

Hood came over and fiddled with Trouble's board. "Never can be too sure with these things. Hm, right. Nothing! Damn planet must have one hell of a fiber backbone. It's radiating nothing but reflected light."

"We ought to be able to pick up something from comm links."

"Not if they're really low power. Means a lot of repeaters, but if you don't want your communications monitored, you do it that way."

"Well, there's got to be some high-powered communication between the planet and the station. Shuttles in between. Something."

"Doesn't look like it." Hood double-checked one of Trouble's readouts. "No, no shuttles in transit at the moment. The station is in a low, two-hour orbit. Maybe they only talk to it when it's above the horizon."

"Hold it." Trouble sat forward, tapping one monitor.

"There's a Global Positioning System. Okay, and there's a weather satellite. Maybe more when we get closer."

Three days later, they knew little more. "GPS and weather satellite system. Nothing else," Trouble reported to Hood. "I've got the main urban area decently mapped"—he glanced at his own readout—"but I'd like a second orbit to verify it."

"Oh, darn," came with no emotion from the ship public address. "We seem to have lost a gyro. Clobbering my burn. If I don't get it fixed real soon, I just might lose my window to the station this orbit. Henry, could you fix that for me?"

"Boss, you ain't given me time to fix the last one that went south on us. Unless you want to try and park this thing with bum gyros, you're gonna have to give me a while."

"Well, get a move on. Time is money."

Trouble laughed; he got three extra passes. The station was no more eager than Henry to have a ship with a bad gyro sidling up close where a sudden failure could mean a lot of bent metal and composites. While the *Loki* was station-keeping with the orbital base, Trouble finally got a brief glimpse of the ground-to-station tight beam. Very tight, and encrypted from the sound of it. *God, these guys are paranoid.*

By the time they docked, Trouble felt good. He had solid visual, electronic, and infrared scans. He might not have intercepted any message traffic, but he had a good handle on where the electric motors, hot sites, and surface disturbances were. As expected, there was a lot of agricultural land, most of it well to the north of the urban sprawl that was centered on a plateau in the southern hemisphere. Mineral extraction showed at a few scattered points, very few. The planet was early in its development and had few mountains. Didn't look like it had a lot of plate tectonic activity, nothing to stir the minerals from the core to the crust.

Just before docking, Trouble finally intercepted signals from two ships also on approach. They'd arrived by different jump points; this system had too many jump points for Trouble's taste. Too many sources for surprise.

"Unusual for them to be quiet so long," Hood advised him, "but the chatter sounds pretty normal now. One claims to have passengers from the core worlds. Other one says it's just cargo from around the rim."

"Cargo?" Trouble asked.

"That's what they say."

"We'll see."

The three extra orbits they'd taken meant that they would see. Captain Hood prided himself on getting in and out of ports fast, before a customs agent could get too interested in him. Riddle Station was small, maintaining about half a gee's worth of fake gravity. Cargo would be easy to move around; Trouble was assigned to help with it as soon as he'd made his first crack at getting past the firewall. Two minutes told him Tru's info war program was dead in its tracks.

Stopped there, Trouble slipped the second disk into his pocket and joined the other six hands moving cargo off as quickly as the captain wanted. The *Loki* was not a container ship. Still, Pier Two seemed designed for such small ships. The large cargo hatch to the *Loki*'s second hold was open, mated to a simple expansion tube from the station. A cable snaked down from the station, limp and curling in half a gee. The crew manhandled eight crates as tall and wide as a man and four times as long. Officially, they were full of miscellaneous high-value goods—videos, wines, other delicacies that couldn't be made locally. Trouble hadn't asked what they really had; some things were best left unknown. Each crate was shoved into a line at the hatch, one behind the other. Then the first one was hitched to the line.

"Trouble, Ken, and Hab, ride this one topside, take care of that half of the business," Hood ordered. "Trouble, you handle the manifest." That would get him up close to a computer he could feed Tru's second disk. The firewall had stopped him; could this disk break the encryption? Trouble and the other two rode the first crate up, hanging on to the central line.

In half a gee, it was easy to hop off, then capture the loose line that let them pull the container away from the hatch and toward a waiting collection of wheeled cradles. While the others bolted the container down, Trouble lowered the cable, then found the cargo computer and fed it Tru's disk. Central control acknowledged the info dump, verified that the weight of the first container matched the manifest, and cleared them to offload the rest of the cargo. They were not to put any cargo on the conveyor moving along the far wall of the concourse. "In use," he was advised. He activated Tru's first "war" program.

While the computer hummed and the next crate worked its way up, Trouble examined his surroundings. A large ship had docked just ahead of him at the next pier to his right. Several passenger elevators disgorged a mixed bag of travelers, who were motioned over to the single conveyor.

"You mean we have to use the cargo belt?" one disheveled passenger complained.

"Listen, Art, we're drawing double the pay we were. So we have to rough it a bit. It's only for three years. Relax, man."

"You said this place had everything. Open air, top service, good housing, even swimming pools. You better have this right."

"Trust me, Art. Have I ever done you wrong?"

Which left Trouble wondering who had done whom. That didn't sound like the kind of job and quarters the boss had been promising him and Ruth. Was somebody in for a surprise? Were there two levels of employment here? Interesting.

The first program gave a defeated beep. Trouble initiated the second, then went to handle the next container. Halfway through the fourth container, that one also beeped that it was whipped. As he finished processing that container, all the foot traffic from his right dried up. A docking horn went off to his left. The second ship was coming in.

Tru's final program was still trying, and he was pushing the last of the *Loki*'s containers around, when the dock to his left started disgorging passengers. No elevator for this bunch; they were dragged up a cargo chute, attached to a single cable. Like his containers, they were collected tightly in an area next to the conveyor. There were a lot of them, well over a hundred.

One of them was Ruth.

Trouble's gut went into free fall. The woman was filthy; the stink from the slave ship spread through the concourse. Still, her walk, the carriage of her shoulders, all of it fit just one woman . . . Ruth.

Shock turned to anger. *God damn it! Not again!*

Trouble fought emotions to keep his head down and push the last container while the other two pulled. *Observe and report back.* Son of a bitch, he didn't even have a sidearm on him. He was eyes today, he snapped at himself bitterly, not power projection. Hell of a situation.

The conveyor was moving now, bringing six containers toward Trouble. "Great, our cargo's right on time," Ken said happily as he got in place to snag the arriving canisters. Trouble joined him, keeping his back to Ruth except for the few furtive glances he couldn't help but cast her way, trying to see if it was her, hoping the next peek would show it wasn't.

It was her.

As soon as they had their cargo off the slide, the slaves were pushed and shoved onto it. Ruth flowed by him, her eyes downcast, her dirty face empty. It took everything Trouble had not to call out to her, do something to give her hope. *This won't last long, honey.*

He turned to the loading with a will. Ken stopped him. "Trouble, help me check this stuff before we stow it."

Together, the two of them broke the seal on the containers and looked inside. "Count them," Ken ordered. So Trouble climbed up on the lip of the container where he could see the tops of the metal Dewars and started counting.

"Fifty by my count. What's in them?"

"Money for us. Dreams for someone else."

Oh, shit, I'm shipping drugs. That spy was one big bastard.

"When we lift the containers, check the weight. We know what these things should weigh. They'd better."

"Right, boss," Trouble told Ken as he resealed the container. Ken sauntered off to check the contents of the rest with Hab. Trouble was weighing the first one when the slave ship disgorged its last passengers.

These two were freshly washed and well dressed. A short man had his arm around the waist of a tall blonde as they slowly made their way to the conveyor. Her high-pitched laugh carried through the concourse.

"We showed them, didn't we?"

"Yes, my dear, we did indeed. I think with us you have finally found your proper place. Ah, what lays before us." The slight emphasis on the "lay" spoke volumes to Trouble. The woman smiled down at her confident friend. Trouble studied her for a second, then turned away. *I've seen her before.* Not a lot. He had no name to go with the face. Still, he had met her. Since she was on the same ship that had carried Ruth, he searched his recollections of Hurtford Corner. He'd met so many people in such a short amount of time.

Public safety! That woman had helped him arrange the security for the dance. The dance he'd been kidnapped at. Hadn't the skipper mentioned someone in Hurtford's Office of Public Safety who had cleared all the questionable crews for mountain travel? Zylon something. Trouble kept his head down. He hadn't said anything to Ruth; he damn sure had nothing to say to this woman. Not yet. Not until he had a full assault team behind him. Then they'd talk. He smiled to himself.

The crew was just lifting the first container as the couple flowed by them on the conveyor. "What's the weight?" Ken called.

"One point three six kilos above tare," Trouble answered, looking up from his screen. Ken nodded. Behind him, the woman on the conveyor glanced at the work party, then ruffled her associate's thin crown of hair. "Yes, Big Al, I can't wait to see what kind of job your friends have waiting for me."

Trouble's heart skipped a beat as he snapped his eyes back to the numbers. They hadn't made eye contact; he was just one of several dockworkers. Right? She was looking forward to her new life, not to holdovers from the last one. He hoped.

As one container went into the ship, one of the arriving ones went onto the belt. Trouble was pretty sure that somewhere, someone was watching. Making sure all was exchanged per agreements. "Trusting lot," he murmured.

They were loading down the second-to-last container when Trouble saw his first evidence that people actually worked on the station. A thin, small man in a white shirt and black slacks came galloping up to Ken. "There's a discrepancy with one of your manifests. Your container is ten kilos short."

"That's not bloody likely," Ken snapped. "T, you weighed them on the lift out. Call up their weights for this man."

The hackles on the back of Trouble's neck rose for no apparent reason. Two men in blue jumpsuits, bags thrown over their backs, exited the passenger ship. They started walking down the concourse, going against the slide. Trouble called up the weights. "Hey, they're good matches. You have to double them to take into account the reduced 'gravity' here, but our cargo's the same as when we got it."

Now three spacers in ragtag civvies hustled out of the slaver, cutting a diagonal toward the slide. Trouble's alarm bells were ringing now. By his estimate, they'd arrive at the conveyor about where Ken was standing. Coincidence? *I don't believe in coincidence.*

The unhappy accountant waved his reader. "Number four weighed in light at my station. I got to talk to your captain."

Ken scowled as he hit his comm link. "Skipper, we got an accountant up here who doesn't like the weight of our cargo."

"I'll be there in a second."

A large man in a brown suit was now briskly walking down the slide. Trouble's quick analysis of trajectories put him, the two spacers, and the other three here no more than a second apart. What he'd give for the automatic he'd been ordered to leave behind. "If you get in trouble, you won't be able to shoot your way out of it," the spy had insisted. Maybe Trouble couldn't, but given the developing situation, he'd rather try than not.

Captain Hood was hoisted up about the time the brown suit arrived. "Hi, Captain, I'm Gunter Hammerman." He held out a beefy hand. "I need to discuss a matter with you."

"Always looking for new business," the skipper replied heartily, taking the hand and shaking it firmly. The five walkers arrived. They came to a halt, surrounding the *Loki*'s four men like crows on a fresh battlefield. From the far end of the conveyor, a half dozen men in gray coveralls were jogging toward them now. Trouble blinked as sweat ran into his eyes; the odds were bad and getting worse. He popped the disk; with no place to dump it, he slipped it into his back pocket.

"We wonder what business you may have taken on."

"Nothing that's eaten into your business," Hood assured him.

"Could I have all your people up here for a few minutes?"

"Sure, sure, no problem." Hood tapped his comm link. In a moment, captain and crew stood loose, waiting. About the same time, the station reinforcements arrived. Shock sticks were visible now; the two in the blue jumpsuits opened their bags and tossed automatic pistols to the other three spacers.

Hammerman glanced around the armed circle, smiling. "Now I believe we can hold a productive conversation. You," he said, pointing at Trouble. "What's your name?"

"Tordon," Trouble answered.

"When did you come aboard the *Loki*?"

"At Jacob's Folly."

"Ever been in the service?"

"Yeah. A marine before I got beached in the drawdown after we kicked you guys' butts. You want to hire someone who knows how to use a weapon, I'm your man." He grinned. "Sorry, Captain Hood, I appreciated the job, but if these guys want to use me in my real line of work, I'll have to take the job offer."

"Ah, yes, the force restructuring." The suit smiled, then shook it off. "Sorry, Lieutenant, but we have a witness who saw you very active recently on Hurtford Corner. Our organization feels you owe us a debt, and we always collect what is owed us."

A shock stick came up hard against Trouble's kidney. In agony, he folded to the deck. Somebody kicked him, though he hardly felt it over the first hit. A shock stick to the neck drove vision from his eyes. He tried to ball himself up, make the pain somehow smaller.

"Captain Hood, I am detaining you and your crew. Will you walk with me, or be carried like this poor fellow?"

"We're coming," "Whatever you say," and similar sounds came from the rest of the crew. None too gently, Trouble was kicked and rolled until he flopped onto the conveyor. The pain ate at him. He could fight it no more, and let himself sink into the many-colored darkness that beckoned.

Trouble came to under a glaring lamp. He was strapped to a chair. The brown suit and two big guys with shock sticks eyed him like hungry birds examining a worm. "Morning," Trouble croaked.

"It is still afternoon, Mr. Tordon. Time moves slowly when you are in my company. Why are you here, Lieutenant?"

"I needed a job. Hood offered me one. I took it." That was his cover story. Trouble saw no reason to change it. He doubted anything would make him change it up to and including death. *Always wondered how I'd handle this,* a distant part of him was muttering. Now he'd find out.

When he awoke the second time, the taste of blood filled his mouth. They'd tried both the new and old-fashioned tools available to modern torturers. He didn't recall telling them anything. The suit had taken his coat off sometime during the last session. He sat in a chair, facing the marine.

"Trouble. That is what they call you, isn't it?"

It hurt to move his lips; the marine nodded.

"Trouble, we hate to use up some of the paying customers' product, but for you, we're gonna. Forest here is going to give you a shot of the pure stuff. Then we're going to work you over again. We'd like your professional opinion. Does it really make the pain five times worse? Ten times? You be the judge."

A needle pricked his right shoulder. Trouble's racing heart counted off a long minute. Then they slapped him. Lightning shot through him; he could feel the pain in every nerve ending of his cheek. The next blow was to his stomach. The agony enveloped his entire body. He wanted to faint. He had to black out. The sheer pain should be enough.

It wasn't.

A very long time later, he resurfaced. His entire body screamed in newfound agony. It took him a moment to remember why. Right. The beating. During it, he'd forgotten who he was. Now he knew himself again, but the long beating was a distantly remembered thing. The aches left in his body reminded him. Oh, they reminded him.

"Want some more?" The suit's tie was now off, sleeves rolled up. With an effort, Trouble froze his body, neither showing nor denying the desire for another session. *How much longer before this kills me?*

"We almost lost you, Trouble. I don't know whether you have a bad heart, or just the drug and all." The suit switched his chair around and rested his arms on the tall back, his chin in his hands. "I've been thinking. I can keep this up until it kills you. You won't enjoy it, but what the hell. It won't hurt me." He waited, let the silence lengthen. Trouble refused to fill it; it hurt too much to move his lips. He kind of enjoyed the momentary rest. *I can listen as long as he can talk.*

The suit finally shook his head. "Why do I suspect that you are not going to tell me what I want?" He stood, pulled Trouble's disk from his pocket, and flipped it absently. "Just your being here told me a lot. Somebody is interested in us and wants to know more. You could be just freelancing, after that first taste of us. Maybe so. Are you just one man?"

A wave of nausea swept over Trouble. He leaned over, tried to empty his gut. Nothing came.

"I guess it doesn't matter. You and the rest of the crew of the good ship *Loki* are just going to disappear. No one will know how or why. We'll keep our eyes open for anyone coming after you. Make them disappear, too. This doesn't have to go on forever, just long enough for us to get what we want and go legit. All we need is time, and your being here, marine, has bought us some of that time."

The suit collected his coat and tie. At the door he paused. "Besides, waste not, want not. You're worth money to me, mister. At least for a while. I figure you'll last six, maybe nine months. Work is work. Enjoy."

The suit left. One big guy collected their gear; the other headed for the door. "Hey, guards, move this one to the farm. We'll make it easy on you."

The equipment fellow placed his shock stick at the base of Trouble's skull and held it there. As he screamed, the marine's world sank into many shades of black.

Trouble came to very slowly the next time. He was bouncing around, in a truck maybe, on a rough road. Each jostle sent waves of red and yellow pain shooting through him. He groaned.

"It's okay, T," Ken's voice softly assured him.

He lay on a truck bed. The rest of the *Loki*'s crew was with him. No, not everyone. "Where's the captain?" Just asking made his lips crack, his mouth fill with fresh blood.

"Bad heart," Ken said.

"Why wouldn't he tell them something?" Hub whined. "Anything."

"Do you think that would have gotten us anywhere?" Ken shot back. "We knew we were dealing with crazies when we took the job. Damn, I just wish I'd skipped after the last payoff. You mess with drug bosses, and you gotta expect weird."

Hub just whimpered. Apparently Hood had been smart to tell them nothing. The truck was sealed, leaving no way to look out. Trouble saw no benefit to struggling at the moment. If he or the captain had cracked under interrogation, he wouldn't be going off to wherever they were headed. *Hell, at least I'm riding this time.* Trouble let himself drift. Despite every cell in his body aching, maybe he could sleep. It had to be better than being awake.

TEN

IZZY WAS BEGINNING to enjoy these meetings between her division heads and the yard foreman overseeing the overhaul work. Even a veteran meeting-hater could enjoy ones where everything went smoothly and everyone liked what was happening and who was doing it. *Yes, I can take meetings like these more often.*

Except then, the work wouldn't get done.

"So, Engineering, any problems?"

If Buddha could be bothered, that was the look on Vu's face as he leaned forward in his chair. "Regretfully, yes."

Quickly, the chief engineer went over the basic problem with all the cruisers converted from prewar merchant ships. The ships had two fusion reactors—the original ship's and a second one, which was a slightly modified version of a surface-based power plant. On planets, the reactors were installed in groups of four. The Navy had quickly discovered that power production from a single unit tended occasionally, for only nanoseconds, to be unstable. No matter how brief the instabilities, they tended to create very spectacular explosions. "As we told you, Captain, both I and Mr. Oberstein believed we had a way around it."

"We also converted cargo ships during the last war," the yard man said, taking up the report. "Out on the rim, our power needs were smaller, so our converts had three small reactors to your one big one. However, it appeared to me that the real problem was in the installation and calibration."

Izzy wished they'd get to the point. She and Guns had agreed that it would be great if they could draw on both reactors for whatever they needed—more guns, more speed, more whatever. As it was, the original reactor was limited to propulsion and maintaining the fusion containment fields. Weapons and general ship's services took some spectacular power hits in the normal course of business. "I take it that your ideas aren't working out," she cut them off.

"It appears that the new software will not do what we had hoped." Vu agreed.

"So we fall back on the original software," Izzy concluded.

Mr. Oberstein cleared his throat. "Unfortunately, the new hardware will not work with the old software configuration."

"Can we reinstall the old hardware?" Izzy asked hopefully.

"No, ma'am." Vu answered. "The old equipment was close to failure as it was. I am afraid just the act of removing it reduced it to scrap."

Izzy drummed her fingers on the table, then forced herself to immobility. "Gentlemen, I agree we have a problem. How did you solve this with that other cruiser, the *Sheffield*?"

"The chief engineer of the *Second Chance* refused to let us do anything but medium-level maintenance. He liked the configuration he had," Oberstein assured her.

"Chips, can you help these people with their software?"

"Yes, ma'am."

"Vu, Oberstein, if you need anything, let me know. The *Patton*'s going nowhere without its engines. You are now the critical path. I don't want to tell Trouble when he gets back here that we've got to delay going after the girl he's

sweet on and who is somebody's slave just because your up-
grade turned into a downgrade. Understood?"

"Yes, ma'am"'s came quickly from around the table.

"I sure as hell don't want to tell a marine that he's got to
sit on his hands cause the Navy can't get off theirs. All right,
folks, let's get back to work." Izzy sent them on their way.
It would be another week before Trouble got back. He'd
have two weeks to convert his recon into a full assault plan.
As soon as he found out Ruth was down there, she'd probably have to weld his boots to the deck to keep him from immediately charging off after her. She'd about had to get the
welding arc out to keep Joe under control. No, the *Patton*
had to be ready to lift on time. It had to be.

The truck screeched to a halt. The locked plastic hood covering its bed was flung open, turning oppressive hot darkness into sweltering heat under a muddy gray sky. "Okay,
out of the truck," shouted the shorter of two guards who
looked to be in a lousy mood. The erstwhile crew of the *Loki*
struggled on unsteady legs to follow orders. Ken helped
Trouble.

He stood in a muddy compound with prefab barracks to
his right and a rough collection of workshops, barns, and
other buildings to his left. Behind him, five or six freshly
painted houses formed a small court next to the one road
out.

Ahead of Trouble, separated from him by a chain-link
fence, were endless fields planted with row upon row of
bushy vegetation. Scattered clumps of men were bent
over, hoeing around plants ranging from small as twigs to
chest-high. Others harvested several rows as tall as themselves.

"Take a good look. That's what you're here for. Now,
over to the sheds with you." A whip of rawhide got their attention. It flicked across Hub's back; the poor man cringed.
For a second, Trouble feared Hub would just collapse in
place, but he managed to move with the rest toward the
pointed-out shed. Legions of insects, most of them species

unknown to Trouble, joined them in the trudge; the slaves swatted more than they walked. The whip cracked, hustling them on.

In the steaming shadows of the shed, the smell of raw plastic and hot metal replaced the stench of raw sewage and standing water. A man greeted them with a half-toothless smile and handfuls of animal control pods. "Some of you may recognize these goodies. Some people put them around folks' waists where they can get your attention in a lot of different ways, from stomachaches to knocking you out. We figure we got your attention." He stepped forward and slipped two around Ken's neck, tightened a thin collar, then reached for Trouble. "You feel a tingle, listen real good. Cause you won't feel nothing next. You'll be dead."

Trouble gulped as two pods nestled down beside his spine. "Understood," he said.

"All you better understand," the short man snapped his whip. "You make us any trouble, there's plenty more where you came from. Work and you live. Become a problem, and we'll solve you real quick."

Once everyone was necklaced, their next stop was a barracks. Tiers of green plastic bunks, three high, stretched in rows on both sides of an aisle. There were no mattresses, no blankets, no cloth of any kind. Muddy plastic bunks stood on muddy brown floors. The windows were open; insects were everywhere.

"Can we have bug netting, or something?" Ken asked.

"Don't worry nothing about the bugs. They don't carry nothing that can kill you. Just make sure your bug bites don't get infected from the muck." The taller guard looked them over. "Some of you look like you tripped over your own feet a lot. Check with the medic once she comes in off the fields. An open sore can make you too sick to work. No work, no food. You don't want to miss one of our delicious meals."

Both guards laughed at that, then left.

"Hey, we got showers!" Hub shouted from the back of the

barracks. Trouble knew Unity prefabs had a latrine in the rear. The crew crowded around the entrance to the latrine as Hub turned on the water. It came out weak and brown. He twisted the hot water handle as far as it would go and stuck his hand under the resulting trickle. "Cold."

"Cold!" Ken started for the water stream.

"Not cold, puke warm," Hub answered. He washed his hands in the lazy flow, then shook them. "Dirtier than when I started."

They returned to the open bay and collapsed into bunks. "Wonder how long the work day is?" Hub asked the torrid air.

"I suspect we better enjoy this rest," Trouble muttered. "I doubt we get much time off."

"What made you such a bloody optimist?" Hub whined. "Maybe it won't be so bad. I mean, we ain't slaves. We ain't prisoners. We ain't been convicted of nothing."

Trouble lay back on the plastic bunk, leaving it to someone else to set Hub straight. Nobody did. Like a good soldier, Trouble took the opportunity to take a nap.

"Hey, if you new guys want something to eat, you better get out here quick," came from a nearly naked man standing in the doorway of the barracks, a bowl in one hand, a biscuit in the other. Quickly the *Loki*'s crew emptied the barracks; with his muscles cramped and screaming, Trouble hobbled up to the end of the line. Slowly, the line moved to where a stack of bowls waited. A dispenser on the side of the barracks sloshed a thin gruel into the bowl, and a biscuit dropped from the box next to it. One per customer.

"You're new guys." A big hulk of a man confronted the eight from the *Loki*. "You ain't hungry. Gimme your biscuits."

Hub was about to hand his over. Trouble gave his bowl and bread to Ken. "Hold these for a moment. There must be one of these in every crowd." He turned to the big guy. "Sorry, but they didn't feed us at all where we came from."

"No work, no eat," the guy growled. He stuffed his biscuit

in his mouth, followed it with the last of his gruel, then flung the bowl hard at Trouble's head. The marine bent to the left, and the heavy dish flew past him. He sidestepped to the right as the big jerk charged; Trouble gave him enough gentle encouragement to send him sprawling into a muddy puddle. Seeing no point in prolonging the fight, Trouble stepped in with a blow to the man's spine, then a chop to his neck. The jerk went limp with a groan. Since his nose was out of the water, Trouble left him where he fell, retrieved his meal, and started eating it slowly.

"Thanks," Ken said. Even Hub muttered something.

"Oh-oh, you're in trouble now, slick."

Trouble looked at the speaker. A scarecrow of a man, he pointed toward the good housing at the other end of the compound. A woman stood on the balcony of the largest house, dressed in something slinky, more appropriate for a ball than the end of the work day. She said something to the man next to her. He nodded and left.

"Who's she?"

"The boss woman. New gal, just been here a couple of days. She figures she owns us, body and soul," another man in a breechcloth answered. This one was more filled out and carried himself like he still wore a three-piece suit. He set his bowl into the washer and turned to Trouble. "I'm Tom Gabon."

"Know your brother," the marine said, offering his hand.

"Stan? You Navy?" The guy's eyes lit up.

"Not at the moment." The marine shrugged. "They call me Trouble."

"Looks like you've been in a lot of it. You better have someone take care of those open wounds. Our new medic should be done eating by now. I'll show you the dispensary."

"Stan said you were due to testify for something. Then you left." *Is this the man who knew too much?*

"Yeah, who wants to talk to a Senate hearing when you have a job offer too good to be true?" Tom glanced around. "Didn't quite work out like I expected."

Tom led Trouble to the clinic, such as it was, among the

work sheds. The door was ajar. "Is the doctor in?" Tom called softly.

"No doctor in sight, but the witch has got her cauldron boiling," came a familiar voice.

"Ruth," Trouble breathed.

The door flew open. "Trouble! What are you doing here?"

"Trying not to track mud into your hospital." He gave her one of his crooked smiles. It hurt.

"Better you don't drip blood all over the place." She pulled him into her aid station, grabbed a wad of cotton, dabbed alcohol on it, and started working over his face.

"I saw you on the station," Trouble said, trying not to wince. "Did you see me?"

"Yeah, but I didn't show it. They catch you because of me?" Ruth turned pale under the mud that seemed to cake everyone.

"No. Someone else from Hurtford. A woman."

"Zylon. That bitch. I saw her on the ship out to here. A lot of people wanted to talk to her back home, but she got away and took about forty of us with her, just to make her point. Whatever that is. She even bragged to us before their ship picked us up. Damn, that woman's crazy." Ruth glanced out the door. "She's also our new boss."

"I thought the woman on the balcony looked familiar."

"Yeah." Ruth started working down from his face. He opened his jumpsuit. "Trouble, who beat you up this time?"

"Some of the best. Got anything to help?"

"Nothing for the aches. The guards have their own painkillers, though I sew them up after their nightly brawls."

"How do we get out of here?" The raw whisper of the words that had been clawing to get out of his throat escaped him.

"You don't." Ruth tapped his control pods. "That necklace is ceramic composite. Nothing here is going to cut it. You wander beyond the planted area, and you're dead."

"There are things out there big and nasty," Tom added. "When they bring the bodies back, they've been chewed and clawed up something horrible."

"I didn't think we could eat the local stuff, or it eat us," Ruth said.

"Most of it, we can't," Tom answered. "But that doesn't keep some of them from trying."

"How do we get off a message?" Trouble tossed out the fallback option.

"We can't do that either," Ruth answered.

Tom nodded in agreement. "Guards have the only radios, and they're very short-ranged. One of the guys in my work group was the network manager who laid this whole planet out. They used fiber optics for everything. Kept radios to the minimum."

Trouble scowled. "Explains why this planet was so silent when I tried listening to it. There's got to be some spare transmitters besides the guards. Tractors, trucks?"

"My tractor has a GPS receiver, but no transmitter. There are no trucks on the compound."

"Zylon has spare wrist systems," Tom added after a pause. "She didn't like the way a silver one looked with her red ensemble last night. She switched to gold. There must have been a dozen units, made up to look like jewelry."

"How can we get our hands on them?" the marine asked.

Tom turned away. "They're in her bedroom. Gida, the overseer before her, had kind of adopted me. She wanted to get ahead in this business. I was her teacher, sort of a MBA bed-warmer. I guess she passed that along to Zylon. She had me in the last two nights. Business and pleasure in one neat package." He glanced back to them, a helpless twist to his empty smile.

"Before Gida, I never thought a woman could rape a man. Zylon . . ." He shook his head. His back was raked with long claw marks. "There's something wrong with that woman."

"Think you could lift one of her wrist units for a day?" Trouble asked. "We could modify it, use Ruth's tractor to power it up, jack up its range."

"For what?" Ruth asked as Trouble zipped up his suit now that she was done dabbing sealant on all his abrasions and contusions. "Where would we send the message?"

"Security is never perfect, or so a friend of mine insists. Tom, you get me the guy who designed the system and a transmitter, and we'll figure out a place to patch into it."

"You are Navy." Tom eyed him hard, maybe almost hopefully.

"And the Navy looks after its own," Ruth quoted.

"Hey, you in there!" A rough voice from the outside cut them off.

"Damn, it that time already?" Tom muttered as he opened the door. "You hunting for me?"

"Naw. She wants the new guy. Tordon, you in there?"

In the cramped quarters of the clinic, Trouble was face to face with Ruth. Her nostrils flared as she took an involuntary step back from him. Without thought, he reached for her and pulled her close. In her ear he whispered, "Hang together. I'll have something for you when I get back."

She nodded as he turned. Her arm held his, trailing out to fall only when he was out of reach. "Be careful" was the last he heard from her.

"I'm Tordon," he said, stepping past Tom.

"Come with me." The fellow leered. Trouble followed him through the compound to the largest of the houses on the square. An open showerhead sprouted from one side. Trouble was ordered to "Strip, and get the mud off ya."

He did. The warm spray washed the aches from his abused muscles, the oil and dirt from his hair and body. Except for where he knew he was headed, he might have enjoyed it. The power of the spray wore away the ointment Ruth had put on his cuts; several began to bleed again. At the order to "Hurry up," he switched to cold water and felt cool for the first time in a week. He turned from the shower to find no towel . . . and his jumpsuit and boots had been kicked aside.

"Follow me." Trouble did, padding along, dripping and naked. On the veranda of several of the smaller houses, guards lounged, bottles in hand. "New meat for the old lady" was the least of the catcalls he got. "Maybe this one'll be good enough to live through the night" didn't match with

Tom's claim to being a regular. The strategist in Trouble evaluated the prospects and options available to him, even as the man in him was hit hard by humiliation and degradation.

His options were few. Be stubborn and die, or do what was wanted of him, exactly as it was wanted, no matter what the cost, and maybe he'd live. Maybe he'd walk out of here with a transmitter. The tough combat marine in Trouble wanted to fight. The man in him wanted to kill someone, wipe out this shame. The officer in him knew payback time would come later, but only if he did this right. The man who loved Ruth would do anything he had to to save her from a night like this with the guards. As the guard led Trouble up the central stairs of the big house, he bowed his head, took a deep breath, and swore to do whatever he had to do—for Ruth, and for revenge.

Zylon Plovdic liked what she saw in the mirror. No more of Hurtford's make-do. She was making it *her* way. Removing the wrist unit that had matched today's outfit, she searched in her jewelry box for one to match tonight's ensemble. The jet-black "living leather" pants and mesh top needed something chrome and black. As befitted a station director, she had plenty to choose from. She smiled; a station director managing four subordinate supervisors, thirty-two employees, and almost two hundred "volunteers." Big Al said it was just a start. The last woman had been boss here over a year. Zylon wouldn't need that long; what was her name, Ruth, right, she knew how to run a farm. Zylon would double production in a lot less than a year.

With a happy smile, she strapped an ebony-and-silver comm unit onto her left wrist, then found a matching holder and slipped it around her right hand. Kick should be here any moment with the controller. There was a knock at her door.

"Yes?" she answered sharply.

"I got what you asked for."

"Come in."

Kick opened the door. He handed her the control pod; she quickly slipped it into her palm holder. The naked man entered, his head low, his eyes darting like those of some cornered animal—or some virgin girl. Zylon tapped the unit in her hand. A tremor shook the man from head to toe. "Everything is working fine, Kick. Thank you." She smiled at her deputy.

With a curt nod, he closed the door.

Zylon studied the man. Tall, light skinned, close-cropped hair. He had everything a man should have, though disappointingly limp at the moment.

"You're Tordon. You were on Hurtford Corner a while back."

Head bowed, his eyes came up to meet hers. "Yes, ma'am."

"You caused me a lot of trouble."

"I imagine from your perspective, I did."

Zylon tapped the controller, held it. The man fell to his knees, his hands helplessly grasping at the pods on his neck. Zylon wondered how long it would take it to kill a man, what he would look like, how he would scream. She might find out tonight. But not yet. This guy had disrupted too much of her life to die quickly. "Is there any other perspective? Besides mine?"

Tordon collapsed on the floor, like a naked savage worshiping his goddess. Zylon liked that image; she let it play in her mind while he groaned. With a well-manicured toe, she tapped him. "Is there?"

"No, ma'am."

"Stand up." He struggled to his feet.

"Hold me." There was fright in his eyes as he put his arms around her. She rested her body against him. There was blood on his chest from a cut; she nuzzled closer, licked him. The coppery taste pleased her. She began stroking his back; he followed suit. She raked him with her nails. He flinched but kept up a slow, gentle massage that left her wanting to purr. She didn't want to purr tonight. She wanted to scream in ecstacy, watch him scream in agony.

She stepped away from him, sat on the edge of the bed, enjoying the feel of silk sheets through the skintight slacks. "Come, take off my boots," she ordered.

He came, knelt before her. So submissive, she wanted to kick him. She did. He started to dodge, then froze. The spikes of her high heels caught his arm. More blood. The night was getting better.

"Take my boots off slowly. Gently. Pleasurably," she whispered. There was fire behind his eyes, but he nodded submissively. *What's driving this man? My controller? His fear of death?* The thoughts excited her as he reached for her boots. His fingers played along her legs, pleasurably. She moaned softly as his fingers massaged and delighted.

Yes, this one knows his place. She'd had another who thought her outfit was a come-on. That she was here for him. It had been a joy, using the controller over and over, until he got the message who was boss here. He hadn't been much use by that time. This one was a fast learner.

"Now take my pants off."

His hands slowly flowed up her flanks, gently undid each fastener that held them in place. His fingers wandered, the living leather transmitting their touch wide over her body. Her inner thighs warmed when a wandering hand passed quickly over them as they searched for her belt. *Damn, I may keep this guy around.*

She reached for him. He was still small in her hand. "What's the matter with you? You like boys or something? Maybe I should have a couple of the foremen in here."

That brought fear to his eyes when the controller had only brought pain. "I'm not wasting it until you want it," he answered her, maybe a tad too quickly. She'd have to consider keeping Kick here the next time she had this one in. Kick did have a way of getting his kicks.

Her pants were off; she leaned back on the bed. "Kiss me," she ordered, tapping the controller. He didn't flinch this time. He also didn't ask where she wanted his kisses. He guessed right.

Much later, she came slowly awake. His slow ministrations to her afterglow had ceased. She rolled over. He was halfway to the door. His night vision must be bad; he was headed for the wall next to her dresser, not the door. "Leaving so soon?" she snapped. His back dripped blood; she'd gotten him good. Without a word, he turned back. Bite marks on his shoulders and chest showed red against his pale skin. *Yep, it had been a fun night.*

He returned to the bed, and the slow, long, strokes that had soothed and relaxed her for sleep. She rolled over, away from him. "I'm cold. Pull up a sheet."

He obeyed. This was good. This was what a woman like her deserved. She kept her finger on the controller as she slowly fell asleep.

Back and forth, slowly, slowly, Trouble worked his hand along her back, trying to relax her, not wanting to excite her again tonight. Dear God, no! He struggled to slow his heart, slow his breathing, become nothing but a hand. He'd already been nothing but a slab of meat. His fingers twitched, wanting to grab the sleeping woman's neck. Choke the life out of her. The sensitivity trainer had said abused women went through these feelings. He never thought a man could.

Used, degraded, nothing but meat on demand. He wanted to shake her, scream "I'm me. I'm a man."

Slowly the hand worked its way down the back covered by the silk sheet. Her breath slowed; he slowed his with her. He had to put her to sleep before he fell asleep himself. Whatever happened, he did not want to be here tomorrow when she awoke.

If he fell asleep, he'd miss his chance to rummage through her jewelry box, lift a comm unit. He bit his lip and used the pain to keep himself awake as she drowsed. The taste of blood came again. She'd bit his lips. He'd been scared she would bite his tongue. How did you have sex with someone who scared you to death? How could a woman do it? He'd heard women could fake it. He couldn't, but somehow he'd dredged up enough to satisfy her.

This time he was sure she was asleep, well asleep, before

he risked rising from her bed. Listening to each slow breath, he walked toward the dresser—freezing in place when she moved in her sleep. It was too dark to make out any colors in the jewelry box; he selected a bracelet from the back. Holding it close to his eyes, he made sure it had a vid and speaker. Palming his prize, he sidestepped to the door. As he let himself out, he gave her one more glance. In the light from the court, she slept.

Between the houses and the barracks a guard sat, half or more asleep. The comm unit was in Trouble's left hand; he edged to the right of the guard. The guard came awake as he passed.

"She kept you a while. Let me see your collar."

Trouble stood while the man ran a scanner over his control pods. "She marked you up good. Better check into the clinic afore you get what little sleep you can." Half asleep, the guard almost sounded human. Then, as Trouble passed him, the guard kicked him. Trouble held tight to his prize as he stumbled, but held his balance. The guard laughed, watching Trouble as he headed for Ruth and meds.

There was a dim light on in the clinic. He tapped on the door; it opened to his touch. Ruth sat on the one bunk; Tom and a short, wiry man squatted on the floor.

Both men were in breechcloths; Trouble was swept by a wave of shame and revulsion at his own nakedness, vulnerability.

"Did you get it?" Tom whispered. Trouble held up his hand and let his prize dangle.

"Bought and paid for."

"You look like you've been through a meat grinder," Ruth said, coming forward with a tray of cotton, cleansers and ointment.

"Not a bad way of putting it," Trouble agreed as the stranger took the comm unit to study under a covered lamp and Ruth directed him to a small stool.

"What do you make of it, Steve?" Tom asked the short guy.

"We can jack it into the tractor's receiver, use its antenna.

The GPS satellite will accept a message. Every satellite's got to send and receive maintenance checks, updates, and the likes. The Surveyor 2000+ series is no different from the rest . . . if I remember the codes for that puppy." Steve headed for the clinic's tiny diagnostic unit.

"You mean we could have sent a message out anytime?" Tom was incredulous.

"You got anybody you want to send a letter to? 'Help, I'm being held hostage on a drug farm.' Right; who do we know who'd pay attention to you or me? Now, Trouble here . . ."

"Who do we send to?" Tom asked.

"Wardhaven, Minister of Science and Technology. Copy to HSS *Patton*."

"I can do that," Steve mumbled as he typed. "What do we say?"

"That I'll be a bit late for dinner," Trouble suggested.

"She really tore you up," Ruth whispered through teeth gritted almost as tightly as Trouble's.

"I'm the one getting alcohol poured in his claw marks. Why are you gritting your teeth?" Trouble hissed at the pain.

"'Cause it hurts me to hurt you. I mean, if you feel anything, you've got to feel with people. How she can do this and that at the same time? How you fellows can . . . and . . ."

Ruth looked close to tears.

He reached for her, held her at arm's length. "I tried not to think of where I was or her. I thought of someone I'd rather be with."

"Who?" came at him so fast he forgot to dodge.

"You." She had refused to meet his eyes. She'd been staring straight down. Now, what had been so quiet was stirring straight back at her. She looked up at him, a hint of her old smile on her face.

"I think I believe you."

"Guys, can I get something to wear?"

"Turn around. Let me get your back," Ruth ordered.

"We'll get you something at the bunkhouse," Tom answered distractedly.

"Trouble, you notice any defense blisters on the station?" Steve was typing away. "It was ordered as a standard T-3-a."

The marine closed his eyes, tried to remember the approach to the station. "Couple of bumps that didn't belong. Say five or six to a side. Probably four times that, all told."

"Okay. Standard set of three Meteorology 6112 weather satellites, Global Positioning System had twenty-four Surveyor 2000+ satellites in low orbit, and there are four repeaters in high stationary orbit to keep the station and Richman City in contact. We bought them straight off the shelf from TRW, but there were suggestions of adding encoders to them before I got the boot," Steve answered. "Bet you didn't get past the firewall or crack the encryption."

"You can tell them that," Trouble growled. "I also didn't get anything on the ground layout."

"Don't worry." Steve smiled. "Couple of us have been here almost from the get-go. I knew they were using the farms for a dumping ground for folks who knew too much and couldn't be trusted close to high-tech gear. I just never figured I'd end up here."

"Pass that along, Steve. If they drop teams on these farms, we could put together a good map of our target even if we can't get into the central map for this shit hole."

"Got it. Message is three K. Ruth, you should be able to send it to a couple dozen satellites. Where's your tractor?"

"In the shed. Tom knows where it is."

The two slipped out into the night, leaving Trouble alone with Ruth. "You okay?" he asked her.

"I'm fine. They need me. Can you imagine? They're trying to run a farm with a bunch of fools that never even held a hoe before they got here. Not just you poor volunteers, but the guards. They know how to crack a whip or thumb a controller button, but they don't know a thing about growing things."

"I remember career development trainers telling me anyone who can manage something can manage anything." Trouble snorted. "Like they pulled Izzy out of commanding defense brigades and gave her a ship. She is managing it okay."

"Well, these folks aren't. They'd never done a soil analysis. They were dumping processed sewage from the city's system and calling that soil preparation. I demanded a soil analysis kit. They had them in the warehouse, but nobody knew how to use one, so they just sat there taking up space. This soil is weak on iron, calcium, phosphates, and a dozen other nutrients. I told them to let me spray the fields, and I'll double the crop yield."

Trouble didn't tell her what she was growing. "You aren't wearing a collar." He fingered his own.

She gave him a look of wounded pride. "I'm no volunteer. I'm an employee. I get paid. Got a labor contract with a signature on it that almost looks like mine. In six years I can go home." Suddenly she got very serious. "That worries me, Trouble. These crooks think they'll have Hurtford Corner working just like this before my contract is up. Could they do that?"

Trouble thought about that while Ruth put sealant on him again, something to keep nasty microbes out and his blood in. "Farms can't afford to lose too many hands. Then there's the problem with the mining contracts. I wouldn't swear they couldn't, but I'll damn sure do what I can to see they don't."

A few moments later, she finished. "You better get some sleep," she suggested.

He stood. She was so close. He reached for her, brought her into his arms and kissed her, first tentatively, gently. Her response was fire on his lips. He let himself sink into the kiss, and the love beneath it. His lips were bleeding again, but it didn't matter. Ruth's kiss cleansed him of the foulness he'd struggled to swim against that night.

Maybe he could have had more. Maybe he should have. But he stank of Zylon sex. Ruth had only washed his back and chest. He broke from the kiss. "I'll try to get some sleep."

• • •

"What do you mean, you can't stabilize the plasma?" Izzy wasn't shouting. Not quite.

"It's a software problem," Vu assured her. "There is nothing wrong with the engines."

"But we don't leave the pier without stable plasma, do we, Lieutenant Commander?"

"No, Captain. We do not." The quiet man wilted under her heated gaze.

"Surely the *Patton* is not the first ship to stabilize plasma," she said, turning on the yard man.

"Yes, ma'am. However, there are slight variations between systems. Software handles those problems. Humanity software and Unity software handled it differently."

"You worked on a Humanity cruiser before," she shot back.

"Yes, ma'am, but the chief engineer limited us to low-level maintenance."

"Surely you made a backup of his operating system files."

"We did, ma'am."

"Then load it."

"I cannot recommend that. We suspect there may have been a bomb buried somewhere in that software. The ship vanished on its first jump."

"Oh, shit!" Such language was not expected of a captain. However, there was a limit to how much a captain could take. The crew better know their captain was way past that. At least, that's what Izzy told herself. She sat back in her chair, rubbed her eyes, took twenty or thirty deep breaths, then came back at the problem from another direction.

"The *Patton* is not the only ship in her class. Call the nearest Navy yard for a set of the standard software."

"We can't do that, ma'am."

Izzy shot to her feet. "And why not?"

The yard man gulped, then started his explanation slowly. "The power control system you brought in on the *Patton* was near failure. We reduced it to junk by the simple process of removing it. The system we installed is similar to that we found on the *Sheffield*; however, it had been modified by its crew outside the standard Navy configuration. We have a call in to Pitt's Hope, where the actual work was done. They are checking their records, but there was a war on, and people were more interested in operational warships than taking time to document how they got operational."

Izzy sat back down. "Chips, is there anything more we can do to support engineering?"

"No, ma'am. They've got three-quarters of my analysts and code writers."

"And Wardhaven has sent us up almost a hundred specialists to help," the yard man assured her. "We are doing all we can."

"You better, 'cause a marine's going to come charging in here any minute. And he won't take this nearly as nicely as I am."

"Yes, ma'am."

Trouble rejoined the living when a guard whacked him on the soles of his feet well before the sun was up. Tom tossed him a breechcloth, and he pulled it on. In the weak predawn light, he gobbled down a breakfast no different from supper. Still hungry, he joined a line of men at the end of the compound taking hoes from racks. He found himself next to Tom and Steve, or maybe they collected him like a stray puppy. Anyway, he ended up assigned to work with them.

"Is it like this every day?" Trouble asked, sweat dripping into his eyes after only five minutes of hoeing weeds.

"Is it like this every day?" Tom repeated to Steve. "You've been here longer than I have."

"Naw." Steve nodded his head. "Some days it's a lot worse. I mean, it's not hailing. There's no hurricane blowing through. Hell, the guard stayed up all night playing poker and must have won. He just wants to find some shade to nap in, not take his losses out on us. Nope, guys, today is a good day."

"You leave me seeds for hope." Trouble scowled, and

swatted at a bug only slightly smaller than a destroyer. "Do these things ever leave you alone?"

"Depends," Steve informed him. Picking an ugly green worm from one of the drug bushes, he smashed it on his left elbow and smeared the sickening fluids along his arm. "Stinks to high heaven, but the stuff that passes for insects don't like the smell either. The little beggars don't really benefit from sucking your blood. Well, maybe they like the salt. But the sores they make can get infected from the shit we're walking in. Smell or die. Which you want?"

Trouble plucked a ugly thing from the bush next to him and put it on his arm.

"No, don't squash it. That's one we eat."

"Eat?"

"Not too many of them, or they'll tear your stomach apart. But a few."

"Eat it." Trouble studied the thing. It was darker than the first, and it left a trail of slime as it flowed up his arm.

"Breakfast, you remember that pause that didn't refresh?" Tom took over from Steve. "There's not enough in the two meals they feed us to keep us alive. If you don't live off the land, you don't live."

"Anybody try eating the plants?" Trouble put the slug in his mouth and swallowed it fast. He choked, but got it down.

"You don't want to go there. Chew the leaves, and they take away your hunger; then they take away your mind and your will to live. Don't touch the plants—and that's not just because the whip gets applied if they catch you. Don't start chewing leaf until you're ready to die."

"Has anybody gotten out of here?" Trouble had to ask the question. Hopefully that message would get them out. Then again, a good marine always had a fallback position.

"I've been here for six months," Steve answered. "Never saw anybody leave any way but feet first. They bury us where they're going to put in a new field." He paused. "We're probably working somebody's grave today."

"Who are we? How did they get us? Slave labor is stupid. Paid workers are always more productive. History shows it." Trouble knew he was sounding like some ivory-tower professor, but damn it, it was true.

"Some are the crews of the freighters captured by pirates. Can't exactly turn them loose to write home. Some are ex-Unity troopers who didn't read their new employment contract very well, though lots of them end up as guards. Some are street people they lifted off one of the developed planets like Earth, though they don't survive too long. Some are like Tom here, a manager who knew too much and is the whispered rumor that will keep others in line. Me, I knew I was working for some bad actors, but I figured I could get my money and run. What I didn't count on was a hostile takeover by an even worse bunch. The pirating, the slaving, all started after the war. We have some really bad hombres calling the shots now."

Trouble found another green bug and smeared it over his face and neck. It stank, but the insects did leave him alone. He kept on hoeing weeds. They were mostly Earth weeds, and they were growing . . . like weeds. "How'd you get here, Tom? Stan's worried sick about you."

"He always was too damn straight to make a living," Tom sighed. "Navy's probably best for him. Me, I got just far enough up the ladder to know too much, and not far enough to know what was really happening. Some senator got my name and thought I knew how corporations were running Unity during the war. Hell, we weren't running them." He paused, picked up a slug, and ate it. "I don't know. Maybe some people thought we were. Maybe they were. Hell, from where I sat, you couldn't tell. Maybe we did have more contacts across the battle lines than a general or admiral would want, but, damn it, the war wasn't going on forever. You have to position yourself for the next economic wave. That's all we were doing."

"You look pretty well positioned." Trouble gave him a toothsome grin.

"Tell me about it. I was coming out here to run an agricultural implements line, production, distribution, sales and service. Our company was one of the thirteen that had a seat on the planetary governing council. It was a big promotion. So I left a week before my scheduled hearing appearance. Let them come out here and find me."

"Doubt they'd find you here." Steve laughed bitterly.

"Yeah, I walked off the ship to a welcoming committee of the other council members. First elevator I come to, I'm stuffed in it, drugged, and I wake up naked in the barracks."

"Quite a comedown" was all Trouble could think to say, punctuated with "God, it's hot."

Steve eyed the sky. "Not even noon, laddie. Better get used to it."

Tom snorted. "Now let me talk to those senators and I'll have a story for them. You know, with this happening, I'm starting to think the worst rumors were right. Maybe we were running Unity."

"We'll just have to get you there" was Trouble's promise.

The guards herded them in maybe an hour before sunset. After they'd finished their slop, Tom took Trouble over to the dispensary, ostensibly to have cuts checked for infection.

As Ruth worked on his wounds, she reported on her day. "Every time I checked in with the GPS, I sent the message. Every satellite up there must have it in its buffer. How long will it take to get where it's going?"

"Your guess is as good as mine." Trouble shrugged, and winced as he shrugged right into Ruth's finger. "Depends on whether Steve knows as much about the inner workings of the surveyor system as the comm system at the station." Trouble stood in silence while Ruth finished tending to him. "How we going to get this thing back in Ms. de Sade's jewelry box?"

"That depends on who gets called in tonight."

"You in there?" came Kick's growl from outside.

"I am," Tom said.

"She wants to talk to you. She's excited about some damn fool idea to get more work out of you guys."

Tom dropped the bracelet into the back of his breechcloth. "I'm always happy to talk with the boss," he said as he swung out the door and closed it behind him.

Ruth and Trouble both kept silent until Tom and Kick's attempt at easy banter disappeared. "Can we really get out of here?" Ruth asked again.

"I think so. A lot depends on that message getting to Wardhaven. And then some gutsy folks being willing to launch a major invasion on a shoestring and a hunch."

"Would you do it?"

"If I knew you were down here, yes."

"But you're here. Who's out there who cares?"

"Captain Izzy Umboto, Ruth. And she doesn't leave until the whole crew is aboard. You can bet your life on that."

The tiny 3K message on Surveyor 14 was the first to be tapped. It rode a routine report on reaction mass remaining up to Repeater 2 and then into the buffer of Satellite Maintenance. There, it hitchhiked a ride to Main Communications when a routine status check was made of the system that kept links open to the rest of human space. There, the message waited. Its next command was to attach itself to any mail going to Wardhaven. A last command would pull it off there and rush it to its final destination. There was no traffic heading for Wardhaven, so the message waited. It had no way of noticing that other copies of itself were collecting in the buffer, duplicates waiting patiently . . . and tying up buffer space for no reason apparent to the technicians running the system. That wasn't unusual; packets were always being lost in transit. When it got too bad, the techs would flush the buffer. Of course messages would be lost, but what the heck, that was what backups were for.

If Steve hadn't been so tired last night, he might have realized Wardhaven was not a popular destination for mail from this corner of hell. He might have given the message alternate initial destinations, from which it could reroute itself to Wardhaven. He didn't, so the messages sat, collecting as more of the Surveyors were queried, taking up more of the large, but not unlimited, buffer.

• • •

Sleep refused to come to Izzy. Usually, she slept like the dead, but that was before she killed several hundred people she'd sworn her oath to protect. During the day, she stayed busy. God knows, the overhaul had enough going on . . . and going wrong . . . to keep her centered. But at night the ghosts came.

Izzy saw them. Dragged into a strange ship. Told nothing about what was happening. Heavy gees without the proper gear. Then wild maneuvering, and wilder fears. Then they were nothing, with no hint of warning. Not to know. Not to know until there was nothing to know.

Their helplessness brought back memories of a helpless kid. The little Izzy bewildered by the slums, the bosses, the drug merchants. Someone was supposed to protect kids, but not there. There, a kid never knew where today's shootout would be, never knew when a street game would turn deadly because somebody was shooting three blocks away and bullets don't stop just because they'd gone past their intended targets. Joie, Angie, little Toby . . . how long was the list that Izzy could still remember? Once in a long while, when Momma was sober, she'd tell Izzy she had to get out. School was a way out, not the run-down building called PS-921, but a real education. Somehow Momma found a way to send her to the school with the nuns. They'd opened up a whole new world for a wide-eyed kid. She'd taken in as much as she could, not nearly enough, but as much as a kid could, holding down a part-time job and cooking for Momma when she came home.

Izzy hiked straight from graduation to the Navy recruiter. The Navy was wonderful. They fed her. They clothed her. They had a job for her that left her wonderful hours of free time to study. And Lieutenant Manon had given her a chance for a real education and a commission. Izzy knew she wasn't as good as the other officers. They came from families, and had real educations. She knew what the Navy had taught her, and what she'd taught herself. They got ship duty; Izzy got the defense brigades, the last choice on the wish list.

And when she finally got her ship—she killed a couple

hundred innocent civilians. She was no better than a drug lord.

"Come on, Trouble. Get back here. I need some new faces, grateful faces of people we've set free. I can't take these faces much longer."

Every day was like the last on the farms. Get up, work the fields, go to bed exhausted and hungry. Every day it rained. Trouble's wounds healed; only one got infected. His visits to Ruth no longer lit up the day. Tom was the boss's regular. He managed to get the bracelet back without its absence being noticed. Unfortunately, Zylon Plovdic was learning from him.

With Ruth's promise of doubling the crop, Zylon looked at improving the end product. Her orders were to strip the leaves off the plants and drop the stalks in the field to rot and support the next crop. That left the field hands with more work. Since only a dozen new hands had arrived, and six others had given up and died, it meant everyone had to speed up. Zylon didn't think to increase the rations, just the work pace.

Trouble went to bed each night wondering where the damn invasion was.

"Walt, the main message buffer is acting flaky. Take it down and reload it."

"Boss, there's only a half hour left on the shift. You want my status report today or tomorrow? Can't the swing or midnight shift do it?"

"Swing's got backups to do, and midnight's too thin to do more than keep the shop up and running. Tomorrow morning, first thing, you reload the buffer."

"Will do, boss."

Ruth was discovering that the reward for a job well done was getting screwed. She'd tested the soil in every field, treated them, and worked herself out of a job. These crops got no pesticide or herbicide, for reasons no one would explain to her, so there was nothing she could do with her tractor there.

Helping your neighbor here was some kind of a joke. Her foreman laughed when she suggested loaning her out to the other farms to do similar tests and treatments. No, he figured, she was about due to be rotated to the vats.

That meant a collar and more attention from management than she cared for. Ruth countered with a suggestion to retest the fields, this time doing four tests to a hectare. "After all, we're terraforming this place pretty unevenly."

"That ought to keep you busy until we get the first crop in that you treated. If it really is double, maybe we can find a permanent place for you." His grin had a twist to it, suggesting that if it was anything less than double, he had a place for her.

Trouble, where's that invasion fleet?

"Art, I told you this place was great," he said, waving his drink at the golf course outside the club's windows.

"That you did, that you did. But damn, the overtime is killing me. When am I gonna have time for a game or a swim?"

"They've posted vacancy notices galore, Art. We just got to recruit some folks to lighten our load. Know any good analysts back on Wardhaven? I could use a construction boss as well as a dozen composite stringers."

"I know a few good-looking ones."

"Be nice to have more women around here, Art."

Art turned the menu into a message pad, called up his address book, and composed a cover note to the vacancy notices.

"Throw in a picture of the condo I built, Art."

"With all that rain?"

"It's not raining today. I told you the rain wouldn't last forever. Six months of rain, six months of blue sky."

"Yeah." Art finished his first message, copied it to another file, put a new name on it, and sent the first.

The message was large, with all its attachments. It almost

overflowed the main comm buffer. However, it was addressed to Wardhaven. Several tiny packages that had been waiting for that address to appear attached themselves to Art's message. They went out with it, leaving the buffer with more room for the next job offer he sent. None of this mattered to Art. He was a manager. So long as his mail went where he wanted it to go, buffers and lost packets meant nothing to him.

They meant a lot to other people.

ELEVEN

"IZZY, CAN YOU get down here quick?" It was Elie on the view. She looked pale.

"Is there a problem? Is Trouble back?"

"We've heard from him."

"Heard?"

"The recon blew up in his face. He's in some kind of slave labor camp."

"On my way." Izzy punched off and headed for the bridge. "Stan, you, me, and Gunny are going dirtside, right now."

"Yes ma'am. Bos'n, have the captain's gig made ready. Quartermaster, have Gunny meet us at the gig." Stan exited the bridge only a step behind Izzy. "What's the problem?" he asked as he caught up with her.

"Recon blew up. They got a message dirtside that may tell us more." Stan looked worried but said nothing. Gunny fell in step as they turned the last corner to the gig. They belted in as the pilot backed the craft away from the station.

"We have a problem?" Gunny asked.

"The recon failed. Lieutenant Tordon is in some sort of slave labor camp. Our rescue mission may be a bit larger in scope and harder to plan."

"That boy got himself enslaved again," Gunny said ruefully. "Maybe this time we ought to let him stew a while."

"I suspect by the time we get there, he will have stewed plenty," Izzy observed dryly.

Trouble was having a bad day. The foreman had lost heavily in last night's poker game. He had a roaring hangover and, rather than sleep it off, was taking it out of their hides, literally. The long black leather bullwhip cracked again.

"You bags of shit are slow as shit," he roared, flicking another six inches of Trouble's hide off. Boss's vocabulary was very limited, as was his intelligence. Apparently, he'd also lost his productivity bonus this month. Trouble wondered what month it was and how long he'd been doing this.

The next crack of the whip hit someone on the opposite side of the work group. Trouble was grateful it wasn't him and ashamed of the thought.

"Ease up, Trouble," Tom whispered. "Your knuckles are white. Ease up, there's nothing we can do about it. Relax, the sun's past noon. This won't go on forever."

Tom got the next whiplash for talking.

Trouble wanted to bury his hoe in the foreman's empty skull. To pry his eyeballs out and see if there was anything but vacuum behind them. "Remember, you got to stay alive," Steve mumbled, as if he could read the marine's mind.

The whip cut into him next.

Out of the corner of his eye, Trouble watched the two corporate men, sweating in the heat, bleeding from the lash, keep their heads down and their hoes going mechanically. If that was what you had to do to make it in a corporation, Trouble wanted none of that. *Give me a rifle and plenty of ammunition. I'll show you how to get ahead.*

The image caught at him. A head. On a hoe handle. Trouble kept the smile to himself. *Come on, Izzy, where's that damn invasion?*

• • •

"I think we best forget an invasion at this time." Major Tran, commander, 2nd Guard, stood before the data displayed on boards behind him and worried his lower lip. "I hate to give the bottom line first, but it's ugly enough you should have my recommendation in mind as we go over the report."

Beside Izzy, Gunny shuffled in his chair, a raging scream from a man who was usually ramrod straight and as responsive as rock. On her other side, Stan rubbed his chin doubtfully. Izzy would have expected him to nod agreement. Had he been around her too long? The commander of the Guard brigade continued.

"You have a copy of the brief message from the recon. For unknown reasons, he was apprehended before he could complete the reconnaissance of the target. That alone is a critical piece of information. Any hope we had of surprise is gone."

"Paranoid bastards," Izzy observed.

"They might feel they have reason to be," the unnamed spy responded.

"The extent to which the recon was unsuccessful before its capture is also of concern. Note that although they used the best systems we have available for hacking networks and cracking crypto systems, the firewall and encryption defeated them."

"Um." Tru Seyd scowled at her equipment's failure.

"They have identified the station as a basic C-3-a structure, though defensive blisters have been added. The satellite suite is minimal, just a GPS, weather, and repeater system. Most communications are limited to fiber optics, leaving us little access for either hacking, cracking, or misinforming. Ladies and gentlemen, this is enough information to tell us an assault by my brigade is suicide and its prospects for success nil. I suggest we look for other options." The major sat.

Nobody spoke for a long time. In the silence, Izzy got up and ambled over to the wall screen showing what they did and didn't know about the Riddle system. Four jumps were

scattered around it, all four or five days' travel from the occupied planet. A station in high orbit, say four hundred miles
up, and orbiting every two hours. The extent of human occupation and its location were unknown.

"A lot we don't know," Izzy agreed.

"We can't plan a planetary assault without knowing what
we are going up against." The major was definite.

"It would be tough planning it as we went along," Gunny
agreed. Or was he opening an option?

Acting Minister Rita Nuu-Longknife shook her head
firmly. "My husband, wherever he is, still walks with a
cane because he tried to force open a pass he knew too
damn little about. I won't send the Second Guard into that
again."

Izzy smiled. "We chewed you up plenty good that day, but
you should have seen the lash-up on our side. Our gear had
been transshipped four times on the way out. We couldn't
find shit. Our fingernails just were a bit stronger that day."

"Your rockets damn near wiped out my transport." Rita
left the challenge hanging.

"I had to bust my butt getting those birds off the ground.
No, it was a damn close thing. We were just a bit luckier."

"Luck doesn't fit into any plan I draw up," Major Tran
spat.

Izzy wouldn't argue that point. Only a fool assumed anything in a battle plan. She stared long at the displays. "If we
could seize the station . . ."

"Unless the hackers and crackers support our move into
that station," the major cut her off, "we'd have to fight for
every level, every space. What you'd have when we were
done wouldn't be worth having. And I wouldn't have much
of a brigade, either."

"And we'd be hanging there with our rear out, skipper,"
Stan added. "Anything come in behind us, we'd have to
fight it off while they were taking the station. Cannons to the
front of us, cannons to the back of us," he misquoted.

"Lousy tactical situation," Izzy agreed. So, how could she

make it better? She turned to Tru. "How could you improve your chances of hacking their system?"

"Trouble went in with a basic one-size-fits-all suite of tricks. If I had been there, with my gear, I'd have hit their system with human-directed input. Nothing beats reaching out and touching a problem yourself."

"You're not a combat trooper," Major Tran cut her off.

"I should hope not. But if you could keep those big hairy guys overdosed on testosterone off my case for a couple of hours, you might be surprised what doors I open."

"So, if we keep things from going terminal for a while after we dock the *Patton*, you might make it an easier nut to crack."

"Maybe" was all the answer Izzy got.

"Says here," Stan broke the silence. "That the fellow who designed the system and several of the people who laid out the urban plan are with Trouble raising drugs."

Izzy nodded, and the major shook his head. "We probably could identify the agricultural areas from the urban areas. However, we would not know which farms were growing drugs and which were growing lettuce. If we drop on the farms, I scatter my troops to hell and gone. Then I'd have to reconcentrate a strike for whatever center of gravity these people suggest. And their data will be at least six months old or older. I could be assaulting a brothel instead of a network center or power station."

Izzy nodded. "Yes, you could. We can't afford to scatter our only troops all to hell and gone." Izzy turned to Rita. "Is the Second Guard all you got?"

The minister patted her swelling belly thoughtfully before answering. "Wardhaven has three Guard brigades. The cabinet would have to decide to commit all three."

"You don't have transport." The major shot that down.

"Stan, how's the *Patton Jr.* coming along?" The *Patton* was his job. The conversion of the captured pirate into a warship of some capabilities was his passion.

"Surprisingly well, ma'am. Local yard's familiar with the design and layout. It's coming together just fine."

"Patton Jr.?" came from several people around the table, including Rita and the major. Not the spy.

"We brought a captured pirate ship in with us. Used to be a Daring class cruiser. Your yard's been working on it in their spare time. What's it got, Stan?"

"Six six-inchers, full sensors, engines in better shape than ours." *He didn't have to say that.* "I think it could take a load of containers as big as the *Patton*. Maybe more."

"Rita, if you got us all three brigades, one could take the station with two in reserve for drops. Trouble got a message out somehow; maybe we can get a message down to them. Know where they are before we drop. Could use my marines for that."

For once, the major was not shaking his head. Now it was Elie. "Am I the only one who sees a problem with this entire idea? I mean, that planet is a member of the Society of Humanity. So is Wardhaven. Can you explain to me again how it is that we can just go off and start blowing it up?"

"Good point," Rita said. "We got too many uniforms at this table, trying to figure out how to do it. Should we do it? Do we have a right to do it?" She leaned back in her chair, eyes locked on the spy. Izzy used the silence to sit down. She had definite opinions about people who made hostages of her crew. Still, she didn't have the right to declare war. The admiral back at District Headquarters might not be very understanding if she did.

"Thank you for the reality check," the nameless one said. "If the leaders of Riddle are indeed trafficking in slavery and piracy, they are in violation of several articles of Society's Declaration of Human Rights. Both of which can be punished by any of the signatories to the constitution. This may surprise you, but I had my legal staff examine our situation." The spy actually smiled. "Captain Umboto, you are covered by the right of hot pursuit, assuming we can identify something hot for you to pursue. One of your crewmen is a hostage. I believe you have a *prima facie* case for investigating. Wardhaven ships have vanished. I believe that you have the right to request our assistance. That should cover the Guard brigades." That sounded encouraging to Izzy, but the spy was no longer smiling. What bad news was he about to add to the good?

"However, if we do not quickly show some cause for our arriving in force in the Riddle system, you can expect the powers that be to log a strong protest and tie us up in legal knots for so long as we all shall live. We need proof, solid proof, before we start shooting up space stations and populated areas. We do not have it at the moment. I agree with the major. We need more information. We will need legal proof to cover our actions."

"Do you think we should stop, then?" Rita asked.

Slowly the spy shook his head. "No, all evidence is that this disease is growing rapidly. It requires radical surgery, and soon. We are prepared to move at this time. If we can, I suggest we do. Captain?"

With that, the spy tossed the ball to Izzy. There was no question in her mind. Go! But an invasion of a planet required better preparation than getting a missile strike off at grounded transports. Her crew might well find hostiles to their front and back. She turned to Stan. "Your thoughts on the matter?"

He raised an eyebrow at that, then leaned back in his chair for a long, silent minute. "Pirates may or may not be in the system when we are," he said softly. "The station may or may not fall to a hack-and-crack assault. We may or may not have to shoot our way into the station and onto the planet. If we can't establish contact with hostages, we really shouldn't do any shooting. That's a lot of bad news." Then he smiled. "The good news is we can hightail it out of Dodge anytime up to the point we start shooting, and nobody is the wiser. What do you say we take it one step at a time, skipper? If it's working, we keep going. If we end up facedown in the mud, we start crawling in reverse as fast as we can."

The major looked none too happy. Rita seemed undecided. The spy was unreadable. "What the hell, they were offering me early retirement when I took this job. I say we go."

The data chief rubbed her hands together. "It's gonna be a fun little puppy if we do."

Rita spent a long time staring at the ceiling. "Has the agency already completed its arrangements?"

"The large container ship *Star of Gdansk* loaded out a hundred thousand tons of prefab buildings and light industrial machinery. Its next port of call is Riddle. I have bribed its captain. My agent will bribe the rest of the crew when the time comes. If we do not go now, I will have paid for nothing. I think we should go forward with the option of reversing if necessary."

The major shot to his feet. "This is no way to conduct a military operation. I will not be a part of it."

"Thank you, Major. I have a meeting scheduled next with your Minister of External Affairs and the Prime Minister. Captain Umboto, will you accompany us?"

"Yes, ma'am. Stan, you and Gunny stand by here."

Thirty minutes later, Izzy was already seated in the back of a conference room when the Prime Minister and the External Affairs Minister took their seat. Rita was now accompanied by the spy, the reluctant dragon, and two other majors, a tall, rail-thin Major Erwin, and a shorter, broad-shouldered Major Murphy. At Rita's invitation, Tran quickly briefed the group on the problem. With broad strokes, he painted the picture, no bleaker nor brighter than he had before.

"You believe the risk is too great." The Prime Minister summed it up.

"To go in with no knowledge, no plan, and hoping that we can discover a basis for our action is to invite disaster."

The Prime Minister shook his head slowly. "And we have had enough disasters in the last war to last us several generations. Yes, but you would require us to allow a snake to grow and breed more snakes. I would much rather this snake was killed now, while it was small. Major Erwin, Major Murphy, is it as bad as Major Tran says it is?"

The two newcomers exchanged glances. One spoke for both. "Yes, Mr. Prime Minister."

"You would recommend we do nothing at this time."

"No, Mr. Prime Minister," said Major Murphy.

"Yes, Mr. Prime Minister," came at the same moment from Major Erwin.

"It seems I have divided counsel. Major Murphy, you said no. You disagree with the others?"

"Mr. Prime Minister, I don't think we should back away from this project without further consideration. We have paid to open a window. We have assets ready. I think we should give the project further consideration."

"What is there to consider?" Erwin snapped. "Until we get a recon in and out of that system, we are just sharing our ignorance. Your brigade got as badly mauled as mine on Elmo Four. Look at us. Majors leading brigades. This Humanity naval officer wants to put three brigades in system, and we don't have a general to command the operation."

Izzy eyed Rita. "You do seem kind of thin on officers."

"A lot died on Elmo Four. More got bullets in the back when they disagreed with Unity politicians who drew a thin line between disagreement and treason." She glanced at the spy. "We have a few generals who survived, but aren't sure who we can trust."

"More reason not to go," Tran snapped.

Izzy watched them; as of this moment, the project was dead. All she had to do was keep her mouth shut, and no one was going anywhere soon. Should she? She wished Andy was here. He could tell her whether the blood rising in her was just a tiger who couldn't pass up a shoot, a woman desperate to avenge her niece, or a captain blinded by loyalty to one marine officer and willing to risk too much to keep her honor unsoiled. There were a lot of reasons to keep quiet. Two hundred innocents had died the last time she shot off her mouth.

But damn it, this wasn't right.

"I know what your brigades faced on Elmo Four. Ship

driving is just my mid-life change. I was the exec of the Ninety-seventh Defense Brigade. I was the one who got the troops in place seconds before you got there. I got the rockets flying just barely in time to send you packing. I organized the five thousand men and women who just barely kept you from winning. We fought off some damn good officers and troops. You telling me the ones left couldn't shine the shit of the ones we killed?"

She had their attention.

"We know how to fight," snapped Erwin. "We just don't know where we'd be fighting. You've got to know the terrain, the target. We didn't know you, and you wiped the floor with us."

"I didn't know the terrain before we got there, either. And I sure as hell didn't know what you sent against us before we even had a chance to unpack. If you're half as good as the troops who damn near kicked us off Elmo Four, you ought to be able to handle anything we find on Riddle."

"You assume we find it before it's eating us for lunch."

"Yes. It's a four-day run from the jump point to the station. We'd have a hundred hours to map things out and make a first cut at a plan. Ms. Seyd says she can peel the station like a ripe banana. If she can't, we back out. The *Patton* and *Junior* can handle anything we meet on the way in and out. We don't move on the station until Seyd sizes it up. We don't drop on the planet until you say we drop."

"You're giving us a veto on the mission. Any time?" Tran asked slowly.

"If I say we run for it, I can't see you staying behind. I can say drop, but it won't do me any good if you say no." Which had to be obvious to everyone and hell on unity of command. If they pulled this off, it would be one for The Book. If not, the next edition of the manual would rip them apart.

Murphy grinned like a thief. "And if my brigade drops, I can just see you guys sitting on your hands back at the station."

Maybe the command structure was even more complicated than Izzy thought it was.

Tran made one last plea. "Mr. Prime Minister, you are not
putting the only three brigades Wardhaven has under the
command of a Humanity Navy three-striper."

The Prime Minister turned to Rita. "I've never been in the
service. Can we do it?"

Rita laughed. "She's an O-5 by their pay scale. Our boys
are O-4s by our pay scale. She outranks them."

"That's not what I mean," Tran snapped.

"I know it isn't," Rita answered. "Mr. Prime Minister, we
lost the war. Society allows us to keep our local military
forces as a militia. They can call them up in an emergency.
We are encouraged to work together at all times. If we're
going after that snake pit, I see no reason we can't put our
troops under a Society officer. I don't see how else we can
do it."

"I won't do it. This woman damn near killed me not a
year ago. Wiped out half my company. Rita, damn it, Ray
uses canes because of this bitch."

"That's enough, Major." The Minister of Exterior Affairs
cut him off. "One more word out of you, and your brigade
lifts with your exec in command." Tran sullenly retreated
deep into his chair. The minister turned to Izzy. "Captain, I
apologize for my subordinate. If you wish, I will have him
removed from his command."

"I think I've brought enough trouble into his life. I'll take
him if he's willing to go." Izzy hoped she wouldn't regret
this magnanimous gesture.

The prime minister stood. "Major Murphy, are you willing to prepare your unit for action and transport? Will you
participate with your superior, Captain Umboto, in a council
of war before commencing hostile actions against High Riddle station, and a similar council before taking hostilities to
the planet surface?"

"Yes, sir."

"Major Erwin?"

240 · Mike Moscoe

"We've eaten enough defeat pie, woman. We could use a taste of victory for a change."

"Victory is to my taste, too, Major. But you don't get to eat either sitting on your hands on post."

"Mr. Prime Minister, the First will lift when ordered."

"Major Tran, will you do as I've asked the others?" the Prime Minister asked.

"I didn't think I had a vote."

Izzy stood. "Major, I'd prefer to have three brigades. I'll lift, if I see a chance to take Riddle, with only two. Why not come along? There will be nothing wrong with the ride."

Tran shook his head ruefully. "I've got to be crazy to go along with this, but include my brigade."

Rita and the other minister stood. "Looks like we need to set Captain Umboto up with a staff." Rita turned to the spy. "I imagine you have a few suggestions."

Switching gears, Izzy tapped her comm unit the second she came aboard the *Patton*. "Vu, Chips, how are my engines coming?"

"We've loaded the software from Pitt's Hope," Chips said. "We're troubleshooting it right now. We've got a print-out of the *Sheffield*'s backup, and we're comparing them line by line."

"You need more help?"

"We just got thirty more software specialists up from Wardhaven. They're new, but they've actually slept in the last thirty-six hours, ma'am. We're confident we've got the problem progressing."

Izzy noted that he didn't say the problem solved, or under control. Progressing. "Stay on it, Chips. I just offered some very demanding army types the *Patton* for their ferryboat across the river Styx. Don't make a liar out of me. I don't want to be the reason Trouble has to take it another day."

Trouble wasn't sure he could take another day of this. Ruth had let slip that her days as an employee were numbered.

Ruth didn't know what to expect if she was shipped to the vats. Ruth shouldn't have to expect anything like that. Every muscle in Trouble's body wanted to do something, anything, to keep her out of there.

And there wasn't a damn thing he could do. He was a marine, trained to solve problems with the appropriate degree of skill, expertise, and violence. And his hands were tied. Rather, his neck was yoked. If he crossed their line, they'd kill him.

And every day they rubbed his nose in it. Every day was slop to eat, whips for any reason the guard felt like, and work without end. Trouble watched the fire go out of men's eyes, beat down by the rain, the heat, and the whip.

A manager Steve knew stuck in Trouble's mind. The man may once have been fat, but now he was a skeleton. His work got slower and slower. The guard reduced his food allowance. The man quit eating entirely. Then he quit working. No amount of beating or pounding could get him out of his bunk. He just lay there curled in a ball.

Trouble brought half of his biscuit, put it under the guy's nose. The vacant eyes did not see the food, or Trouble. The marine lingered with him until total darkness, as much to keep someone else from stealing the half biscuit as to study the dying man. He just lay there. Not moving, hardly breathing.

"You better get some sleep," Tom whispered in the darkness. Trouble ate his half biscuit as he crawled into an empty bunk.

"How do you keep going?" he asked Tom.

"I wanted to die, right after they dumped me here. Steve kept me from attacking a guard, getting him to kill me. After a while, I followed his example. Put one foot in front of the other. Everything changes. Sooner or later, if I live long enough, this will change. I don't know why or when. Hell, most of the time in my real career I didn't know why things happened. They just did, and most of them were good, so I claimed them for my work. Truth is, much of it was just damn luck and good hunches. So now my luck's bad. It'll change." Tom rolled over, said nothing for a while.

"Your problem, marine, is you want to make it change. You want your invasion. You're going to end up like that poor slob real soon if you keep waiting for a squad of big, hairy, gun-lugging marines to come blasting into the farm, and they don't come soon enough. Maybe they need to send another spy in. Maybe they'll do a legal approach. Those take time. A long time. If you can't manage for the long haul, you may die five minutes before they show up."

"Just my luck."

"Get some sleep. Everything changes."

Change came over the *Patton* slowly, but it came. She was coming back to life. Some changes were easy to recognize. The network worked noticeably faster. When they reinitiated fusion, the ship didn't blow up. Guns chortled when all his batteries took a full charge; he was dying to play with his new rangefinder. Izzy managed to squeeze in a six-hour cruise. The *Patton* and *Patton Jr.* had only that practice being cruisers before it was back to the pier to be loaded as freighters.

The gripe sheets from the live fire exercise were a lot shorter than Izzy had any right to expect. Stan, who had commanded *Junior* for the short run out, was back aboard, the *Patton* still his first responsibility. "Yard will handle all of this while we take on containers and troops," he observed over the paperwork before his eyes lit up. "Damn, Guns, your shooting was good. *Junior*'s stuck with the old fire control, and our shooting showed it."

Guns pursed his lips thoughtfully. "Let me have a look-see. Maybe, if we're fighting in line, if I got a good bearing on you and another good bearing on the target. It might work."

"Would that limit us to one target at a time?" Izzy asked. In battle, it was critical to keep all hostiles busy. Leaving one comfortable to plan its shooting at leisure was a good way to get yourself converted to atoms.

"We've got upgraded computers, both central and fire control. We might have the spare resources," Guns answered.

"Check it out, if you have time."

The madly ordered disorder of getting a warship under way now took over, made worse by the obligation to be both a warship and a troopship. There were never enough minutes in an hour and far too many problems.

And now the ship wasn't her only problem. She had a Guard command staff, drawn from officers and civilians. The spy vouched for their trustworthiness; Rita made sure they knew the job. The duties were familiar: operations, supply, intelligence, personnel. Wardhaven's solutions to them were no different from those the 97th applied. Her chief of staff was a major swiped from Wardhaven's War College. A lost arm five years ago had sidetracked Urimi from Unity's war. Intelligence was Ms. Seyd; she brought with her a dozen youngsters and boxes of computer gear. Izzy had to remind her there was more to battlefield intelligence than interrogating electrons. Urimi dug up a team of mappers and interrogators to handle the less sexy side of data gathering and dissemination. Supply and personnel was a balding fellow, Captain Von Kerkin. Izzy handed him off to her supply officer; together they went off to figure out how many containers they could hang on the *Patton* before Guns screamed.

And now she had a place to settle Joe Edris; the spy sent up a civic action team: a hotshot manager from Nuu's shop, a lawyer and three guys who swore they could manage a city's full range of services, water, sewer, transportation. Izzy hoped she wouldn't have to count on just three people to run a city. That was one of many things she didn't know.

The days were full of meetings, the nights full of ghosts. She was tired, and getting cranky.

"Comm for you, Captain."

"Yes," Izzy answered, trying to use her voice as a calming influence on whoever it was bringing her a new problem.

"So, my tiger's got herself a ship and a ground task force for her next fine show."

"Captain Anderson." Izzy's voice lit up. Her old commander from the 97th's timing was lousy, but what the heck.

"How's it going, Izzy?"

"Could be better. Has been worse."

"Hasn't it, though?"

"You picked a hell of a time to show up, sir."

"As usual, I have little control over my time. I hear from Elie that this won't be your first shoot."

Izzy sighed. "No."

"Got a few seconds we can talk?"

"Not really."

"I'm on the station. Got a table reserved for us at the Wharf Rat."

Izzy scanned the confusion around her. "Stan, can you take over for an hour?"

"No trouble, Captain."

"Okay, Andy, you got one hour of your tiger's time."

"I think you need it."

Izzy found Andy in a quiet corner of the lounge. He put down his well-worn volume of Shakespeare as he stood to greet her. "What's it been, three, four months?" He smiled.

"Seems longer." Izzy found her throat going dry on her. She slid into the booth across from Andy.

"I took the liberty of ordering steaks with all the trimmings . . . and water. You're headed out, aren't you?"

"As soon as we're loaded." Izzy found that one an easy answer. "I wish you'd been here when I first showed up. Had a hell of a time deciding to trust this bunch."

"Things can get a bit weird when enemies become allies almost overnight. I've enjoyed working with them."

"Now that's something I've done a lot of, lately, once we got this mission on. Sure wished you'd been at that batch of meetings. This tiger was having second thoughts. Was I just running off to do something, or was this something that needed doing?"

"But my tiger was thinking." Andy smiled. "Woman, you may just grow up some day."

"I feel like a million years old. Andy, I knew in my head that being Navy, we killed people. But twenty-plus years of peace, I guess I never really knew it."

"It was in your head, but not your heart," Andy offered.

"Yeah. Then the war hit and we were too busy staying one step ahead of dead to worry. Now, this universe is crazy and I don't know who's trying to kill me and who I should be killing."

"And you wish I'd tell you." Andy's smile was warm and fatherly. Izzy had never known her father.

"Silly of me. You don't know any more than I do."

"Of the evil lurking out there, maybe I do. It is out there, and it has to be stopped. Who must die to stop it? Ah, Izzy, that is the quandary we all live with. For most, it is purely philosophical. But you wear the uniform. You have the power to stop it. You can kill it . . . and you can kill others, too."

Izzy let that sink into her slowly. "So I'm headed out to meet that evil with a full gunnery kit and three brigades of Wardhaven's best." At that she could not help but laugh. "Eight months ago, I was trying to kill them. Now, I'm praying they are as good as advertised."

Andy nodded. "Peace has given us a very strange world. Enemies become friends, friends become unknowns, and legitimate targets become . . ."

Izzy swallowed hard. "I fall asleep exhausted, but somewhere in the middle of the night, they show up. People I'll never know, that I had no quarrel with . . . and that I killed."

Andy sighed. "Forty years I put in the Navy. Never harmed a fly. Then comes last year. Lord God, the slaughter of good men and women, ours and theirs."

"But that was a fair fight, Andy. We knew what we were heading into. So did the Unity troops. These folks, women, men, kids, had no beef with me. No chance. No chance at all. I just killed them." Izzy's eyes were rimming. In a moment she'd be crying. She looked away from Andy. *Where are the damn steaks?* Andy said nothing. His silence was a vacuum, pulling words out of her.

"You told me tigers got people killed. You warned me I was too damn trigger-happy. You told me, and I laughed and went right on. I didn't want to be bothered by prisoners. I *wanted* the pirates wondering what happened to their raider. I had it all thought out. All thought out. Except for what might be in their brig. Damn!" Now Izzy was crying. She never cried. You didn't cry in the slums. You didn't cry in the Navy. You didn't cry for yourself or for your dead.

Andy handed her a small box of tissues. She took a handful. "You came prepared."

"I've used enough of them, the last six months."

"You!"

Andy thumped his book. "I've read Will's plays and sonnets since I was a boy. I think I only began to understand them this year. Maybe I only began to understand the pain that's behind them now, after I've . . . commanded death and fled from it in all its myriad faces. The dead and the might-have-beens that would have given them longer life haunt my wakings and sleepings. Izzy, we are not alone, and"—Andy opened the book at random—"and we are not the first. Prince Hal gave his God full credit for victory at Agincourt, not because he was a saint, but because it liberated him from the responsibility for the slaughter. You have a god, Izzy?"

"There's no god in the slums. Just devils to hide from."

"Elie's been a good person to talk to. College professors don't think the way Navy does. Softer or something."

"I always told you she was soft in the head." Izzy tried to laugh; Andy smiled.

"You probably figure I'm going soft between the ears, too, but I found myself a padre to talk to. Old, retired trooper from Wardhaven's army. Someone I didn't have to explain how a place shakes when a shell goes off next door to you. In your buddy's hole, but, thank God, not yours."

"Think I should talk to him?"

"She's dirtside, and you're headed out again. What you gonna do if you get pirates shooting at you?"

Izzy leaned back in the booth and rested her eyes on the fake wooden timbers. "I don't let them kill my people. I'm not putting any of the joes in any more danger than I have to." The words came out so sure, so absolute. That part was rock solid in her heart. "Beyond that, Andy, I will try to take prisoners."

"How hard?"

"I wish I knew."

"Good hunting."

TWELVE

IZZY GOT LITTLE rest on the voyage out. If she wasn't on the bridge, she was at the CP established in the pod of containers just outside the midships radial 90 hatch. Majors Murphy and Erwin rode the *Patton*. Tran was with Stan on the *Junior*. Command relationships were cordial, if somewhat cool. Izzy's chief of staff, Major Urimi, had designed an operations order with gaping holes in it. "We'll fill these in as we go along. If not, maybe we don't go." He smiled encouragement to both Izzy and the majors. Urimi did a great balancing act.

Tru Seyd took time away from planning her assault on the station's data stream to develop and test a network between all the brigades' officers and troopers. As soon as Izzy knew something, it would be passed to everyone. First tests were a disaster. Every squad leader did not need to know *everything* Izzy knew. Urimi, the brigade commanders, and Tru worked out a decision tree for the network to keep it from bogging down at every turn.

Now that Riddle was in sight, the intelligence crew was hard at it. "About what we were led to expect. System layout has no surprises. Riddle has very little radio traffic. We're mapping it as best we can from this distance," Tru reported.

Izzy's chief of staff began filling in the blanks on his operations plan. "Only one major urban area. I expect that is where we will land. I'll keep an open mind about that until we hear from your man Trouble."

"Good idea," Izzy agreed. "Dealing with minds that go in for piracy, slavery, and drugs, don't bet their center of gravity is where you'd put it."

"We will need more data," Urimi said.

"Shit, look how tall that stuff is," Steve marveled as they pulled up the first field fully grown under Ruth's management. The stalks were taller than Trouble, the leaves broad and a pale green that almost seemed transparent. They worked their way down the rows, pulling each stalk, then stripping it of leaves. Those went into bags dragging behind them. The stalks were left to dry in the field, rotting to feed the next crop.

From one viewpoint, the thugs ought to be glad. Ruth had come through with a damn fine crop. On the other hand, would Zylon see it in her best interest to keep a professional farmer like Ruth happy, or was she now excess baggage to be tossed to the dogs? If Trouble worried about that, Ruth must be half crazy. Still, when he saw her testing the field next to the one he was working, she moved with her usual self-possession and purpose. Maybe there wasn't a problem.

"It'll be fun bringing that one down a peg or three," Trouble heard one guard mutter to another while eyeing Ruth at work.

"Depends on what the boss girl says," the one beside him answered, then cracked a whip. Zylon had come out to look the work over. She eyed the field hands, then glanced at Ruth and her tractor. Trouble wasn't close enough to catch her expression. *Zylon couldn't be that stupid.* Then again, those who used piracy and slaves had already shown a certain lack of grasp for human motivation. *Damn, where is that invasion fleet?*

· · ·

Damn, this isn't telling us a hell of a lot. Izzy studied the information decorating the walls of her command post. It was thin. Maps of the planet had too many question marks. The general layout of the station was updated with blisters and pods of unknown origin and use. A lot of unknowns. Too many?

"Don't worry." Tru must have taken up mind reading along with tea leaves and electron bits. "Once we're docked, we'll hitch into their net and access all kinds of maps, blueprints, guides. That'll fill in the blanks fast enough for you to pass it along to the assault troops."

"Trouble didn't have much luck cracking their firewall and encryption," Izzy reminded her.

Tru's enthusiasm was unfazed. "I have access to the latest published tools, their backdoor accesses, keys, and plenty of computing power to crack them. If I can't get through their firewall, Major Erwin has loaned me a squad to drill a hole in a bulkhead and plug me into the other side of the damn firewall. One way or another, I'll hand you this station on a platter."

Izzy hoped Tru was as good as she claimed. Taking this station apart piece by piece would not only slow them down but tip their hand big time. Izzy's legal staff warned her that the sooner this task force started shooting, the sooner someone would show up with a court order to shut them down. This task force was a combined operation of the weirdest sort, from cruisers to techies, from troopers to lawyers.

"Captain, Sensors here. A ship just jumped into the system."

Damn! Izzy groaned. "Which jump and what kind of ship?"

"Beta jump. We don't have a good fix on the ship, but its jump pulse was medium power. Say a large freighter."

"Or a light cruiser," Izzy sighed.

Major Urimi tapped a screen; it changed to a sim of the Riddle system. Izzy rapidly explained the problem. "We're two days out from the station. Beta jump is usually a four-day cruise in at one gee. So, if there are no more surprises, this shouldn't be a problem. However, our line of retreat is starting to look a bit threatened."

Urimi rubbed his chin, deep in thought. "Our margin for error is getting thinner and thinner."

"Did you actually think it would get better as we went along?" Izzy tried to laugh, but it came out more like a growl.

"One could hope. I'll keep you up to date on what we find about our target. Do you want to return to your bridge?"

Six hours later, Izzy had made a lot more calls to keep Urimi up to date than he had made to her. The planet refused to give up its secrets. Izzy now had three unknown ships in-system.

"They all came through the Beta jump, and they're about an hour apart," Sensors informed her. "All we've got on them is an engine signature."

"Let me guess. Daring class." Izzy sighed.

"You got it, skipper."

"What are they, cheaper by the dozen?" Stan chimed in on tight beam from the bridge of the *Junior*.

"I swear," Izzy growled, "when this is over, I'm gonna look up somebody in warship disposal sales and hang 'em."

"First we got to get this over," Stan reminded her.

"Can we put on extra acceleration?" Urimi asked.

"No benefit, Major, we're decelerating," Izzy answered.

"So we wait," her chief of staff concluded.

"And make sure Tru has all her tools laid out and ready to go as soon as we dock."

It took three days to harvest Ruth's first crop, three hot days of yanking, ripping, and tearing. Rough work on the back and hands. Trouble had splinters and blisters to show for it. Tom had a gash in his foot. After supper, Trouble helped his friend hobble to the clinic. Actually, he just wanted to see Ruth. Her smile made the trip and the pain almost worth it. She cleaned out Tom's foot, then treated it. Seeming to understand he was extra, Tom limped off. That left Trouble tongue-tied, hunting for something to say to Ruth. Trying to figure out what he really wanted to say.

How do you tell a woman you admire her? That you appreciate her cool approach to tough situations, that you like being around her. It was easy to tell a man that . . . or another marine. It was a job. You did it. Well done.

The words didn't quite match what he felt for Ruth.

"Crop's good. Best I've ever seen," he ended up saying.

"Damn right it is. If these idiots knew anything about farming, they'd have done more than just toss a seed on the ground. But then, if you're dumb enough to grow dope, you've already shown you're not too smart."

"You figured out what we're growing."

"Yeah. We grew pharmaceutical feed stocks back on Hurtford Corner. 'Course, no company would buy a crop from uncertified fields and farming methods. Drugs are the only things it could be. How much longer we gonna be here?"

That was a slap that brought the marine up short. "I don't know. I'd thought they'd be here already. Then again, I'm none too sure what day it is."

"Me neither."

"I want you out of here, Ruth. They're changing you. Making you rougher. I don't want them changing you."

"I always thought a man wanted to change his woman."

"I liked you just the way you were the first time I saw you."

"Drugged and hogtied. That's a man for you." She slugged him in the arm. Gently, hardly more than a rub. He wanted to roll over like a puppy and have her rub him all over.

"You know what I mean—the woman who took over caring for those who needed help. Who stood up to the slaver when no one else would. Who had him begging out of her hand for fungus. That's quite a woman."

"I had to. I couldn't let a guy like you take all the risks. A girl's got her pride."

"I'm a marine." Trouble shot back the usual answer. "I'm supposed to take chances."

She took his face in her hands, held his eyes so he had to look deep into hers. "And here I thought it was just for me."

"It was."

There was a rap at the door. "Tordon, Ruth, you in there?"

"Kick," Trouble whispered. "Yes," he answered.

"Get out here. Both of you."

Trouble led the way, keeping Ruth behind him. Opening the door, he preceded her down the steps of the clinic. "You want me?" he asked.

"Ms. Plovdic wants both of you. Ruth here's been little miss queen bee long enough. You've just been a lot of trouble. A guy came over from one of the other farms. Wanted to see our crop. He also shared a little idea of his for something special tonight. Plovdic loved it, thought it might be fun. Couple of guards here would like a go at Ruthie. To make it more fun, you get to fight them naked, with knives. They kill you, they get her. They yield, Zylon gets you, or what they leave of you. What do you think of that?" he grunted. "Follow me."

Trouble didn't waste breath answering Kick's question. Like a good slave, he'd bowed his head, knowing what was coming even before the head guard got to the punch line. A slave had to accept it, do what he was told. The guards had beaten that into the field hands with casual whips and senseless brutality. Trouble shambled after Kick, not even letting the indrawn hiss of fear in Ruth's breath change the facade he wore for the guard.

"Hurry up," Kick growled, and he reached back to slap Trouble. Kick was so confident he controlled the beaten and starved field hands that he, like so many of the other guards, had taken to leaving his pod controllers in his pockets.

The marine broke Kick's neck before he could scream, much less reach for his controller. The crack of the bones sent a shiver through Trouble, a quake that shattered the passive, take-it person who had been a slave. With a feral grin, he turned to Ruth. "I didn't really like that idea. Did you?"

"Wasn't on my short list of things to do tonight. Now what do we do?"

Trouble glanced around. Nobody in sight. "Back to the clinic. I want to see what he's got."

They spent a precious minute going through Kick's pockets. Trouble stripped off his wrist unit and his shirt; the pants were ruined when Kick's bowels let go. "Not much to show for a life of crime," the marine judged as he stuffed everything from the dead man's pockets into a first aid pouch. "You know any good places to disappear?"

"Girls at the vats have a few places they lay low from the guards. You can get away with it once in a while."

"Think they'll tell on us?"

"It ought to take the guards a while to realize we've hid and ask them, don't you think?"

"Worth a try." Trouble stashed the body under a tarp behind machinery away from the clinic. He followed Ruth through a maze of buildings before she edged into a warehouse through splits in its corrugated metal wall. The dirt floor was covered three to five deep with stacks of hundred-liter drums.

"Some are full. Most empty," Ruth whispered. "Follow me."

Trouble helped her scale the stack; then they crawled along the top until they came to a dip. Nine barrels were missing, giving them a place to hole up out of sight. There was even a tarp and some rags. A place to rest. To hide. Maybe to cry yourself to sleep when the terrors outside were worse than any nightmare that had disturbed a woman's sleep. A place to rest before going back to the horror. Trouble settled in with Ruth beside him.

Her fingers were soft on his neck. He turned to her as she whispered in his ear, "Let's have a look at your collar."

Zylon Plovdic didn't like to be kept waiting, especially when she had a man present she wanted to impress. She had never been a patient woman. Patience was for people whose time was worthless. Zylon counted every moment of her life like gold.

"Where is Kick? How long does it take to find one worthless field hand and a ninny of a woman in love with her tractor?" Ruth really frosted Zylon, prancing around like she was the queen of green, using a few bits of know-how to lord it over all of them. She probably thought she could do a better job of running this farm than Zylon. Well, tonight she'd learn.

"Sounds like my ex-wife," Mordy snickered. "Loved her tractor more than me. That's why I left her."

Zylon would show Ruth. A couple of the boys swore they could work that little mud analyzer just as well as tractor girl. Tomorrow, they'd show her and Mordy. And they wouldn't ride around all day with their noses stuck up in the air. Yes, it was time Ruth learned how you really ran a farm.

"Damn it! Hicks, Bascom, go find those little shits and bring them to me. Now!" Zylon relished the look of fear on the two men's faces as they jumped at her words, grabbed three others, and hustled off to do her bidding.

"Damn it!" Tru hated to be reduced to vulgarities. At the moment, that was all she had. "The Great Wall 4630s have five generally available back doors," she muttered so the majors hovering over her shoulder could know something of her problem, "and two that even the production crew didn't know about. All seven have been locked out on this installation. Every one! Nobody closes all the work-arounds. You have to leave an opening in case everything blows up."

"One might suspect these people of being paranoid," Urimi muttered. "Or that they didn't want people doing unto them what they'd done unto others."

"Sounds like it, sir."

"How's our cracker doing?" came from the comm unit, in the all too familiar voice of the ship's captain.

"Not so good. Firewall doesn't seem to have any of the usual holes. We're ready to go to plan B."

"Figures. I got the station folks wanting to start unloading. Can she be ready to offload in five minutes?"

Tru stood, a soldier at her elbow, loaded with most of her gear, ready to run her up to the first cargo container. "Go," Urimi ordered, and the soldier took off at the double. Tru galloped with him, breaking into a sweat, which she detested, and wondering why she'd volunteered for this in the first place.

Ruth ran her fingers lovingly over Trouble's throat. She wanted to hug him, kiss him, have him make love to her. What she did was yank at the pods on the thin plastic cord around his neck. No surprise; they didn't move. "Try cutting them off," Trouble said, pulling out the knife they had taken from Kick.

Working the blade between Trouble's vulnerable throat and the cord, Ruth tried. The knife refused to even dent the thin strap. "There's got to be some way to get at these pods," she finally gasped in exasperation.

"Look it over. Batteries or damaged parts have to be replaced," Trouble suggested.

To Ruth's eyes, the pod was smooth metal or plastic. In the fading light, she saw no seam in the casing's surface. She ran her fingernail over the pod. Something snagged. Trouble handed her a lighter Kick had no further use for. She didn't want to risk fire, for fear either of it being seen or of burning Trouble. She flicked it on. Yes, there was a small indent, neither for a blade nor Phillips head screwdriver, but for an L-shape. She went back to the knife. Like her father's, it had plenty of blades to choose from. Where Pa's had a Phillips head, this one had one L-shaped. She applied it to Trouble's pod and turned the screwdriver clockwise. Nothing. Counterclockwise didn't work either. She put her hand between the pod and Trouble's neck, leaned with all her weight and slowly twisted it clockwise.

It moved.

She kept the pressure up, slowly turning the knife in her hand. It slipped once. Trouble stifled a cry of pain as the blade cut into him, but urged her back to work. She tried going light on the pressure, but the blade lost its grip. Weighing heavy on her man's neck, she turned it again and again and again. Finally, it got easier. She paused for a moment's rest; a crack showed down the middle of the pod.

"It's coming apart," she whispered. And went back to work. A long minute later, half of the pod fell into her hand. "It's got three batteries in there. I'm gonna pull them out."

"Nothing beats a try but a failure, my mom used to say," the marine answered, and clenched his jaw for a shot of pain. None came. The batteries dropped into Ruth's hand with no sign of a farewell jolt to Trouble.

"There are some chips and stuff in here. Should I do anything to them?"

"Probably the receiver for the controller's signals. Use the knife to mess them up."

She did. Then she attacked the second pod. It didn't come apart any easier, but now she knew what to do. Ruth just had the batteries in hand and was attacking the rest of the pod's circuitry when the door to the warehouse slid open noisily.

"Check it out," a rough voice ordered. Flashlight beams worked along the ceiling and through the cracks between the barrels. Someone climbed up the stack and played a beam along the tops of the barrels. "Nothing here. I told you they'd be heading for the fence."

"Hicks and his boys are covering the fence. We check all the buildings. So check them."

When they left, they didn't shut the door.

"Think they'll be back?" Ruth asked.

"I'd figured to hide here until early tomorrow, then run." Trouble produced Kick's wrist unit. "We can monitor their chatter to decide when to move. Now, at least, they can't zap me silly."

Ruth gave him a hug. "If we can get to my tractor, we can get out of here fast."

Zylon was unhappy and getting unhappier. This was not supposed to happen to a senior farm manager, definitely not when she was entertaining company. She was the boss. People did what she ordered. When she wanted results, they produced them.

"Vahan, get me the serial numbers on that Tordon's control units. Then rig a controller to them. Let's see how well he can hide when he's screaming." She smiled at Mordy.

Vahan ran to do her bidding; he was back in less than five minutes. Zylon tapped her comm unit. "I'm about to send a wake-up call to Mr. Tordon's neck pods. Listen up for the scream."

"Why didn't we do that in the first place?" she heard on net. She recognized the voice. He'd look great naked in a knife fight; for now, she pushed Tordon's button.

There was no answering scream.

"That's impossible," Vahan breathed.

"Did Kick have a pod repair kit?" Zylon asked on net.

"I think so" came from several sources.

"Okay, we do this the old-fashioned way. I know these people slough off on me. Where do they hide when there's work to be done?" Zylon snapped.

"We got the field hands in sight every minute of the day," Vahan whined. "They slough off, they get a taste of the whip."

"Sometimes, the gals at the vats seem hard to find," a guard said slowly. "You go hunting and you don't find her 'til next day. Ask girls, and they say she's over there. Girls yonder say, no, somewhere else." He shrugged. "Maybe they do hide."

"Bring me the vat girls."

That didn't take long at all. Zylon took their measure; none met her eyes. No back talk here. "Where do you girls hide when you want to duck work? Or a guard?"

There was a general shake of the head and a mumbled "We don't do that." Why didn't Zylon believe that? She grabbed one who stood a little straighter than the others. "Where do you hide?"

The answer was slow in coming. Zylon reached for a guard's dagger. "We don't," the woman answered quickly.

"You dodge work, you get beat and lose a meal. We all work."

That was the official line. Stupid answer. Zylon slit the woman's throat, reaching for a second woman even as the first collapsed. "Where do you hide? Where are the two runners?"

"The warehouse, ma'am. Sometimes, some of the girls hide among the barrels. Deep among them. I never done it."

Zylon sent the woman sprawling. "I knew one of you girls would remember." She tapped her comm unit. "Search the warehouse. Take the barrels down one at a time if you have to. They're in there."

Izzy had her hands full. The station manager was demanding she unload. "We got three more coming in right behind you." As if she wasn't all too aware of them. She wanted to offload . . . the first couple dozen containers, the ones that put the hackers in contact with the station's hull. However, as more containers were shifted to the station, the sleek and glistening lines of a cruiser would become all too visible. Izzy had hoped the confident cracker's plan A would open the station up for a friendly takeover. Now it was plan B. Plan C involved shooting the station up or running like hell. *Which one, tiger?*

Not time to decide yet. Still, breathing down her neck were three Daring class cruisers. With a trio to work over, Sensors had caught enough leaks to get a clear picture of them this time. No way to tell if they were carrying slaves or captured crews. There was no question they were still gunned.

Stan ambled over from his own command; the *Junior* was docked next to the *Patton*. With luck, the two loads of containers would provide a good excuse for slow unloading. If not, a couple of the winching systems would have to develop the flu. "How long we got?" was Stan's greeting as he crossed the bridge hatch.

"Six hours, maybe a tad more." Izzy waved him to a side screen where she was planning her space battle. "Can't af-

ford a head-on pass. That would put them between us and
the station with us doing a slow turnaround to get back. No,
we swing around Riddle and cross their paths as they come
into orbit. That ought to give us thirty to forty-five minutes
of shooting before they can get a bead on the station."

"Why, thank you, Commodore," Urimi said as he entered
the bridge and the conversation simultaneously.

"How's Tru doing?"

"Her container, with the rest of Erwin's best nutcrackers,
are now in contact with the station hull, as close as any container gets. They should be forcing an entry to the station in
about five minutes."

"Well, Major, here's the schedule she's got to meet. To
handle the three incoming cruisers, Stan and I got to back
away from this station in five hours. To do that, we got to offload all of our containers by then. I figure in about two
hours, we'll have offloaded enough containers that the little fan dance we've been doing with them won't work any
longer, and my cruiser's fine lines will be bare-ass naked
to the lusty eyes of station security. If we don't have the
station the easy way in two hours, Erwin's First will have
to take it the hard way."

"That was my estimate too." Urimi tapped his comm link.
"Tell Goldilocks she's got ninety minutes to heat up that
porridge." He eyed Izzy's board. "That what you plan to do
for fun?"

"Can't have three pirates interfering with you ground-
pounders' fun and games. How's the assault planning coming?"

"You know more about those pirates than I do about that
damn planet. Never heard of an urban area so silent on the
electromagnetic spectrum. We figured out where the power
plant is. A few factories, too. Beyond that, I can't even guess
where the comm hub is."

Izzy had reviewed the planet data an hour ago. Beyond
separating agricultural and urban, they were pretty much in
the dark. Was a tall building full of apartments or pirate

offices? Was that a country club or the city hall? With no microwave intercepts, it was impossible to tell.

"We need Trouble and the guys he's found," Izzy said.

Trouble knew they were in trouble when he heard the shouting. The men were being whipped out of their barracks and driven over to the warehouse. He and Ruth had heard the women being trooped off to Zylon a few minutes earlier and decided it was time to make a move . . . just in time. Under the cover of the shouting and carrying on as barrels were knocked over, shoved aside, and pushed around, he fueled the tractor and lifted two spare gas cans into its cab.

"Why doesn't Zylon use the comm link to issue orders?" Trouble muttered. He was learning a lot more from the yelling and shouting than he was from the captured link.

"I don't think these people are real comfortable with their gear," Ruth whispered back. "Look at them. Trying to grow stuff by tossing a bunch of seeds on the ground. Running around whipping you guys. That's no way to run a profitable farm. Now most of those ex-Unity draftees are bawling orders at the top of their lungs and using the comm links for chattering. Trouble, these people are stupid."

"But the last three I saw were toting guns. Let's put them down as stupid, but dangerous."

"So, when do we get out of here?" Ruth asked.

That was the question: how to time their dash? "The more time they spend knocking around the warehouse," Trouble whispered, "the more tired they'll be chasing us when we bolt. Maybe they'll work themselves to exhaustion and we can tiptoe out of here when everyone's dead asleep."

"You ever seen a tractor tiptoe?"

"No."

"Well, I've done everything else with one. Why not tiptoe it? I guess we wait."

"I think so."

Ruth snuggled up close to him, huddled down, out of sight. It would be nice to come home to her every night for a snuggle like this. Maybe not like this. He could skip the smell of gasoline, the hounds out for their blood. Still, the feel of her flesh against his. Yes, she would be nice to come home to.

If a marine had a home.

"Damn it, there's not supposed to be cabling here," Tru snorted as she eyed the results of the first drill probe through the station's hull. With nothing better to rely on, they were using the standard design prints. Clearly, this was no standard design. "Try again, twenty centimeters to the right."

The corporal started drilling, while the private patched the station's hull. Next visual showed an open compartment; a full spectrum analysis revealed no activity of any sort. The cable that had spoofed them the first time was a water pipe.

It took them the better part of fifteen minutes to establish themselves in the compartment and determine the next compartment over had a cable run and was not under observation. They cut a big hole in the wall and moved over.

"Place stinks," the private muttered.

"It's a paint locker, Joe," the corporal informed him . . . and Tru. "None too smart to run fiber optics through a fire hazard." That was the first dumb move Tru had found these puppies in. *Nice to know they aren't perfect.*

They might as well have been, for all the good it did Tru. Skelly, her technician, jacked Tru into the fiber-optic run, then grinned as she finished. "It's all yours, boss."

Tru returned the grin as she went to work . . . and scowled as she hit a concrete wall. "It's encrypted. Every damn package is encrypted like it's a bleeding bank."

"How bad?" Skelly asked.

"Give me a minute." Tru suspected she already knew the answer, but she had to prove it to herself. As she thought, these folks didn't do anything in halfway measures. "They're using the latest bank encryption. Two-fifty-six bit encryption with a double key." With sinking heart, she tried the code the developer swore would let anyone in. It had been disabled.

"Damn. Don't these guys trust anyone?"

"Would you, if you were the bloody bastards doing unto everyone else?" the sergeant reminded her.

"No."

"We got to report something." Skelly reminded Tru of practical matters. Tru searched for public nodes. There had to be a map of the station that wasn't encrypted. She found one, transmitted it back to the command post.

"Got anything without all these blanks?" was her thank-you. The map showed public corridors, rest rooms and restaurants, and not much more.

"This whole station is encrypted like a rock," she answered.

"Well, in one hour, we start taking this rock apart, one atom at a time. Let us know if you've got any suggestions in the meantime."

Tru didn't like failing. Failed relationships were one thing. Failed hacks were another. Given three weeks, she could crack this encryption system. They didn't have three weeks, and the bad guys would probably change codes in the meantime. "Damn, these guys are good."

"Too bad we don't have them working for us, instead of her," the private whispered to the corporal, loud enough for Tru to hear. The sergeant scowled at the private, and he shrank back to his place. Tru wondered if any of the folks causing her so much trouble had ever worked for her. She'd lost a few people recently to better job offers farther out on the rim. Unusual, since normally Wardhaven paid a lot better than the rim.

Whom had she lost lately? Kim. Fred. Did any of them have pet codes? She tried a few of her office favorites. Nothing.

Damn! Of course these codes were tough; they were designed to be tough. It took time to crack them, and by then, you changed the code. Tru stared at the ceiling; she wasn't getting anywhere. What do you do when your nose is hard up against a wall you can't get through? Go over it. She'd tried. Go around it. She'd tried. She'd tried everything in her bag of tricks, and it wasn't working. "Damn, these guys are good."

"You said that before," Skelly reminded her.

Her unit beeped. She'd been running a search on the system, hunting for anything she could read. Her pet computer proudly pointed to a file on some maintenance unit. With nothing better to do, she opened it.

"What is it?" Tru asked.

"Some repair tech has his own layout of the station," the corporal opined.

"What's it show?" the sergeant asked.

"Air flow, I think," Skelly tossed in as she pointed at the layout. "Though why would these sections be venting to space?"

"Firefighting. That's what this is," Tru crowed. "This guy doesn't want to be fighting a fire with no blueprints because somebody changed the codes. I like this guy." She passed it along to the command post.

"Got anything that shows the locations of automatic weapons?" was her thank-you. "Few folks we let out on the station report lots of surveillance cameras and something extra. Things that look like remote machine guns. Sure would like to have something on them before we start shooting up the place."

"Why do I not think we'll find that in an unencrypted file?" Skelly laughed. While the others enjoyed his joke, Tru studied the map, letting her fingers rove the layout. "We know where the power plant is. That accounts for one venting to space. There are two others. Yep, both are using Halon-3000. That means computers. I bet one is security, the other data central."

"Assault teams will be happy to hear that, but which one?"

Tru grinned; the original map showed, among other things, the personnel office. One of the two unknowns was close to the power station. The other was close to personnel. "I think I know where the Admin Division is," she chortled.

"So what?" the private tossed her off.

"So, Sergeant, get the assault team ready. I'll want the entire specialist team to follow me in five minutes. If you don't hear from me by then, come in shooting there." She stabbed her preferred site. There were no locked doors between here and there. None except the one that mattered. Tru stripped off her armored space suit, retrieved a scarf from her kit bag while she printed out a dozen of the right forms, and headed for the door.

"What are you doing?" There was actually worry in the sergeant's question.

"Following the private's orders." She curtsied, and closed the door behind her.

Trouble was having trouble staying awake; maybe it was the gas fumes. Certainly it had been a long day. The racket from the warehouse was down to a dull roar. Then the comm link finally contributed something worthwhile.

"We found their hideout," said a man.

"You sure?" That was pure Zylon.

"There was a tarp hid among the barrels."

"What makes you think they were there?"

"We found two halves of pain pods. They took them apart."

"But they're not there anymore." That was pure Zylon venom.

"No, ma'am."

"Bring all the field hands and vat girls back to our end of the compound. Then start them walking for the other end. Tell them the one that spots those two runners gets food, real food, for the next month. If none of them raise a holler, I'll use the pods every night for the next month. You make sure they listen good. Nobody's escaped a farm. I'm not gonna be the first."

"Ruth." Trouble gently shook the sleeping form beside him. She came awake with a start. "Honey, it's time we start moving."

"You say the nicest things to me, dear."

• • •

Tru's humor didn't last much past the first turn. If her guess was wrong, she was headed for security goons. Unlike the fabled dilemma of the tiger and the woman, Tru was making her own call. *Besides, if I guessed wrong, I'll just keep on walking.*

Unfortunately, the other potential location for the computer center was several locked bulkheads away. Keeping one eye on the corridor and the other on her wrist unit, she navigated herself to . . . a familiar glass window, complete with buzzer to call for attention. She buzzed.

"May I help you?" a young woman asked. She wore a bored look and a tee-shirt from the latest band craze. *Swing shifts if I ever saw one.*

Tru smiled. "Yes. I'm recruiting for network specialist vacancies on Wardhaven. I wonder if I might talk to your boss."

That brought the music lover up short. Tru was betting there wasn't a standard operating procedure for personnel raiders. The length of the wait while the young woman sorted out Tru's request was long enough to start her worrying.

"Karin, can you handle this?" the woman finally said.

"Hey, we're working as hard as we can to get the D server back up. Give us another hour."

"No, K, it's not about the network."

"What is it?"

"I think she wants to offer some of us a job."

"Who?"

"Who?" the band follower asked.

"I've got quite a few vacancies to fill," Tru said in her most suggestive voice. "May I come in?"

"I don't know." The woman worried her lower lip, but the door was buzzing. Tru opened it and walked right in. The center had over a dozen people in it, half gathered around one large unit with its cover off and boards scattered around it, and the rest around a system showing a black screen and code. *Yep, server's down. And I had nothing to do with it.*

"What d'ya want?" came from a short man in a green

checkered shirt and a tie that screamed it didn't match. Since he was the only one not in a tee-shirt, Tru took him for the shift supervisor.

"I'm Trudy Seyd, IT manager for a large corporate entity on Wardhaven. I need to staff up a major new unit."

"How'd she get in here?" came from someone around the dead server. Tru ignored the question.

"We are quite competitive in both salary and benefits. We expect this unit to have a long run and are willing to make a lengthy commitment to its staff," Tru finished, tossing the bait out. Now she waited.

"We're all on two-year contracts here, and you don't walk out on our management," an older man pointed out.

"Two weeks' notice is all it ever takes to terminate a contract," a young optimist put in. From the shaking of heads around him, Tru saw few held his view.

"I want to hire you right now. Tonight. Wardhaven will provide transport off-station tomorrow morning." Tru tossed that card on the table. When frowns showed that had sunk in, she played her last card. "I will triple whatever salary you are presently receiving." She handed an employment contract to the foreman, then started passing around copies to anyone in reach.

"Right now?" the foreman said slowly.

"I've worked on Wardhaven. Great place" came from someone around the server. "And at this pay. Wow."

"Right *now*!" Tru answered, glancing at her wrist unit. "I can give you thirty seconds to consider. I need the papers signed by then."

"It's not as if we owe management anything. You saw the way they fired Borden last week. Anyone heard from him since they took him dirtside?"

"Yeah, but do you really want to piss them off?"

"For triple pay on Wardhaven with a ten-year contract, I'd piss off the devil himself."

"You got to get to Wardhaven to spend that money. Lady, how you gonna get us out of here without the boss man knowing?"

"I have a ship docked at the moment. Accommodations are rather spartan, no better than those on a troopship, but the food is plentiful, and its next stop is Wardhaven." Well, maybe not. Next stop after a bit of a space battle, but no need to worry the new recruits.

"Troopship?" the shift foreman echoed.

"I need signatures," Tru emphasized. Around the server and station, pens were out, poised to sign, waiting for the first one to break the ice.

The supervisor pulled out a pen and signed with a flourish. "Okay, boss. What do you want?"

Tru docked her wrist unit with a workstation and brought up the map of the station. "Any security cameras between here and there?" She pointed to the assault teams' compartment.

"Three of them," the supervisor said, calling up a different schematic. "However, since no one is in those corridors, we ought to power down the lights and save electricity. Right, Randy?"

"Lights off."

Tru tapped her comm unit. "Friends, Goldilocks has the porridge warming. Breakfast time."

"On our way" was her answer.

The woman from the window handed Tru her employment agreement. "I hope I can get some training. I want to be an analyst."

"Trust me, friend," Tru assured her. The woman got over to the door and opened it just in time for the sergeant to lead a stampede through it, gunners followed by specialists and more gunners pulling up the rear. There was little consternation among Tru's new hires. "Folks, we've got a little hostile takeover going on here. Consider yourselves the first people to benefit from picking the right side. Now, we need to open up some parts of this station, and close down others. You probably have a pretty good idea of what we have in mind. Enthusiastic improvisation will be duly noted and rewarded."

The supervisor attacked his keyboard. Without looking

up, he asked Tru, "Those the only employment contracts you got? I know a dozen more folks that have been looking at vacancies and would come in quite handy for what you have in mind."

"I can print them out as fast as you can make the job offers," Tru answered.

"What do we do about that security office?" the sergeant asked over Tru's shoulder.

"I don't think that will be any trouble," the supervisor answered. "My station is showing a fire in there. That set off the fire extinguishing system, and in a moment, we'll vent it to space." He swung around in his chair, grinning. "I always hated those smug bastards in security."

Izzy chuckled. It had turned into a race; could the ships finish offloading their containers before the station was fully pacified? It ended in a tie. That left her with an extra thirty minutes to get her task force ready for combat. As all hands set about that, Major Urimi called.

"You all set?"

"Getting there," she answered. "And yourself?"

"Not as far along as we'd hoped. The station is ours, lock, stock, and barrel, with a lot of enthusiastic help from Tru's new contract employees. Still, there's little on the station about the planet layout. Found an advertising video, but it's three months out of date and doesn't show us anything about the command and control setup dirtside. We've got the high ground, but still don't know anything about the ground underneath us."

"You need to connect with Trouble and his brain trust."

"Right, but how? They've got no radios, and we can't very well go invading every drug farm down there, asking if they've seen a marine lieutenant. We're at a dead end again."

"They sent their only message up piggybacked on a GPS satellite. Any way you could send a message from a GPS?"

Tru sidestepped into view. "GPS satellites send a continuous message. Stations react to those. They're pretty dumb."

"When Trouble was a hostage dirtside, he sent me a help message using three fires in a triangle. Anything that basic you could use?"

"What about Morse code?" came from Gunny just behind Urimi. Izzy didn't need marines to fight three cruisers; Gunny and his crew wanted their lieutenant back. "Could you turn the GPS signal on and off to send a message in old Morse code?"

"Does your guy know that old code?" Tru asked.

Izzy shrugged. "I have no idea. But if Gunny thinks it's worth a try, why not? I've given up guessing what Trouble does and doesn't know. Good luck finding him."

"Good luck to you, Commodore." Urimi took back center screen. "We're counting on you for a lift out of here."

"I won't forget, Major." *Nor will I forget these damn pirates are probably carrying hostages like the last ones. How do I protect my own without murdering a lot of innocent people?*

"Ship's ready for departure," the ship's lieutenant, standing in for the exec, informed her.

"Stan, you and *Junior* ready?"

"As ready as we'll ever be, Commodore."

"Fine. *Patton* will take the lead. Conform to my movements. Watch, all hands to underway stations."

There was only one way out of the garage for the tractor, so Ruth looked for another way. She was not about to parade herself down the middle of the compound for Zylon to shoot at like some cornered rat. "Trouble, how solid is that back wall?"

The marine checked it. "Don't see any supports." She fired the tractor up, backed slowly to the wall, and began gently to push. The wall bulged agreeably.

Trouble peeked through one of the cracked wall sections. "They're about a hundred meters away. Near the clinic."

"Climb in, boy, we're going for a ride in the country." She loved the lopsided grin he gave her as he settled down beside her. She gunned the engine, slipped the tractor into gear, and the wall of the garage came tumbling down.

The wrist unit squawked all kinds of shouts that boiled down to "Something's happening," but told nothing. Ruth slammed the rig into first and roared down the back alley, past the drug factory, heading for the fence. As Ruth and Trouble ducked shots, the tractor sideswiped a few buildings. Ruth didn't care. Now in high gear, she aimed for the fence. Never had she wanted so much to be out among growing things.

The fence went down with a crunch, and the tractor's wheels spun a bit as they shot across mud. She intended to race halfway down the newly cut rows, then zig over into tall dope. That would let them hit the outer fence unseen. Once they were past the lighted farm center, it was dark. She glanced at her GPS, counting on her own memory to tell her the coordinates of the fields.

"Trouble, what's wrong with the GPS?"

"Did we take a hit?" He glanced down at the locator unit. "It's working."

"Yeah, but it's not supposed to be flashing on and off."

"It's telling you where you are."

"Right."

"Drive," He snapped. She did. Still, his eyes were locked on the small, dim numbers, as if he were trying to make something out of this unusual system failure.

"You've never seen it go crazy like this?"

"Never," she answered.

"There's a pattern to it. One long blink, then six short blinks. I could be starting in the wrong place. No there's breaks between some of the shorts. Dit, dit, dit, dit, pause, dit, dit, dash. No, a break before the dash. Hit. Hit?"

"Hit. Hit what?"

"It's spelling out H, I, T, in Morse code. Ancient stuff."

"As old as the three fires in a triangle you used back on Hurtford Corner?"

"Somebody wants something hit or . . ."

They said it in unison. "Hi, T."

"The fleet's here! Finally!" Trouble shouted.

"What do we do?"

"Tell 'em where we are."

"Once we're out of here?" Ruth knew she should have made that a statement, not a question, but she already knew from the way Trouble was thumping the fuel cans that when the Navy asked a question, it expected an answer "soonest."

"They got to know which farm to land at, where the people are like Tom and Steve. We got to answer here . . . now."

There was a definite downside to falling in love with a marine. They did stupid things, and if you weren't careful, you ended up cheering them along instead of doing the mature, adult thing like telling them to shut up while you drive.

She slowed. Without a word, he tipped over a gas can, drenching the dead stalks on the ground. When one can was empty, he hollered, "Stop!" She did, left the tractor running, and got away from it quick. He doused the tractor, took a few steps back, and rummaged in the first aid kit for the lighter. She found herself grinning like a fool as he flicked it to life and tossed it at the tractor.

"Run!" he shouted. She already was . . . heading for the tall dope. In the bright light of the burning tractor, it was easy to keep her footing. It was also easy to spot her. Shots rang out. Bullets slapped into the ground around her. Trouble caught up with her, tackled her, and slid her into the mud.

"No use getting yourself killed just before the cavalry arrives. Let's take it easy."

"How long will it take?" she whispered back.

"Not long, I hope," he said, taking in the running guards, rifles out, grinning like they'd got them all by themselves.

"What was that?" Gunny pointed at the screen.

"Somebody's had a fire," Tru answered, dialing in on the spot for further analysis. "Automotive fire, gas, oil, rubber. Must have hit a tree."

"That fire's got a tail."

"So?"

"You've been sending Morse code on the GPS channel for half an hour. Now you got something unusual. Just a coincidence?"

"Looks like that to me, Sarge."

"It's in farm territory."

"Yes. We haven't observed internal combustion technology anywhere else."

"Ma'am, tractors don't drive fast enough to explode when they hit a tree." The marine turned to Major Urimi. "Sir, with your permission, I'll drop my platoon on that location."

"Could be nothing." Urimi eyed the screen, neither persuaded nor opposed.

"Yes, sir, then it could be what we're looking for. Tomorrow morning, do you plan to scatter a brigade over farm territory looking for my lieutenant and a few civilians who might know what we're after?"

"I don't want to."

"Maybe I could save you the trouble."

"Sir," Tru interrupted. "That fire is over the horizon now. I could study it more next pass."

"If the lieutenant sent us that message, we aren't the only ones seeing it. If we drop now, we can be there next orbit. Ninety minutes. If we drop next round, that's three hours."

"Ms. Seyd," Urimi ordered quickly, "pass the sergeant all the information we have about the locale of the fire. Sergeant, let me know as soon as possible what you find."

"Yes sir." The sergeant saluted, then did an about-face. As he double-timed away, he growled into his comm link. "Boots and saddles, crew. Drop mission departs in ten minutes."

Tru shook her head. "You sure you want to send him? I think he enjoys that stuff."

Urimi smiled. "I wouldn't let him go if he didn't."

"Shuttle four has departed from the station. It's dropping into lower orbit or heading for a landing," Sensors reported to Izzy. She hoped Gunny and the platoon had a good lead on Trouble. Right now the ground problem was Urimi's. The space around Riddle had to stay in Navy hands, or the brigades wouldn't be invading anything in the morning, no matter what Trouble and his friends might know.

Three pirates wanted her space; she was headed for a fight. It shouldn't be much of one. Two professionally commanded and crewed warships should make short order of three irregular ships, even if they had once been cruisers just as deadly as the *Patton*. Her crew fought for loyalty to the Society of Humanity. Those bandits fought for money. A mental image of Tru hiring the network services team flitted across Izzy's mind's eye. Could she just offer this bunch a better employment contract and buy out the fight? She shook her head sadly.

The computer geeks might have no idea who they were working for. These guys were killers. They'd shot freighters out of space, lugged slaves from planet to planet. They were at the center of this cancer, its willing purveyors. These guys would fight, and if they surrendered, she would gladly hang them once their day in court was done.

No, this would be done the old-fashion way.

So how do I get their hostages out alive? How do I separate those under a death sentence from the innocent? It was going to be one hell of a fight. Unless . . . "Comm, send to *Junior*. Stan, I got another batty idea. You up to a masquerade?"

THIRTEEN

THEY DRAGGED TROUBLE and Ruth back to the compound; Trouble expected rougher handling. He didn't waste effort resisting. Everything he had—mind, flesh, soul—concentrated on keeping him and Ruth alive for the hour or two it would take a Fast Reaction Team to show up. So, he went limp and made them half carry, half drag him through the field, across the compound, and past the crowd of field hands and vat girls to the brightly lit common between the guards' houses and the big house where Zylon waited.

"Took you long enough," she snapped. "Why'd you blow up the tractor?"

"Didn't blow it up." Ruth shook off her two guards and stood free to face Zylon. "Injectors were shot. I told you we needed a real mechanic to go over it. The damn thing blew up in our face. If you'd given us decent equipment, this farm would not only be making money hand over fist, I'd be long gone and you'd never have found us."

"Sounds to me like a good reason to do it my way." Zylon grinned. "But then, I always get my way, don't I, boys?"

That brought a series of snorts and laughs from the guards. Ruth shook her head. "You know this is stupid. Back on Hurtford Corner, my pa and the family bring in twice the crop with no whips, no beatings."

"Yeah, but where was the fun in it?" A voice from the guards cut her off.

"Mordy?" Under all the mud, Ruth went even paler than the glaring white light made her.

"Your ex?" Trouble asked.

"Her ex." A smirking man, little taller than Ruth, hardly more muscled, stepped out from among the guards. "Long time no see, Ruthie."

"Not long enough. So this is where you went."

"Lot more fun."

"Enough philosophy," Zylon snapped. "Vahan, get the long knives. Who wants first go at the girl philosopher?"

Two grinning guards stepped past Mordy, taking their shirts off. Trouble measured them, and didn't like the odds. Both had the reach on him. Probably more muscle on them, mixed with fat. They took him in and swaggered into the square with confidence.

"This will be a fair fight," Zylon announced with a total lack of sincerity. "After the boys kill this piece of trouble, they get the girl. You won't mind that, Mordy?" Ruth's ex shook his head. "If they yield to him"—she sniffed at that dim prospect—"he gets to spend tonight in my bed, with a new set of pods. You'll like that." The smile she awarded Trouble would make a cobra flinch. He bowed in mock gratitude.

"I believe you're overdressed." Zylon pointed, and a quick flick from a guard's Bowie knife cut off Trouble's breechcloth. Trouble had plans for it, not modesty, but protection. The guard kicked it into the crowd before he could wrap it around an arm.

Ruth stripped off her shirt; her bare breasts glistened with sweat in the harsh light. Mordy cackled while the guards hooted their glee; the two across the square added leer to their broad grins. "Wrap this around your left arm," she ordered, handing her shirt to Trouble.

"Where'd you learn that?" Trouble was glad she had, but he didn't expect that from a farm girl raised on a quiet planet like Hurtford Corner.

"Mordy brought a few of his star-wandering vices with him. Saturday nights could get real exciting if he found some young kids dumb enough to take him up on his dares."

"Hey, that's not part of the fight!" came from one of the two expectant thugs across the ring.

The guard who'd cut off Trouble's excuse for clothes reached for the shirt. Trouble batted his hand away. His Bowie knife came up. Trouble kicked him in the gut. He sailed back into the crowd of watchers.

"No problem." Zylon cut the fight off. "It's not interfering with my view," she leered. At that moment, Vahan returned with a polished wooden chest. His mistress removed one of the gleaming blades. Ceramic composite, it gleamed wicked in the light. When she turned it edge on, it disappeared.

Trouble whistled low. Ruth's shirt wouldn't stop that blade. He didn't give it back to her; if Ruth didn't know what she was looking at, he didn't want to let her in on the secret. He was sweating enough for both of them.

Zylon put the knife back in the chest. Her lackey let the two bully boys have first choice. Trouble took the one left. Vahan snapped the case shut with the finality of a coffin. "They cut nice," he smirked. The marine passed up the temptation to use the flunkey's throat for a demonstration.

"Step back, Ruth." Trouble nudged her toward the edge of the ring.

"Oh, no," Zylon corrected. "She stays with her stud. Right, guys?" The guards roared agreement. Mordy's grin took on stellar proportions.

"Stay behind me, but not too close."

"I won't trip you up," Ruth assured him.

From across the lit square, the two advanced. Trouble went into a low crouch and danced out quickly to meet them. He wanted maneuvering room for this fight. The three met in the middle. For a long minute, they just eyed each other, knives weaving a threatening pattern. Maybe they too were getting used to the light weight of the blades. Almost too light; Trouble's hand hardly knew it held a twelve-inch extension of pure death.

The big one on the right made a thrust. Trouble backed up. The tall one on the left now stabbed out like lightning. Trouble was far from its reach; still he backpedaled again. The big guy closed the distance in two quick steps Trouble wouldn't have believed him capable of, then thrust for the marine's gut. Trouble took a step back, then ducked to the left, just in time to parry on the side of his knife a strike from the tall one.

Surprised to find Trouble waiting for him, the tall man backed to the left. For the first time, Trouble had them moving apart. "Watch the guy on the right," he shouted to Ruth as he faked to the right; then, as the big guy backed up a half step, Trouble two-stepped forward and grabbed down with his left.

The tall guy on the left had seen his chance and jabbed for where Trouble's bare side would have been had he repeated his usual thrust-and-back on the big guy. The tall fellow howled as Trouble grabbed his wrist and pulled him forward, off balance. Swinging his knife hand around, Trouble brought the hilt up hard against the tall guy's skull, further urging him forward, and into the big fellow. The two went down in a wreck of too many arms and legs in too little space.

Trouble shot over to them, spotted the big guy's ribs poking out the side of the pile, and dropped, landing both his knees hard on the big guy's chest. Ribs snapped and the air went out of the thug. The tall guy's knife arm flailed. Trouble pulled it back and wrapped it around the wrong way. It shattered noisily.

Trouble stepped back from the two broken thugs, knife still in hand. "Are we done?" He wasn't even breathing hard. From among the watching field hands and vat girls there was a smattering of a cheer. The crack of a whip ended that.

Two of the guards stepped into the ring, pistols out, aimed at Trouble. He gave them a submissive bow.

"This shit needs new control pods," Zylon snarled.

Vahan hustled off to do his boss's bidding. Ruth came to Trouble. "You okay?" she whispered.

"Hardly broke a sweat, buddy." He unwrapped her shirt from his left arm and hung it modestly around her shoulders. Trouble's back was to Zylon, but Ruth's eyes repeatedly flicked back to their problem boss.

"She's not going to let you live through tonight," Ruth whispered.

"I suspect so. When the marines get here, make sure Tom and Steve get right to the sergeant. He has to know what they know. Also, you tell Gunny I expect him to personally see to it that you get back to Hurtford Corner."

"Can't you do something?"

The marine did not turn around. In his mind's eye he measured the distance to Zylon. Hefting the knife, he wondered how it would throw. He'd never been good at knife throwing. Why toss away a perfectly good weapon? He had no idea how this one would fly. If he did try for Zylon, the two guards would empty their automatics at him. Kill him. Probably Ruth. Possibly a lot of the field hands behind him. The way Trouble's luck had been going lately, they'd probably hit Tom and Steve. "No, farm girl, there's nothing I can do."

"I love you, marine."

"That's a dumb thing to say."

Ruth looked around. "Good night to be stupid."

She came to him; and he held her. He could almost hear Zylon sizzling behind him. Let her; Gunny would be here before the night was over. Zylon might kill him, but there wouldn't be enough time to get around to Ruth. She'd live if Trouble and his marines didn't do something stupid.

Damn it, Gunny. Where are my marines?

Zylon's toady returned with a new necklace for Trouble; this one had four pods. While Trouble was being fitted for his noose, he noticed a huddle across the ring around Mordy. They seemed to reach some agreement; Mordy stepped into the ring.

"Zylon, as some of your boys see it, that wasn't quite the

fair fight they expected for little Ruthie. It was supposed to be two to one, but that girl ended up on the ring. I saw her trip Komhen. Me and three of the boys would like a rematch." Here his swagger seemed to leak a bit. "If you don't mind?"

"Why should I?" Zylon paused. "In fact, I like the idea."

That brought a lot of hoots.

Somewhere to the west, there was a peal of thunder. A double peal. "Don't smell like rain," a guard observed. Trouble agreed. That thunder had no lightning attached to it, just an assault shuttle coming in fast and hot. Only thing the sky would rain tonight was marines.

Trouble stepped forward. "That's not fair," he whined. "I already fought two guys tonight. Shouldn't I have a day to rest up before I got to take on four more?" *Stall, man, stall. I'll waltz with half your guard tonight if you want. Just don't take me upstairs and turn these pods on.*

There was a chance he just might not die tonight.

"Whoever said life was fair?" Zylon cooed. "You caused me a lot of trouble tonight. Why shouldn't we have a lot of fun with you? Yes, guys. Two of you'll have to use your own knives."

Ruth started to take off her shirt. Trouble took her hand before she undid the second button. "Don't bother. These knives are too sharp." The others started for the center of the ring. He hastened out to meet them, Ruth beside him. She'd taken her belt off, wrapped it around her right hand. For the first time, the marine noticed how heavy the buckle was.

She swung it with meaning at Mordy and the thug on the right. "You wanted a fair fight, two against four, didn't you?" They backed up.

"Where'd you learn to use that?"

"Ask Mordy," she said, flipping the weighted leather strap. "You may not have given me kids, but you showed me some weird ideas of a fun time. I learned."

Mordy's answer was a wicked laugh.

"If it's okay by you, Ruth, let me take the lead on this." He couldn't afford an argument with the woman who pro-

THE PRICE OF PEACE · 283

fessed to love him, and whom he might very much love in return. Still, he had some practice fighting four guys with knives and he wasn't sure how to fit her into his plan without extensive training.

"You lead, I'll follow," Ruth said, and took two steps back.

The four—tall, short, Mordy, and thin, from left to right—advanced on Trouble, keeping their interval and distance. No one edged ahead. No hole opened up between them. Short was even calling a cadence of sort. "Step," he'd whisper, and all four of them would take a step forward. And Trouble would take a step back. If this kept up, they'd back him against a wall and cut him to bits when he had no more room to dodge.

Next whispered "Step," Trouble faked left. Tall and short shuffled their feet but stayed in place. The marine slashed to his right. Mordy and thin held their ground. Tall and short inched forward to dress on their buddies. Trouble was another pace closer to the wall, but he'd bought time. He reached behind him with his left hand and waved Ruth to move over to his left side. She did.

They'd lost their rhythm, so shorty did a count. "One, two, three, step." While they concentrated on their little dance, Trouble sidestepped for the left of the line and slashed at the tall one's arm.

He stumbled back, and the entire line collapsed as the four thugs tried to change front to meet a target that would not stay where they wanted it.

There was laughter among the slaves. Trouble grinned. He could keep this up all night. "What you guys need is a good drill sergeant. Want me to help?" he taunted them.

Shorty snarled and charged the marine. Trouble sidestepped him. Ruth slammed him in the side of the face with her heavy buckle as he went by. He screamed and made a blind grab for her. Since the other three weren't doing anything, Trouble risked turning his back on them. He spun, ready to put himself between the knife and the woman he loved and . . .

The night got light as day. Overhead, an assault landing craft launched rockets at something beyond the big house. In a blink, the landing craft was gone, and the night was lit only by the lights around the farm. In comparison, it almost seemed dark.

Shorty had made the mistake of looking up. Puzzled by what he'd seen, he stood there, knife half thrust toward Ruth, mouth hanging open. Trouble slashed for his throat.

The knife was better than Trouble expected. Like a surgical instrument, it took the guy's head off. Trouble felt only slight resistance. *That must have been the spine,* he marveled. This was a knife worth keeping.

Trouble whirled back to face his three remaining threats. They had lost interest. There was no guard behind him, the path to the crowd of field hands was open. He grabbed Ruth and started backing toward the others. Then the lights went out.

Smart move, Gunny. She can't zap us if she's got no power to her transmitter. A scream of rage from Zylon probably verified that she had gone thumb down on her pain controller . . . and found a dead central power meant a dead central transmitter. The pain pods were as worthless as last week's chow.

A rifle shot rang out. Civilian rifle. Gunner probably panicked. "Down, everyone. Down!" Trouble shouted and gently took Ruth's legs out from underneath her. Covering her with his body, he tried to spot his marines.

"Wondered when you'd get me on my back." Ruth shoved him off her. "Keep your own head down," she growled.

Somebody was firing into the night. Wild, ragged volleys. A single shot answered it. There was a scream, then silence. From the house came the tinkle of breaking glass and several pistol rounds. The shots were well over Trouble's head. "Ruth, can I borrow your shirt again?"

"You get a girl on her back in the dark, and all you want is her shirt off. What kind of marine are you?"

"One who wants to wave something to attract his sergeant's

attention and hasn't got a stitch on." Ruth slipped out of her shirt, and started waving it herself.

"What marine's gonna pass up a bare-breasted girl waving her shirt at him?"

"One that's busy staying alive." Trouble reached for the shirt, tried to take over waving it from Ruth. She wouldn't let him. They ended up each waving one end.

"That's got to be the lieutenant. Only he wouldn't know what to do with a half-naked girl on her back."

"That you, Taylor?"

"Yessir."

"Corporal, the good guys are on the ground. Anyone up and moving is a target. Cover me, I'm coming in."

"Squad, cover the lieutenant."

At a crouch, Trouble headed for his corporal's voice at the corner of the nearest barracks. Cover fire was limited to a few high rounds, since no one was offering to fight the marines at the moment. The lieutenant relaxed only when he had the building between himself and the big house.

"Lend me your helmet, Taylor." The corporal quickly passed over his headgear with all its command and control information reflected on his faceplate. It looked like a good drop. Most of the platoon was in a loose circle around the big house—except for one squad floundering around out in the fields.

"Gunny, this is Trouble."

"Glad to have you back, sir."

"Very glad to see you. Our objective is the large house. Resistance consists of thirty to fifty lightly armed civilians. Let's use weapons of nonlethal intent to start with. Anybody aims a gun, use all force necessary."

"Roger that, sir. First and second squad, concentrate on the east and south side of the target. Third and fifth, cover north and west. Fourth, as soon as you've finished making mud pies, we'd appreciate you up here." Fourth's reply was vintage marine.

"Duke, prepare to lay smoke, noise, and light on the objective." Trouble watched the situation develop for a minute.

Gunny arrived at his CP. Moss had Trouble's battle gear. "Sorry, sir. If I knew you was bare-ass naked, I'd have brought you pants to go with the armor."

"Every officer ought to try giving orders that way. See if they really got command presence," someone drawled. Trouble had other worries besides putting Craig on report.

"We go in in one minute," Gunny announced.

There was a roar from the far side of the house. "Second squad here. A large air-cushioned vehicle just busted out of a basement garage, and it's heading south like Gunny for a beer bust. Do we shoot it down?"

"Got nothing to do it with," Gunny growled on net. "Sorry, sir," he added to Trouble. "We dropped kind of in a hurry. Grabbed what looked important. No report of hostile aircraft or heavy assault vehicles, so I kept us light."

"No problem, Gunny. Glad to see you when I saw you. Five more minutes and I might not have been alive to say hi."

"Only got a glimpse of what was going on, sir, but it didn't look up to your usual level of entertainment."

"Been a rough couple of months."

"And tomorrow looks to be tougher."

"Got a few friends who might be able to help there."

"Put me through to Security Central," Zylon screamed into the phone.

"This is Security Central. Please state the nature of your problem," the maddening voice repeated.

"Not you, you idiot, your boss, or boss's boss. Someone who knows what's going on here." That was the problem with this setup. Most of the idiots thought it was just a nine-to-five job. Only a handful knew who the real bosses were. There was no market on Riddle for organizational charts, at least not the real one. Before, Zylon didn't mind the paranoia; why let everyone know the fortune that was there for the taking? Tonight it was a problem.

A totally wasted half minute went by before she heard

"This is Captain Wallace. I'm shift supervisor. Can I help you?"

"Yes. I am Zylon Plovdic, Manager of Farm Forty-one. I just evacuated the farm one step ahead of an attack shuttle full of marines or something. We're being attacked from off-planet."

"Pardon me, ma'am. This number is a service of your planet Security Center. It is not to be used for entertainment purposes. May I suggest you rejoin your gaming friends and not use standard communications units as part of your simulation."

The phone went dead with a click.

"Why, you stupid . . ." Zylon couldn't come up with more words to pile on that clock-puncher. She'd have him assigned to her farm when all this was straightened out. He'd listen to her when he wore a slave collar and she held the controller.

She searched for Big Al's number in her system. His day phone wouldn't pass her along to his home. She had to search her old calls to find one from him at home. She almost broke the phone dialing it. "Al, we got a problem," she said, cutting off his groggy bitching. He listened for her quick explanation.

"If that's true, we do have a problem. If not . . ." The observation that she might end up working beside her vat girls was left unsaid. "I'll call you back."

Zylon glanced at the clock and matched it against the craft's speed; Mordy had it maxed. "I'll be at Richman in two hours."

"This is Betsy Corbel of the *Pride of Portland*. I'm gonna be crossing kind of close to you, so I thought I might introduce myself." Izzy sat on the *Patton*'s bridge, wearing a pair of khaki cutoffs and an oversize tee-shirt the chief of the boat had just had tie-dyed. It was almost dry. If her in a wet tee-shirt added a level of distraction to the man just coming on the view screen, so much the better. Eyes locked on their boards, no one on the bridge was paying any attention to her.

If the program Izzy's countermeasures officer had picked up on Wardhaven was as good as promised, only Izzy and the helmswoman were visible.

"Hello, I'm Sam Hill of the *Hot Bottom Line*. Glad to hear from you. High Riddle still hot?"

"Hottest this side of Earth," Izzy promised. *Very hot.*

"Well, watch out where you're headed. Hear the pirates are getting worse around the rim."

Not after today. But Izzy nodded agreeably. "We're headed back to the core. Taking Alpha jump. So long." Communications ended, and Izzy let her breath out slowly. The course to Alpha jump took her directly across the sterns of the three incoming bandits. If she'd timed it right, they'd be within fifteen thousand klicks at the closest point of closure. Perfect. She and Stan could take out the engines on two before they knew what hit them.

Izzy glanced around the bridge; most boards were straight lines. Countermeasures promised she'd cover all emissions from *Patton* and *Junior*. Still, Izzy took no chances. Anything that didn't belong on a merchant ship was cold metal, and would remain so until thirty seconds before they needed it. She checked the bridge chronometer; rechecked the paths of the five ships. Exactly four more minutes to wait.

Izzy leaned back in her chair and did a great imitation of a woman without a care in the universe. Everything that could be done had been done. Now all that was left was the doing.

One minute stretched by, followed by an eternity that only saw another sixty seconds pass. The third minute was longer, if that was possible. The final thirty seconds flew.

"Activate all combat systems. Guns, we do not range the targets until all batteries are charged." Assuming they all took a charge. Why not be an optimist?

"Roger, ma'am."

Umboto watched the seconds pass. Twenty seconds into the warm-up period, the acting XO announced. "All combat systems on line. Performance is optimal. All batteries are charged. We are ready, ma'am."

"Sensors, how is *Junior*?"

"All up and operational. However, countermeasures give my readings only a moderate confidence level."

Maybe they were working. "Talk to me about the targets."

"Three Daring class cruisers. Triple reactors active. No military systems on line."

"Guns, I want a firing solution on the first one, and a solution for the last one passed to *Junior.* Activate range finders."

"We've pinged the targets," Sensors reported.

"We have a firing solution. *Junior* has hers."

"Put on spin. Begin jink mode. Fire ranging shot," Umboto ordered. The *Pride of Portland* cover vanished as the *Patton* took on a warship's defensive spin and slipped into a random dance of up, down, and sideways zigs. A single shot reached out from the cruiser to the *Hot Bottom Line.* It sliced into the target just aft of amidships, and immediately winked out. The targeting solution was perfect. Without orders, Guns adjusted the remaining turrets and opened fire. The *Patton*'s lights did not dim, thanks to the yard's work. Five laser beams cut into the stern of the *Bottom Line,* slicing engines, smashing plasma conduits. Misdirected plasma shot into space at all angles as the ship took off in a wobbling flat spin.

"Check fire," Umboto ordered. "Switch to second target." She had only the three guns that the ship's spin now brought to bear. One reached out for the middle ship. It wasn't there. It had bounced up. The other two turrets tried for it, but missed.

"What the hell do you think you're doing?" Sam Hill was back on the screen, holding on tight to his bridge chair as his ship continued its wild gyrations. Another captain came on screen, but didn't bother identifying himself. His ship didn't look any better controlled than Hill's. Stan had done good.

"This is Captain Umboto of the Society of Humanity cruiser *Patton.* You are ordered to cease all acceleration, close down all systems except basic life support, and prepare to be boarded."

"You're crazy. You got no right," the unidentified captain started.

"You are charged with numerous counts of piracy and involuntary servitude, as well as conspiracy to commit same." Umboto cut him off. "I repeat, close down and be boarded."

"I'll see you in hell first," Hill snarled.

"That can be arranged. We know the location of your bridges, and you are sitting ducks. Comply with my orders." Umboto cut off the two captains. "Comm, send to *Junior.* Two cripples are yours. I will engage the undamaged ship. Good luck."

All batteries were again charged, but the lone target was jitterbugging through space, never holding a constant course or acceleration. This one was going to be tough.

"Comm, send a hail to the evading ship."

"He's calling us, Captain."

A new face appeared on screen. "I am Johnnie Romijn, of the *Diamond Cold Heart.* What the hell are you doing?"

If he'd monitored her last transmission, he knew the answer. "Cease your evasive maneuvering," she ordered.

"No way. Some crazy woman's shooting up ships. I'm gonna do what I can to keep my hull from being made Swiss cheese."

"If you're a normal businessman, boarding will cause you no problem."

"Don't have the reaction mass to cruise around this system all week. I need to refuel at the station."

"You are not approaching the station without being boarded and searched."

"Listen, lady, I'm just a man trying to make money on a very slim profit margin. I got no time for this silly business."

That was the problem; there was a slim chance he might be telling the truth. Umboto had nothing to go on but assumptions and intelligence. But if he was a gunship, she could not let him near the station's collection of troop containers and landing craft. *Has my trigger finger gone off too quickly and too wrong, again?* "Sensors, talk to me."

"She's a Daring. She's got all three of her reactors going.

I'm hearing no combat systems. Visual shows she's got containers around her hull. They are not covering her gun turrets, but that could just be . . ."

Right, everything or nothing. Umboto's countermeasures officer was running a new package that covered the *Patton*'s emissions. Had this one bought the same gear? Time to choose. Attack, or allow the *Diamond Cold Heart* to pass. Umboto did not like that name, but that was no reason to shoot it out of space.

"Captain, Countermeasures here. Something's interfering with my systems. I'm getting spikes and valleys in my coverage."

"Like there was another system operating nearby?"

"Maybe, ma'am, but no guarantee."

Life didn't come with a guarantee. That ship might be innocent. Then again, it might be guilty as sin but crammed with innocent victims. "My ship will escort you into the station."

"No way I show you my stern. I'll pull even with you."

"As you will," Umboto said and killed the main screen. "Comm, send to *Junior*. Advise me soonest you get a report from your boarding parties. Must know if they are what we expected."

"Yes, ma'am" answered her, but she was already lost in her problem. If that was a pirate off her port quarter, how could she entice it to fire? And make sure it didn't blow her out of space with the first broadside? That was the game they played. Death was the payoff. Her and her crew's deaths. If that was a pirate, she still had to take it relatively intact. She would not slaughter hundreds of innocents. Not if she could help it.

"Unknown is pulling aft," the helm reported.

"Match the unknown. Keep it right off our port quarter. Sensors, I'd really like to know more about our unknown."

"Captain, I got nothing new to add. Some emissions, but they could be background." Igor shook his head. "I can't tell shit."

Not a regulation report, but appropriate to the moment. "Is the unknown still zigging and spinning?"

"Yes, ma'am."

"Let's tempt him. All his systems should be up by now. Cease jink pattern. Reduce spin to five RPMs. Helm, you have discretion to return to evasive maneuvers if you perceive any threat. But for now, let's see how good he is."

She was answered by "Aye aye"s and dubious glances. She would have been willing to wait this one out 'til the sun went dark, but the station was only twenty minutes from coming in range. She couldn't afford for the bastard's first broadside to take out half a brigade. Maybe the command post. No, time was on the bastard's side. Umboto needed an answer, and it was up to the Navy to get it before the troopers bought it the hard way.

She leaned forward in her chair. "Come on, you son of a bitch. Do something." Nothing happened. Had she screwed up? Had she shot up two poor merchant ships that just happened to show up at the wrong time and place? The clock was in slow motion, stretching each second into hours.

"Unknown has stopped evasive maneuvers. Hull rotation is same as ours, five RPMs," Sensors whispered.

"Take all rotation off the ship. Countermeasures, close down all systems."

Sweet Jesus. I killed two hundred innocent people on a pirate, and now I've shot up two ships for pirates that weren't.

"Unknown has closed to ten thousand klicks," Sensors reported. "I'm getting something, ma'am. Very low band; nothing should be down there."

One thousand one, Umboto counted. "Jink! Down!"

"Down jink," Helm answered.

"Enemy firing!" Sensors shouted.

"Guns, fire."

"Firing A," came the gunnery officer's familiar twang.

The *Patton* wobbled as the ship took on spin and absorbed hits in the same second. The helmswoman, good at her job, had rigged her board to put on rotation as soon as she zigged again. Pumps screamed, struggling to move reaction mass fast to balance the *Patton* as the spin increased. The ship bucked and danced until the pumps did their job, then settled on course.

"Hull breach at frame forty-eight, radial two-eighty," the acting XO reported. "We've lost number two bow thruster set. Ship is manageable. No loss of combat capability."

Umboto was glad for the damage summary; she stayed concentrated on offense. The *Patton*'s one shot had pinned the *Diamond Cold Heart*. "Take out her engines, Guns," she ordered.

"Full broadside, target aft," Guns answered. Five slashes fixed the target, shattered its stern, left the ship cartwheeling through space. New turrets rolled into view on the hostile ship, reached out, but, unable to adjust to their own mad dance, came nowhere near the *Patton*.

"All right, you bastard." Umboto mashed her comm button. "*Diamond,* close down all systems, or the next target is your bridge. You've got five seconds."

The *Patton* continued its jink pattern. Gunnery, thanks to the refit, adjusted for each dance step beforehand and modified its firing solution accordingly. If Umboto ordered that bridge peeled, it would be open to space before the broadside was done.

"Fuck you" was the *Diamond Cold Heart*'s response.

"Fire!" was Umboto's. The *Patton*'s guns obeyed, catching the hostile in her wild dance, slicing into the ship's heart.

"I repeat my previous order, *Diamond.* Close down all systems and prepare to be boarded."

"Captain, Comm here. There's no carrier wave from the target vessel." Now would be a good time to shatter their reactors, let their own plasma turn them to atoms. Unfortunately, Umboto could not take that easy out again.

"Sensors, what's target's status?"

"Countermeasures are gone. Forward batteries are armed. Amidships are not there anymore. Aft batteries appear to be uncharged."

"Guns, check fire. Target forward battery for full broadside on my command." God willing, she wouldn't have to give that command.

"Dear God, make them stand down." The whispered prayer came from somewhere on the bridge. Umboto concentrated on her target.

"Sensors?"

"No change, ma'am."

"Recommendations, Guns?"

"She's wiped. But as long as she's got power and loaded batteries . . ."

Right. She's deadly. Umboto would hate herself for the next order she gave.

"Sir," Sensors barked. "Target is powering down her reactors. I repeat, one reactor is off line. Second one is dropping off. Third is at eighty percent. Make that seventy."

"Somebody wants to call it quits." Umboto sighed. "What about the forward battery?"

"Still loaded."

With plasma being dumped, the wild cavorting of the target slowly became tame. The message of surrender was loud; it also simplified the firing solution for the forward guns. Umboto held her breath.

"Target is firing," Sensors shouted.

"Guns . . . check fire. They're firing away from us. They are discharging their lasers on their disengaged side," Izzy sighed. She had fought the bastard, and he hadn't made her murder innocents. Well, maybe not. They'd have to board and find out how much damage they'd done.

"Comm, message from *Junior.* First boarded hostile had crew from a pirated ship and slaves. Repeat, they are pirates and slavers."

"Now you tell me, Stan." Izzy laughed with relief. She'd done it. She'd gone into battle, beat two bastards, and killed no more than she had to. And she had not risked her crew to do it. *Damn fine ship handling! Now let's see what Urimi and I can do on the ground.*

FOURTEEN

THE ASSAULT LANDING craft rested in the farm compound in front of the barracks. Trouble sat in its command center, surrounded by his noncoms and civilians. Tom would keep his next date with Senate investigators. Trouble wouldn't let Steve out of his sight; Ruth, he didn't want to.

"That's all we've got on Richman." Major Urimi finished updating Trouble on the situation. It hadn't taken long.

"They didn't want info out on the place." Steve stepped forward. "I had my suspicions as to why, but I never guessed at anything like this." Trouble would give Steve the benefit of the doubt because of what he'd been through. Still . . .

"They started a major new city hall a year ago. That really got me wondering. Most buildings go up. This one went down, twenty-five stories. Only two above ground." Steve's fingers roved the map, then stopped. "This place, the one you've got labeled 'Country Club ??.' That's the place. A lot more underground than above."

"It is on a hill," someone behind Urimi observed.

"Then it's more a command bunker than a city hall."

"A fallback position to hold until they can get some kind of relief force through," Trouble muttered.

"They've already got a call out," Tru Seyd added. "Half an hour ago a coded message came up from the surface, shot through the station's comm service using hidden protocols, then headed out to all four of the jump point buoys and caused them to make immediate pass-throughs. Damnedest thing I ever saw."

"Elevate things to the political realm." The skipper joined them on line. "Then thumb their noses at us when observers arrive and tell us to back off by a seventy-five, seventy-four Senate vote."

"Not if we take that bunker apart before the observers get here," Trouble pointed out.

"Might not be that easy," Urimi noted. "We've looked over the station. It's got a hell of a lot of remote machine guns. Tru closed down the security center before they used them. If they've got the same stuff covering that bunker and the 'golf course,' it'll be damn costly to do a frontal assault."

"Then maybe we better take the redoubt tonight," Trouble suggested.

"Too late," came again from off Urimi's screen. "It's active, making music like a division in full combat kit. Lots of people headed in. If we dropped tonight, we might keep some out, but we might also run into other stuff. I'm reading an antiair envelope stretching fifty miles out around that town."

"If they've got missiles to back up the radar."

"You want to guess which garage or condo hides the SAM?"

That seemed to exhaust that idea.

"Might be some advantage to letting the bunker fill up," Urimi muttered. "Not everyone here is into the illegal side. We got the station when the computer geeks took a better job offer. If they don't know enough to run and hide, they probably aren't guilty of anything worse than failing to ask around about the company they hired on with. In this mission, we got to separate the sheep from the goats."

"And if all the bad guys dig into the bunker, all our sour apples are in one barrel," the skipper said, mixing her metaphors.

"That might be a good idea," Steve said slowly.

"Because?" Trouble egged him on.

"There's a lot of water around here. You may have noticed the frequent and excessive rainfall." Steve grinned at Trouble.

"Not lately," Trouble countered.

"Even Riddle has to have a dry season. Anyway, when they started digging city hall, they ran into all kinds of springs in the hill. Had to work out a whole series of drains, or the ten bottom floors would have been flooded half the year. Anyway, there's a major drain pipe running from under that bunker directly into the main city sewer. Since it hasn't rained for a couple of days, it might not be underwater at the moment."

"Worth a try." Trouble glanced at Gunny. He was grinning as he nodded his head.

"They'll have sensors covering that access," Tru opined, "Can I go dirtside with you boys?"

"If we put a load of explosives in there, then give them thirty minutes to surrender and evacuate." The skipper spoke slowly, weighing each thought as she said it. "I like it. At oh-four-hundred, I'll drop the brigades to surround the city and begin moving in toward the center. By noon, we ought to have the bunker isolated. I could drop a demolition team and full countermeasures squad to support you. Think your engineers could map that sewer system between now and then?"

"We got sixth squad with us," Gunny said.

"I think we can," Trouble assured his skipper.

"Any questions?" Umboto asked.

There were none.

"Hell of a slim brief. You know the objectives. Keep in touch with the units on your flanks. Let's not kill each other, or any civilians we can avoid. Good luck to us and Godspeed."

Trouble turned to Gunny. "Sergeant, mount 'em up. We're moving out." Gunny did that with his usual ease. The civilians were Trouble's problem. "Steve, you're coming with us. Tom, I got to keep you safe. You and Ruth stay here."

"I don't think all the guards bugged out with Zylon." Tom shook his head. "I'm not hanging around here."

What was safer, the frying pan or the fire? "I'll send you topside with this lander once we're in town," Trouble decided.

Ruth took a seat like a mountain settling onto a tectonic plate. "You too," Trouble said. Ruth gave him a wide-eyed look that neither agreed or disagreed.

"Thought we might need some extra gear, sir," Moss said, handing out weapons and battle suits to the civilians. "Just like on Hurtford Corner." Trouble had no choice about having civilians in that fight. Here, it seemed he had none either.

Zylon Plovdic did not like being turned away at the front door of company headquarters. "You'll have to park that rig in the garage down the hill," she was ordered. "We can't have a lot of cars in our parking lot here." Zylon dismounted her entire staff and led them into the rambling two-story building while Mordy disposed of the vehicle. Aboveground, all you saw was a health club. As with so much of her life, it was what you couldn't see that mattered.

Immediately, Zylon realized her staff was underdressed. Everyone here sported coats, ties, even three-piece suits; her guards still had mud on their boots. "Where's Big Al?" she asked one of the security people seated at the information desk.

He glanced up, took in Zylon and her associates with a single sweep, and went back to the board he was watching intensely. "Tied up in meetings. Not seeing anyone today. Ned, is there anything we can do about that bogey?"

Nobody ignored Zylon Plovdic. "Listen up, boy. I'm the one who got Big Al out of bed this morning. I'm the one who let all of you know we had a little problem here. If it wasn't for me, you'd be waking up tomorrow morning to find this place under new management, you without a job and no idea how it happened. Now, if you don't want to be handed a hoe and put to work for some of my boys, you'll tell me where Big Al is."

That got the fellow's attention. He cast a very worried look to the man on his right, apparently his supervisor. That one didn't even look up from his board. "Mr. Alexander Popov is presently tied up in meetings in the seventeenth-floor conference room," he said evenly. "Those in attendance have asked not to be disturbed. Rod, I've called in the unknown. No reaction team available. They don't want to call out the junior militia."

"Thank you," Zylon huffed. "Maybe Big Al will send me and my boys out to settle your little problem." That got a rise out of them. She signaled her crew to a bank of elevators; Mordy rejoined them. For not yet three in the morning, the place was alive. She shared the elevator with suits who got off at the fifth floor, Acquisitions and Contracts; seventh floor, Legal; and ninth floor, Promotions and Sales. Aware of the stares her crew got, she deposited them at the tenth-floor cafeteria before going on to seventeen.

As soon as she exited the elevator, the receptionist looked up from his desk. "May I help you?"

"Big Al told me to see him as soon as I got in. I'm the one who raised the alarm."

"Ms. Plovdic, yes. He asks you to wait for him. As you understand, things are a bit unusual this morning. At the moment, the board is facing some very challenging opportunities."

The loud voices overflowing the two thick wooden doors and flooding the heavily carpeted foyer told Zylon everyone didn't see the same opportunities in this morning's challenges.

She sat.

The assault craft flew low, heading up the river that flowed through Richman. A hundred miles out, they picked up a search radar. "Military issue," the spacer at the counter-measures station announced.

"I think they bought it cheap at an army surplus sale," Steve contributed. Trouble wasn't sure he'd trust that data.

Fifty miles out, a computer demanded their access code

and insisted they surrender control of their vehicle. The bos'n ducked lower and yanked the craft around to an easterly heading. They made a couple more nudges into radar coverage, got queried each time, but saw no sign of a lock-on or a missile.

"Would be nice to know if they could land the troops in closer," Steve suggested.

"Be nicer still to get where we're going," Trouble reminded the bos'n at the controls. They stayed low and outside radar.

South of town, a series of ridges ran east–west. They used those to close in, staying in their shadows to avoid the radar. Ducking over the ridges got them noticed, queried, but still not shot at. No human voice objected to their presence. Trouble called their experience in to the command post.

"We've been following you," the skipper told him. "I think I'll skip a few fast movers over town at the start of the drop. If they don't draw fire, I'll move our landing zones up to the outskirts of town. No use wasting an hour driving in if we can land there."

The assault craft rose above the final ridge, hanging in air, ready to duck. When nothing came their way, it slipped over to land in a park's meadow. The platoon took nearly five minutes to exit the craft, unusually long, but this load out included sixth squad and its full set of engineering gear. It also included a few choice words with Tom and Ruth; they refused to stay aboard. Giving up on commanding civilians, Trouble waved the craft off to return to the station for the demolition team and countermeasures he wanted before he would even think of assaulting the bunker.

It was 0300 hours as fire teams moved from the woods into the outlying streets. Here, among condos and convenience stores, nothing moved. Still, Trouble wanted his crew off the streets as soon as possible. An engineer released several "tunnel gnats" at the first sewer drain they came to.

The tiny flyers, less than three centimeters across and supported by a single spinning blade, hovered for a moment, then dove down the drain. Trouble watched the corporal's board as the gnats spread out. Reporting back by laser comm beam to a base gnat that hovered in the first drain, they split up. Half went right, the others left. The right-hand team quickly hit the end of the pipe. The left team reported a six-foot-high sewer pipe two blocks over. The platoon headed in that direction.

There was traffic on that road. The first car caught half a squad down a manhole, the other half waiting. Everybody scrambled. The manhole cover was back in place when a duded-up gal, late getting home, passed by. Trouble never sent more than a four-trooper fire team out at one time after that. There were more drive-bys, fancy dressed, finally heading home, or work clothed, heading for an early shift. In between them, Trouble slipped his marines down the manhole.

By 0320 Trouble had his team out of sight. Now the tunnel gnats went to work in full force. As the marines slowly made their way toward the center of town, the gnats mapped the sewer. Trouble let them go in all directions until he was confident they had a good route toward the bunker, then had the gnat boss recall those headed in the wrong direction. Every five minutes, they raised an antenna up a drain to listen for traffic aimed at them.

Everything was quiet, frighteningly quiet.

"Zylon, my dear, so glad to see you." Big Al was his usual positive self. Two dozen Very Important Managers had left the meeting quickly, their faces showing various levels of confidence and anger. Behind Big Al, five more trailed from the room looking a lot less sure of themselves. "Thank you for the call. Seems High Riddle has had a change of management that went unnoticed by the security watch office down here. Disgusting oversight." Al eyed a man in a gray-and-black uniform. Zylon smiled at him. The thought of adding him to her field hands was a pleasant image to contemplate.

"However"—Al turned back to her—"at the moment, we have everything well in hand. We've sent out an emergency call and expect to have a full Senate investigation launched on this atrocious matter by tomorrow. We should have no trouble holding out until they arrive, should we, Carl?"

The uniformed man nodded. He would have looked more assuring if his face were not so ashen. "All the weapon pits are active and under positive control. Every inch of our 'golf course' is under automatic weapon, mortar, and antiarmor rocket coverage. If they'd only bought the surface-to-air missiles I asked for . . ."

"Yes, yes, Carl." Big Al cut him off. "No one in uniform is ever content with his toys. You must make do with what management can afford. So long as you use what you have to the utmost, I am confident we will be left here unmolested until our lawyers can sort this out."

"Sir." A young suit with the nose of a rat broke in. "Has security checked our asshole, as you named it?"

"Yes." Big Al fixed his gaze on the security boss.

Carl's face drained from gray to translucent white. "I will make sure of that as soon as I return to my command post."

"Darling Zylon, why don't you go along with Carl? Your team would be a fine addition to his people."

"Covering our asshole?" Zylon echoed.

"Water drainage system," Big Al tossed off. "Normally quite full, but Riddle does indeed have a dry season. May not be quite as underwater as we assumed. Right, Carl?"

"I shall see to it." He headed, stiff-legged, for the elevator.

"So shall I," Zylon answered, following the fellow. She wouldn't mind wearing a cute uniform like that. Colors would look good on her. She'd want a floor-length skirt, slit up the side. Yes. She had plenty of security experience on her résumé. If Carl's job became vacant, she'd fill it.

Trouble had an antenna up at 0400, but he needn't have bothered. Fifty assault landing craft dropping out of orbit set off enough sonic booms to wake the dead and send people racing from their houses, putting on whatever they found handy.

"Okay, crew, the show is on," Trouble announced over the laser network maintained by tunnel gnats clinging to the roof of the sewer. "These civilians know this isn't their average Monday morning, so keep your heads up and your asses low. Fourth squad, fall back and spread out to maintain contact with our initial entry point. Taylor, you and a private return to the LZ and get ready to lead in our support teams."

"Should never have laughed at the LT's butt," Taylor muttered, but he headed back the way they'd come, leaving pairs of troopers at each major intersection.

"Lieutenant, gnat boss here. I think I've found our target."

"Show me."

On Trouble's heads-up, a maze of lines appeared. Most were yellow. One ran off to the left of the rest before branching into four other lines. "There are bars at the mouth of that red one."

"Have the gnats mapped that branch?"

"Yes, sir."

"Pull them back, then. I want to be real careful exploring that one." Beside Trouble, Steve nodded.

"Be real careful," he whispered. "Don't make so much as an extra drop of water fall before we got that puppy wired *our* way."

Izzy was having a much better day than she'd expected. Pirates had not shot up her troops. The landing was going down unopposed. Well, almost. Some irate fools felt that having their sleep disturbed gave them the authority to scream at armed men. The stupidity of civilians never ceased to amaze her. Faced with strong men, armed, her first goal would have been to be elsewhere, fast.

With the first companies of each brigade moving in rapidly, she assigned LZs closer to the center of town and moved the second wave into them. Things were going so smoothly, there had to be a rub. She checked the "city hall/bunker." None of her troops were near it. Why did she expect a rub there—big time?

"Has Trouble gotten his support units?"

"They're on the ground and moving up," Urimi answered.

Good. Or rather, as good as it was going to get. If she isolated all her problems in the redoubt, and then couldn't get at them, what then? Could she really blow them up?

That bridge she would wait to burn until she was on it.

Zylon liked the Security command post. It was full of tight butts going purposefully about their business. She could really enjoy this place. A few people would have to go, like Carl and the pasty-faced woman who brought him the bad news.

"We've lost the sensors in the tunnels," said pasty-face. "They're always full of water, and we couldn't keep cameras working. Last time the camera circuit went down, we let it go."

"Has anybody actually taken a look at them today?"

"Not yet, sir."

"Have a repair team do it immediately."

"And a fire team," Zylon added coldly. "We move out in five minutes. I'll be back by then with my team. I'll need twenty full sets of automatic weapons and night visual gear."

"I'll see to that," the woman said and cringed away.

"This is going to be fun," Zylon crowed. She turned on her heel and went to find her men.

Trouble left his platoon strung out behind him and waved Tru forward. For once, the three civilians did what he signaled them to do—stay put. That was the first time Steve, Tom, and Ruth had paid any attention to him. Nobody should have to go to war with civilians around who took his orders for suggestions.

Trouble and Tru rounded a corner. Down the eight-foot-diameter pipe he could just make out a branch off to the left. Tru signaled the marine to halt, then produced a gizmo from her satchel. It skittered forward like a spider, trailing a web out behind it. A window on Trouble's heads-up opened, showing a bug's-eye view of the tunnel. He saw nothing unexpected, which did not relieve the tension growing in his gut. Today, what he didn't know would be what killed him.

Tru's heads-up dimly showed several windows. The lieutenant waited for the expert to send him one she considered important. He had a long wait. Even after the multilegged scout reached the side entry, all Trouble got was a picture of mesh, bars, and a dribbling stream of one-centimeter-deep water. Ten years of high-tech mayhem gave him the patience to wait.

"Damn," Tru finally whispered, and retreated to the last side tunnel. "They got that place covered. Video, motion, laser, the works, and probably the best available. This is going to be a challenge." The woman grinned.

"Let me know when you're done with your challenge. I'm not moving anyone in there until you're downright bored."

"Good move, marine." Tru aimed her comm unit down the tunnel. "Measures and counters, I need all you got. We got to sink our own tunnels, hack their cables, and set up our own feedback to them. Get a move on, folks."

"How long?" Trouble asked.

"Best guess two, maybe three hours. Could be four. In the meantime, sit tight, trooper. Catch a nap, relax."

Trouble passed the word to Gunny. Half his platoon probably would flake out. He headed back to the demolition team. He wanted them in and out fast, like a millionaire's spoiled brat at boot camp. He got no objections from the swabbies, and drafted third and fourth squads to support them.

He was leaving as Corporal Taylor faced a leadership challenge. "Man, Corporal, how do I get out of this squad? The LT ain't ever gonna forget you."

Back in front, Tru was a happy camper. "I heard from some ex-miners how fast these little beggars cut through, but you got to see it to believe it." She grinned at several one-centimeter holes in the pipe's wall, fiber-optic lines flowing smoothly into them. Tru's handheld screen showed new lines reaching out toward the target one. "Got to isolate their sensor pods, cut into their network, record their reports, then

randomize them and rerun them for public consumption
while we close down their whole sensor suite. Neat, no?"

"Neat, yes. Just let me know when I can get that place
rigged for booms."

"Two, three hours."

Zylon bossed a crew of forty; she liked that. Each of her
guys now had someone else working for them. She doubted
the gray-suited security personnel saw it that way, but that
didn't matter. What Zylon saw was real; the rest were fanta-
sizing.

Down here, it was cold and damp. They'd found a break
in the cabling, just as the fiber optics left the sensor ring. A
quick patch, and she was watching a very boring hole in the
ground. "No problem," she reported to Security with a voice
mail to Big Al. "I have everything under control. Nothing
will happen down here we can't handle."

Beside her, Mordy slung his automatic weapon and jug-
gled three grenades. His grin showed that he agreed with
Zylon; anybody came in here, they were dead before they
got their head in the hole. "Tell me about your board," she
said, caressing the neck of the tech concentrating on the
readouts. Might as well learn something, as well as have
fun.

"Marine, you there?" The skipper's voice startled Trouble.

"Yes, Captain, we're working on getting in." He eyed Tru;
she held up a finger. "One hour, maybe less."

"Well, the bunker has stopped us in our tracks. They got
machine guns, mortars, rockets dug in everywhere you look.
All controlled from somewhere else. We move within a hundred meters of their perimeter, and we take fire. Tried everything, smoke, decoys. They got a sensor suite that won't
quit. No heavy artillery until tomorrow to start plowing
ground. Even then, I suspect they got backups for their
backups."

"We wait them out," Trouble surmised.

"We got problems up here from the civilian population."

"They up in arms?"

"Quite the contrary. Except for a few shouters, they're very easy to get along with."

"So why isn't declaring martial law and locking them down for a day or two gonna work?"

"Because nobody's got any food in their refrigerator. Would you believe that every meal around here is eaten out? Every block's got a restaurant, or a fast-food place. Nobody cooks." Trouble waited. You don't rush the skipper.

"And nobody's got any cash in their pocket. Everything is credit card."

"And the bastards closed down the credit network," Trouble and the skipper ended together.

"Nobody up here can buy a sandwich or a plate of waffles or pay for a load of vegetables the farmer just brought to market. We got eighty thousand hungry people and no way to feed them."

Trouble had a mental image of an old Sunday-school story with Izzy trying to multiply loaves and fishes. He didn't dare laugh. "So we got to close these people down."

"Close them down, dig them out. Something. How does it look from our side?"

"Give us another hour. We'll move the demolition charges in there fast, then weld all entrances from the bunker shut. You give them thirty minutes to call it quits, or else."

"Or else I blow them out. That will be an interesting order." The skipper's voice had a choke in it as she closed out.

Could she give such an order? Could Trouble legally and morally execute it? Interesting. He'd damn sure rather blow a big hole in the ground than see a lot of good troopers pay for that bit of real estate. But if the bad guys just sat quiet, neither giving in nor taking action. Like Izzy said, take things one step at a time.

"I got good recordings on all their sensors." Tru cut into his thoughts. "I'm ready to randomize, cut out the original signal, and begin replay."

"Demolition team, third and fourth squads, ready to move out?"

"Yessir"'s echoed down the tunnel.

"Do it, Tru. Let me know when it's safe to move."

Zylon had learned that the tech was a very married man. In addition, she'd learned more about the sensors than she ever wanted to know. From a purely technical point of view, they were wonders. The video gave her a boring picture of empty sewers with only a trickle of water flowing through them. The motion detectors were good enough to note ripples in that flow—and the footfalls of rats in the adjoining tunnels. The metal mesh at the mouth of the tunnel at least kept those filthy things out of her line of vision. Just to make sure, lasers randomly laced the tunnels to check air or water density. Nothing got past these suckers. Now, if only the tech was more interesting.

"What was that?" Several of the sensors had tiny spikes rising minimally above the background squiggles.

"Probably nothing. Just another lander's sonic boom. You pick those up even down here. That's how good my babies are."

Right, tell me about it. No. Don't tell me about it. Zylon wondered what was happening upstairs. There'd been a few probes along the perimeter, but those had died away quickly. With emphasis on the died. She hoped someone tried her little hole in the ground. She wanted to have something to show for all her boring commitment to duty.

"Bad guy's sensors are down. That tunnel is yours," Tru announced.

"Gunny, occupy those tunnels,"

"You heard the man. Move it, move it, move it."

First squad moved out, rifles sweeping up, down, right, left. One fire team established itself at the next junction. Second team cut the wiring off the entrance to the target tunnel, then they and second squad disappeared down the hole with Gunny.

Trouble joined the demolition team. "Let's move that stuff up there quickly and gently," he said. The Navy types trotted out with loads of explosives on their backs. And damned if Steve and Tom didn't grab a load and follow them.

Trouble reached the mouth of the tunnel as Gunny reported back. "Four tunnels secured. There are eight entry ports. I've got Private Harz welding them down."

"Good." Trouble stood aside; the head of the demolition team, a grizzled chief, handed him a box. "Don't lose that, sir. I've timed the charges to drop this tunnel first, then blow up the other four. That way, we'll have a plug in place. Force won't have anyplace to go but up." The chief's grin was deadly. He'd done it right. Now it was up to the officers to decide if it was done at all.

"Four of the exits sealed," Gunny reported. "Now we start on the right side."

"What's that smell?" Mordy growled.

"Damned if I know" seemed to be the general response, as if any of them cared.

"Smells like welding. I got stuck on a welding crew once. That's welding."

"And who do you think has a welding torch around here?" That got the other guards laughing at him. Mordy shut up.

Zylon didn't laugh. Who would be welding? She studied the squiggles on her no longer talkative tech's board. All of them stayed low, where they were supposed to be. None of the video showed anything new, certainly not a welding torch. The tech had told her about a test you could run; see if the system was picking up random inputs, or if the inputs were too orderly to be random. He only ran that test once a day; had to shut down input for five minutes to evaluate one minute.

Zylon punched the test button. All screens went blank. They stayed that way for a long minute. When the screens

came back to life, red letters streamed across them: 52%
PROBABILITY THE SIGNAL IS GENERATED. TEST STILL RUNNING.

"Somebody stick their head down an access hole. I want
one eyeballed," Zylon ordered.

There was a pause while one of her men raced up the corridor to the first access hatch. "It won't turn," he shouted.

"Put your back into it, wimp."

"It won't turn. It's hot, like it's been welded."

"I told you so," Mordy bellowed.

"Everybody, check all the access hatches. Take your guns,
you idiots. Move." With and without guns, then all with
guns, the mob scattered unevenly in different directions.

"This one's hot and won't open, too," one shouted.

"Mine, too."

"Mine turns. I can open it," Mordy hollered.

"Get back here, you stupid idiots," Zylon screeched.
"Back this way. Those hatches are open. To them."

Eighteen or twenty armed men pelted back up one maintenance corridor and headed down another. Zylon followed
them. Not too closely. She wouldn't want to be hit by a stray
bullet. She would supervise this, but from a safe distance.

"We got problems." Tru came over the net smooth and even.
"They're shouting and moving up there."

"Gunny, clear teams out of the left-hand side. I'll take the
right," shouted Trouble. That was where the hatches weren't
yet sealed. Gunny ran; so did Trouble.

At the first right-hand branch, Trouble skidded to a halt.
"Clear out, folks, we got company coming. Keep an eye on
the service hatches."

"You heard the man," Corporal Taylor shouted. "Lock
and load. We got targets coming."

With a cheer, marine gunners readied themselves. Demolition people kept their heads down, going from pallet to pallet, pulling red-flagged pins from their charges and flipping
switches.

Trouble headed farther down the tunnel. He got there as
the first hatch swung open. The fire team was only four

strong; still, the private first class had deployed his crew to cover both hatches. Unconsciously, the teams had gone to cover—behind stacks of explosives. Trouble had read somewhere that direct bullet hits weren't supposed to set the stuff off. Like all marines, he didn't trust what he read in manufacturer's flack ads. "Get away from the explosives," he shouted as he opened fire on the first one to drop to the floor of the tunnel.

That one crumbled. He looked familiar—Mordy? Others fired long, unaimed bursts from the lip of the hatch. One ducked his head down to get a better picture of what was happening. Trouble put a three-shot burst into his skull. As if in slow motion, the guy who wanted to know too much fell through the hole to land atop the first one. There was a break in the racket of rapid but unaimed fire.

"Quick, close the doors. Don't let them get through!" came a familiar scream from up above. Zylon!

Is that bitch everywhere?

Both hatches clanged shut, almost in one sound.

"Any of you demolition guys got booby traps for those hatches?" A chief was already pulling something out of a satchel at his waist. He underhanded one to a blue-suiter close to Trouble; then both clambered up the rungs in the tunnel. The explosives slapped onto the hatches with a solid plop.

"Don't want to be the joker who opens that the next time," the chief said, dropping to the tunnel floor. "Now, ladies, gentlemen, and marines, I suggest we get the hell out of here."

"You first," Trouble offered. Navy men ran. Marines backed up quickly, weapons at the ready.

"Keep the exits covered. Anybody comes through them, shoot. You, tech, call Central. Tell them we need more guns. They're coming in the back."

"But they were welding the hatches shut," the tech answered.

"Weren't those explosives down there in the tunnels?"

"I didn't get a good look; were they?"

"Shut up. Call Big Al. Tell him I've got the army stopped, but I need more guns. Do it now," she shrieked.

Trouble was the last one out. Gunny waited for him at the main tunnel.

"No more after you, sir. Everybody's accounted for."

"Good, folks. Let's back up some. Chief, if one of those booby traps goes off, will it take everything with it?"

"Don't know, sir, but it sure won't give me the blow I planned. By the way, sir, that's no way to handle the detonator." To use his rifle, Trouble had slipped the little finger of his left hand through a strap on the detonator. It dangled there rather firmly, Trouble thought.

"I'll take it," Tom said. He stepped forward, gently removed the device from Trouble's finger, and tossed it toward the chief. He threw high. Steve caught it.

Trouble was already jogging down the tunnel, headed for the next junction where Ruth and Tru waited with the rest of the platoon. He patched himself through to the command post to bring them up to date. "The demolition charges are in place, but we were discovered. I suggest you issue your ultimatum and give them five minutes to respond. Otherwise, we're going to have to go back in there and fight them for the explosives. Not something I want to do."

"Fire in the hole!" came from behind Trouble. He twisted as he ran. Tom and Steve had the detonator. Tom took the safety cover off. Steve yelled, "Fire in the hole!" once more.

Trouble yelled, "No!"

Steve pushed the button.

The mountain danced around them; Trouble dove for the mud at the bottom of the pipe. For the next week or two he bounced around, a ping-pong ball in the devil's own game. When the dust settled, the ceiling was still above him, not on top of him. He sat up, facing where Tom and Steve lay laughing like maniacs.

"When they ask you what happened," Steve said as he gasped for breath.

"Tell them it was two disgruntled ex-employees," Tom finished. "I think we had good cause to be disgruntled," he said, slapping Steve on the back.

"Very good cause," Steve agreed.

Trouble shook his head. Would he ever finish the paperwork on this one?

FIFTEEN

PAPERWORK COULD WAIT: mopping up took priority. People had to be fed and the basic laws enforced. Using her recent hires, Tru cobbled together a complete credit system. That took care of a big part of getting Riddle going again. Closing down the drug farms and feeding their displaced workers had to be started, and started quickly. Trouble volunteered for that.

The guards on the farm compounds vanished. The second day they found most of the farm rigs in a garage across from the bunker. Apparently all the farm managers like Zylon made it to the bunker before it blew. That explosion not only took out all or most of the criminals, but every record of their crimes. Trouble was passing the redoubt when a crane lifted out a mass of computer hardware. Tru was standing by with a team of her techs, grinning from ear to ear. Trouble figured if there was any way to recover that data, Tru would do it.

Trouble was too busy to stop. He had several thousand hungry, naked people to bring in. What Riddle had done to them was Riddle's problem and expense.

Late on the fourth day, Trouble was enjoying his first real dinner in a restaurant the occupation army had taken over for an "O" Club. Everything was on the house. He'd just ordered when Ruth walked in. She quickly dismissed herself from the five she was with and approached Trouble's table. If he hadn't seen her damn near naked, he'd have thought her shy.

"Are you waiting for someone?" she asked softly.

"I was kind of hoping to find you." The honesty of his own words surprised him. The smile that swept her face was worth it. She settled at his table, sweeping the skirt of her dress effortlessly away from the chair as she sat. He'd never seen her in a dress. He thought she should wear one more often.

Her smile was the first sign he'd spoken his thought aloud. Now it was his turn to retreat behind shyness. Damn strange feeling for a combat marine.

"Sorry I haven't seen you. I've been busy bringing in slaves from the farms. Tomorrow we start burning the crops." That would feel good. A good job for a hard-charging, fire-breathing marine. Burning death masquerading in green drag.

"I know about the folks you've been bringing in. Izzy has me working in a displaced bureau of some sorts. We see they get fed, housed, clothed, tickets home with some kind of pay settlement. Trouble, they look so pathetic."

"We looked just like them five days ago," he reminded her.

"Hard to believe."

"Yes, kids younger than I was when I ran off and joined the Corps. Hell of an introduction to life as a grown-up."

Their waiter took her order. She studied the tablecloth for a long minute after the interruption. "You ran off to join the marines?" she said.

"Not really. Mom was only too happy to sign me in. I was a handful. Best to let a DI straighten me out."

"Mom? What about your dad?"

"He was deployed, more often than not, and when he was back, he was training his platoon and getting ready to go back out. Not much difference between the two. My first word, I am told, was 'mama,' and my second was 'Ops Tempo.'"

"Ops Tempo?"

"Marine for Operations Tempo, or how long can you keep guys away from home before they do horrible things to you? Even in a long peace, there's always somebody who wants marines in somebody's backyard. The only reason we were on Hurtford Corner was a businessman's complaint about being gouged."

"I'm glad you were on Hurtford Corner," she said simply.

"A dozen or so wives of my troops probably weren't."

"So that's what the wife of a marine has to look forward to."

"Gone, and getting set to go. It's no life for a woman. No way to raise a kid. Swore I'd never do that to anyone I loved."

That seemed to leave her with nothing more to say. Trouble sat as the silence between them stretched out and started to twist into knots. "What's it like farming?" he finally said.

"After the last couple of weeks, I figured you'd tell me."

"I mean real farming. Facing a field with a full belly and pride that what you planted will mean life to someone, not an empty death."

She pursed her lips. "It's nice like that. I remember some beautiful mornings and wonderful sunsets." She paused and studied her hands. "They haven't found Mordy; at least they haven't identified a body. There were thousands in the bunker when it blew. Some of the bodies are in pretty bad shape. It's going to take a while." She looked up, hard into Trouble's eyes. He searched for the words to tell her he had probably shot Mordy himself. "I don't give a damn about him. They can toss him out with the rest of the sewage. You and I watched them use better men than him to fertilize the next crop. He's gone. I'm glad."

"I am too," Trouble added with a gulp.

"So what do we do?" Ruth rushed on. "If we were back home, I'd move in with you until the first child came. It would cause a scandal, but it would give you time to try me out before you had to make any commitment. Where can a marine keep a woman?"

"This marine doesn't need to try you out, woman. You've stood toe to toe with me through hell and back. I'd take you as a sergeant, I'd take you as my CO. Damned if I won't take you as my wife . . . if that's what you want." Suddenly he was afraid she'd tell him thanks for the offer, but no thanks.

"Tru really is a wizard with computers." Ruth talked softly to her hands. "If she doesn't know it, she knows someone who does. I think she's got the civil register recreated for this burg. If she hasn't, I'm sure I can talk her into cobbling something together. Do you want to finish supper before we get married?"

"I'm not hungry," Trouble discovered.

"So there you two are. I've been looking all over for you."

Trying to keep confusion from piling on top of confusion, Trouble stumbled to his feet. "Captain Umboto," he said. Ruth stood too. He'd have to explain to her that wives did not stand for officers.

"Sit down, sit down. I've got to talk to you."

"I've been on net since I got my combat gear back," Trouble assured her.

"I understand you didn't have much in the way of gear when they found you."

"All the essentials were there, ma'am," Ruth assured his CO. The two women exchanged knowing looks. Trouble found his face getting warm. *Marines do not blush.*

"Well, I'm sorry I didn't connect with you sooner. These last four days have been wild, and today a full Senate investigative team showed up. Damned if they didn't find two junketing senators out this way and add them in. Demanded to know what we thought we were doing out here." The skipper grinned. "I think they planned to shut us down. Showed them what we had. Crew members of thirty-seven pirated ships. Four pirate crews in the brig. Over two thousand slaves. Suggested they go find the people responsible for this lash-up and ask them about paying the slaves and explaining the rest. Mr. Nuu's rep is betting they won't find anything. He's put in a bid to buy all this—debts, penalties, everything."

"Is there going to be any trouble about that hole in the ground?" Trouble figured he'd spend the next year in front of a court-martial trying to get to the bottom of that pile of rubble.

"Your report is being taken at face value. Two disgruntled employees did it. We assume they perished in the explosion. Heaven knows there's enough here to make a lot more than two people disgruntled with the goings-on. Now when Stan caught up with his brother yesterday, it was a good bet he'd kill him."

"Is Tom all right?" Ruth missed the humor and was concerned.

"Stan just busted into tears and hugged him. Then stuffed him in *Junior* along with all the data Tru's dug out of the rubble of their computer system. They're headed back to Wardhaven. Spy wants to debrief Tom before he turns him over to an Earth inquisition. My guess is, once the spy guy has the full picture, he'll make sure it comes out in the nicest way possible. I would not care to be the bastards who ran this show when that happens."

Trouble listened. For himself, he was glad to be off the hook and find Steve off it, too. What Steve and Tom did was out of line. But what had been done to them was way across the line. Best leave lines to other people.

And it didn't sound like Tom was headed back for an easy life. The spy would drain Tom of every scrap of truth and rumor in him. The bomb they'd set off under the bunker was nothing compared to the bomb the spy would set off under some very deserving higher-ups. Izzy's good news set Trouble's blood to racing, but it couldn't outrun Ruth's marriage proposal.

"Captain, I've got an announcement to make." Trouble eyed Ruth; she gave him a lovely smile and a nod.

"Announce it, Lieutenant."

"I am going to marry this young woman, and we are going to raise whatever she wants on a farm wherever she wants." Trouble had expected the skipper to take it one of several different ways—all bad. Instead, she beamed.

"I'll be leaving the Corps," he added.

"Maybe, maybe not."

"I'm not leaving my wife and kids behind in base housing while I'm gone half the year."

"Wouldn't ask you to. That's why I've been looking for you. Both of you, not just you, Lieutenant. Navy department has come up with some new wild-assed ideas. Most of them would be a laugh if they didn't come with an execute date. I just got one that says our ships are spending too much time deployed."

"God, whatever gave them that idea?"

"That's their studied opinion," the skipper assured him. "And it's costing the Navy a small fortune buying fresh vegetables on the open market. We pay a premium to have them certified disease- and bug-free. Did you know that?"

Trouble didn't.

"So, they're requiring each ship set up hydroponic gardens in the voids between armor and hull, just like the merchies do. There's plenty of room. Then there's the second departmental instruction. They want us to reduce crews by twenty percent. It's peacetime, don't you know? Nobody's shooting at us. Don't need all those damage repair teams. They did a study. It's cheaper to abandon an old ship every year or so than keep all the fleet in a full crew. God, I got to get a few more promotions under my belt so I can get assigned back there. They must be drinking some powerful stuff to come up with this shit."

"So you won't mind if I ask for an early out bonus and leave?" Trouble summed up what he'd heard.

"Who's talking to you, marine? I'm asking *her* if she'll contract to run the hydroponic farm I'm setting up on the *Patton.* I know some great hands that would be glad to work with you. Experienced. Won't get sick on you first time gravity goes out."

"And when they aren't farming, you wouldn't happen to

have a part-time job for them?" Ruth had liked Izzy at first sight. It would be fun working with this woman.

"Well, it wouldn't surprise me if a lot of them were in the Navy Reserve."

"And if the *Patton* gets into a hot spot?"

"I imagine they could be recalled to active duty real fast," Izzy said with a grin, "unless it's harvest time. I understand that's a real do-or-die time for farmers."

"On planets, ma'am. I don't think they have the same problems with hydroponics."

"Good. There's one more thing."

Trouble looked around for a ten-ton truck. That was about all they and Izzy hadn't run across this table.

"Your dad wants to head back to Hurtford Corner. He figures he's done all he can, and wants to go home."

"Ma will like that." Ruth nodded.

"I need an Alcohol, Tobacco, and Firearms agent, maybe a Drug Enforcement Agent, too. Know anyone willing to take a When Actually Employed appointment with those outfits? Means associating with hard cases like Trouble here. Not much pay, but all kinds of excitement."

"I'd get to close down two or three joints like this one?" Ruth asked, glancing around. She didn't mean the restaurant.

"God, there can't be more than one of these," Trouble sighed.

"We can hope so. Won't know until we turn over a few rocks," Izzy assured them.

Ruth reached for Trouble's hand and clasped it firmly. "If it means I won't get left cooling my heels at some backwater base six months out of the year, you got a deal."

Guns entered the restaurant and plowed straight for them. "I thought I left you minding the store," Izzy tossed his way.

"As if somebody could swipe a cruiser in orbit," Guns shot back. Trouble raised an eyebrow. After the last three months, he wouldn't put it past some people. "I got a message for you, *Captain*." There was an inflection in the way he said the skipper's rank that caught Trouble's attention.

While Izzy read the orders, Guns rummaged in his pockets and came up with two shoulder tabs with four stripes on them.

"You're out of uniform, skipper." Guns grinned.

"So are you," Izzy shot back. "We're all promoted!"

"Yeah, I double-checked with BuPers. They swear they're just correcting an oversight from when you took command."

"When gravity grows soft," Izzy snarled. Then she broke into a wide smile. "Then again, maybe somebody up there does like what we've done."

"Be glad to do more of it," Guns chortled.

"Lots more of it," Ruth added.

"Somebody has to." Trouble nodded.

"Then let's do it," said Izzy.

ABOUT THE AUTHOR

Mike Moscoe grew up Navy. It taught him early about change and the chain of command. He's worked as a bartender and cabdriver, personnel advisor and labor negotiator. Now retired from building databases about the endangered critters of the Northwest, he's looking forward to some fun reading and writing.

Mike lives in Vancouver, Washington, with his wife, Ellen, and close to his daughter and grandchildren. He enjoys reading, writing, dreaming, watching grandchildren for story ideas, and upgrading his computer—all are never-ending pursuits.

You can learn more about Mike and all his books at his website www.mikemoscoe.com, e-mail him at Mike_Shepherd@comcast.net, or follow Kris Longknife on Facebook.

An original military science fiction novella from
MIKE SHEPHERD

KRIS LONGKNIFE:
Welcome Home / Go Away

A Penguin Group eSpecial from Ace

Kris Longknife is back home from her galactic adventures, but her entire Fleet of Discovery has been annihilated. And the alien race that she fought has now declared war on humanity. Some people think Kris is to blame, and it may take more than the efforts of her war-hero great-grandfather to save her from the wrath of the angry—and frightened—citizens of her home planet!

• • •

Praise for the Kris Longknife series

"A rousing space opera that has extremely entertaining characters."   —*Night Owl Reviews*

"Kris can kick, shoot, and punch her way out of any dangerous situation, and she can do it while wearing stilettos and a tight cocktail dress."   —*Sci Fi Weekly*

Only available as an e-book!
Download it today!

facebook.com/AceRocBooks
mikeshepherd.org
penguin.com

From National Bestselling Author
MIKE SHEPHERD

. . .

The Kris Longknife Series

MUTINEER
DESERTER
DEFIANT
RESOLUTE
AUDACIOUS
INTREPID
UNDAUNTED
REDOUBTABLE
DARING
FURIOUS

. . .

Praise for the Kris Longknife novels:

"A whopping good read . . . fast-paced, exciting, nicely detailed, with some innovative touches."

—Elizabeth Moon, Nebula Award–winning author of *Echoes of Betrayal*

mikeshepherd.org
penguin.com

M905AS0612